THE MESSENGER

THE FIVE REALMS VOLUME 2

M.L. DARLOW

CONTENTS

Part III
NEW FIRE

"With power comes great responsibility,"

— VOLTAIRE

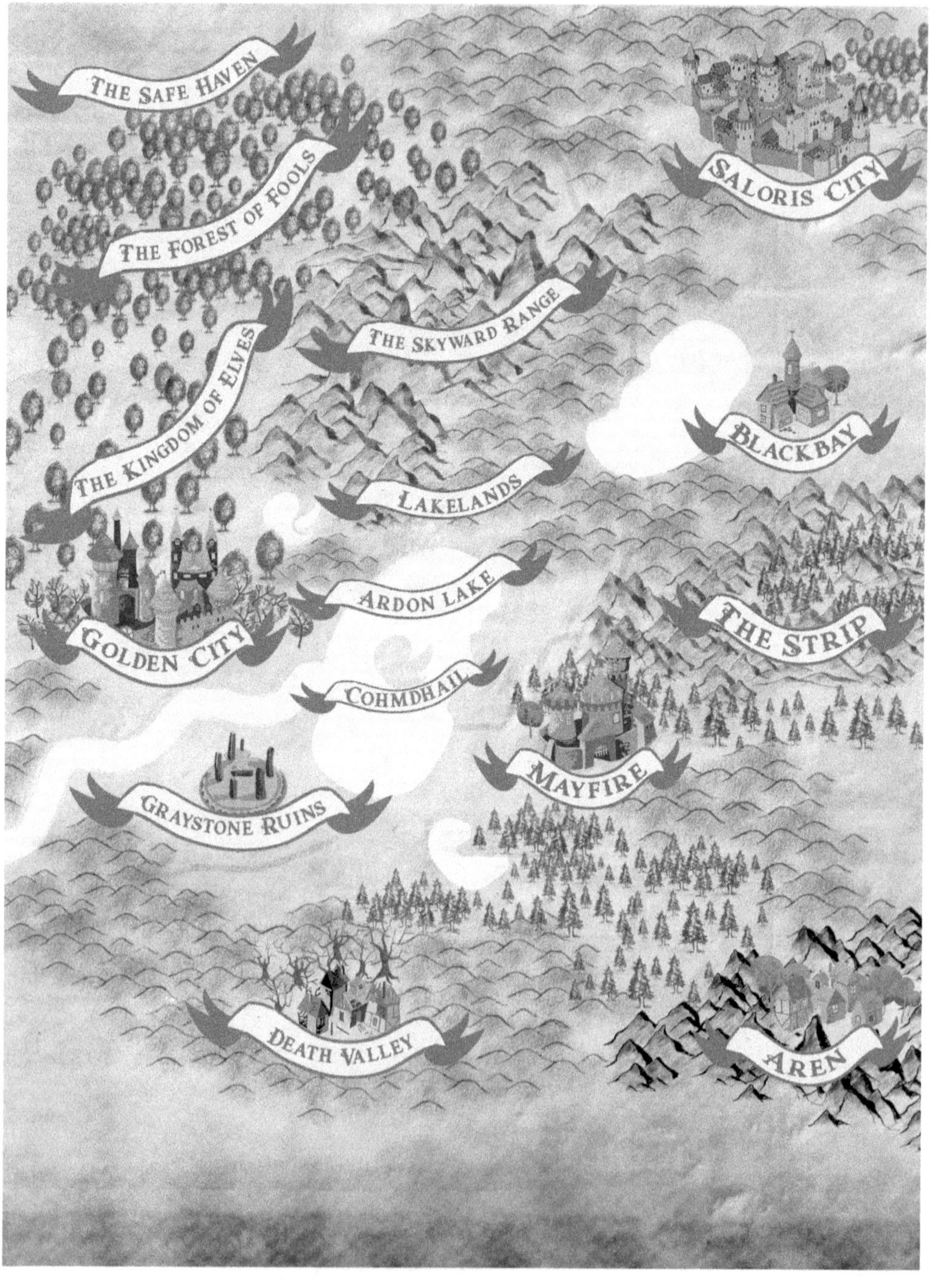

THE SAFE HAVEN
THE FOREST OF FOOLS
SALORIS CITY
THE KINGDOM OF ELVES
THE SKYWARD RANGE
BLACKBAY
LAKELANDS
GOLDEN CITY
ARDON LAKE
THE STRIP
COHMDHAIL
GRAYSTONE RUINS
MAYFIRE
DEATH VALLEY
AREN

THE IDONIAN KINGDOM
GALACTIC GATES
THE IDONIAN FOREST
ENDURION LAKE
WITHEROW
REDDING
DRACUS
CRANE
OLAIGON
LORCAN
DAIRTH
THE REGAL MOUNTAINS
THE EDGE OF THE UNDERWORLD
N
W
E
S

RED WINTER

ROLOGUE

edric Chamberlain was a chaser of legends. There was nothing he loved more than to indulge in Idona's history and find mysteries waiting to be solved. For years before the Dark War began, he would travel throughout all of Si Realtra and learn everything there was to know about each of the Five Realms: Idona, Erim, Minora, Zerin, and Ryiah.

Now, dark times had fallen upon Idona, and the High King had shut the Galactic Gates without warning. Since then, matters had only gotten worse, and Cedric could see the Realm he'd always called home falling apart.

The Mortals and Immortals throughout Idona were now at odds as everyone waited for the prophesied Messenger to surface. At first, Cedric hadn't believed that a single person would be strong enough to slay the Dark King and end the war. He couldn't fathom the Immortal Kingdoms' reason for waiting and not striking back. He didn't understand why it was that the different kingdoms and communities through Idona couldn't band together and take the Idonian Kingdom back.

When Cedric had learned of the legend in Idona, it

was only natural that he found its truth. Perhaps if he approached the Sovereign's Scepter in the Forest of Fools, he might be able to break the spell surrounding it. He *did* happen to have a vast knowledge of spells and had evolved to be a bit of a novice sorcerer himself. And if he *could* break the spell, he'd be able to end the Immortal Silence, and unite the Realm. He'd be able to slay Xavier and return Idona to its peaceful state.

All Cedric wanted was to keep his Realm from falling apart at the seams, therefore he braved the Forest of Fools. He'd skittered around its plethora of deadly deceptions until he'd found the very cavern the legend spoke of. For four days he searched the forest, while avoiding its lethal traps at the same time. But he'd finally made it.

The Elf had faced a whirlwind of emotions as he'd traveled through the complicated cavern. Yet, after traveling beneath water and through tunnels nearly too small for him to fit through, he encountered a beast placed there by the Dark King himself. Cedric's only saving grace had been his wand, and after using the *Inceptstasis* spell to keep it from moving, he approached the scepter with a dagger in hand.

The blade bit at his palm as he dragged it across. His deep red blood swam from the wound and he pressed it to the earth surrounding the scepter and waited. Nothing occurred. The ground didn't tremble, as the legend said it would. The Scepter remained chained to the earth around it. Imprisoned.

Cedric had failed. He would not be able to break the spell and wield the weapon. He would not be able to slay the Dark King and return Idona to its peaceful state. He would not be the one to end the Dark War.

Even though it was hopeless, Cedric wrapped his bloodied grip around the scepter and offered a silent prayer to the Moons. If he could not break the spell himself and unify the citizens of Idona, he asked that they show him another way. He would not sit around and wait. As he removed his hands from the ancient weapon and turned his back on the cavern, he began to devise a plan. He would find a way to keep the peace between the Immortals and Mortals by gathering as many people as he could find that would listen to what he had to say. Together they would rebel against Xavier's dark reign.

Eliza Snow never thought she'd see the day the Idonian Kingdom fell. But now, she could smell it burning. Ash and smoke sailed through the wind, surrounding her as she left the comfort of her cottage. As a Mortal, Eliza didn't share the impeccable vision of an Elf. But she knew all that remained of the Kingdom was nothing more than a glowing red ember in the distance, smoldering beneath a cold winter's night.

And though the night had begun like any other, Eliza couldn't shake the fear consuming her since the Red Winter began a fortnight ago. She couldn't rid herself of the feeling that this year, the Pandora's vicious nature would change the course of history. And now, with tears beginning to prick her icy blue eyes, Eliza needed to accept the fact that she'd been right.

News of the High Queen's death had traveled across the main Realm as quickly as wildfire ripped through dry brush in the fourth Realm, Zerin. By midnight, all of Idona had learned of what had occurred in the Idonian Kingdom, and that a Dark King now sat on Si Realtra's High Throne.

Once Eliza had learned of the queen's demise, she knew any chance of resting had escaped her. Now, she found herself out in the cold with her bow clutched tightly in her grip and her quiver fastened at her thigh. A chill crept down Eliza's spine as the frigid air bit at her exposed face. She watched her icy breath curl in tendrils before disappearing. Sucking in a deep breath, she pushed forward, now leaving the village of Crane behind.

Throughout her youth, during a time where Idonians hadn't needed to fear what lurked in the shadows of night, Eliza would often find herself in the mountains that surrounded Crane. When her thoughts began to spin wildly in her mind, the views from the East Cliff, or a hunt never failed to calm her. Now, dark times had fallen upon Idona. Midnight hunts and breathtaking views were a thing of the past. Yet tonight, Eliza knew there would be no Pandora in sight. It was evident that they were currently occupied in the Idonian Kingdom.

Eliza's eyes fell on the forest trail leading up to the mountains that surrounded Crane. So far, Winter Solstice had made quick work of covering the trail in sheets of icy snow, but she would still be able to find her way around using the village symbol carved into the trees, marking the safest route for villagers.

For centuries, Crane had gone unnoticed. While it had been the inspiration for songs, riddles and legends, very few dared to seek it out. Nestled within the center of Idona's longest mountain range, The Strip, it was nearly impossible to get to. Idonians had long referred to the Strip's center as its swirl because of its peculiar shape. There are many stories about the Strip's intriguing center, but storytellers know little of the people who reside there.

Eliza, herself, was only aware of two occasions where strangers crossed through its deadly borders. And while deadly they may be, those borders were no match for the Pandora. For the first time in the history of Crane, the villagers lay awake at night, waiting for their turn to die.

Four years ago, when the Pandora first attacked the hidden village, Eliza had lost her husband, Erick. She could still feel his warm blood seeping through her fingers, staining the snow around his lifeless body. Her breath hitched as she endured the painful memory. Tears that she had been fighting to hold back sprung from her eyes and rolled down her cheeks. Her hands instinctively reached to wipe them away before they froze in the winter air. Eliza's breath became ragged as she fought to calm herself.

On this night, the seventh day of the second week of Winter Solstice in the year one thousand and thirty-one, the Idonian Kingdom has fallen to the proclaimed Dark King, Xavier.

The voice of Crane's Justice Keeper, Drake Waters, rang in Eliza's mind as she maneuvered through the complicated mountain terrain, the snow crunching beneath her boots. "May the High Queen rest in peace," she muttered to herself as her eyes fell on lights flickering off in the distance, casting a warm glow upon the freezing forest.

The McBride Estate.

Eliza's lips curled into a smile as she saw it, knowing her dearest friend lived within.

Right now, Claire was likely fast asleep, nearly full term with her third son. However, she could see that she wasn't the only one tormented by today's events.

Pat McBride kicked at chunks of ice as he made his way down the stone path leading away from the miraculous cabin-like mansion that he had built for himself. It was unlike any cabin Eliza had ever seen, forged from logs that had once belonged to the trees that covered the land he'd built his home upon. The path led up to the large front porch where two rocking chairs swayed in the harsh winter winds. A candle flickered in each window throughout all three stories, which only made the magnificent estate seem even more inviting. And to think, it had all been built by one man.

Eliza could recall when she'd first met Pat, the day he'd appeared in Crane. Like many, she'd feared him at first. *Who was he? Where had he come from?* But, soon enough, Drake had begun to trust the stranger, and Claire had fallen deeply in love with his dark chocolate locks and sparkling blue eyes, which meant Eliza had no choice but to put up with him after all.

After he'd finished building his cabin, Pat planted crops that he donated to the village, providing for tables that were often lacking. He became a living legend within Crane, the first man to successfully grow anything so deep into the mountains. People had often whispered that he'd put Magic in the soil, and it was thought that he was a Sorcerer who'd gone rogue. But, despite all the curiosity and rumors surrounding Pat McBride, it wasn't long before every villager depended on him for fresh fruits and vegetables. He delivered a bounty every harvest season that would last the village through the Red Winter. Without him, Eliza was sure that many villagers would have starved since the Dark War began.

"You shouldn't be out here alone," Pat chastised once he caught sight of her, standing at the end of his pathway.

"Something tells me the Pandora are busy elsewhere this evening," Eliza replied, her face twisting into a scowl as he arrived before her. "And where do you think you're going? Claire could go into labor any minute," she groused, using the long end of her bow to poke him square in the chest.

"Turn that accusing stare of yours in a different direction," Pat sneered as he pushed her bow aside and passed her, heading off into the forest.

Eliza huffed, a cloud of icy tendrils erupting into the air before her. "I was going to go on a hunt," she explained as she turned to follow him.

"At three in the morning?" Pat snorted, looking over his shoulder to give her a long disbelieving look.

"If I wait until sunrise, I'll have to compete with everyone else. Besides, we all know now that Xavier took over the Idonian Kingdom, nothing will come out of it, which means the village of Witherow will no longer be able to assist us. We'll have to survive off of your farm, and hunt for protein," Eliza began to rant, her pulse beginning to quicken, pounding in her ears. The future was uncertain, and the idea of what might happen now that the Idonian Kingdom was lost led her stomach to churn. "Starvation is not a part of my five-year plan."

Pat nodded slowly as he ceased his walking and turned around to face her completely. Eliza's lips pulled down into a frown as she took in Pat's expression. He looked at her the way he always did, with a single lifted brow and a crooked smile that made her feel foolish.

Eliza found herself fighting the urge to load her bow and mount him above her fireplace.

"You're lucky Claire loves you so much," he teased, his lips spreading out into the smirk that always caused the blood to boil in her veins. "It just so happens that I'm an expert at tracking at night. Truth be told, I saw a deer big enough to last you all winter around sundown."

Eliza's jaw clenched, her glare lingering upon him for a few moments longer as she attempted to figure out if he was luring her into some sort of embarrassing trap. "Are you messing with me?" she asked.

"Would I do such a thing?" Pat scoffed, raising a hand to his chest, fawning offense before resuming his walk.

"If you are, I'll tell Claire." Eliza warned as she followed.

"I'm not afraid of many things," Pat replied softly as he broke away from the forest trail, moving effortlessly through mounds of thick snow, "but I am afraid of my wife."

Eliza gripped the freezing bark of trees as she worked to keep her balance, her eyes like daggers upon Pat's back. How could he move so easily? *Maybe he's a Sorcerer after all,* she mused.

After a while, Eliza began to realize that they were approaching uncharted territory. An empty feeling evolved in the pit of her stomach as her mouth grew dry. None of the trees were marked, and if she were alone, she wasn't sure that she'd be able to find her way back. She'd been born and raised in Crane, but she'd never left its borders. And now, she was sure Pat had led her past them.

"Where are we going? I thought you said we were tracking a deer," Eliza asked, fighting to hide the fear quivering in her voice. She could feel her stomach beginning to twist into knots as she silently gave into the suspicion that he may have been lying after all.

"I just need to check something," Pat admitted. "Don't worry, I'll make sure you don't starve."

Eliza bit her lip hard enough to draw blood as she surveyed her surroundings. Rays of moonlight seeped through the forest canopy, illuminating the snow around her. The beauty seemed surreal, as if it might be an illusion. She doubted she'd ever seen anything quite so alluring in her life.

The sound of a baby's cry pierced through the silence, jolting Eliza where she stood. Her heart hammered against her rib cage as her gaze darted to Pat. He was already running, having abandoned her at speeds so incredible that her eyes bulged.

Frozen in both fear and shock, Eliza stared for a moment at the spot he'd just been standing before she rushed after him. She wasn't able to run nearly as fast as he could, and the only clue as to which direction he'd gone were his footprints in the snow. When she finally caught up to him, the sight set before her caused her to stop dead in her tracks. She swallowed against bile creeping up her throat, fearing she might wretch all over the sparkling white snow.

A newborn baby shivered in Pat's arms. Its flesh was pale and bore a blue hue. She was shocked that it hadn't frozen to death in temperatures so frigid. "How?" Eliza heard herself ask, tears of both rage and devastation beginning to swarm her vision. "Who would leave a baby here?"

Pat's lips formed a hard line as he remained silent. He sucked in a breath, appearing to know exactly what to do next. His jaw set, his demeanor grave as he unzipped his jacket and moved to unbutton his flannel shirt. As he brought the baby to his bare chest, tears began to stream from his eyes. "Come here," he told Eliza, trembling as he turned to face her.

Eliza didn't hesitate. She approached him, unsure of what to do. An intense shiver ran through her, rattling her bones as she pulled in a shaky breath. She fought to keep her emotions at bay, her mind still whirling from what they'd discovered. "I don't see any other footprints but ours," she said softly. "How did it get here?"

"Grab a hold of me," Pat ordered.

Wrinkling her brow, Eliza reached out and placed a gentle hand upon his shoulder. He stiffened beneath her touch, his eyes squinting shut as he cursed under his breath.

"Hold on tight, and tell no one of what we're about to do," Pat hissed. Eliza gripped the cloth of his jacket harder within her grasp.

Within a matter of seconds, Eliza found herself standing in the foyer of the McBride Estate. A warm fire crackled nearby, causing her eyes to widen and her mouth to fall open. No words escaped her lips as she turned to stare at the man beside her.

"Tell no one," he repeated before rushing toward the fire. He dropped to his knees, continuing to hold the baby tightly to his chest as he rocked back and forth. She could hear him whispering. Praying, perhaps.

Pat was painful to watch as he worked to warm the baby. The blue tint began to fade from its complexion, and Eliza couldn't help but weep with joy as yet another loud cry escaped its lungs. And then another. And another. Before long, small footsteps could be heard coming down the stairs. Eliza looked over her shoulder, only to find Claire and Pat's eldest child staring back at her.

"Did Mama have the baby?" Four-year-old Quinn asked with wide cerulean eyes.

"No, lovely," Eliza answered softly. "Go back up to bed. Right now, your father and I need to take care of something."

It was abundantly clear that Quinn was too curious about what was happening to want to go back to bed, but even still, he obeyed. Sticking out his lower lip, Quinn lowered his chin to his chest and slouched his shoulders before turning his back on Eliza, and beginning his climb back up the stairwell.

Eliza sighed as she turned her gaze back toward Pat, just in time to witness a note falling from the wool wrapped around the baby's small frame. She gasped, lifting her hands to cover her mouth. Her heart thrummed harder in her chest. "Pat!" she squealed, rushing to grab it as it grazed the fire. Her fingers wrapped around the parchment and she was quick to blow out the small flame blooming on the corner of the letter.

Pat blanched and the baby's cries faded into soft whimpers in his arms. "What does it say?" he croaked, his eyes darting between Eliza and the baby.

Eliza gently opened the letter, praying that the fire hadn't burned away any of the script written upon it. She sighed as relief washed over her. The ink was untouched.

"To my darling, Ash," Eliza began, her heart breaking as she realized that this letter was from a mother to her infant daughter. A letter that explained everything. A lump formed in Eliza's throat as she prepared for the words she was about to read. Tears spilled from her eyes as she read the letter's contents, her heart breaking for the baby in Pat's arms and the late High Queen who had birthed her.

Eliza's hand trembled as the letter fell from her grasp, landing delicately on the floor beside her. She was sure she'd never be able to speak again. She looked toward Pat and found him staring down into the eyes of the baby, with tears welling up inside his own.

"S-she's a VanCamp," Eliza rasped. "We need to take her to the Elves.".

"No," Pat replied. "*We* can protect her. The Elves have never been trusted. How can we trust them now? Besides, she wasn't directed to go to the Elves. It wasn't what Meera wanted. Even so, if we were to bring her to Dracus, she'd live with a target on her back. That is no life for a child."

It was very clear to Eliza that Pat was struggling with the idea of how this baby would live if they were to turn her over. It led her to believe that it was possible he may have lived through a similar childhood. The idea of it sent a chill down her spine that caused her to shiver in front of the fire.

"We?" Eliza's stomach began to twist.

"You," Pat clarified. "*You* always wanted a baby, didn't you?"

"But they'll be looking for her."

"Yes, they will. But they'll never find her here," Pat whispered, running one of his fingers along the VanCamp's soft, pink cheek. "And if they do, we'll make sure she's strong enough to face them all."

Six Red Winters had come to pass since Eliza had brought Ash home to raise her. She'd even given her a new name, Ashlyn Snow. The sensation of guilt and fear overwhelmed her every time she'd curl her arms around the warm bundle. Each week, the village of Witherow would send Crane their recycled papers to keep them informed about what was happening throughout the Realm. And each week, Eliza would hold her breath as she read through the pleas from Dracus and the cries from the Kingdom of Elves. The remaining kingdoms within Idona were searching desperately for the baby she'd rocked to sleep every night, and they wouldn't stop until they found her.

The Missing VanCamp.

Eliza's parents hadn't raised her to be a liar. Hatred evolved deep inside Eliza as she recited over and over the story Pat had insisted she tell everyone about Ashlyn. After all, people were bound to ask about the baby. But not all villagers were kept in the dark. The Justice Keeper, Drake, knew who Ash really was. As did the rest of his small council. However, they didn't know the entire truth. As well as Eliza thought she might know her fellow villagers, Pat had been clear that when it came to a VanCamp, no one could be trusted.

So, Eliza continued to lie until eventually the curiosity of those around her dissipated. What were once constant questions came to a halt. Finally, she achieved the peace she'd been longing for. Together, she and Ash could be a normal family. Until one day, when tragedy struck the hidden village once again.

Mortal or Immortal, no being's strength would ever make them strong enough to get used to another name on another headstone. Eliza, as well as every other citizen of Idona, had lost far too many people since the Dark War had begun. But she had never imagined, even during her darkest moments, that she would see the name *Pat McBride* etched in stone.

Tears swam down her porcelain cheeks as Eliza took in the faces of Pat's children. She wished she could be concerned about her own breaking heart, but that was impossible when four orphans stood before her. They listened to the kind words Drake had to say about their father, their eyes large, wet, and filled with a pain no child should ever know.

It was difficult enough for the McBride children when Claire died giving birth to their youngest sibling, two-year-old Lilly. The entire ordeal nearly shattered the village. Claire had been such a kind soul with a strong presence, and an endearing mother. After three unruly boys, all she'd ever wanted was a little girl of her own. No one had ever thought that after three successful labors, the fourth one would take her life.

Pat had nearly lost himself when Claire took her last

breath, but he'd never stopped protecting his children and Crane. Mourning wasn't something allowed during this day and age. So, Pat named his daughter after Claire's favorite flower, enlisted Eliza's help in taking care of her, and went back to work. The farm was always waiting. The villagers needed to eat. And before long, the Red Winter would come again, and his farming tools would be swapped for his bow and sword. Pat never stopped.

Not until this Red Winter got the best of him. Pat McBride died trying to protect Drake's wife, Celine, who perished as well. Eliza had been nowhere near the village when the Pandora had attacked. Instead, she and Ash had been at the McBride Estate, where she'd been caring for Lilly as she normally did.

Pat never returned to the estate, and instead, it was Drake knocking on the door in the middle of the night with bright red eyes and bloodstained clothes. Eliza knew the worst had happened. Crane had lost two people they'd grown to care for deeply. Two people who were once outsiders, but were now cherished and loved.

Every soul in Crane had come to the meadow they'd buried Claire in two years ago to bid their respects to Pat. In Spring Solstice, lilies and lavender covered the bright green grass, but now snow fell from the thick clouds above, covering the disturbed earth in front of Pat's headstone.

With Celine gone, Drake would now have to raise his eight-year-old son and six-year-old daughter on his own, and try to forget that his beloved wife was four months away from giving him a third beautiful baby. Right now, he fought to appear strong as he addressed the villagers. Eliza could see right through him. He may pretend to be alright, but the truth was, after this, he would have to return home and take down the crib he and Celine had been excited to set up in the nursery. He'd have to pack away the baby clothes and donate them. He'd have to go lie in his bed alone, his wife's spot empty and cold beside him, the smell of her hair still fresh on their pillows. He'd have to endure that pain, and there wasn't anything Eliza could do to ease it. She knew that pain all too well.

The McBride children would have to live a life without either one of their parents to guide them. But they weren't alone. Eliza would never allow that. Claire meant too much to her. She would never let her best friend's children go through life alone, especially during a war like this one.

"They say when it comes to raising children, it takes a village." Drake spoke to the crowd of villagers who pressed handkerchiefs to their damp eyes and sniffled in the cold. His eyes were on the three boys in front of him, and Lilly swaying in the wind. She gripped her elder brother, six-year-old Cooper's hand as Drake's voice cracked against the breeze. "Pat McBride has done wonders for Crane, and we owe it to him to ensure his children live on to carry on his name."

"That's not my biggest concern," the eldest McBride child, ten-year-old Quinn, snarled. "I'd rather live on to avenge him."

"I agree," eight-year-old Lincoln said. "I'd rather slaughter them all."

The crowd remained silent, their eyes revealing their shock. No one expected such harsh and chilling words to escape the mouths of young children. But during times as dark as these, even children couldn't afford to keep their innocence.

Eliza bit her lip, her eyes falling on her own daughter. Ash stood off to the side, her gaze fixated on the mountains surrounding the ravine the estate was built within. Her bright hazel eyes were filled with curiosity as to what existed beyond the Strip. She stared with such a longing that it caused Eliza's breath to catch in her throat. There had always been something off about the child. It was as if, even at six years old, Ashlyn knew this wasn't where she belonged.

She belonged in the fight.

3

As time went on, the Dark War intensified. The Pandora no longer appeared only during the colder solstices. Their presence was felt throughout the Realm all year round. However, each Red Winter was bloodier than the last, for it was during the Winter Solstice that the Dark King punished the villagers still daring to defy him by either forcing them to bow down and raise his flag or destroying them altogether.

Eliza remained in the business of keeping secrets. Pat was gone, but she would never forget how insistent he'd been about keeping Ash's identity a secret. Those who knew kept their lips shut tight, and Eliza fought every day to convince herself that that was for the best.

In the beginning, Eliza had collected the papers the village of Witherow provided. Over the years, she imagined that King Loren would call off his trackers and the updates to find the Missing VanCamp would stop. But she'd been wrong. To this day, every week she'd pick up a paper and read through the same similar articles.

By now, the trackers had been through the Realm at

least ten times. They'd combed through village after village in every jurisdiction, from the Regal Mountains to the Forest of Fools.

Not *every* village, though.

If King Loren's trackers were going to locate Crane, they would have done it by now. After all, it had been sixteen years. Sixteen years of people roaming aimlessly around the Realm, either looking for a child that looks like her twin brother, Vincent, and her older sister, Penelope, or looking for the bones of a newborn. If they hadn't stumbled upon the hidden village yet, it was unlikely that they ever would. This put Eliza's mind at ease for a time, but now the kings and queens of the Realm weren't the only ones asking questions.

Ashlyn had never been daft, and Eliza had known it was only a matter of time before the girl looked in the mirror and realized they weren't related. If she had at one point or another already, Ash never said a thing about it. She'd looked at her mother with only love in her eyes. It was because of that, that Eliza needed to break her promise to Pat.

Time means nothing to an Immortal, but to a Mortal like Eliza, it means everything. Her body had aged, worn and tired from the stress of living one Red Winter after another. When she began to feel her body withering away, she was struck with the realization that she would die the same way her mother had.

The sickness starts slowly, going unnoticed for quite a while before one wakes up one day and realizes that they can barely open their eyes or get out of bed. For Eliza, it was rapidly getting worse, just like it had for her mother. With what little time she had left, Eliza knew that she couldn't leave Ash without telling her the truth.

The only concern that Eliza had was the influence the

Rebels had over central Idona. Each McBride, and Ash herself, had connected with them over their hatred for Immortals and a need to defeat the Dark King and the Pandora. Not only was Ash the Missing VanCamp, the letter the High Queen Meera had left for her revealed her true nature, the result of a potion used during her birth, one powerful enough to turn a Mortal into an Immortal. Now, Eliza worried for Ash's fate, and how the other Rebels, and even the McBride's, would treat her once her true identity came to light.

Over time, Eliza had begun to notice how different Ash was compared to her peers. She may not be as tall as the other Immortals one might encounter, but she radiated as if she'd been crafted from the Moons themselves. Her eyes grew brighter, and her hair longer, glistening in the low light of Crane's nights. She was faster than those around her and could hear every whisper on the wind. Eliza wondered if she'd noticed how different she was on her own and hoped she had. It would be far easier on her if she didn't need to explain everything all at once.

Each day that passed brought Eliza closer to the moment she would leave this Galaxy forever, and what she feared most was leaving Ash to handle the truth on her own. She couldn't allow that. She needed to tell someone else as well. Someone that she could trust as much as she'd once trusted Pat.

Since moving into the Estate, Ash and Lincoln immediately took a liking to one another. As children, they were attached at the hip, and as young adults they seemed to be much more than that. Eliza could see the love they had for one another as they all sat around the dinner table each night, the little gestures that gave off that they were more than friends — a push here, a peck on the cheek there. But Lincoln couldn't be Ash's confidant. It needed to be someone else. Someone capable of withstanding the fear and the pressure.

Eliza sucked in a breath and winced at the pain in her abdomen as she let out a sigh. She sorted through the papers she'd gathered throughout the years when the face of another McBride brother popped into her mind. Ash would need someone strong and trustworthy. Someone like Quinn. Eliza scanned the papers, each article displaying a piece of her daughter. They would tell Ash everything she would need to know to move forward and become the girl Eliza knew she needed to become. Articles about her parents' deaths, about the Missing VanCamp, and about her siblings as they were raised in the Kingdom of Elves. She would need Quinn's help to survive long enough for her to make a decision as to what to do.

Now, all the boxes that once stored Eliza's collection of papers sat empty in the corner of her room. A glance at the clock revealed that it would soon be dusk, and that the McBride brothers and Ash would soon return home from a long day of harvesting. She could already hear Lilly rustling around in the kitchen, working hard to prepare a meal for her family. She may only be twelve, but mentally, the girl was well beyond her years. Pat's children had needed to grow up quickly, adjusting to their father's untimely death. It saddened Eliza, but Lilly would have been an old soul even if the war hadn't torn her family to shreds.

Stars began to speckle in the night sky as Eliza approached her window, the final piece to her display in her hands. The parchment Meera had used to write her letter to Ash had grown delicate with time, but then again, so had Eliza. She held it close to her heart as the sound of laughter pierced through the silence that surrounded the Estate.

Eliza's heart began to quicken as she turned to face her creation, spread across her bedroom floor. Papers arranged by date took up the entirety of the surface. She was careful to step, not wanting to cause any of them to become askew as she moved to place Meera's letter upon her bed.

The sound of the front door opening and shutting caused Eliza to jump. She wasn't ready. Perhaps everything was in order, but her heart was not. She could hear the sound of boots being kicked off, the sound of someone tripping and falling, and then a slur of curses from Cooper.

"Really, Lincoln?" the youngest brother snapped.

Oh, how Eliza would miss their playful sibling rivalry. Deep down, she hoped that rivalry would remain as innocent as it was now. That the pokes and jabs of fingers would never turn into the pokes and jabs of blades. That flicks on the ear would never turn into the quick flick of their fingers releasing a bow string. But Eliza's actions that evening would divide them, even if they couldn't see it yet.

With a depressive sigh, Eliza approached the door. Voices of the McBride boys and her sweet girl, Ashlyn, filled the foyer. The rip of zippers and thump of discarded weapons rattled Eliza's ears. Hoping to catch them before they entered the kitchen, Eliza called from the landing.

"Ash," her feeble voice croaked. With a view of the foyer, she could see her daughter's smile. Her cheeks were flushed from the brisk autumn air and her bright green eyes were wet from tears of laughter. Her mahogany hair fell from its braid in wispy strands that made her look feral. Eliza smiled at her wild girl.

"Yes?" Ash asked, turning to face her mother. Eliza watched her daughter's smile falter, and the light in her eyes dim. Her lips pressed into a thin line as she took in Eliza's appearance.

"I'd like to speak with you upstairs," Eliza replied. "Quinn, too please."

The pair looked at one another with curious gazes and furrowed brows before quickly obeying Eliza's request, abandoning Lincoln and Cooper in the foyer.

Quinn took Eliza's arm and helped her back up the stairs. It was no secret that she was ill, and she appreciated the gesture more than he'd ever know.

Arriving at her bedroom door, Eliza released Quinn's arm and turned to face them. "There is something I need to show you both," she began. "What lies behind this door might be difficult to comprehend at first. Please keep an open mind."

Eliza watched as Ash bit her bottom lip, her eyes dropping quickly to the floor. Her fingers flexed and curled into fists at her sides. Quinn, on the other hand, remained stoic. He stood, his chin high and his back straight as if to say, *I can handle whatever you throw at me.*

Eliza turned slowly, reaching for the doorknob, twisting it gently. The door clicked, causing her heart to skip a beat. *This is it.* Her mind whirled as she allowed the door to swing open.

4

$\mathcal{A}$sh felt her breath catch in her throat as she took in the sight set before her. Newspapers covered nearly every inch of her mother's hardwood floors. Some were yellow and appeared to be even older than she was, displaying titles relating to the High King's demise. Despite the empty feeling in the pit of her stomach, she dropped to her knees beside it, her eyes scanning the late king's face.

"What is all this?" Ash whispered, fighting to understand as she moved on to the next article. "Is this from when the Idonian Kingdom fell?"

"Yes," Eliza replied.

Silently, Ash began to move from paper to paper. Her mind swam with each article she read. The Missing VanCamp, the Trackers, the VanCamp siblings, the wait for the Messenger, Rebel activity throughout the Realm, and so much more. As she read further, she found it difficult to swallow.

"What is all this?" Quinn asked, growing impatient as he reached to pick up an article. "*The Prince of Darkness obliterates Death Valley.*" He read the title, his lips curving into a frown as he put the paper back in its place before following Ash as she made her way around the room.

Ash drowned out his plea for answers, determined to figure them out for herself. There were stories of the Immortals and Dracus, but King Loren's search for the Missing VanCamp began to stick out the most. Every royal in the Realm wanted answers as much as Quinn did.

One name seemed to sink into Ash's heart the most as she moved forward. *Marcus Bonaventure.* She sunk to her knees beside an article displaying a photo of him and a small group of other trackers in Mayfire. The picture had been dated a year ago. Her heart skipped a beat as she realized that this man was still looking for the Missing VanCamp. That he hadn't given up after all these years.

The rest of the papers were more political, reporting visions the Draconian Prophetess, Valentina Gold, had received about the Dark War. Chilling stories of the Pandora and the destruction that followed them throughout the Realm sent a chill down Ash's spine. Her palms became clammy as she read through an article about Princess Penelope's kidnapping last spring. Fury blossomed within her, heating her cheeks as she tried to understand why the Rebels would do such a thing.

Ash stood and looked at her mother, noting the tears in her eyes. She swallowed hard as she glanced at Quinn, who'd made his way back to where the papers began.

"This article," Quinn began, "speaks about how Vincent VanCamp was found the night the Idonian Kingdom fell, alone in the woods beside a murdered Black Knight. Does that sound familiar?" he asked, his voice breaking as the words left his mouth.

Ash pulled in a breath and slowly released it. She had so many questions, but her mind wouldn't allow her to form any words into sentences. "Are you trying to tell us that *I'm* the baby they've been looking for?" she blurted.

Silence hung in the air as Ash held her mother's gaze. Her heart dropped into her stomach the second she saw Eliza begin to nod slowly.

Quinn remained silent as he dropped the paper, allowing it to fall to the floor with the others. The faint sound of it landing on another article was the only sound to be heard as Ash continued to stare at Eliza, now expecting an explanation.

Everything Ash had believed up until this very moment seemed to crash down around her. All she'd ever known was Eliza's motherly love and the McBrides'. The people she'd grown up beside. She'd studied with them, farmed with them, laughed with them and had learned to fight beside them. It was impossible for her to believe that she'd ever been destined to be anywhere else.

"Why are you telling me this now?" Ash broke their painful silence as tears began to prick at her eyes. Her heart began to hammer in her chest and blood raced in her ears, blocking out the silence around them.

"Are-are you expecting her to go to them?" Quinn stammered. "I mean, why would she? This is her home. Let them continue to look. They'll never find her here."

Ash pursed her lips and watched Eliza turn toward her bed, retrieving the envelope that had been sitting on her bedspread. Her stomach twisted into knots as she took note of the name upon it, written in delicate and careful script.

"This was left for you. It was wrapped in the wool I found you swaddled in," Eliza admitted as she slowly approached Ash, gently placing the letter in her hand. "Please try not to be angry with me for keeping this to myself. I only did as I was instructed because I thought I would always be here to protect you. But my future here is uncertain. That letter," she nodded toward the envelope, "will tell you about yours."

Ash's fingers fumbled with the paper as she peeled the letter from the envelope, fighting against the emotions threatening to overwhelm her. She blinked, willing away her tears. She knew that if she gave in, if she let one tear escape, the dam holding them back would break. The ink in her hands would bleed and her future would be lost.

To my darling daughter, Ash,

I wish more than anything that you live a long and happy life, and it breaks my heart that I won't be able to see it myself. I can only be grateful that the Moons blessed me with you and your siblings. Bringing you and your brother into the world during this dark time, has been the only thing to bring me joy. I'm willing to protect you at all costs.

Magic was the only answer I could find.

I will not be beside you as you transition throughout the many milestones of your life, and there are so many things I need to tell you, some of which I'm not proud of.

Fearing there was no other way to give you strength, I used a forbidden potion during your birth. Saving you both is the best thing that I could have done, but because of my actions, you will become something our family has never seen before. The potion I used is unpredictable, and you and your brother will probably transition into Immortals when you reach transition age. Normally, this is at eighteen, but it could occur earlier or later. This I do not know. I want you to know how sorry I am, to take such an important decision, such as your mortality, away from you.

Immortals are not always treated kindly in our beloved Mortal

Realm. I ask that you stay in tune with yourself and your changes. If you ever feel you may be in danger, no matter where you are or how much time has passed, I ask that you go to Dracus. You'll be safe there. I trust King Loren and his comrades more than I trust myself at times.

Ash, I can't apologize enough for all that may happen or has happened to you. But if there's one thing that I'm sure of, it's that you have the blood of VanCamp running through your veins. You will not allow the darkness consuming Idona to win. I knew you were a warrior the second I saw you. Penelope may be the heir to my throne, but something tells me you'll be the one that puts her there.

I'll love you always,
Your mother, Meera.

Ash's lungs burned as her vision ebbed, blurring her biological mother's final words to her. For a few moments, it was as if she'd been thrown back in time, lost in an image of the High Queen dipping her quill in ink mixed with tears to write what she'd just read. She wanted to be angry at everyone—at Eliza for keeping the truth from her, at the Pandora for the decade's worth of terror and destruction, and even at Meera for not running when she should have and allowing her children to have to live a life without her.

It wasn't just that Ash was dealing with the sudden realization that all of Idona had been searching for her since the night she arrived in Crane, there was something about the letter that bothered her even more.

"I'm an Immortal," she whispered, clutching the letter in her shaking hands. "Do you realize where we are? Rebels surround our village. They stand against the

Immortals for their lack of action against Xavier's dark reign. We," she growled, gesturing to Quinn and Eliza, "are Rebels!"

"What do you mean *Immortal?*" Quinn gaped at her, the color draining from his sun-kissed complexion.

"Read it." Ash hissed her demand, thrusting the letter toward him. "She used some sort of potion, and now everyone I know is going to try and kill me the second I transition."

Quinn was silent as he read, shaking his head in disbelief. When he finished, he quickly handed the letter off to Eliza, as if it was poisonous to touch. "So, why am I here then?" he snarled.

"I'm not going to be here forever," Eliza replied coldly. "I can barely handle the stairs. It's getting worse and I don't know how long I have." Her words caused Quinn's features to soften, and a chill to run down Ash's spine. "I couldn't leave you alone with the truth. You needed someone you could trust."

"Why me, then? Why not Lincoln?" Quinn asked, growing tense beside Ash. His gaze darted toward the door as though someone was listening on the other side.

Ash couldn't help but become confused as she waited for her mother to reply. She and Quinn had never been close. It was Cooper she considered her twin because of their close birthdays, not the *brother* she'd apparently shared Meera's womb with. Lincoln had been her closest friend, and perhaps more than that as of late. So, why had Eliza chosen Quinn?

"You're older and wiser than the others," Eliza told him. "Quite possibly even stronger, and far more open-minded. Your concern isn't with the Immortals walking the Realm and their lack of actions against the Dark King. It's with the Pandora and your carnal need to destroy them.

You don't share the same values as the Rebels. You don't share the same hatred. If there's anyone in this village who can protect Ash from those who'd wish to harm her, it's you."

"Are you saying that you think Lincoln and Cooper might wish to kill me?" Ash swallowed hard, her throat growing dry as she pondered the idea. Would they turn on her so easily?

Eliza reached out a hand, placing it softly upon Ash's trembling shoulder. "Up until a few moments ago, you shared the same thoughts about Immortals as they do. What would you have done?" she whispered.

"She's right, Ash," Quinn agreed as he stared down at his empty hands, taking in all he'd just learned. "You…" he trailed off. "You can't trust them."

"So, what do I do? Go to Dracus and pretend I was never here? That I never knew you all? Sit and wonder if you're still alive every time a Red Winter ends?" Ash shook her head, refusing to allow that. "I can't."

"Can't or won't?" Eliza countered.

"No," Quinn snapped, surprising her. "You're not going anywhere. Not now. We'll do our research. We'll figure out how to stop the transition. And if we can't, you can hide it."

Eliza shook her head, drawing their attention. "What if she's a Draconian and needs blood? What if she's an Elf and bears pointed ears? What if she's a Fae and sprouts wings? You must be open to the possibility that staying here might not be an option."

"Then why Dracus? Why not to the Kingdom of Elves where her family members are?" Quinn asked, his strong arms crossing tightly across his chest.

Eliza exhaled slowly before turning to face Ash. "Meera said you're a warrior." Her voice was soft and determined as she stared directly into Ash's eyes. Ash felt the heaviness of her adoptive mother's words. Felt the words that came straight from her dying soul. "The Elves are keeping the other two under lock and key. Go where they'll let you fight."

5

$\mathcal{E}$liza died the fall before Ash's sixteenth birthday, and despite how hard her mother had tried to prepare her for the moment she was no longer there, it hadn't been enough. She felt more alone than ever, and day after day, she found herself standing before her mother's grave. She'd been buried in the same meadow she'd always taken Ash to play in as a child. Back when it had just been the two of them living in a cottage along Main Street in the village.

Now, the meadow's happy memories began to fade and all Ash could remember was how it felt to watch the McBride brothers, Drake Waters, and his son, Sam, carry Eliza's casket through the woods. Her heart would never heal from the moment she watched them lower her into the grave. She would never forget the scream that tore from her throat as they began to fill the hole with dirt or the moment a piece of herself was buried.

Now, nearly two years later, Ash still found herself in that meadow. She wondered if she was losing her mind. She'd rather sit and pour her heart out for hours to Eliza's tombstone than talk to anyone else these days. It wasn't as though people hadn't tried to reach out to her after her mother's passing, many in the village had, but Ash pushed them away. They didn't know about the void in her heart and their kind words would never fill it.

"It was better than most deaths these days," Drake had once said. *"She's happier now."*

"But, what about me?" Ash seethed, digging her nails into her palms at her sides, drawing blood. The scent swam in the air, filling her nostrils, gagging her. Not because she didn't like it, but because she liked it a little *too* much.

"It's been two years since you told me," Ash said softly as she tried her best not to be consumed by her emotions. "Winter Solstice is arriving, and with that comes another Red Winter. And of course, my birthday."

Ash fought against the urge to hyperventilate as she leaned over, placing her hands on her knees. The inevitable was arriving too quickly for her to bear, and she still hadn't made up her mind. She and Quinn had spent the last few years searching for answers, digging for any information on Immortals that Crane had. Yet, the only things they'd discovered were scarce books about the Fae, the Sovereign of Light, and an old crazed bookkeeper who'd gifted her a set of enchanted daggers that he said someone from the past had left for her.

Despite how strange the bookkeeper seemed, and how curious Ash was to know what he really meant, she had far more pressing matters to worry about. So, she took the daggers, having always been a fan of throwing them, and decided to worry more about her coming transition instead.

Although she and Quinn had failed to come up with answers, that wasn't what bothered Ash the most. It was lying to those around her. She'd had no choice but to sever her bond with Lincoln in order to keep him from discovering the truth.

Since Ash and Quinn had first learned the truth about her origin, they'd both abandoned their positions with the Rebels. However, Lincoln and Cooper disagreed and had even considered summoning them all to the tunnels beneath the Realm to hold a Gathering, where they would prepare to take their stand against Xavier and the Immortals who failed to stop him.

But as of today, the Rebels were all in hiding, and Lincoln hadn't found a way to reach them. That was thanks to the Prince of Darkness. Now, Ash no longer needed to worry about the Rebel influence in Crane, but that didn't mean the villagers didn't share the same opinions they always had—a hatred for Immortals.

The second Ash read about how Malachai had killed Walsh, she felt like she could breathe again. She was almost thankful until he'd killed Cedric Chamberlain. The Realm, including Ash, was outraged.

With Walsh and Cedric dead, all Rebel activity in Idona seemed to silence, immediately, until Lincoln decided *he* wanted to replace their perished leaders. Now, it seemed that Ash's choice was clear. She needed to leave, especially if Lincoln *did* find a way to reach the remaining Rebels scattered throughout the Realm.

Footsteps sounded behind her, and Ash was quick to stand up straight and wipe her tears away, hoping to hide her anguish. "I thought I said I wanted to be left alone," she growled.

"You did, but I disagree," Quinn teased, arriving beside her. "Don't you know we still have work to do?"

"Our time has run out. My birthday is in five days," Ash reminded him. "I could transition at any second, even right here in front of you."

Quinn grunted, jabbing her gently in the ribs with his elbow. "At least *try* not to be so negative. We both know you won't transition into a Hybrid. You're clearly a Fae. I mean, look at your ears," he directed as he brushed her hair aside, revealing her pointed tips. She bit back a hiss as she pushed his hand away. "That's at least something. As long as you're not a Hybrid, you're fine."

Ash swallowed hard as she recalled the wounds her sharp nails had left in her palms. How she'd smelled the blood seeping from them.

"Yeah, sure," she mumbled.

"Listen." Quinn sighed. "We can talk more about this later. Lincoln wants us to go on a hunt. It's not every day we're all off watch."

Ash nodded, surprised that none of them had needed to report for duty in the village that day. Watch rotations had begun last week, and each night, able villagers were supposed to report to the watchtowers to search for any glowing red eyes lurking in the distance. The construction of the towers had begun over Summer Solstice a year and a half ago, and this would be Ash and the McBride family's second year participating.

"Fine," Ash agreed, knowing a hunt and some fresh mountain air would do her some good. "Let me just grab my daggers."

"What do you need those for?" Quinn asked as the pair started their short journey home. "What are you going to do, use them to turn a buck to dust? You've seen what they do to Pandora, what makes you think they won't cause our dinner to disappear?"

Ash was quiet for a moment, a slight smile spreading across her plump lips.

"You have a point."

WHEN ASH AND QUINN RETURNED HOME, LINCOLN AND Cooper were already waiting in the foyer. Bows were bound to each of their backs, their quivers well stocked with arrows and fastened to their thighs. Swords were sheathed at their hips, and even though it was unlikely that they would find themselves in full combat with a deer this time of year, it was too risky to leave the house without them.

Ash ran upstairs to gather her own weapons, placing her largest enchanted dagger in her boot before binding her bow to her back. She may not plan to use it during their hunt, but one never knew when the raven perched in the trees might turn out to be a savage beast.

"Why do you always take so damn long?" Lincoln scowled at Ash as she descended the stairs. "I saw the tracks of a deer big enough to stock our freezer for the entire winter and I'm not willing to let Sam get to it first. You all know he's been ruthless this year."

"I swear he's turning this into a competition," Quinn said, rolling his eyes. "Except, it's the kind of competition where the loser starves."

"Good old-fashioned Dark Age fun and games." Ash snorted as she moved toward the front door. "Let's get this over with. Lilly's going to want something to cook before midnight."

"She's right!" Lilly shouted from the kitchen. "Unless you all want eggs and toast again for supper!"

The four of them exited the foyer, and Ash shut the front door behind her harder than she'd intended. The brothers jumped in front of her as the door slammed. Lincoln glanced over his shoulder, meeting her gaze before turning his attention back to the path before them.

The journey to where Lincoln had spotted the tracks was nearly silent, the only sound to be heard was Cooper's occasional whistling. Ash found her eyes falling upon Lincoln's back far too often. She wanted him to turn around. Wanted to give him a silent apology. One that he deserved. She knew he was angry with her. She'd shut him out and shared her secrets only with his elder brother without so much as an explanation. She knew that had wounded him.

Ash stopped dead in her tracks at the sound of a twig snapping off in the distance. "It's further south," she said, watching confusion sweep over Cooper and Lincoln.

Quinn stiffened as Ash realized that she'd heard the twigs break, but the others hadn't.

"Huh? What makes you say that?" Lincoln's brow arched as he looked over his shoulder, his blue eyes narrowing in Ash's direction.

Ash gulped, dropping her gaze from his face. She fought to think of a response, fighting the intense urge to flee. She cleared her throat. "The tracks," she began, gesturing to the soft, muddied, earth. "They lead south."

"Well, duh," Quinn chuckled, trying his best to cover for her.

Ash's stomach churned as Lincoln slowly turned around to face her, crossing his arms tightly in front of his defined chest. Ash's eyes darted between the brothers, resting on Cooper, who refused to meet her gaze. Flexing her fingers, Ash knew this wasn't a normal family hunt. This was a trap.

"What's this?" Quinn gestured to Lincoln's defensive stance. "You're wasting daylight by just standing here. The deer is south. Go fucking *south*," he ordered.

"There is no deer," Lincoln sneered, flaring his nostrils.

Ash set her jaw, her chest growing tight as anxiety

began to grip her. "What do you mean? The tracks are right here. We've been following them for over an hour."

"These tracks were from a deer Sam killed this morning," Lincoln replied. "His sister, Constance, told me *all* about it."

"Since when are you spending time with Constance?" Quinn asked with a damning glare.

"Don't be mad at Constance just because she'd rather see me than you." Lincoln smirked and Ash began to wonder if the man standing before her was the boy she had once loved at all. "I wanted to prove my suspicions were right all along," Lincoln added, gnashing his teeth.

"What suspicions?" Ash's fists balled at her sides. She shifted her weight and the dagger in her boot made its presence known, as it ground against her wool sock. "Being suspicious of me is one thing, but dragging Quinn's betrothed into the mix is crossing the line."

"You think I give a bloody shit about crossing lines?" Lincoln took a step toward her, causing Ash to stagger backward. "You didn't think I'd notice your hair, your skin, your eyes, your ears, and especially your *body* changing?" he gritted out between clenched teeth. His eyes bearing into hers. Lincoln was close enough to Ash that she could feel his hot breath on her cheeks. His shoulder-length dark hair blew in the breeze, brushing her neck. A chill ran down her spine and goosebumps arose along the flesh of her arms.

"I wanted to tell you," Ash admitted, her voice no higher than a whisper.

"But you didn't," Lincoln spat. "At first I thought that you and Quinn were spending time together because you liked one another. I wouldn't blame him for disliking the idea of an arranged marriage. Yeah, it hurt, but, do you want to know what hurt more? Watching you jump down forty feet from a tree last week, only to walk away without a scratch. I realized that you were lying to us all. For fuck's sake, I broke my arm falling ten feet from a tree when I was nine. You just walked away, unscathed."

Ash stood as still as a statue. She was at a loss for words, staring into Lincoln's cold, cruel eyes. She hadn't heard Quinn move from her side, pushing himself between them, barricading her from his brother.

"So, if you knew, then why did you wait until now?!" Quinn roared, shoving Lincoln back with sheer force. He fell to the ground, landing on his back as the forest around them quaked. Birds rose into the sky, cawing and cackling.

"This isn't fair to her and you know it!" Quinn insisted as Lincoln pushed himself up, trembling with rage.

"You want to know what's not fair? Being left in the dark. Holding back secrets from her family and acting like her change isn't something Cooper, Lilly and I should know about. What? Are we not trustworthy?" His eyes flashed to Ash, burning with a fury she knew she'd invoked. "I thought we told each other everything! I guess I was wrong."

"Lincoln, stop." Cooper's low voice cut in, attempting to calm the situation. "We shouldn't talk about this here." Ash remained frozen in place, her eyes wide with fear and confusion. There was nothing to say. Nothing she could do to defend herself.

"No, this happens now," Lincoln demanded as he approached Ash, once again. "Move," he ordered Quinn.

Quinn remained still, refusing to obey. His jaw twitched, his body quivering with anger. Ash appreciated his protection but knew she didn't need it. Whatever was coming to her, she deserved. Stepping around the eldest McBride, Ash approached Lincoln. She moved so quickly that he jumped backward, his harsh eyes widening with surprise.

"What?" Ash snapped, no longer afraid to let her own anger show. "What do you wanna do now? Kill me? Drag my body off to your little Rebel friends? Put me on display and make an example out of me, the same way the Rebels made an example out of that Elf?"

Lincoln's expression softened as he continued to stare down at her, hurt replacing the anger that had once raged so intensely in his eyes. "Do you honestly think I would do any of those things to you?" he whispered before backing away from Ash. His pain-filled gaze darted from her to his brothers before he turned his back on them all and disappeared into the trees.

As Ash and the others began their journey home, the fact that she no longer needed to hide her abilities from Cooper offered a small shred of relief. She took to the trees and jumped effortlessly from limb to limb, allowing the late fall breeze to unravel her braid and snarl her soft locks. The chill air invaded her lungs and froze the tears that ran silently down her cheeks.

They returned home at dusk with empty hands—with no deer, and with no Lincoln in sight. As they sat around the dining room table, Quinn and Cooper explained to Lilly what had transpired during the hunt. Ash drowned out their conversation, her eyes on Lincoln's empty seat across the table. She pushed her plate of steamed vegetables away, her stomach churning as she fought to escape the harsh words that had been said as they replayed endlessly in her mind.

Ash and Lincoln had always bickered in the past, but they'd always made up at the end of the day. Things were different this time. She'd watched her sharp words sting him and had never seen such hurt reflecting in his eyes before he'd stormed off. Perhaps, he hadn't planned for their conversation to turn out as badly as it had. Maybe their emotions had just gotten the best of them all.

Once dinner was through, Ash helped Lilly clear the table and rinse the dishes. She solemnly ran a towel over the plates to dry them before putting them in the cupboard.

"You know," Lilly said in a soft tone as she placed a hand on Ash's shoulder, "I don't think of you any differently."

Shutting the cupboard, Ash turned to face the fourteen-year-old. There was much she wanted to say to her, however, she couldn't bring herself to speak. Instead, she stared back at her, unable to miss the compassion portrayed in Lilly's bright blue eyes, before wordlessly pulling her into a warm embrace.

They retreated to the family room, as they always did after their final meal of the day. Normally, Ash and the McBrides would use the time to discuss their days, or their plans for tomorrow. But today, an uneasy silence hung in the air.

Ash curled into her favorite spot on the couch, her fingers running over the smooth leather spine of a book she knew she wouldn't be able to concentrate on. She pulled in a deep, painful breath as her eyes drifted shut. She wanted to go back in time and tell Lincoln the truth from the start. She wasn't sure how she could fix what had happened between them, but she was determined to try.

The clock struck ten, and what was left of Ash's patience vanished. Lincoln may be angry with her and Quinn, but his anger wasn't worth staying out this late. *Alone.*

"I'm going to look for him," she announced as she stood from her place on the couch, then darted into the foyer. Slipping her feet into her worn boots, Ash turned as footsteps approached her from behind.

"Ash, I wouldn't," Cooper cautioned, his voice wavering.

Ash had tried to stifle her blossoming anger for Cooper but failed. If he had warned her and Quinn about Lincoln's plans, what had occurred on the hunt could have been avoided.

"I don't care what *you* would do," she snapped, catching sight of Lilly's head snapping up from her book. She stared in their direction with wide, fearful eyes. "You know where he would go. I know you do. Tell me where he is."

Cooper's eyes fell to the floor, his shoulders drooping. "Listen, I tried to convince him otherwise," he admitted softly. "But if you really want to go and get into *another* fight with him, by all means, go. He's probably with Constance."

Ash watched as he turned on his heel and walked back into the family room. She sucked in a deep breath, her gaze halting on Quinn. He was staring down at his clenched fists, his expression slack. Her heart dropped at the thought of how he must feel. After all, she felt the same way. No pain compared to the bitter sting of betrayal.

Frowning, Ash tore her eyes from his face and approached the weapons closet, retrieving her bow, sword, and daggers. She quickly armed herself before advancing toward the front door. As her hand wrapped around the cold brass doorknob, a subtle tremor began to bloom beneath her boots. Her brows pulled together as she kneeled, pressing her palms against the dark hardwood floor. The tremor continued, intensifying as the seconds passed by.

"Do you guys feel that?" Ash asked as she shot to her feet, then moved toward the threshold to the family room.

At first, the McBride siblings didn't appear to notice anything, but after a moment, the entire house began to shake. They braced themselves, gripping onto furniture as if the quaking might bring the entire estate down upon them.

"What's happening?" Lilly shrieked.

A horrifying conclusion as to what could be causing it began to gnaw at the back of Ash's mind, and she rushed to take action. "Help me shut off all the lights," she demanded, running to flick every switch she could find. Darkness flooded the entire house as the brothers and Lilly hurried to do the same.

Ash made her way toward the kitchen where a lonely candle flickered in the dark, casting eerie shadows on the walls. She blew it out, her eyes falling on the window above the sink. Her heart began to race, her pulse pounding in her ears as she caught sight of the fields behind the house. Starlight illuminated the sky above, casting a gentle glow onto the pastures below. Thousands of red eyes glinted in the night as Pandora raced toward Crane with Immortal speed. The ground shook with every step they took, rattling the ceiling fan above her. Wind chimes hanging off the back porch flung back and forth, ringing as metal rods crashed together.

"Oh no," Ash whispered as she thought of Lincoln and the other villagers. Her skin crawled as she imagined what would happen to them.

Her heart thundered against her ribcage, threatening to burst through her chest as Ash made her way back into the foyer. She halted as she took in Quinn's form. He stood with his bow in hand and his favored claymore sheathed at his hip. His face was stony and his eyes fierce.

He gave Ash a curt nod, and she knew exactly what he was thinking.

They were going after them.

"You two," Quinn turned his attention toward his siblings, "go in the basement and don't make a sound until morning."

Cooper opened his mouth to object, but he was quickly silenced by his brother. "This isn't a debate. Lilly needs you here. Protect her," Quinn ordered. " If I'm not back by morning, you know what to do."

It was clear that Cooper disagreed, but he inclined his head to both Ash and Quinn and said, "Good luck," before taking Lilly into the basement.

With no time to waste, Ash and Quinn bolted from the house and into the forest beyond the estate.

The ground was still rumbling, and the Pandora were too close for comfort. Ash swallowed against the lump in her throat, fighting against the fear beginning to consume her. She began to wonder if she was dreaming, because everything she and Quinn were doing reminded her of what nightmares were made of. She held her breath as they raced after the Pandora, knowing that if they weren't careful, they were only seconds away from death.

This couldn't possibly end well. She groaned. *Who in their right mind runs* after *the Pandora?*

The swarm of Pandora was larger than any other Crane had faced before, and that could only mean one thing. Destruction.

The realization hit Ash like a blow to the gut. Had the Dark King and his demented prince really sent so many Pandora to destroy the hidden village once and for all? An animalistic snarl escaped her as she looked toward Quinn.

"You know what this is, right?" Ash asked in a whisper, watching as he fought to keep up with her. He nodded slowly, his face pale beneath the moonlight that streamed through the forest canopy above.

"There's no point in destroying us. He wouldn't be able to flaunt his work in front of the Realm. What matters about an obliterated village no one knew about in the first place?"

Ash silently wondered why Xavier would want to destroy Crane in such a way. How did the village compare to Mayfire, or Greystone? Both were large establishments, reduced to nothing but ash and smoke. Blood likely still stained the earth where they used to thrive. So, why Crane? Ash shook her head, willing her thoughts away. The battle she and Quinn were about to throw themselves into would be the worst they'd ever endured and could be the worst they ever would. She needed to focus.

Warm light streamed from the streetlights around Crane, illuminating the village as it came into view. Sirens began to wail, vibrating painfully in Ash's ears as the harsh noise bounced off the surrounding mountains. She could hear everything. The bloodcurdling screams of villagers caught in the swarm, and the quick breaths of women and children running from their fate.

Ash and Quinn waited, concealed by the tree line's shadows as the Pandora continued to barrel over the stone wall surrounding the village. She found it difficult to breathe as she watched an army of thousands invade her home in a blur of black fur and glowing red eyes.

The beasts began to slow to a stop, and Ash blinked a few times to be sure she wasn't imagining it.

"Why are they stopping?" she growled, her brow wrinkling. Once again, the earth began to tremble beneath her. The same way it had when the Pandora had passed the estate. Only this time, it felt different. She pressed her palm against the cold, damp grass to feel more. "The tunnels." Her eyes bulged. "There are people in the tunnels."

Ash could hear Quinn's breathing stagger beside her, his eyes still fixed on the Pandora. The beasts were walking, pushing into the village streets as if they'd been summoned. "We need to find Drake," he told her, rising to his feet.

Ash closed her eyes for a moment as she did the same, slowly removing her sword from its sheath. She focused on her hearing, searching through an endless sea of rapidly beating hearts.

The Pandora.

They were nervous. Ash smirked, finding that quite amusing. With nervousness came hesitation, and hesitation in battle always led to death. That had been the first lesson she and the McBride siblings had learned in training. *Don't think and certainly don't blink.* Ash could still hear Drake's words echo in her mind as she found his voice past the sea of beating hearts. He'd gathered a small army of his own, and they were preparing to strike.

"I found him. Northside of the village. In the fields over there. He's gathered the others," she whispered. "We're late to the party. They're already in formation."

"What formation?" Quinn grunted.

Sighing, Ash focused on Drake's voice once again. The sound of the Justice Keeper's words led her heart to leap into her throat. "Formation Z," she whispered, a shiver skittering down her spine.

Quinn's eyes bulged as he turned to face to her. "As in *the* Formation Z?"

Ash nodded as she fought to master her growing fear. "That explains why the Pandora stopped. They can smell the explosives."

7

The Prince of Darkness had done many difficult and dreary deeds throughout his fifty years of life. Some of them he hadn't wanted to, but most of them he had. He'd yearned for bloodthirsty battles. *Especially* battles where the stakes were high. The adrenaline racing through his veins during a risky fight was something he desperately craved. There was nothing quite like curling his fist around an enemy's neck, digging his sharp talon-like nails into their flesh and watching the life leave their eyes.

But this time, his heart was beating too quickly for his liking. His father had forced his hand, and now Malachai was overcome with nerves. His mouth became dry and his chest tight as he thought of how this night would determine the future.

The Strip had many cliffs and peaks with beautiful views, but, the view set before Malachai only made him grow uneasy. His palms grew sweaty as he stood within the invisible barrier, his eyes set upon a series of glowing lights off in the distance.

Crane.

"You knew it would happen, eventually," Alrich

reminded the prince from behind. "Xavier's been begging for this for years."

A low hiss sailed past Malachai's lips as he turned around, his long black coat swirling around with him. "And what the King wants, he gets," he drawled sarcastically. "Let's just get what we need and get out of here. We'll watch the destruction of the next village."

Alrich led the way, while Malachai followed slowly. He scanned the forest around them, hoping to find someone or something that would stop him from what he was about to do. When they did fall on someone, his breath hitched in his throat. He could feel his heart pounding against the walls of his chest as he stared the man in the eye.

Malachai paused, his eyes narrowing. He wondered if the man would approach him. If he did choose to step forward, would the prince even bother to draw his sword? Did Malachai want to fight him at all? Before he could make up his mind on the matter, the man slowly turned around and walked out of view.

Has my entire *past come back to haunt me today?*

GETTING TO DRAKE BEFORE HE FOLLOWED THROUGH WITH his plan was crucial, or else there was a large chance they'd be swallowed by the flames about to swarm throughout their village. Ash wondered if she'd ever moved so fast in her entire life. The village blurred as she ran around it, her eyes darting in every direction, searching for anything that might strike her.

Ash could feel Quinn behind her and realized that he kept up with her well enough—for a Mortal. Perhaps it was the adrenaline making him move faster as they fought to get to Drake before the chaos unraveled.

Drake and his small army of villagers came into view, and Ash slowed her running as she scanned their faces, searching for Lincoln. Her heart faltered in her chest as she realized he wasn't beside Sam, where he should have been. *Shit.* She grimaced, now imagining the worst. He'd been caught up in the swarm. What if one of those bloodcurdling screams from before had been his?

When Drake spotted the pair running toward him, Ash could see relief flash in his dark, misty eyes. "Draw your bows, get in line with the archers," he ordered.

Ash and Quinn did as they were asked and took their places beside one another on the frontline. She watched as Sam rushed over with two bundles of explosive arrows before taking his place on her left. As she filled her quiver with them, Ash wondered if this was necessary. If this was *truly* their only option. She looked up, focusing on the thousands of beasts crowding the village. She could feel her blood chilling in her veins as she took in how vicious they appeared. They were so black that they nearly blended in with the night around them, but their eyes gave them away. The same eyes that haunted the nightmares of every man, woman, and child in Idona.

As if Quinn could hear her thoughts, he took her hand for a moment and gave it a gentle squeeze. "It's better we destroy our home than them," he whispered in her ear, his warm breath brushing against her neck. "At least we'll still be here to rebuild it."

Ash's breathing became ragged as a frigid winter breeze swam around her, rustling her long locks. Behind her, Crane's north field was covered with men and women, armed with swords and shields. She could sense them all trying not to tremble, and could hear them whisper prayers to whoever might listen.

This was it.

The Pandora remained still, their backs arched, their fur spiked along their spines. The beasts in the form of birds perched on rooftops, staring down their beaks in the Mortals' direction. Ash shivered beneath their stares, wondering why they didn't flee. Their rapid heartbeats gave their fear away so easily, but they refused to move a muscle. They refused to run. They would fight until the last man stood victorious. That was their way.

"There are four hundred of us and thousands of them," Drake announced. "Those odds don't sound great. Nevertheless, we've prepared for a day like this for decades. We're ready. They're not. Stay in formation. Don't let them in. If we separate, they'll pick us off like vultures. Don't give them the chance."

The Archers loaded their bows in perfect unison. The weapon in Ash's hands was far more dangerous than anything she'd held before, and she refused to let that scare her any more than she already was. The arrows would imbed themselves in the flesh of the Pandora, and their body heat would ignite them. It would take no less than thirty seconds. Then, Ash would watch her home burn.

"Archers, on three!" Drake shouted, his own bow gripped tightly in his trembling hands.

The second the Justice Keeper said "*Three*", Ash let her arrow fly, watching as a hundred more joined hers in the sky. Their entire army moved back as they watched the arrows sail with the breeze. Wails shattered the deafening silence and Ash's heart skipped a beat as she pinned her bow between her thighs so she could cover her ears with trembling hands.

Chaos unfolded throughout the village as the arrows erupted. The blast was powerful enough to nearly knock both armies onto their backs. An intense heat over-whelmed the north fields as an eruption filled with bits and pieces of burning enemy flesh swallowed main street whole. Ash steeled herself as her eyes began to water, stinging as smoke from the village began to surround the army. She growled, her vision blurring as the Pandora began to leap through the flames.

"Load!" Drake ordered and the Archers readied themselves, again. There was no time to waste. The Pandora were moving too quickly for them to wait for the Justice Leader's count. A second set of arrows flew through the air, one of them hitting the large stone justice building that sat in the center of the village square.

The building exploded, sending an array of shrapnel into the Dark Army as they fought to escape. Screams and yelps rang in Ash's ears. Her skin was slick with sweat as the intense heat radiated from the burning village. Hot air filled her lungs as she gasped, watching the Pandora as they ran frantically from the flames threatening to swallow them.

Ash would never forget the smell of singed fur as the Pandora erupted through the black smoke billowing above the raging fire. She swallowed hard, moving aside as shielded warriors took their place on the frontline. The screech of metal rose up in her ears as her fellow archers drew their swords, tossing their bows to the ground.

Light glittered off Drake's blade as he held it in the air. The army awaited his signal to begin their march toward the enemy. Ash stiffened as she observed the beasts, some of them transitioning from wolves to large felines. All determined to pick up speed.

Drake lowered his sword and the army pushed forward. The villagers ran quickly, slamming their shields and thrusting their swords into the enemy as they met on the field. Ash snatched the dagger from her thigh and began to thrust it into any black-furred being within her reach.

Dusty black mist hung in the air around the battle as the enemy's remains were carried away by the breeze. Snow began to fall, covering the battlefield in a thick blanket of white. The storm had a negative impact on their visibility, but Ash was thankful that the Pandora were naturally dark, standing out in stark contrast against the snow.

Blood from both armies painted the snowy battlefield. Saliva pooled in Ash's mouth, the coppery scent pushing her senses into overdrive. She snarled, shoving herself further into the shields, yearning to get closer to the enemy.

Another Red Winter had officially arrived.

Drake's army forced Pandora back toward the flames. Smoke filtered through the air as the Pandora transitioned into black bears, towering over the Mortals. Foamy saliva dripped from their sharp teeth as they pushed against them with all their profound strength. The Mortal warriors fought to hold them back, their feet dragging in the snow as they were driven backward.

Snow coated the grass and everything around Ash grew slick. She fought to keep her traction, losing as she held off the Pandora bears. The beasts lunged toward her, and despite valiant effort, Ash fell to the hard, damp ground. Claws gripped at her ankles, dragging her beneath the line of shields. She rolled onto her stomach, her nails dragging into the earth as she struggled to free herself from the bear's grip. Her eyes fell on her dagger, and she reached for it, her entire torso stretching painfully as her fingers grazed its silver pommel. She hissed, her entire body tense as she attempted to stretch herself even more, determined to grasp the enchanted weapon.

Before Ash could wrap her fingers around it, the Pandora wrenched her even further. She cried out, its claws digging deeper into her ankle as she rolled back onto her back. She forgot how to breathe as she stared up into its hungry red eyes. Drops of foamy saliva fell on her face as she squirmed, her hand running down her leg as she reached for another dagger in her boot.

She grabbed it, thrusting it upward into the Pandora's right eye. Dark blood spewed from the wound before the beast faded to mist. Its grip on Ash's ankle disappeared, and she trembled with relief as she began to inch backward toward the Mortal army. Before she could make it back behind the shields, pain rippled through her entire form. Her back arched as she cried out in agony, her fingers curling. Her heart felt as if it had been lit aflame as her blood turned to magma in her veins.

Ash gasped for air, only to choke on blood as it crept up her throat. Her eyes widened, bulging as her lungs grew leaden in her chest. *Transition.* She shook her head, hot tears spilling from her eyes. *Not now.*

A hand curled around Ash's hood, pulling her back behind the shields. Sam and Quinn hovered above her, concern flashing through their eyes. They were both covered in blood that wasn't their own, and her stomach churned at the sight of it.

"What's happening to her?" Constance shrieked from behind her elder brother.

Blood dribbled down Ash's chin, rolling down her neck in thick streams. She focused on Quinn's face as she fought an internal battle to keep the transition at bay. *Not now,* she silently repeated.

"Get her out of here," Drake thundered.

Ash swallowed the blood in her mouth. It coated her teeth, staining them red. She felt her body responding to its taste as an array of sensations ran through her. Her nerves felt as if they were on fire, yet a strange new energy overcame her.

"No," Ash insisted, forcing herself to her feet. She coughed, spitting more blood out onto the snow before wiping her mouth with her sleeve.

"Did one of them inject you with something?" Sam asked, his brow furrowing as he looked her up and down, examining her.

Ash scoffed at the sound of his question. "Don't worry about me," she groused. "Worry about the enemy."

The surviving Pandora had begun encircling Drake's army as they pushed further back into the fields. While the blasts had certainly dwindled their numbers, the Mortals were still severely outnumbered and completely surrounded.

It was abundantly clear the Dark Army had developed a strategy as the Mortals were forced to huddle closer together. Those who had shields and spears formed a shielded circle around their army, but Ash knew it wouldn't be enough.

As Quinn handed her back her sword, she held his gaze for a few moments. He gave her a long look, his brows pulling together as if to ask *Are you okay?* She gave him a nod, though she certainly wasn't. The second the Pandora advanced on them; they'd be overrun. Her coming transition was the *least* of her concerns right now, even if it had nearly become a public show.

"Drake, we need to do something," Ash warned.

The Justice Leader was at a loss for words, his expression grave. "Any ideas?" he asked warily.

Ash bit her bloody lip, running her tongue across her teeth, stealing what's left of the blood. Her heart faltered as her tongue ran over a sharp set of fangs. *This* can't *be happening right now.*

"We need to figure something out *now*," Sam declared as the Pandora began to dig their feet into the snow, preparing to launch themselves toward the small crowd of Mortals.

Without thinking, Ash reached for a bow on the ground beside her and loaded it with another explosive arrow.

"What the hell are you doing? Are you *trying* to blow us all up?" Constance growled.

Ash bit back a vicious snarl as she turned her icy glare toward Constance. "Whatever it takes to get us out of this," she barked before turning to face Quinn. "Lift me up."

Quinn hesitantly lowered himself, driving a knee into the snow. "I sure hope you've thought this through," he grumbled as Ash climbed onto his shoulders before he rose to his full height.

The Pandora noticed her immediately, snarling as she aimed her arrow toward the thickest part of their army. "The second I let this arrow go, run," she instructed the other Mortals as she released her bowstring.

The arrow spiraled toward the Dark Army, striking a single Pandora. The flames spread from each beast to the next, spreading rapidly through their fur, burning through them as they frantically tried to escape.

"Keep them coming!" Ash insisted as she leaped off Quinn's shoulders and loaded her bow with a second arrow. Fire was the only way to force the Pandora to retreat, even if that meant risking what was left of the village. Or her own life.

The Mortals began to spread out, running to different parts of the battlefield. Explosions scattered throughout the hidden village as they emptied their quivers. The Pandora were frantic, far more focused on escaping the flames than attacking the Mortals. Some of them began to transition into birds and attempted to escape Crane altogether.

Something deep in Ash's gut stirred, refusing to let her take the opportunity to flee. She snarled through her clenched teeth, rage coursing through her like a rushing, angry river. She wouldn't allow them to retreat after all they'd done. Instead of running into the mountains like most of the other villagers, she drew her sword and began to advance on the enemy, cutting down any beast her blade would reach. She swung ruthlessly, blood spewing in every direction.

The sound of bones cracking beneath Ash's forceful blows thrilled her, sending a shiver swimming down her spine.

Snow continued to fall in thick, icy flakes, slowly smothering the flames as Ash made her way around them. The wind intensified, blurring her surroundings as she continued to slay any Pandora that dared to cross her path. If they wanted to fight until the last man stood victorious then *she* would be the victor.

Quinn moved to fight beside her, and Ash spared him a sidelong glance as she continued to tear through the beasts. "If you keep this up, the entire village is going to know you're not so Mortal," he warned.

Ash wanted to tell him everything. What she'd felt on the battlefield. How sharp the fangs were in her mouth, but she couldn't risk the distraction. "I'm not sure I can control that anymore," she told him.

When the snow abruptly ceased falling, Ash slowly stopped swinging her sword. The Pandora were cowering in front of her, and her lips twitched toward a smirk.

Although, there was something strange about the way they appeared. She looked around, catching sight of the snow still falling in the distance.

Confused, Ash looked toward Quinn. His wide, fearful eyes were fixed on the sky, as were the other villagers around her. She looked up, her breath immediately evading her lungs.

A massive black Dragon, the color of midnight itself, hovered above the village. Its large, glowing sapphire eyes ignited the dark sky around it as it peered down at the battle. Ash's eyes began to bulge as she watched its nostrils flare, tendrils of smoke flowing from them. She gulped as its mouth opened, revealing rows of razor-sharp teeth and a blue glow emitting from the back of its throat.

"She's gonna blow!" Ash roared before grabbing Quinn and bolting toward the tree line.

She flew into the trees, sucking in deep breaths as she watched blue fire rain down from the sky. The Pandora began to burn, their bones dissipating, leaving nothing but piles of ash behind.

Ash was sure her heart was going to beat straight out of her chest as her eyes fell on Drake. She watched as he stood in the center of the battlefield with his children, their eyes fixed on the Dragon. The blue fire circled them, yet they didn't burn. Ash's mouth fell open as she watched it all unfold, at a loss for words.

The fire eventually halted, and the only flames that remained were the ones caused by the explosive arrows. Most of them had dwindled down, but pillars of black smoke still rose to the sky as the sun began to rise over the mountains.

Ash and Quinn abandoned their spot in the trees and joined the others on the battlefield. She looked over what remained of the village, her knees wobbling as a sigh of relief escaped her. Main street had been obliterated. The shops and the justice building were now nothing more than piles of burned stone and wood, but the rest of the village, the houses, and school, didn't suffer nearly as much damage.

The Mortals who had escaped through the tunnels would be able to return to their beds, and that was a miracle.

"I thought Dragons were extinct." Sam was awestruck, his eyes still fixed on the sky.

Ash shrugged as she followed his gaze toward where the Dragon had appeared. "Not anymore."

8

*M*arcus Bonaventure had begun to believe that there was nothing that could surprise him anymore. He'd witnessed enough strange happenings to last him the length of an Immortal lifetime. However, when his communications chip began to buzz incessantly before dawn this morning, he realized he'd been wrong. Some things *could* still stun the Draconian.

As he rushed to get ready so he could report to the Kingdom of Dracus's Training Center, where he'd been summoned, Marcus's mind swam. His favorite communications officer, Grant Miller, had been so frazzled on their call that he'd barely been able to form any words, but the word Marcus was able to comprehend left him more shocked than he'd ever been before.

Dragon.

Thousands of questions were forming in Marcus's mind as he rushed through the castle and out into the city beyond. He wanted answers. So much so that he was willing to break the law by using Immortal speed within the kingdom's perimeters. For a few moments, he couldn't care less that he was a council member, and that he would likely be given a lot of grief if he were to be seen by King Loren or one of his confidants.

Marcus burst through the Training Center's front doors, barging into the large arena-like building. The first floor was where he worked every day. As the Head Mentor, he trained recently transitioned Immortals and Draconians coming of age. The second and third floors were comprised of dozens of arenas containing different climates and surroundings scattered about the building, designed to teach their warriors how to fight in every possible scenario.

The two underground floors belonged to Communications, operated by Marcus's fellow Council member, Benjamin Buttler. The Mentor bolted to the back of the building, where he flew down the stairs. He'd expected to find Grant, and possibly Benjamin as well, in one of the conference rooms. But after pushing open every door along the hall, it became obvious that they were likely on the last floor—the lab.

Marcus grumbled on his way down the stairs, his patience wearing thin.

When he arrived in the lab, Marcus cleared his throat nervously as he took in his surroundings. Massive screens displayed maps of Idona everywhere that he looked. Some scanned the skies, while others were covered in red dots, displaying familiar locations. Locations where he'd looked for the Missing VanCamp.

Marcus's stomach churned, his eyes falling on Grant, who was typing furiously at his preferred station. Benjamin paced nearby, circling his temples with his fingers.

"What is all this? Did you say something about a Dragon? Why are my Missing VanCamp search locations being displayed?" Marcus questioned, crossing his arms.

Grant glanced over his shoulder, his eyes meeting

Marcus's. "Once Aries connects and Loren arrives, we'll explain everything."

"Have a little patience," Benjamin added, his tone less than kind.

Marcus scowled in his direction, having never been Benjamin's biggest fan. In his opinion, the Head of Communications was nothing but a womanizing socialite with a knack for major technological breakthroughs. Sure, Benjamin was incredibly smart and extremely talented. He could design anything from weapons and armor to communications devices that couldn't be rivaled by anything else in Si Realtra. And while Marcus appreciated everything Benjamin had done to help Idona evolve, that didn't mean he liked him. Not one bit.

"I'd have had more patience had I not been woken up in the middle of the night and told to come here immediately, only to find no one is ready to tell me a damn reason why." Marcus glowered, filling his lungs to the brim. He'd sought for far too long and too hard for answers to be toyed with in this manner.

The sound of footsteps echoing in the hall outside caused Marcus to stiffen. His eyes fell on the door where Loren stood. Bags sat under the king's eyes, and he wore no crown. He was dressed in only a pair of black slacks and a white shirt he hadn't bothered to button all the way. It was clear, Marcus hadn't been the only one suffering due to Grant's early morning panic.

"Finally," Benjamin muttered.

"You know I need at least one glass of blood and four cups of coffee before I can fathom the idea of leaving my quarters, let alone my bed." Loren frowned as he made his way over to a coffee station in the corner of the lab where Marcus watched him fill a tall cup.

The king left it black and barely gave it a chance to cool before he began to chug.

A shrill, repetitive ring began to sound, bouncing off the lab's opaque glass walls. Marcus's hands flew to his ears in an effort to block out the noise. The ringing ceased, and Aries appeared on the screen above Grant's desk. The communications officer rolled back to get a better look at them, and Marcus and the other Draconians gathered behind him.

Aries, the Fae Queen Cleo's advisor, seemed pale and exhausted. Marcus had met the Immortal on plenty of occasions, and this was the first time he didn't appear angry. His burgundy eyes weren't set in an eternal glare for a change. Instead, his features were soft and solemn.

"Were you able to confirm the scout's sighting?" Aries asked.

Grant gave the Fae a curt nod. "Our jurisdiction's transmission tower picked up an unusually high level of skyward activity," he confirmed. "We lost track of it once it crossed over into the Elven jurisdiction, heading northwest it appears. Toward you."

"I've sent my own scouts into the Forest of Fools to keep an eye out," Aries replied.

"What exactly are we talking about here?" Marcus interjected.

"One of our Draconian scouts was investigating something in central Idona on the Strip when he noticed an unusual amount of Pandora in the area," Benjamin explained. "He followed them and witnessed one heck of an attack. But that wasn't the most interesting thing. He saw a Dragon."

Benjamin began to fiddle with his information tablet, a device no bigger than a large book, yet as thin as a sheet of glass, that contained various files and allowed him to communicate with people across the Realm. A few seconds later, an image was displayed on another screen across the lab.

Marcus gawked at the sight of it. The scout had been able to get a clear picture of the Dragon as it was breathing blue fire above the village. There was no denying that it was one of the supposedly extinct beasts that used to fly near Mayfire and the Skyward mountain range. "I thought Erminian soldiers took out the last of our Dragons during the Five Realm War." Marcus shook his head disbelievingly.

"Apparently not," Loren sighed. "This has to be some sort of miracle."

"What makes it even more intriguing is that our scout says that the Dragon had a *Rider*," Grant added matter-of-factly, wearing a wide, toothy grin.

While it would be wonderful for Dragons to fly through Idonian skies with Riders upon their backs, Marcus wouldn't believe it until he saw it with his own two eyes. "So, let me guess," he drawled. "You want me to track it."

"No," Benjamin revealed. "Dragons have always been free to roam our skies, why bother tracking them? It's clear that this particular Dragon has something against the Pandora."

"And it clearly wanted to protect that village," Marcus added. "Wait, what village was it? And which scout?" he asked, curiously lifting a single brow.

Loren paled beside the Mentor. "Aries, care to explain?" the King requested, offering the Fae a dashing smile.

"Why me?" Aries' eternal glare returned, as prominent as ever. "I didn't send him. I just sent the letter."

Loren huffed, and it was clear to Marcus that there was

plenty he had yet to learn. He waited patiently beside the King, his eyes narrowing as he stared him down.

"Vincent found a letter addressed to Cedric from Aries that the Elf had never opened." Loren's voice wavered as he began his explanation. "It turns out he'd been on to something shortly before his tragic death."

Aries nodded, clearing his throat. "A few weeks before he died, Cedric paid me a visit. He asked me if the Fae had any records pertaining to those hatch exits and their locations. I told him I'd give them a look and mail him whatever I found. It took me a bit, but I was able to locate an original list of where they were built. So, I copied it and mailed it out to him.

"I didn't know he'd never opened it, or I'd have brought it up to the Council. When Loren reached out to me a while later, saying that Vincent had found the letter and opened it, I was shocked. I'd figured Cedric had read it and confirmed that all the locations Meera had were correct. But it turns out, that wasn't the case." The Fae shivered in his seat, his feathered black wings ruffling at his back.

Marcus felt the blood rush from his face, his heart quickening its pace in his chest. His throat felt as if it might be swelling shut as he stared at his king.

"Vincent came to Dracus and requested we allow him to investigate the unknown exit about a week ago. He was convinced the coordinates to the location we hadn't originally had on Meera's list were the coordinates pertaining to that hidden village you and Cedric were investigating a few years prior." Loren reached out for Marcus, placing a calming hand upon his shoulder. "He found it."

The entire Realm around Marcus seemed to freeze in time, and he quickly became furious. "Cedric and I were *there*," he began to argue. "There was nothing at the center of the Strip's swirl!"

"An invisible barrier," Aries mentioned softly. "It's likely there was one placed around it. You couldn't possibly know that. You're not trained in the ways of Magic. But Cedric was. I'm surprised he didn't."

Marcus felt his blood beginning to boil as it rushed through his veins. "Did he find her?" he asked, gnashing his teeth.

Benjamin swiped the screen of his information tablet with a single finger, revealing a second picture. Marcus felt his knees weaken at the sight of it and quickly grabbed on to the back of Grant's chair to brace himself. He examined the picture, sucking in a deep, shaky breath.

The picture was of a girl, standing with a Mortal army. Marcus's stomach fluttered as he examined her face. Everything about her features reminded him of a VanCamp. It was her. It *had* to be.

"Vincent says she fought like an Immortal," Benjamin added softly. "She could have transitioned already. It's hard to tell. Her hair covers her ears. But she *looks* like an Immortal."

Aries nodded, agreeing with the Draconian. "She has the stature of a Fae, but no wings. Yet. She may not have completed the transition. But, central Idona has been under the Rebel influence for decades now. It's possible that all of those people around her share those values. If she hasn't transitioned already, once she does, she could be in deep shit."

"We need to send a team." Loren winced at Marcus's side. "Where is Vincent now?"

"From my understanding, he went after the Dragon," Benjamin admitted, cringing as the words left his mouth.

"I can't believe you let *Vincent* out into the field."

Marcus scowled, his eyes on both Benjamin and Loren. "He's not a Draconian scout. We have no idea if he's even finished training."

Loren shook his head, disagreeing. "Vincent is a fine warrior. He trained under Aveo for years and has learned a great deal from Beck and Thaddeus as well. I trust him. He's not a baby anymore."

"Oh? He just ran after a fucking Dragon!" Marcus bellowed. "Where is he now? Alone, right as the Red Winter has begun?"

"I'll find him," Aries offered.

"We need to concentrate more on getting people into that village," Benjamin declared, tossing his information tablet to the side. "I've already reached out to Lucinda. If there's a barrier involved, you'll need her help."

Marcus's features softened at the thought of working with the Realm Sorceress once again. "I request Humphrey Adams and Craven Amsterdam as well."

Loren's brows raised, a faint smile spreading across his lips. "I couldn't think of anyone better."

9

*V*incent VanCamp had never been any good at making rash decisions. He was a man of caution. There had never been a time where he'd done anything without thinking it through, imagining every possible scenario. Everything the Elf had ever done had been precise and planned. One might believe that Vincent even had an itinerary to follow throughout his entire Immortal life.

However, the second Vincent had caught sight of a Dragon, all prior caution he'd had was gone with the wind. What made matters worse was what *else* he'd seen in the hidden village. *All* he had seen and *who* he had seen. His heart was still racing, even now—three days later.

Vincent had needed to make a choice, on impulse, which was something he'd never done before. Sure, one might say fleeing from the Kingdom of Elves and running off to Dracus might have been impulsive, but the truth was, he'd been planning his escape for as long as he could remember.

As he'd perched upon a tree and watched complete and utter chaos unfold in the hidden village, Vincent had needed to make a choice. Follow the Dragon, or approach who he believed *could* be the Missing VanCamp. His twin. A girl whom he'd shared his mother's womb with long ago. The desire to find out the truth about the girl he'd watched burned deep in his gut. But, going into such a secretive village on his own and announcing his arrival seemed like a horrible idea.

So, all Vincent could do was send the pictures and the information he'd gathered to Benjamin. He took off after the Dragon instead, yet another desire for even *more* answers completely consuming him.

"Marcus is better suited to approach the girl, anyway," Vincent told himself as he traveled through the trees. The Dragon had flown northwest, and he'd been quick to follow it. While he hadn't seen the majestic beast since, a gut feeling had led him there. Yet his whereabouts made his stomach flutter with nerves.

As Vincent approached a tree line, he was faced with a large valley with rolling hills that stretched on for miles, and another forest on the other side of it. The Forest of Fools. His blood turned to ice in his veins at the sight of it.

As a child, Vincent had always known he would grow up to turn into some sort of Immortal. He hadn't known what, but it was moments like these that he was happy to have transitioned into an Elf. His superior vision allowed him to see all the things his once Mortal eyes could never see.

While he hoped the Dragon wouldn't be there, a sinking feeling in his stomach made him believe that it would. His suspicions were confirmed as he watched the large beast dive from the clouds above, flying above the forest in anxious circles.

This is what Esmeralda would call *Elven intuition.* Vincent frowned, focusing his vision on the Dragon's back.

When he had first witnessed the beast in the skies, back at the hidden village, he was positive that there had been a Rider upon it. To his dismay, there was no one there.

Vincent's brow wrinkled as he relaxed against the tree and continued to watch the Dragon. His muscles ached terribly, and his stomach growled every few moments. His journey had been long, but it was certainly far from over. A deep sigh escaped him as he began to analyze the Dragon's behavior, as well as his surroundings and what he might do next.

Everywhere the Elf looked, there was danger. He couldn't help but think of Cedric, and what he might do in this scenario. His heart sank at the thought of him. Oh, how he missed the man he thought he might eventually call his brother.

Although Vincent disagreed, it was clear what Cedric would do and say. He'd say *There's something wrong with that Dragon.* Vincent groaned as he prepared to leap from the tree. *And to find out what.*

Vincent jumped from the branch he'd settled himself upon, landing in a crouch on the ground below. He scanned the field in front of him, beads of sweat forming along his brow. He'd stick out like a sore thumb as he walked across it, clad in a red-and-black Draconian uniform against the snow-covered hills. The only thing he could hope for was that the Dragon's presence steered any Pandora away.

And that the Dragon itself wouldn't tear him apart.

They say Dragon's blood runs through VanCamp veins, Vincent reminded himself warily as he began his trek through the field, toward the Forest of Fools. *Perhaps it'll smell that and won't kill me.*

Thoughts of what Loren might think began to creep into Vincent's mind. If the Draconian King knew what he was about to do, the odds of him ever letting the Elf back into the field were slim to none.

"It's best he doesn't know," Vincent told himself, quickening his pace. The beast was still frantically circling above the forest as he halted before the tree line. He could see fear reflecting in the beast's large blue eyes. Panic, even.

Vincent swallowed against his tightening throat as he considered the idea of the Dragon having had a Rider. Was it possible that that was why the beast was in such disarray? He drew his sword, squinting as he peered into the forest, attempting to locate any visible traps.

"From the looks of it," Vincent muttered to himself, "the Dragon is hovering above the north east side of the forest, which means it'll be a long walk to see why. And who knows what sort of traps the Fae have scattered about the place."

Sighing, Vincent took his first step into the forest. He recalled his training with Aveo and focused all of his senses on his surroundings. He began to move throughout the complicated terrain with light, careful steps. "Aveo wouldn't have been dumb enough to go in here without the help of a Fae," Vincent groused, forcing himself to continue.

The coppery scent of blood began to fill the air around the Elf. He stiffened, his nostrils flaring. "Mortal blood," he whispered, nearly gagging. He would never understand how Draconians found the scent so alluring.

Now, it was clear why the Dragon was in such a state. There *had* been a Rider, and they were injured. Vincent began to move faster through the frightening forest, his feet remaining nimble as he carefully planned every step he took. He encountered a large gap in the earth and leaped across, just barely clearing it. His breath escaped him as he stumbled, nearly toppling over. Steadying himself, Vincent brought a hand to his chest and worked to control his breathing, the brush with death having left his nerves a mess.

The scent of blood strengthened, thickening in the air, and Vincent knew he was getting closer. A harsh wind blew through the forest from above, rustling his hair, likely caused by the Dragon's wings. He fought to keep himself steady, the breeze strong enough to knock him off his feet as his eyes fell on a man lying lifelessly up ahead.

The Dragon roared above as Vincent neared the body, bile creeping up his throat at the sight of him. The man appeared to have been mauled by something. Crimson blood seeped from multiple gashes on the man's flesh, soaking the forest floor around him.

Unsure of what to do, Vincent's mind raced as nausea swept through him. He shook his head, willing the feeling away as he reached for the man's wrist. He pressed his trembling fingers against the man's veins, feeling for a pulse as he caught sight of the sword sheathed at the man's hip.

Vincent felt the blood rush from his face as he examined the hilt. A glass Dragon's eye sat on the pommel, while the silver was engraved with fierce flames. "Dragons Breath." Vincent's pulse vibrated in his ears as he rolled the man over. "It can't be," he whispered, stumbling backward, his eyes widening from pure shock.

The man's pale hair looked as if it hadn't been cut in years, and was caked with blood, sticking to his pale forehead. He seemed to be no older than twenty-five, and Vincent could see Idonian knot patterns running down his arms, spreading on his chest beneath his tattered shirt.

"The mark of a Dragon." Vincent nearly choked on the words as he glanced toward the sky. The Dragon's eyes were upon him, burning into him from above, begging him to save the man before him.

Unsure of anything else to do, Vincent rose to his full height, his breathing raspy and shallow. "ARIES!" he screamed at the top of his lungs, silently pleading that the Fae would hear him. "CLEO!"

Tears began to well in Vincent's eyes as he listened for the man's heartbeat. It was weakening more and more as the seconds passed by. His mind was in shambles as he tried to make sense of everything around him. He shouted the names of every Fae he knew over and over again until one of them finally appeared in front of him.

"Vincent." Aries' burgundy eyes were set in a vicious glare, his black wings fanned out behind him. The Fae glanced at the Mortal man, his face twisting with disgust before he looked toward the sky and paled beneath the moonlight. "What in the eight layers of the Underworld…" he trailed off.

"We need to get this man to Dracus *now*," Vincent demanded, sparing the Dragon one last look. He hoped the beast understood what he was about to do, and that its heart wouldn't break when he vanished with the Rider right before its eyes.

Aries sank to his knees, checking for a pulse himself. "It's weak, but it's there," he muttered. "He might have a chance."

"Let's go then. Unless you have a better idea," Vincent snapped.

Aries was quiet for a moment, his brow furrowing. "Draconian venom would be faster than anything we could do here." He sighed, reaching for Vincent's arm and taking it firmly in his grip. His other hand wrapped around the Rider's torn jacket. "I'd close your eyes if I were you."

Vincent did as the Fae suggested, clamping his eyes shut. Wind whooshed in his ears as a tingling sensation prickled along every inch of his flesh. The Realm felt as if it were spinning around him, leaving him dizzy and even more nauseous than he was to begin with. He opened his eyes, immediately blinded by the bright white tiles coating every inch of the Draconian Infirmary. His eyes adjusted and he watched as Aries laid the Rider down on a stretcher. One more sight of the gore only caused the Elf to find the nearest trash bin and wretch into it.

Healers were already fussing around the Rider, hooking him up to machines and putting pressure on his wounds, when Vincent finished hurling. The head Healer, Ebony, was already paging both the Mentor and the King using a system that'll broadcast her message throughout the entire Kingdom.

"One of them better get here immediately," Ebony growled as she turned to work on the Rider. "He's fading fast."

Aries moved to stand beside Vincent, placing a calming hand on the Elf's shoulder. "You did good, VanCamp," he acknowledged.

Vincent bit at his nails, watching as the Healers rushed about the room. He wondered silently if he'd be sick again, his eyes glued to the enchanted sword still sheathed at the man's hip.

Shouts sounded out in the hall and Vincent backed against the wall, wishing he could shrink against it. He could hear Marcus's voice as he barked something at Craven. Lucinda was frantic as she chased after them both.

Marcus burst into the room, and Ebony immediately handed him an empty vial that he quickly brought to his exposed fangs. Vincent's eyes widened as he watched it fill with yellow-tinted, bubbling liquid. *Venom*, he cringed, having heard how painful the substance was as it raced through veins and into vital organs, triggering the Draconian transition.

Once the Mentor filled the vial, he handed it to Ebony, who dipped a syringe into it and retrieved the venom. Marcus took it back from her and approached the bed, barely paying any mind to the man or his current condition as he drove the syringe into his heart.

Vincent winced as he watched everything unfold, swallowing hard against the vomit racing up his throat to keep it from spewing onto the sanitized floors.

"You're going to have to get over that," Aries told him.

When Marcus finished, he turned to face Vincent with the worst scowl the Elf had ever seen. He held his breath, waiting for the inevitable.

"You're a bloody idiot," Marcus accused. "Who in their right mind chases after a *Dragon* into the Forest of fucking Fools, of all places!"

"He did the right thing." Aries moved to defend him. "Like Loren said, he's not a baby now. Look, he just saved the Dragon's Rider!"

"Not just any Rider." Vincent's voice wavered as he pushed himself off the wall, striding toward the bed. His hand curled around the hilt of Dragons Breath as he pulled the enchanted sword free from its sheath.

Marcus's jaw dropped at the sight of it.

"I'm pretty sure this is Alistair Ward." Vincent gulped.

10

Three long, tiresome days had passed by since the Pandora's attack on Crane, and Ash could still feel every bit of exhaustion in her aching limbs. Her sore muscles screamed with every step she took, but that hadn't stopped her from searching for Lincoln. From the moment the Dragon had disappeared from the skies above her, she and Quinn has rushed back to the estate to wash themselves of the gore covering them and check on Cooper and Lilly. They hadn't stopped long enough to eat or rest before the four of them took off into the mountains.

The McBride siblings were each in pieces without their brother, but they had still joined Ash on that first day. They had called Lincoln's name, shouting it over and over again until their lungs burned, but to no avail.

Since then, Ash had combed through the forests that surrounded the massive ravine Crane was built within, and the mountains beyond. She refused to think about the fangs she'd noticed in her mouth that night, or the surge of power she'd felt coursing through her.

Lincoln's disappearance mattered more to her than coming to terms with what she was turning into. She wanted to find him. She wanted to make things right, before she was forced to leave Crane behind for good, and the McBrides as well.

There was nothing Ash could do to make up for the last two years, and she silently vowed to never tell another lie. Even if the truth killed her. Even if it drove those she loved away.

The other villagers believed Lincoln to be dead. It was safe to assume that while he'd been storming off in the forest, the Pandora had run him through. But Ash wouldn't believe that, not unless she saw it with her own eyes.

Now, Ash found herself looking for his corpse. She expected to encounter the scent of rotting flesh and follow it to its source. While she wanted to succumb to her grief and to weep until her tears ran dry, she couldn't allow herself to. She wanted to find him and bury him alongside his father and mother.

After she gave Lincoln a proper burial, Ash would have to make her choice. Quinn had returned home yesterday evening after assisting the other villagers with Crane's repairs, only to reveal that the villagers were growing suspicious of her. There was plenty of talk about what had occurred during the attack. Many of the Mortals in the army had witnessed her endure the pain of a transition, or at the very least, part of one. Ash could only hope that they hadn't realized what exactly they'd seen.

They thought she'd been bitten by a Pandora, and that she was turning into one. The very idea made Ash chuckle, rolling her eyes as she maneuvered through the Strip's uneven terrain. The rubber tread of her boots gripped snow and slippery earth. She stepped over exposed roots, gripping the trunks of trees as she climbed over jagged rocks.

At first, Ash kept to the mountain paths the villagers had created over the last few centuries. But it was clear Lincoln wasn't anywhere upon them, which meant she'd needed to broaden her search.

The Strip wasn't a safe place for anyone to indulge in their desire to mountain climb. It was dangerous, with plenty of opportunities to fall from extreme heights. Wolves and bears had made the mountain range their home, and while they might not be Pandora, Ash still wished to avoid them at all costs.

Not a single villager had offered to help her after the first day, and that was incredibly bothersome. They believed her ventures to be pointless, and that Lincoln was truly lost to them all.

Ash would cover far more ground if she had some assistance, but she understood why the McBride's might want to avoid finding their brother's body. Sometimes it was easier to just believe a missing person to be dead rather than go looking for them.

Everyone wanted answers, but sometimes those answers weren't the ones you'd hoped for. Ash knew that fact all too well. It had been easier for her to believe that she'd transition into a Fae, due to her short stature and her small, pointed ears. She may still be Immortal, but at least she wouldn't be slaughtered by the other Immortals. Now, she was forced to face the truth. She was, indeed, a Fae, and she was also a Draconian.

She was a Hybrid.

The one thing she'd prayed *not* to be.

For a moment, Ash allowed herself to consider what her great, great-grandfather might have done if he'd known what she would become today. Would he have banned Hybrids? Would the law exist at all? She was selfish to think of such a thing after so many Hybrids before her had been slaughtered due to their unpredictability and dangerous natures.

Ash swallowed; her mouth having gone dry. Coming to the realization that she was Hybrid and accepting that fact was only part of her problem. It complicated everything, but most importantly her decision as to where to run to. She certainly couldn't go to the Kingdom of Elves. If they didn't kill her, they'd lock her up.

"Like hell they will." Ash scowled as she found herself approaching one of the mountain paths she'd walked upon that morning. "Great, I've officially gone in a circle. What great progress I've made," she groused sarcastically, leaning against a tree as she thought about what she should do next.

Maybe the others were right. Maybe she should give up.

Snow began to trickle down from the skies once again, swirling in flurries around Ash as she sucked in a few calming breaths. "Why did you have to storm off," she whispered. "Why couldn't we just continue to scream and fight until this whole thing was resolved. I could have gone my own way then. I wouldn't have to be here, looking for your body."

The sound of nearby footsteps pulled Ash from her thoughts. She instinctively reached for the dagger in her boot, her eyes scanning the forest around her.

Ash believed that it was possible one of the McBrides had come to retrieve her. Dusk would arrive soon, and just because they had managed to defeat the Pandora, that didn't mean the beasts wouldn't come back for revenge.

A shiver ran down Ash's spine at the thought as she crouched beside the tree, shielding herself with the surrounding brush. Her muscles tensed as she kept still, her hot breath turning into icy clouds in front of her. She pressed one of her hands against the earth, feeling for vibrations. *South*. Her gaze darted in that direction, her breath catching in her throat when her eyes fell on a man.

It was clear he was an Immortal. Ash could practically smell it, her nostrils flaring. While he didn't appear aggressive, she imagined he was deadly. He was tall with a tanned complexion. His dark golden hair fell in waves to his broad shoulders. His caramel-colored eyes were upon her, shining bright in the fading sunlight. Ash fought not to squirm beneath his gaze as she rose to her full height.

They stared at one another in silence. Ash examined him, attempting to figure out exactly who and *what* he was, and it was likely that he was doing the same to her. She might be able to hide her differences from the Mortals, but she doubted she could do that so easily in the presence of another Immortal.

"And why would a girl like you be in these mountains alone, at the start of a Red Winter?" the man asked, tilting his head as he continued to peer at her with narrowing eyes.

Ash jumped at the sound of his deep, husky voice and nervously cleared her throat. "I could ask you the same thing," she retorted with a shrug. "You don't belong here."

The man mockingly mimicked her shrug. "I roam where I like," he quipped, taking a step in her direction. "You don't belong here either."

Ash stiffened at the sound of his accusation, biting back a vicious snarl. "Well, unlike you, I *live* here," she said, her fingers curling into fists at her sides.

"If you say so." The man replied with a smirk. "What are you, anyway?"

Ash's heart surged into a gallop in response to the question. Her stomach twisted into knots as she fought to think of a reply that wouldn't get her killed. "What are you?" she deflected, crossing her arms and tucking her dagger against her ribs.

"I asked you first," he sneered.

"Yeah, well, my mountains, my rules," Ash told him, her grip tightening around the dagger's hilt.

The man arched a perfect brow, now standing a mere foot away from her. This was the closest Ash had ever been to another Immortal. *Well, one that isn't a Pandora,* she thought as she stared him down. She could see why the Mortals wouldn't like them. Power practically radiated off the man's form, seeping from his pores. She wondered exactly what he was capable of in battle and imagined quite a lot more than the Mortals she was used to fighting alongside. It was no wonder the Immortal Silence had infuriated everyone. They wanted the Immortals to use that power that came so easily and do something. *Anything.*

"My name is Morghan Henning," the man revealed.

The name struck a nerve deep in Ash. Her brows pulled together as she thought back to the papers Eliza had once displayed across her bedroom floor. *Morghan Henning.* A subtle gasp escaped as she realized exactly who she was looking at.

"You're the last Werewolf," Ash blurted, her eyes widening.

"And you are?" Morghan pressed, pursing his lips.

"Ashlyn," she reluctantly admitted. "Ashlyn Snow."

Morghan held out his hand, and Ash hesitantly took it in her own. She shook it lightly, now deep in thought about what might happen next. Would he realize what she was? Could he *smell* what she was? The thought caused a lump to form in her throat. She swallowed against it, her pulse beginning to pound in her ears.

"You haven't answered my question," Morghan mentioned curiously as he released her hand. It fell limply to her side. "I saw what happened to your village the other night. It's far too dangerous for anyone to be out here alone. The Pandora don't take defeat lightly."

Ash nodded, shivering at the thought of how they might retaliate as she slipped her dagger back into her boot. "I'm looking for someone."

Morghan's brows raised, his lips dipping into a slight frown. "These days, people that go missing *stay* missing," he told her softly.

"I know," Ash snapped. "But that doesn't mean I won't try to find him. I owe him at least that."

Morghan shifted his weight uncomfortably in front of her. "I'd advise you to stop your search. Go home," he said, and Ash's blood quickly began to boil in her veins.

Rage began to heat Ash's cheeks, her jaw clenching. "I don't take orders," she informed him, baring her teeth. "Especially from strangers."

"Listen kid," Morghan growled, his expression grim. "You don't know what you're getting yourself into."

Ash's heart sank into her stomach as she held his gaze, noting the warning in his eyes. "You know something I don't, don't you?" she accused, curling her fingers into her palms.

Morghan's jaw twitched, and Ash could sense his reluctance to tell her the truth. "Who are you looking for?" he questioned, his tone as cold as the snow falling around them.

For a moment, Ash considered why this Werewolf would be so worrisome about her continuing to look for Lincoln. Or why he wanted to know who he was. "His name is Lincoln McBride. He's around six foot two, nineteen years old, with blue eyes and dark hair about as long as yours," she explained softly.

Morghan's frown deepened, his eyes drifting away from

her and toward the forest floor. "Go home," he repeated, turning his back on her.

"What do you know?" Ash fumed, her eyes bearing into his back.

"Nothing you *want* to know," Morghan shot over his shoulder.

"Tell me." Ash reached for her dagger once again. "Or I'll make you."

She held her breath as she watched Morghan tense in front of her. She imagined he could transition into a Wolf larger than any she's ever seen and tear her to ribbons. He slowly turned around, and Ash could see the pupils in his eyes widening, nearly swallowing his brown irises whole. She forced herself not to tremble or show her fear, but knew he could likely smell it.

"If you even so much as point that dagger at me, I'll bite your hand off," Morghan hissed.

Ash lowered the dagger, now pointing it toward the earth below. "Tell me what happened to him," she whispered, debating whether she should beg.

"Listen, I don't know who you are or *what* you are," Morghan told her, his pupils relaxing. "I don't know what the deal is with this village, or the people in it. I don't know why the Dark Army is so obsessed with it. To be truthful, I came here to find out. I think I have my answers now."

Ash sucked in a long shaky breath to keep herself from losing what's left of her patience. Her arms continued to hang at her sides, when all she wanted to do was take her hands and use them to shake the information she needed out of the Werewolf.

"What answers?" Ash barked, gnashing her teeth.

Morghan grunted frustratedly as he ran a hand through his hair, brushing it away from his face. "If I tell you, promise me you won't do anything rash. You don't know what you're up against."

"I promise." Ash silently cursed herself for telling another lie.

"The Prince took him," Morghan admitted and Ash's knees became weak. She fell back against the tree, bracing herself against it, hoping to remain on her feet. "Likely because of his last name. If this McBride you speak of is what I *think* he is, then Xavier has just gained one *powerful* asset. This war would be as good as over."

Confusion swept through Ash, her mind whirling. "The McBride's are farmers. *Mortal* farmers," she insisted, giving the Wolf a damning glare. "Whatever you *think* Lincoln is, you're wrong."

"Sure." Morghan scoffed. "I'd believe you if I hadn't seen a fucking *Dragon* the other day. But if *they're* going to bounce back from extinction, the Arebus might as well too."

Ash shook her head. "I don't know what you're talking about," she told him. "But if the Prince took Lincoln because he *thinks* he's one of these Archers you're referring to, well, he's going to be pretty damn disappointed," she declared, her heart pounding against the walls of her chest. "We need to get Lincoln back before the Prince realizes he's useless."

A hysterical laugh escaped Morghan, tears welling in his eyes. "*We?*" he chuckled. "*We* are not doing anything. You want to cross the Prince of Darkness? By all means, go right ahead. But you're doing it on your own."

Ash released an exasperated sigh. "What if I said I know of someone who can help?" she asked him. "And all *you* need to do is get me to him."

Morghan's laughing dwindled, though his smirk remained. "And what makes you think I'm willing to leave my new humble abode to take you anywhere? Ashlynn, we just met. It's not appropriate for us to run away together."

"I need to go there anyway," Ash admitted softly, her gaze dropping from the Wolf's face and drifting toward the falling snow. "It's not safe for me in this village anymore. If you can take me to Dracus, I promise I'll make it worth your while."

"Ah, so that's what you are," Morghan mused. "How did you wind up so far away from home?"

"Dracus was never my home," Ash grunted. "But it's Marcus Bonaventure's, and there's no way I'll get Lincoln back without his help."

The Werewolf was clearly struggling to stifle another bout of laughter as he looked her over. Ash froze beneath his gaze, having never appreciated the feeling of being examined. "What makes you think he'll help you run after Malachai, of all people?"

"I have something he wants," she replied, revealing no emotion in her tone. "So, will you take me there?"

Morghan was quiet for a few moments, his facial expressions changing as he thought about the matter. Ash fought against the urge to tap her foot impatiently, her pulse quickening as she imagined what she might do if he said no. Or even if he said yes.

"Fine," Morghan reluctantly agreed.

Ash's eyes widened with surprise. "Really?"

"I'll take you as far as the Endurion River," Morghan added. "But I won't go into that kingdom. Everyone wants a piece of the last Werewolf." He shivered, his nose wrinkling with disgust. "Meet me on the East Cliff tomorrow morning."

By the time Ash returned to the McBride Estate later that evening, the three moons were hanging high in the sky. She spared them a glance, glowering in their direction. Most of the citizens in Si Realtra believed that the Sovereign of Light, the being who breathed life into the Realms long ago, retreated to the Moons. That she lived there, guiding her people from above.

Ash scoffed at the thought. What she needed now more than ever was guidance, yet she found none. And tomorrow, she'd head to Dracus with a stranger, leaving everyone she'd ever known behind. All on a whim. All because of one single hope that Lincoln might be able to be saved.

The alluring scent of apple pie wafted from the house, and Ash's stomach groaned as she took it in. "Lilly must be stress-baking again." She sighed, her fingers wrapping around the cold, brass doorknob.

As she entered the house, Ash bit at her bottom lip. There wasn't a soul to be seen as she kicked her boots off and slipped out of her jacket. The wooden coat rack wobbled as she hung it on a hook, and she reached to steady it before walking further into the foyer. Her eyes drifted into the family room on her right, a smile creeping across her lips.

A fire was lit in the hearth at the back of the family room, fresh logs burning brightly. She eyed the flames for a moment, shivering as the fire began to heat her cold and tired flesh. Prickling sensations ran through her fingers and toes as they adjusted to the heat.

Ash would prefer to enter the family room further and stay near the fire, cherishing its warmth before she embarked on her journey to Dracus, but the scent of apple pie had only grown stronger since she'd entered the house. Her mouth watered as she tore her eyes from the fireplace and made her way down the hall to the kitchen. Candle-light flickered from sconces along the wall, the scent of matches still hanging in the air around them.

Ash sighed dreamily, reveling in the cozy feeling of home as she entered the kitchen. She reached for the switch on the wall beside the threshold and flicked it upward. Light flooded the room, revealing the people who'd been hiding within. The McBride's and the Waters' siblings all grinned in her direction.

"Surprise!" Lilly squealed excitedly.

Ash's jaw dropped as she looked around. White paper streamers hung from the ceiling in intricate dips. A fresh apple pie was set on the kitchen table beside a small pile of gifts. "What is all this?"

"What, we're not allowed to celebrate your birthday?" Quinn teased with a crooked smile.

No part of Ash was in the mood for a celebration, especially one that involved Constance Waters. Her eyes fell on the girl who sat at the kitchen table. Hair the shade of black silk swam over Constance's shoulders, framing her heart-shaped face. Large pale eyes hid beneath thick eyelashes, staring down a narrow nose in Ash's direction.

A rage-fueled heat coiled in Ash's stomach as she stared back at Constance. Lincoln's disappearance and the Pandora attack had been enough to distract her from what she'd learned during the hunt for a short time, but, not anymore. Memories of Constance's betrayal rushed to the front of Ash's mind as a vicious hiss rolled off her tongue.

"Let me guess," Ash began slowly. "You're just here to see if it's true that I'm turning into a Pandora."

Constance's lashes fluttered as her eyes grew wide. "I'm here because I was invited," she replied innocently.

"Mm-hm." Ash's eyes rolled, her heart quickening its pace as her anger intensified. "That's a shock, considering what you've done," she snarled.

Quinn held up a single hand, silencing Ash as he drew her attention. Her lips pursed at the sight of his glower. He didn't say a word, but the warning in his cerulean eyes was enough to get her to bite her tongue. A furious blush crept onto Ash's cheeks as she fought to stifle her hatred for Constance.

"My birthday isn't for two more days," Ash declared, changing the subject.

"Hence why this was a *surprise* party," Cooper chuckled.

Ash scanned the faces throughout the room, wishing she could appreciate them all more. She *wanted* to be happy about what they'd done for her, but far too much weight had fallen upon her shoulders. Sharp pains radiated through Ash's chest as she thought of all Morghan had said earlier, and what she would do tomorrow. She cleared her throat, forcing a smile.

"Thank you," she told them all.

Sam smiled back at her, his sky-blue eyes shining

brightly. "We just want to make sure that you know we care about you,"

Ash's breath caught in her throat as an eerie silence developed between them. She stared at Sam, her stomach lurching. *They know,* she gulped, her eyes darting from face to face. Every muscle in her body tensed as she watched Lilly turn to face the counter, her head falling into her hands.

Ash's gaze drifted toward the back door, her heart thrashing against her ribcage. "This is another trap, isn't it?" she asked warily, glancing toward Cooper. She scowled at him as his eyes dropped to the floor.

"Not the kind you think," Quinn assured her, holding out his hands as if to stop Ash from doing anything reckless.

"Really?" Ash snapped. "It sure feels like an intervention!"

Constance stood from her seat, resting her hands on the kitchen table as she leaned forward. "You do understand that they *had* to tell us, right?" she asked, her fingers wrapping around the white lace tablecloth. "We're not idiots, Ash. Thankfully they spilled the beans before we *really* started to believe you were turning into a Pandora. I wouldn't have thought twice about slitting your throat!"

"What's going to make me believe that you still won't try?" Ash gnashed her teeth, her white-knuckled fists trembling at her sides.

Constance's cheeks burned red, fury reflecting in her harsh gaze. "Did you want me to?"

"That's enough!" Quinn bellowed, slamming his fist on the kitchen counter. The ceiling fan above them rattled, the paper streamers swaying as Lilly nearly jumped out of her apron. "We aren't here to fight. We've done enough of that lately. We're here to help you."

Ash pressed her lips into a hard line as she stared at him. "Help me do what, Quinn?" she asked, her sinuses burning as tears fueled by her anger formed in her eyes.

"Make your choice," he told her softly.

Little did he know that she'd already made her choice. "Don't worry about what I'm going to do," Ash spat, her heart faltering as she watched hurt flash across his face. She'd seen that hurt before. Once, when she'd pushed Lincoln away to keep him from learning the truth. Now, she needed to do the same to Quinn. If he knew what she was going to do tomorrow morning, he'd follow her— straight into the lion's den.

Lilly cleared her throat as she straightened her apron. Bits of flour flew into the air around her, coating her hands. "I say everyone just calms down and has some pie," she suggested, her cyan eyes smiling as she stared at Ash. "Why not open your gifts as well?"

Ash eyed the small pile on the table, her eyes narrowing. She'd never been fond of receiving gifts. She'd prefer people spend their hard-earned coin on the things they needed. "Fine," she muttered, striding toward the table.

The first gift was a long and narrow box, wrapped in plain brown paper with a bow made of twine. Ash pulled the twine away and gently dislodged the paper, revealing a wooden box. She stared down at it, running her fingers over the smooth surface. Her name was etched in elegant script on the top, which brought a faint smile to her lips. As she turned it in her hands, she heard something rattle inside. Her stomach fluttered as her fingers ran over the golden latch on the side of the box.

Ash opened it, her eyes bulging slightly at the sight of a silver pocket watch. The letter *A* was engraved on the front, surrounded by an elegant pattern of vines twisted into

Idonian knots. A small clasp protruded just below where the long, sparkling chain began. She pressed her thumb against it and the watch swung open. Her heart sank as she gazed down at the face of a clock and a picture of the McBrides, Sam Waters, and herself from last Giving Day.

"I took that picture," Constance mused with a smirk.

Ash blinked against the tears forming in her eyes, swallowing the lump in her throat as she stared at the picture. She was nestled between Lincoln and Cooper, while Lilly sat in front of them. Quinn grinned from beside Cooper, while Sam laughed beside Lincoln. Her heart warmed as she looked up at those watching her.

"Whose idea was this?" she asked, her voice little more than a shaky whisper.

"Lincoln and I split the cost," Sam revealed with a wide smile. "You've been a tad bit grumpy the last few years. We just wanted to make you smile on your birthday, especially since you've reached such a huge milestone this year."

Ash's breath staggered at the thought of their thoughtfulness. Her heart broke in her chest as she began to wish Lincoln was here more than ever before. She fought the urge to curse beneath her breath. *I'm going to get him back, even if it kills me.*

"Mine next!" Cooper insisted as he pointed to the second gift. Ash placed the watch back inside its box and set it gently on the table, taking the next gift in her hands. She could tell immediately that it was a book, and a thick one.

Ash tore at the paper once again and gawked down at the cover. The book looked ancient and was made with delicate and careful hands. The leather cover was centered by the Idonian symbol, embossed in gold foil. Three intersecting triangles stared back at her, shining beneath the kitchen light.

"It's about Immortals!" Cooper exclaimed excitedly as he moved to her side and gestured for her to open the book. "It's handwritten and filled to the brim with information. There are even spells in here. And potions!"

Ash examined the first few pages, her mouth hanging open as she skimmed the script upon them. *The Fall of the Arebus Archers.* She cleared her throat nervously as she recalled what Morghan had said to her earlier. Her eyes flitted to Quinn, who was wearing a grin that stretched from ear to ear.

"Where the hell was this two years ago?" Ash grumbled, and he laughed musically.

"I found it in my dad's barn, amongst plenty of other things. There were all sorts of journals, books about farming, and then this," Cooper told her, nearly trembling with excitement. "Of course, if I had known about your... predicament a bit sooner, I'd have given it to you a year ago when I found it."

Ash's lips curved into a deep frown as she looked up at Cooper. "Very funny," she growled.

"Don't expect a gift from me!" Lilly warned with a playful smile. "I slaved over that apple pie for hours!"

"Okay, last thing!" Quinn began to fish through the pocket of his worn jeans. When he pulled out a small ring box, Ash felt her blood rush from her face. She glanced toward Constance, who was eyeing Quinn warily from her seat at the table.

"Uh…" Ash squeaked; her eyes fixed on the box.

Quinn began to walk toward her, his eyes twinkling in the kitchen light. Ash held her breath, watching every move he made with scrutinizing eyes.

A knock on the front door caused everyone in the

kitchen to jump, and Lilly cursed beneath her breath. Both of her brothers glared in her direction as she moved to answer it. A few moments later, Ash began to hear Drake's voice in the foyer, and the familiar sound of Lilly complaining.

Sighing, Ash turned to head into the foyer herself to find out why the two of them were becoming so irate. The others followed on her heels.

"No, they can't go out. We're in the middle of Ash's birthday party!" Lilly argued, her hands planted firmly on her narrow hips.

The Justice Leader's lips were pressed into a thin line, his jaw set. While Lilly may be the youngest at just fourteen years of age, she was a small force to be reckoned with. Arguing with her about anything was pointless, especially when it came to interrupting the family time she adored.

"You can resume the party when we get to the bottom of this," Drake said, and Ash winced as the words left his mouth.

"My brothers and Ash aren't the only warriors in Crane!" Lilly roared.

"What's the meaning of this?" Constance pushed passed Ash, lightly shoving her to the side. Ash bit back a hiss as she fought not to return the favor.

Drake turned to face his daughter, his face pale and grave. He looked as if he'd seen a ghost. Ash's spine straightened, the hairs on the back of her neck beginning to raise as she anticipated what he might say. Whatever it was, it was clearly dangerous enough for him to want to travel all the way up to the McBride Estate and request their help.

"Billy Sanders ran back down the mountain in the middle of his shift, yelling and screaming that he'd seen a Werewolf," Drake explained slowly.

Ash felt her breath escape her as her knees weakened. She reached out, placing a hand on Cooper's shoulder to keep herself from falling to the foyer floor. Her mind began to race with thoughts of what might happen next. What did Drake expect them to do? Kill Morghan? She couldn't! Without him, how would she get to Dracus? Sure, she might be able to find her own way, but how long would that take? She could get lost. Or worse, find herself caught in a swarm of Pandora.

A queasy feeling began to develop deep in Ash's stomach, and the heat wafting from the fire in the family room quickly became too hot for her to bear, beads of sweat forming along her brow. As she fought to remain calm, a searing headache pierced through her thoughts and sent her crumbling to her knees. Every nerve in her body felt as if it were on fire, burning beneath her skin. She gasped, sucking in as much air her lungs would allow as darkness began to creep along the edges of her vision. She could feel herself slipping into an unconscious state as the taste of blood appeared in her mouth once again.

ight had fallen in Dracus, and the Kingdom was silent. More silent than Marcus had ever noticed before as he found himself approaching the black butterfly fountain in the city square. Lucinda was already waiting for him, clad in black, as if to blend in with the shadows. While she might try, her wine-red hair would always give her away.

Throughout his adult life, Marcus had only attended two missions alongside the Realm Sorceress. The first had been during his first year as a Black Knight. All they'd done was mediate a dispute between the Giants and Trolls that roamed the Regal Mountains. At first, Marcus had considered that mission to be the scariest he'd completed. He may be a man of great height, standing just over six foot three, but as he'd stood beside eleven-foot-tall giants, he'd felt like a child's toy. He shivered at the thought. Marcus had seen far worse things since then.

The second mission Marcus had attended with Lucinda had been the same one that haunted him to this day. In fact, *finishing* that mission was the reason they were both here.

"You're late," Lucinda told him as she paced around the fountain.

"Not as late as Humphrey and Craven," Marcus retorted, forcing a smile. He wanted to believe that this night would end well. He desperately wanted his eighteen-year search for the Missing VanCamp to end in the best way he'd ever imagined. With Ash VanCamp right in front of him, not a hair touched on her head. But time was running short. For all he knew, she could have already transitioned. Her fellow villagers could have turned on her.

Marcus's stomach churned as he imagined what he might be walking into. The hidden village had been protected by an invisible barrier for a reason. The people that lived there, who'd built it from the ground up, didn't want to be found. They didn't want strangers lurking in their shadows, or to be put on a map. They didn't want any truth to come to their legend.

"How do you suppose the Pandora found this village?" Marcus asked curiously, having thought long and hard about the matter.

Lucinda ceased her pacing, her eyes finding his own. "It's likely one of them was in the form of a bird and accidentally flew through the barrier." She shrugged. "At least, that's the only explanation I can think of."

The sound of footsteps approaching drew the pair's attention. Marcus turned to view Craven walking toward them, with Humphrey following suit. The famed Draconian with unique, electric abilities appeared as he always did—in uniform and prepared for anything—Shadow Strike sheathed proudly at his back, its silver hilt visible above his left shoulder.

However, Humphrey's complexion was as pale as the Moons above. His honey-colored eyes danced from face to face as he arrived beside Lucinda, his throat bobbing as he gave Marcus a nod to greet him.

"This is by far the most important mission that we've ever done," Lucinda began with a quivering lip. "The four of us worked harder than we'd ever had before to survive the night the Idonian Kingdom fell. This mission has lasted us eighteen years. We're going to finish it today."

Marcus's breath staggered as he watched Lucinda hold out the chrome sphere. He fought not to think of how long he'd been looking for the Missing VanCamp, and how often he'd failed. Every village he'd searched through flashed through his mind. A sea of memories began to overwhelm him as the Realm Sorceress tossed the sphere onto the ground.

A portal to a place Marcus had never seen appeared. The *one* place he hadn't looked. The *only* option left. As he walked through the shimmering wall, Marcus couldn't escape the feeling that Meera was watching him, begging for him to succeed.

Ash's eyes opened to dozens of faces hovering above her. She blinked, only to realize she'd been seeing double. Blood rushed in a thick stream from her nose, the scent instantly intensifying her senses, nearly driving her wild. She exhaled slowly, forcing herself to remain calm as Lilly brought a warm, damp cloth to her face to wipe it away.

"What... the... f-" Ash began, but a sharp pain sliced through her already aching head, silencing her. She winced, only to cry out as her sore muscles screamed in response.

"It's safe to say we're leaving you out of the hunt this time around," Cooper told her, his tone wavering.

Ash glared into his turquoise-colored eyes. *Did he just say hunt?*

"I think it's best we just take you up to bed," Sam cautioned.

Ash shook her head, trembling as she pushed herself to her feet. "I don't think so," she growled, brushing blood-caked hairs away from her brow.

Quinn stared down at her, setting his jaw as he crossed his arms in front of his chest. "If you could see yourself right now…" his voice trailed off.

For a moment, Ash scowled at them all. The taste of sweet, coppery blood lingered in her watering mouth. Her lips were pressed into a thin line as she thought of a way to convince them she was fine enough to go on their *hunt*. Her fingers clenched into trembling fists at the thought of what they might do to Morghan if they found him. Sure, he was an Immortal, but both the McBride and the Waters' men were strong. And what if what the Werewolf had said was true? What if there *was* something about the McBride's that would make the Prince of Darkness, of all people, want to snatch them up in the woods?

Ash's heart began to race, her blood beginning to boil. If what Morghan had said was true, Malachai had been willing to *destroy* Crane just to get his hands on Lincoln. Ash needed answers, and Morghan was her only ticket to Dracus.

"I'm fine." Ash broke their lingering silence. "Don't you remember when this happened, during the battle? I went on alright then, why wouldn't I now?" she pressed, planting her hands on the curves of her hips.

Drake gave her a wary look, his dark eyes squinting. Ash held her breath, her stomach twisting as she thought about what he might say.

"Fine," the Justice Leader mumbled. "We go in pairs.

Constance, you'll stay with me. Sam, you'll go with Quinn. Ash, do *not* leave Cooper's side."

Ash kicked at chunks of ice as she and Cooper made their way up into the tall mountains that surrounded Crane. She'd specifically requested to go toward the east, having recalled where she had met Morghan earlier that day. While it was unlikely he was still standing in the same place she'd left him, Ash hoped she'd be able track him from there. If she *did* manage to find a trail that might lead her to the Werewolf, Ash knew she'd need to find a way to escape Cooper's watch.

"I know, you'd normally do these things with Lincoln," Cooper mentioned softly as they made their way through the east mountain trails.

Grimacing at the sound of his words, Ash bit her inner cheek. She imagined how Cooper might feel if he learned what Morghan had told her earlier. She glanced toward him, scanning his solemn features, and knew exactly what he would do. He'd do anything to get his brother back. He'd get himself killed.

"Maybe." Ash shrugged. "But, you're my twin, remember? I'd much prefer to do this with you. Besides, Lincoln would always grumble. You know what he was like if he didn't want to do something."

Cooper's lips split into a wide smile, his bright eyes twinkling beneath the moonlight streaming from above. "He would always tell me that I was *too* optimistic about everything." He chuckled softly. "But truly, he was just too pessimistic."

"You all might look alike," Ash replied as she scanned

the forest around her, "but you couldn't be more different, if you ask me."

The sight of two sets of tracks sent the pair skidding to a stop. Ash examined them, her mouth growing dry. One set revealed a set of men's boots, while the other were large paw prints. Large enough to belong to a Werewolf. She swallowed against the lump forming in her throat, rising to her feet. "We should split up."

"That's the exact opposite of what Drake said to do," Cooper grunted, instinctively drawing his sword. "I say we stick together and follow the paw prints."

Ash shook her head, preparing to protest. "But what if the men's footprints are Lincoln's?" The lie sailed past her lips.

Cooper scowled in response. "But what if they're not? Didn't Drake say that Billy saw the Werewolf in this area? What if those boot prints are his?"

Frowning, Ash bit her tongue. Convincing Cooper to follow the large paw prints on his own was turning out to be one daunting task. "Those don't look like frantic footprints to me," she retorted, arching a brow.

Silence spread out between the pair as they stared into each other's eyes. Ash fought to remain placid, knowing that Cooper knew her well enough to be able to tell when she had ulterior motives. She slowly crossed her arms, tapping her foot impatiently.

After a while, Cooper groaned. His eye scanned the trees surrounding them as if he feared someone might overhear what he was about to say. "Meet me on the East Cliff in no more than an hour," he demanded, sulking as if he was admitting defeat.

Ash fought to hide her joy, reaching up to ruffle his sandy locks. "Don't forget the signal, if things go wrong," she reminded him as she drew her own sword.

"A Raven's call." Cooper's nose wrinkled. "And if that doesn't work, the most wretched bloodcurdling scream your lungs will allow."

Ash gave him a nod and then sighed with relief as she and Cooper went their separate ways, her gaze dropping to the boot prints. She followed their path, walking beside them as she pushed further east. The mountain was growing steeper, and her muscles were far too tired for her to make the journey easily.

While it was possible the paw prints had belonged to Morghan, Ash couldn't escape the idea that he'd been in his Mortal form. Perhaps Billy had witnessed him transitioning, and that's what had frightened him so badly. She nodded, knowing this was more than likely to be true as she continued.

"If Morghan wanted to meet by the East Cliff, he must live nearby. Maybe I'll start there," Ash said as she approached an incline. She drove her sword into the earth, using it to hoist herself upward. A dull ache pulsated throughout her head as she pushed herself to continue, her legs nearly buckling, begging her to stop for at least a few moments.

Quinn and the others were scanning other areas on this side of the Strip, and unlike Ash, they hadn't just spent three days wandering the mountain range aimlessly. She was exhausted, and they were not. If she didn't push herself to move faster, they would get to Morghan before she could. If that happened, she didn't know what they would do. Would they kill him on the spot, or tie him up somewhere? Either way, she doubted that she and the Werewolf would be able to continue with her plans.

Ash had fallen deep into her thoughts when the sound of wings nearby startled her. While some species of birds remained on the Strip throughout Winter Solstice, most fled to warmer areas of the Realm. They flew closer to the Edge of the Underworld, or toward the Forest of Fools, where Queen Cleo had spelled the forest surrounding her Safe Haven to remain a neutral temperature.

The most common species of bird to be found on the Strip during the cold winter months were Pandora. Ash's stomach roiled, her heartbeat growing sluggish as she thought of the beasts and their inevitable vengeance. The familiar sensation of her pulse thrumming in her ears began to overwhelm her hearing, distracting her from any other sounds coming from her surroundings.

Ash's limbs began to shake, panic beginning to set in as her thoughts took her to places darker than she'd ever been. She was alone, and undeniably weak. The scent of her blood likely still lingered on her clothes and her flesh.

The sudden flapping of more wings caused Ash to nearly leap out of her skin. Tears began to well in her eyes as she clutched the hilt of her sword with both her hands. Slow, deep breaths began to fill her lungs as she forced herself to swallow her fear and scan her surroundings.

The sound of a raven screeching nearby caused every muscle in Ash's body to tense. The sound hadn't come from Cooper. It hadn't been followed by a bloodcurdling scream.

What had been the screech of a raven quickly turned into the low growl of a bear. Ash could feel its hot breath on her back, the hairs on the back of her neck rising. Goosebumps pebbled along her flesh, her mind racing as she tried to find a way to escape. *Move*, she begged herself, but her entire form had become leaden. She doubted she'd be able to lift her sword.

The beast was so close to her that Ash could feel its cold, wet snout brush against her hair. Tears began to roll down her cheeks. *Move*, she internally screamed as a large shadow began to form in the snow in front of her—the shadow of a bear, on its hind legs. Its claws were outstretched, ready to drag through her skin.

Snarls erupted from the nearby brush, and Ash watched a second shadow barrel into the bear. She fell forward, her sword falling into the snow beside her as she rolled onto her back. Her eyes widened, her jaw dropping as she watched the massive gray wolf tear into the Pandora. The beast struggled, fighting to get the wolf off its back, but it was no use. The wolf was too strong, its jaws clamped tightly around the bear's neck.

The sound of the Pandora's neck snapping led Ash's breath to catch in her throat. She stared at the wolf, her lip quivering. It was larger than any of the other wolves she'd seen. The gray fur around its mouth was stained red, blood dripping from canines longer than Ash's fingers.

Familiar caramel eyes stared back at Ash as she surveyed the beast, a smile creeping onto her lips. She opened her mouth to say thank you but caught the sight of at least a dozen sets of red eyes beginning to pierce through the night around her.

"Morghan." Ash began to warn the wolf as she reached for her sword, scrambling to her feet. However, he was already aware of the enemy's presence. His demeanor changed, his back arching, the fur along his spine raising as his gaze darted in every direction. When his eyes fell on Ash again, he said everything he wanted her to hear without speaking a single word.

Run.

Normally, Ash would have scoffed at anyone for telling her to flee from a fight, but all she could feel right now was pain. Every nerve throughout her body felt as if it were on fire, and she could feel blood creeping up her esophagus. A hot stream of the substance began to drip from her nose as she turned her back on the Werewolf, cursing beneath her breath.

Ash wanted her legs to move, and her feet to push her faster than she'd ever gone before, but her body didn't want to obey her commands. She barely managed to sprint away from the gruesome scene she'd just witnessed, fleeing further east. She sheathed her sword, using her hands to grip the icy earth as she endured yet another steep incline.

The sound of a vicious fight echoed through the night as Ash's hearing began to dull. At first, she wanted to blame it on the heights, having gone so far up into the mountains, but she began to feel warm, damp streams running down her neck. She reached to inspect it with her hand as she stumbled over the top of the incline, falling onto her knees. When she pulled it away, her palm was stained with her own blood.

A spectacular view sat before Ash as she crawled further away from the trees. Shades of orange and pink began to overwhelm the night sky as the sun began its ascent over the mountains. Darkness began to creep along the edges of Ash's vision as she felt steaming hot liquid erupt from her throat and fill her mouth. She spit it out, coughing as she fought to remain conscious.

Ash's hands curled around the icy substance as she wretched, her heart racing at impeccable speeds. Every bone in her body screamed, quaking from a force she couldn't possibly comprehend. Her body gave way, causing her to fall into her own mess of blood. She shivered in the snow, red watery tears flowing from her eyes as she used what was left of her vision to look toward the trees. She opened her mouth to scream for Cooper, Quinn, or even Morghan. Anyone. But no sound came out.

13

raven found himself crouched in the brush surrounding a large estate he and the others had stumbled upon. It was higher in the mountains, surrounded by beautiful rolling hills. A farm sat nearly a mile from the large cabin-like mansion in front of him. He could hear the squeals of pigs and the hooves of horses rubbing against hay as they paced in their stalls.

Candles flickered in every window, the scent of apple pie wafting through the air. A cobblestone pathway led up to a large porch where two chairs rocked with the winter breeze.

"It's beautiful," Lucinda said dreamily from Craven's right side.

Nodding, Craven couldn't disagree. As he stared up at the house, his heart skipped a beat in his chest. The sight made him daydream about days without war, where he might settle down and raise a family. He thought of how his black-haired and violet-eyed children would look as they ran through the fields. A smile spread across his lips as he imagined how their laughter would sound.

"We're not here to drool over the house," Marcus

reminded the others, his tone stern. "There's someone home."

"She's too small to be the girl we're looking for." Craven had already noted the girl's presence. He could hear the clattering of dishes being washed and put away as she rifled around in the kitchen. Rising to his full height, Craven began to move toward the back of the house, using the trees to conceal his form. The others followed him, their steps quieter than a mouse crawling its way through the fields surrounding them.

The scent of blood lingered in the air, causing Craven's senses to intensify. It was a familiar scent, in more ways than one. His mind whirled, drifting back to a time that felt so long ago now. The Ballroom Battle. The throne room. Xavier's dark form sinking onto a throne that was never meant to be his while the High Queen lay limp at his feet. A trail of blood ran down her lips, her eyes open wide, as if she were staring up into the stars, maybe even beyond them.

The High Queen's blood.

Craven's heart faltered in his chest as he ceased his walking, glancing over his shoulder to view Marcus's expression. The color had drained from the Mentor's face, his vivid green eyes tearing as they stared toward the house. It was clear that he'd picked up on the scent as well, and for that, Craven was thankful. For a moment, he'd thought the mission's high stakes had begun to get the best of him.

"There are six sets of footsteps leading further into the mountains," Lucinda mentioned as she pushed past Craven. "I'd bet my life's savings that one of those sets belongs to *her*."

Nodding slowly, Craven swallowed hard as he spared the house another glance. He watched as the girl inside shut off the lights in the kitchen, likely retreating to bed at this hour of night. His breath staggered as he stepped out of the brush, silently praying that she didn't spot him or the others as they entered the field.

The group followed the footsteps through the field and onto a mountain trail. The trees were marked with a symbol of three mountain peaks, and Craven eyed them curiously. He ran his fingers over the grooves in the bark, his gaze drifting back to the footprints.

They were led up a sharp incline, forced to leave the trail behind. If it weren't for Lucinda's sphere, Craven would be concerned. This part of the Strip wasn't documented on any map, meaning the chances of getting lost were extremely high. Craven shivered at the thought of it, his mind drifting to what it would be like to be abandoned in a place such as this. He imagined that it was just as deadly as it was beautiful.

At the top of the incline, Craven and the others found themselves at a loss. The six sets of prints had all gone in different directions, and it was impossible to tell exactly which set belonged to the girl they were looking for.

"Two of these are women's prints," Humphrey mentioned, kneeling in the snow to examine them. "Did Vincent say what her stature was like? Perhaps we can determine the size of her shoe?" he suggested, his tone hopeful.

Craven dropped to a knee beside the first set of women's prints, his brow wrinkling as he rubbed his temples. His gaze darted between the pairs, his frustration growing as each second passed by. "They're nearly the same," he snapped, rising to his full height. "We're going to have to split up and track them both."

Marcus frowned, clearly not fond of the idea. "That's risky," he insisted. "The four of us together would stand much more of a chance if the Pandora decided to make another appearance here."

"Do you have another idea?" Craven crossed his arms.

Silence spread out between their small group, and Craven watched as Lucinda's amber eyes flitted between him and the others. It didn't matter that Marcus was a former Black Knight and Guardian to the High Queen, or that Craven had been named the Dark Army's biggest threat by reporters across the Realm. Lucinda was not only the oldest out of the bunch, at over four centuries old, she was an Idonian Council Member. She was the Sorceress everyone working in the ways of Magic strived to become. She called the shots.

"I'll take Humphrey," Lucinda revealed as her diamond encrusted wand fell out of her sleeve, landing perfectly in her grasp. "You two take the sphere," she added, causing Craven's eyes to widen with surprise.

"But what about you? What if you run into trouble?" Marcus questioned, biting his lip as the Sorceress forced the sphere into his hand.

Lucinda gave the Mentor a disbelieving look, her mouth slackening as she cocked her head to the side. "Have you no faith in me?" she asked, waving her wand in Marcus's face.

Craven chuckled lightly as he tied his dark hair away from his face. Once he finished, he drew Shadow Strike, his heart pounding as he thought of how this night would end. "Whoever finds the VanCamp wins a round of shots," he smirked, turning his back on the others.

Marcus reluctantly followed, moving to the Draconian's side. Craven's gaze drifted between the Mentor and the prints they were following, watching as his expression changed constantly. He imagined the worry he was seeing in Marcus's eyes would quickly change to relief once they made their way back to Dracus with Ash VanCamp.

They traveled in silence, moving through the shadows in order to keep out of view. If they stumbled upon anyone, they would prefer to be able to plan their approach.

The only sound to be heard was the subtle thrum of electricity coursing through Craven's form, and Marcus's erratic heartbeat. But that quickly changed when the scent of Immortal blood began to travel through the air with the breeze, surrounding Craven as he maneuvered through the uneven terrain.

The scent caused Craven's stomach to flip as he ceased his walking, his eyes falling on Marcus. "It isn't hers," the Mentor mentioned, deep in thought.

"What other Immortals could there be around here?" Craven asked slowly, his eyes narrowing. "Hmm?"

The sound of vicious, animalistic snarls began to echo throughout the mountains. Craven immediately fell into action, bolting in the direction the sounds were coming from. His sweaty grip tightened around Shadow Strike's hilt as he forced any thoughts of hesitation and fear from his mind.

Marcus abandoned his position in the shadows to take off after Craven. "Don't do anything rash," he warned as he arrived beside him.

"You're joking right?" Craven spat, his eyes narrowing in Marcus's direction. Electricity began to spread from his palms, now surrounding the enchanted sword. Purple-shaded sparks ignited the night around them as they ran. "Eighteen years, Marcus. Eighteen fucking years you've been working for this moment and you're going to tell *me* not do anything rash? Those Pandora could be attacking *her*."

Marcus's lips pressed into a thin lie, determination flooding his face. "Just don't draw too much attention," he hissed.

"I can't help but be flashy," Craven grunted as he picked up speed. He ran against the harsh wind, snow blowing around him, obscuring his vision as shocks bounced off his sword, popping in his ears. Threads began to swim from the fingertips on his free hand as the snarls grew louder and the scent of Pandora blood stronger.

When the pair of footsteps they had been following split into different directions, Craven instantly grew uneasy. Another set of boot prints and one set of paw prints were visible, causing him to wonder exactly what had led the six people he knew had left the estate to travel out into these mountains after dark.

Craven could feel Marcus behind him as he pushed up another incline. He fought not to slip on the ice and lose his balance, knowing if he so much as grazed the Mentor, he'd be electrocuted. Craven's gift was both a blessing and a curse. While it would do him a great deal of good in a few moments when he barreled into battle, he would never escape the fear that he might injure someone he cared for.

The pair approached a small clearing after they made their way up the incline, and it was there that they found the source of all the noise. Craven's mouth fell open, his eyes widening at the sight of the Werewolf fighting his way through a swarm of Pandora. The beast caught the birds between his razor-sharp teeth, crushing them with his jaw's impeccable strength. He cringed as the sound of bones breaking crunched in his ears.

Craven quickly gathered his thoughts, and while he wasn't sure exactly how much of an ally the Werewolf truly was, he couldn't allow a fellow Immortal to fall so harshly right in front of his eyes. He rushed to aid the beast, driving his sword into anything with black fur, scales, or feathers.

Blood splattered around them, covering Craven's red-and-black uniform and the Werewolf's gray fur. It dripped from the Draconian's hair, the taste of it lingering upon his tongue. His jaw ached as his fangs extracted, begging to sink into the flesh of anything with a beating heart.

A fury-fueled combination of adrenaline and bloodlust pushed Craven harder, intensifying his will to obliterate the enemy. While they could transition into massive beasts, and he could not, Craven wouldn't allow them to intimidate him. He kept moving, slashing his sword with one hand while electricity weaved through his fingers on the other.

The Werewolf's eyes widened as he glanced toward Craven, and the beast quickly fled into the shadows. Craven's lips twitched toward a smirk as he drove his sword into the earth. Electricity bounced off the obsidian blade, spreading through the snow and shocking the Pandora. Yelps pierced through the night while Craven raised his hand, aiming his abilities at the beasts in the sky. Feathers flew in the air as the birds fell dead to the ground.

Craven pulled in a series of deep breaths as the sound of slow clapping flooded his ears. He glanced over his shoulder, his eyes rolling at the sight of Marcus's grin.

"You're good." The Mentor gave him an appreciative nod. "One might think I trained you myself."

Craven scoffed, brushing his damp hair away from his eyes. While he wanted so desperately to put the Mentor in his place, there were far more pressing matters to deal with. "Where'd that Werewolf go?" he growled, scanning the trees around them.

Marcus shrugged, his gaze dropping from Craven's face, falling on the ground. "I will admit, I didn't expect to find Morghan here." He sighed, his brow wrinkling as he began to cross the small clearing.

Craven could see that the woman's footprints resumed, though they'd been smeared during the fight. His stomach churned as he examined them, unable to help but notice how different they appeared now opposed to before. "She was struggling," he said, his voice little more than a whisper.

The scent of her blood suddenly hit the two Draconians, causing them both to jump, startled. It flowed through the air so thick that Craven could nearly choke on it as he forced himself up the incline. Dots of deep red were visible in the snow, marking a sickening path that he followed urgently. His heart pounded against the walls of his chest as he flew through the trees, his stomach twisting as he skidded to a stop before a cliff.

The girl was lying in a heap of her own blood, her dark hair fanned out around her, shielding her face. Craven swallowed hard, forcing bile back down his throat as he sank to his knees beside her, pulling her onto his lap. He brushed the damp, bloodied locks away from her face. Her flesh was tinted blue, freezing to the touch as he felt for her pulse.

"It's weak, but still there," Craven warned as he glanced over his shoulder, where Marcus stood frozen, his eyes wide with shock. He watched as the Mentor trembled, his grip loosening on his sword. Whitefire dropped to the snow as silent tears streamed down Marcus's cheeks.

Craven bit his inner cheek, knowing he would never understand what Marcus was feeling right now. But, even so, his patience was wearing thin. "Open the damn portal!" he demanded.

Marcus blinked as if he were waking up from a nightmare. Craven could hear every deep breath he inhaled as the Mentor dropped to his knees into the snow beside him. He reached for the girl's wrist, pushing up her sleeve.

Time seemed to stop as Craven watched Marcus inject the girl with his venom. His stomach dropped as he fought to comprehend all that had just happened. He continued to monitor the girl's pulse while Marcus hurried to open the portal back to Dracus. He ran a hand over her cheek as he fought to calm himself, his eyes falling on her lips. His brow furrowed as he noticed a sharp tooth he hadn't realized was there before. His pulse thrummed loudly in his ears as he gently pushed her top lip up, revealing a set of sharp fangs.

Horrified, Craven looked toward Marcus. "What did you just *do?*"

THE SUN HAD BEGUN TO RISE ABOVE THE MOUNTAINS AS Quinn and Sam made their way toward the East Cliff. While they hadn't found any sign of a Werewolf, or even a Pandora, it seemed only fitting to watch the sunrise before heading home to finally catch some rest.

As the pair approached the cliff, Quinn was stunned when they came across a clearing covered in shredded Pandora. His stomach churned, and he feared he might wretch as he took in the sight before him.

"What the bloody hell?" Sam gasped as he kneeled to examine a bird. Its feathers were smoking, its meat fully cooked and partially charred as if it had been fried. "It's like it was set on fire, or something."

Quinn shivered, the deep cold of the mountains seeping into his bones. "Let's just move on. Whoever is responsible for this, they clearly did us a favor," he declared as he moved across the clearing.

The East Cliffs were right ahead, and Quinn couldn't help but notice the drops of blood and sets of footprints leading up to it. His breathing became uneven, his stomach twisting into knots as he pushed through the tree line. His hand rose to his mouth as he took in all the blood around him, the sound of his heartbeat flooding his ears.

Cooper stood nearby, whimpering as he hovered over the large pool of blood as if it were his own. The sun continued to rise, streaks of orange and pink piercing through the star-speckled sky.

"What happened?" Quinn asked slowly, beginning to tremble with an evolving rage. "Where is she?"

Cooper shook his head, his lip quivering. "I don't know," he croaked.

Sam growled as he began to pace, his hands rising to cradle his head. He kicked at the snow, a slur of curses sailing past his lips. Quinn watched him, beginning to piece everything together in his mind. Cooper had been with Ash. They passed the remnants of what was clearly a small Pandora attack, and now, his brother was standing over a pool of blood larger than any other Quinn had ever seen.

"What's this?" Sam's question pulled Quinn from his dreary thoughts. He glanced over to view his friend kneeling in the snow, his fingers tracing some sort of print.

Quinn warily approached him, his heart in his throat. He stared down at what appeared to be the print of a sword in the snow, one with an extravagant hilt and a large blade. His thoughts began to race once again as his gaze darted between the snow and the blood. While he'd originally begun to think that Ash had died, it was clear there was more to what had happened overnight.

"She was taken," Quinn insisted, his fists curling at his sides.

"But this sword," Sam breathed, rising to his full height.

While Quinn couldn't be sure, he had a feeling he knew exactly what sword had been dropped in the snow. His jaw clenched; his entire form rigid as he looked toward his younger brother. "Are you thinking what I'm thinking?" he asked, crossing his arms.

Cooper nodded slowly. "We need to go to Dracus."

14

The past few hours for Marcus had gone by in a blur. The scent of blood and mountain air still lingered upon his clothes, overwhelming his senses. He would never escape the gruesome image of how the girl appeared when he and Craven had found her. Adrenaline still raced through his veins, even now as he tried to calm himself by pacing the length of King Loren's office.

Craven sat in a chair nearby, his head in his hands. Marcus imagined he was trying to wrap his mind around all that happened last night. The Pandora, the Werewolf, the girl. The scent of VanCamp blood hanging heavily in the air.

It could all have been a waste. Marcus winced at the thought of his venom, sinking into the girl's flesh, and the look on Craven's face when he realized she'd already had fangs. *What have I done? Have I killed the girl I've searched so long for? Have I failed Meera once again?*

The door to Loren's office opened abruptly, causing Marcus to nearly leap out of his skin. His eyes darted over to the threshold where Lucinda stood with flushed cheeks, snow-caked hair, and a damning scowl.

"You *bit* her?" The Sorceress thundered.

Marcus sighed heavily as he sulked against the glass walls of the king's study. "She was dying…" he trailed off.

"Marcus is the Mentor, it is up to his discretion whether or not anyone needs changing." Craven came to Marcus's defense, slowly rising to his feet. "You weren't there, you didn't see how she appeared. Every ounce of her blood was smeared on the snow!"

Lucinda stepped further into the room, rage reflecting in her amber eyes. "Do you idiots know nothing of Immortal transitions?" she chastised.

Craven's lips dipped into a frown. "What are you getting at?"

A scoff escaped Lucinda. "When a Mortal transitions into an Immortal of any sort, they're rid of all their mortal blood. Over the next few days that blood is replaced by Immortal blood."

Marcus felt his knees weaken as he pressed his back against the wall, slowly sliding down into a crouch. Of course, he'd known that fact. His position in this kingdom revolved around transitions. Yet, in the heat of the moment, fear got the best of him. He'd been so afraid that the girl would die, that he'd forgotten everything he'd ever learned.

Craven's face twisted, confusion beginning to set in. Having been born an Immortal, he would have never experienced what Lucinda had just described. He was trained to be a warrior; therefore, he likely never paid any mind as to what went on in the infirmary.

"So, what does that mean for the girl then?" Craven asked warily.

Marcus's chest grew tight as he thought of what might happen next. "Do you think she'll live?"

Lucinda's features softened at the sound of the question. She stared at Marcus, her eyes beginning to sparkle brightly as the morning sun spread through the walls. "They're doing everything they can," she said, releasing a depressive sigh. "But this has never happened before. No Draconian has ever injected venom into another. The head Healer, Ebony, is worried it might be too much for the girl to handle. She's small, and it's apparent that she's more than just a Draconian. She has the ears of a Fae, as well as the stature. There's a chance she might be too weak to endure a complete change."

Craven sank back into his seat, the color rushing from his face. He began to stare blankly in Marcus's direction, which only led the Mentor's heart to sink into his stomach. His throat began to feel as if it were closing up, his mind racing as he thought of what he might have done.

Silence spread throughout the room as Marcus pinched the bridge of his nose, squinting his eyes shut. Thoughts of Penelope and Vincent flooded his mind. What would they think of him when they found out? If Cedric were still alive, what would he say? What would Loren do with Marcus? He swallowed hard at the thought.

As if the King had heard Marcus's dreadful thoughts, he entered his office, slamming the door so hard behind him that the chandelier shook above them.

Marcus forced himself to his feet, bowing slightly in the King's direction along with the others. He held his breath, fearing the words that would escape Loren's lips.

"The Elves are going to have a field day with this," Loren grumbled as he sat behind his desk, opening one of its many drawers where he retrieved a large bottle of whiskey. His gaze lifted, falling on Craven. "Retrieve some glasses from the cabinet over there, would you?"

Craven's brow raised with surprise, but he quickly

complied. The Draconian returned to Loren's desk, his arms cradling four crystal classes.

"I think we could all use a drink," Loren announced as he poured the whiskey. "This night has been nearly as stressful as the night the Idonian Kingdom fell."

Lucinda nodded slowly as she retrieved her glass from the King's desk. "What shall we do now?" she inquired as she took her first sip.

Marcus was hesitant to do the same as the King beckoned him over, forcing the whiskey into his hands. He eyed Loren curiously, wondering what was going through his mind. "Shouldn't you be stoning me right about now?" he asked, his eyes narrowing.

"Valentina told me not to," Loren told him quickly, rolling his eyes. "You should have known not to do what you did. Something like this will make the rest of the Council rethink whether you should be in your position."

A subtle relief washed over Marcus as he thought of the Prophetess intervening, but his stomach quickly began to sour at the thought of what the other Council members would think. Richard wouldn't stand for a mistake such as this one, and Axel would be more than pleased to retire from being General and take Marcus's place as Mentor.

"What else did Valentina say?" Craven questioned, his glass already half empty.

A faint smile spread across Loren's mouth as he brushed strands of messy black hair away from his brow. "She believes the girl will live," he revealed.

"Should we reach out to Penelope?" Lucinda chirped excitedly.

Loren shook his head, his smile faltering. "Not until we're in the clear. Ebony has called for Vincent so she can compare their DNA. For now, this news stays in Dracus. No one is to know anything until we're certain."

Everyone nodded in agreement, finishing off their whiskey. Marcus watched as Craven rubbed at his tired violet eyes but forced his own thoughts of exhaustion away. There was still one more thing the Mentor needed to do before he succumbed to sleep.

THE INFIRMARY HALLS WERE EMPTY. THERE WASN'T A Healer or a visitor in sight. The guard hadn't even wanted to allow the Mentor in the building due to the two high-profile patients being cared for within. If it weren't for his position, Marcus might not have been able to get through the doors.

It was silent as Marcus traveled to the third floor, where patients spent most of their recovery process. Right now, he imagined the girl was on the basement floor, where intense care was given to patients. He forced thoughts of her from his mind as the elevator ceased its rising. The doors opened slowly, revealing yet another stark-white tiled hall. Lemon-scented cleaning supplies lingered in the air, and the floors sparkled as if they'd just been polished.

Marcus began to make his way around the third level, peeking into the small window in every door until he found who he was looking for. His breath caught in his throat as he watched Vincent pass through his view, a cup of ice in his hands.

Although Marcus had tried not to be angry with Loren allowing Vincent into the field on his own, it was difficult. Vincent was the late High King's only son. There was a bright and shining target on his back, and Marcus had vowed to protect Meera's children. Although, now he was beginning to doubt that he was very good at it.

Sighing, Marcus pushed open the door, not bothering

to knock. He walked further into the room; his fists clenched at his sides as his eyes fell on Vincent once again.

The Elf's eyes widened at the sight of him, his gaze drifting down his bloodied form. He paled at the sight of Marcus's stained uniform. "The look of you makes me think things didn't exactly go as planned," he said in a whisper, cringing.

Marcus set his jaw, his eyes drifting to the man in the bed. Surprise quickly struck the Mentor as he looked him over. The tattoos he'd had on his wrists of Idonian knots had spread widely up his arms, covering his chest and part of his neck. Marcus had never seen anything like it in all his life, though he'd heard of how the warriors in Zerin would mark themselves every time they aged another year or participated in another battle.

Pale blond hair fell around the man's face, nearly shielding familiar blue eyes staring back at Marcus. The corners of the man's mouth curled upward into a cocky smile, and the Mentor wasn't sure whether to laugh or cry.

"You're supposed to be dead, Ward," he chastised.

Alistair shrugged as if that didn't matter much to him. "Is anyone ever *really* dead?" he inquired, arching a brow. "Besides, aren't you glad to see me?"

An annoyed grunt escaped Marcus as his tense muscles relaxed. "Something like that," he replied. "I'm glad you're alright. I'd prefer not to have to tell Penelope of your demise twice."

Alistair's cocky smile disappeared. "I heard about what happened to Cedric," he admitted, his gaze falling to the floor. "I wanted to send a letter, but I was afraid the Pandora would intercept it. We all know they don't like when people escape. I feared they'd find me and finish the job."

Marcus's brow furrowed. "How exactly *did* you escape?"

"I was thinking the same thing myself," Vincent blurted. "I saw what a destruction-level Pandora attack looks like recently. There are thousands of Pandora, and for a city the size of Mayfire, there would have been ten thousand or more."

Sadness began to reflect in Alistair's eyes, his shoulders drooping as he leaned forward in the bed. His hands curled around his white blankets, and Marcus could see how much he hated to think of what had happened that night.

"The tunnels," Alistair replied softly.

Marcus couldn't imagine how Alistair might feel. He wondered exactly how it must have felt to run, leaving your parents and little sister behind. Memories of his own abandonment caused Marcus's heart to race in his chest. How had his family felt when they left *him*? Was it hard or effortless? Did they even care?

"I fled to the Skyward Range. I thought about heading to the Strip, since it was closer, but I figured I'd only get lost and die," Alistair continued, his expression pained. "I hid in the mountains and found a nice cave to live in. I ate snow for water and trapped animals for protein. I would travel to every peak, searching for supplies and streams once spring arrived. I didn't dare head into a village, even when I was at my worst. I once considered traveling to Blackbay, but that was too close to the Idonian Jurisdiction for my liking. I wouldn't have survived the journey, anyway."

Vincent was staring at Alistair, his bright sage-colored eyes filled with childlike curiosity. "But how did you find a Dragon?"

Marcus lowered himself into a chair, fatigue beginning to get the best of him. He leaned back, his hair falling away from his face. The bright lights above him were nearly blinding, and he blinked rapidly until the black spots faded from his vision.

"I'm getting to that," Alistair grumbled. "I thought I was going to die. I most likely was. So, I figured if I was going to die, I might as well do it with one hell of a view. I decided to climb the tallest mountain in Idona. It took me four days, but the higher I got, the colder it got. There was more snow for me to drink. I was able to kill a rabbit, and I used Dragon's Breath to cook it. I began to feel better, but knew I still wasn't far off from death.

"Once I made it to the top, I couldn't help but laugh. The view was so beautiful. I felt like I could see everything. Every jurisdiction. I could see the Regal Mountains and the orange glow of the Edge of the Underworld beyond them. But then I noticed something else. Some sort of statue. It was worn, the elements having broken it down over time. It looked like it had once been a Dragon, but the wings had broken off and the horns had fallen apart. There was an engraving, in the old language. I could still make out some writing though. I don't know much of it, only what my parents and teachers forced me to learn, but I was able to figure out what it said. *Call of the Dragon.*" Alistair began to smirk, and Marcus found himself leaning forward, yearning to hear more.

Alistair reached for his glass of water, chugging it quickly before he continued. "The statue was caked with dirt, so I cleaned it off as best as I could. There was more to it. More symbols. Some of them I didn't understand, but one of them I did. The Dragon's eye. It looked just like the one on the hilt of my sword, so I unsheathed Dragons Breath to compare it. But as my sword got closer to the statue, it began to glow, and then something strange happened."

"What happened?" Marcus pressed, his words escaping him before he gave permission.

Alistair chuckled, clearly enjoying himself. "I don't know."

"What?" Vincent gawked. "What do you mean you don't know?"

"I passed out," Alistair revealed. "And when I woke up, I was in some sort of different Realm. Well, maybe not a Realm. I'm not entirely sure where *it* was. I just knew *what* it was. The Dragon's Den."

A TWIST OF
FATE

The scent of musk, salty tears, sweat, and damp stone surrounded Lincoln McBride as he pulled against the chains that bound him. A blindfold was wrapped tightly around his eyes, blocking his vision. Sweat covered his form, dripping down his face and causing his shirt to stick to his chest. He choked on the gag in his mouth, tears silently streaming down his cheeks.

Defeat washed over Lincoln as he sank back against the wall. Cool metal bit at his wrists and ankles, cutting into them. The sound of rats rushing across the floor around him made him cringe. Their fur tickled his flesh, causing his stomach to roil. A muffled scream escaped him as he thought of his family. Quinn, Cooper, Lilly, and Ash. He whimpered as their faces flashed through his mind. Was their feud worth this fate?

The thought of Constance only made Lincoln sick to his stomach. He would never forgive himself for the hurt he'd inflicted upon those he cared about The damage he'd done to those he cared for was irreparable. But did he deserve *this*?

The sound of footsteps nearby caused the hairs on the

back of Lincoln's neck to stick up straight. Since the moment he'd awoken in this misery, he hadn't heard another soul. *Unless I count the rats.* He groaned as he waited impatiently for the inevitable.

Lincoln had no recollection of who had taken him and didn't have the slightest clue as to where he was. Millions of possibilities ran through his mind. Had it been the Immortals? Did they know he had planned to take Walsh's place and light a new fire in the Rebels? The thought made his chest tighten.

The footsteps grew closer, and Lincoln realized there was more than one person headed his way. Possibly one to hold him down while the other did the killing? Lincoln tensed beneath his chains, only to cry out as the metal rubbed against his raw flesh.

"Sounds like he's awake," the voice of a woman crooned nearby, muffled by what was likely a thick metal door. "Do you think he's strong enough?"

"His strength doesn't matter," a man said. "We have our orders."

The woman giggled before releasing a sigh. "Well, now that Malachai's dropped off the injections, we have no choice but to begin. I wonder how long it'll take."

"Knowing your brother, Your Highness, not very long," the man told her.

The sound of a key being forced into a lock caused Lincoln's heart to cease its beating. He shrunk against the wall, knowing there was no way he could escape his fate now. The horror of the realization he was forced to face began to overwhelm him, and all Lincoln could do was shake his head, the cloth over his eyes now soaked from his tears.

The pair entered the room, and Lincoln winced at the sound of the woman's heels tapping along the stone floor.

Her scent pierced through the thick aroma of his own manly musk after days without washing. She smelled of lilacs, just like the ones that bloomed right outside the living room windows at the beginning of Summer Solstice. The thought only made Lincoln yearn for his home more than he ever had.

"This is the man my father wanted so badly?" The woman sounded as if she were struck with disbelief. Lincoln could feel her disapproving stare upon him. His skin crawled as she neared him, her gentle hand grazing his shoulder. He flinched beneath her touch, every muscle in his body sore from the stress he'd endured.

The woman whispered something beneath her breath, and Lincoln felt himself calm. His body relaxed, as if he'd just chugged a glass of chilled ale after a long day of tiresome work, yet his mind screamed. This woman wasn't the run-of-the-mill lass he would have encountered in Crane. *Witch.*

"I'd hurry," the woman directed. "The sooner this is over, we can get him clean and put him to work."

The sensation of a sharp needle appeared on Lincoln's neck, and while he wanted to attempt to squirm away from it, he felt as if he'd been sedated. His body wouldn't obey him, and before he had a chance to even suck in a deep breath, the needle was deep into his flesh. A rush of hot fluid sailed into his veins, burning as it raced through them.

Lincoln opened his mouth to scream, but no sound came out. He found himself growing weaker, his arms falling limply to his sides as he sagged further against the wall. Darkness began to swallow him whole. The man and the woman began to speak once again, but their voices sounded farther away. Lincoln could feel himself slipping into a state of unconsciousness as he fell further onto the filthy stone. His body weakened as he writhed painfully atop the cold ground. Silently, he began to pray that one day he might escape the terror he'd found himself in. But a small voice in his head told him that he never would.

XAVIER HAD NEVER BEEN SO JOYFUL. FINALLY, ALL HE HAD planned for was falling perfectly into place. A celebration was in order. Therefore, he called upon all of his servants and commanded they prepare the most delicious of feasts for the guests he had summoned.

You really think your children want to have dinner with their father, the voice mocked Xavier from within his mind as he made his way to his extravagant dining hall. *Can't you see they despise you?*

Xavier shrugged, brushing the voice off. He wouldn't allow Meera to destroy this evening that he had so intricately planned. Anything she could say wouldn't ruin his mood.

Oh, so you're ignoring me now?

Still, Xavier said nothing as his guard opened the large arched wooden doors for him, revealing the dining hall in all of its glory. The table, long enough to sit fifty people, was clothed in black satin. Lit candlesticks lined the surface, flickering beautifully, casting eerie shadows upon the leafy centerpieces. Warmth radiated from a bright fire burning in the hearth, the scent of firewood filling the room.

"Oh, it's just as I imagined." Xavier grinned as he lowered himself into his seat at the head of the table. "Absolutely perfect."

It's a bit dark for my taste, Meera sighed.

Xavier rolled his eyes as he reached for a glass of wine.

He took a long sip, hoping to drown the voice out by the time he found himself at the bottom of a bottle.

Ah, it's dry, Meera gagged. *Much like your personality.*

Leaning back in his chair, Xavier looked over all he'd won. He imagined a day when nobles would rise at their seats when he entered the room. Of course, he'd need to kill the Messenger first. That would be a difficult task. But still, what would follow her death would be worth far more than the stress leading up to it.

Where are your guests now? Meera questioned. *Isn't it custom for the king to arrive last?*

"My children are busy individuals," Xavier finally replied. "They aren't lazy like yours."

My children are far from lazy, Meera hissed.

"Oh, really? All they do is sit behind golden walls, waiting for some prophesied being to arrive and do their dirty work for them. Mine are out there in the Realm, doing everything they can for their cause. Making scientific breakthroughs and training, although they're already skilled beyond belief."

You don't need to remind me how skilled your children are, Meera reminded him coldly. *It's a good thing you haven't ruined them all.*

Xavier's grip tightened around his wine glass. The stem began to crack as he fought to calm himself. "Do me a favor and at least pretend to be dead for the evening," he snapped.

As the words escaped the wicked king's lips, the doors to the dining hall flung open once again. Soroya passed through the threshold gracefully, holding her head high. She was dressed in black lace, her long dark hair braided delicately down her back. "Father," she greeted Xavier, offering him a slight curtsy as a servant rushed to pull out her chair for her.

Xavier beamed at the sight of her green eyes sparkling in the candlelight. He doubted he could have ever wished for a more beautiful, smart woman to call his daughter. "You look more and more like your mother every day," he told her proudly.

"She was much kinder, or at least that's what Chai tells me." Soroya giggled as she raised her glass of wine to her red-painted lips.

"Speaking of your brother," Xavier grumbled. "Where is he?"

Soroya sighed in her seat, her back as straight as a bored. "I haven't seen him, though I know he's here in the kingdom *somewhere*. He did drop off those injections this morning," she revealed with a smile, flashing her stark-white teeth.

"And?" Xavier pressed.

"Alrich and I administered the first one shortly after we received them. The man didn't handle it very well. For safety reasons, we might need to push the injections from every day to every other day. I'm not sure he'd withstand it otherwise. Archers are weak without their bows," Soroya explained disapprovingly as she swirled her glass of wine in her grip, sticking out her bottom lip.

The doors swung open again, and Malachai gracefully passed through. He kept his red-tinted gaze on the floor as he made his way to the table. His dark suit clung to him as he lowered into a seat. "What's all this?" the prince grumbled as he gestured to the extravagantly decorated table.

"A celebration." Xavier glared.

"For what?" Malachai finally looked up at him, his face twisting with annoyance. "Is it your birthday? Sorry if I've forgotten, I've been a little busy."

Xavier scoffed in his son's direction. "You don't see

finally retrieving that Archer as an accomplishment worth celebrating?" The king could hardly believe it.

Malachai stared blankly at his father. "You didn't bake me a cake when I destroyed Death Valley," he reminded him with an arched brow.

"This is different," Xavier insisted.

"How so?" Malachai sneered.

"Now that we have the Archer, we can make further advances in the war," Soroya told her brother kindly, as if he hadn't already known this fact. "He'll serve us well."

Malachai's lips dipped into a frown as he fell back into his chair. "Now we begin phase three." The prince grunted as he reached for his own glass. "If only there weren't three hundred more phases to get through."

"Must you be so negative?" Soroya chastised.

The sound of shouting in the hall only caused Xavier's brow to furrow as he rose from his seat, his fingers curling around the satin tablecloth.

And here we go, Meera mused from within.

The chaos eventually made its way into the dining hall as the doors were thrust open. Guard rushed in after an infuriated commander by the name of Ryole. Xavier scowled at the sight of him, his blood beginning to boil.

"Can't you see we're having dinner?" Xavier bellowed.

No respect, I swear. Meera clicked her tongue.

Ryole stiffened as he approached the king, a crumpled note in his hand. "This is urgent," he assured Xavier.

Malachai chuckled in his seat, gingerly sipping his wine.

"We just received this from the Rat." Ryole paid no mind to the prince and stepped forward, bowing before handing his king the note.

Xavier glared at the torn paper in his grip. "And what does that bastard have to say now?" he asked, squinting down at the messy script. His informant had never had the best handwriting. It bothered the king to no end.

"Dracus has the Missing VanCamp," Ryole announced.

Xavier felt himself freeze in place, his heart pounding viciously in his chest. Meera snickered in his mind, but he refused to acknowledge her. "Bloody hell," he heard himself say, his grip loosening on the letter. It fell delicately upon the table, grazing a flickering candlewick nearby. Flames began to swallow the paper, and Xavier quickly extinguished them with his fist.

"*Now* do you see why I'm so negative?" Malachai asked his sister.

16

$\mathscr{A}$sh's eyes fluttered open, and she was instantly blinded by bright luminescent lights. Her vision grew spotty as she fought to adjust to the intense lighting, her heart quickening its pace. The sound of beeping in the distance slowly began to drive her mad as she shifted upon a mattress far firmer than the one she was used to. She could feel the sensation of clean cotton sheets rubbing against her bare legs.

These sheets are too soft. Ash's mouth grew dry as she brought the sheet up to her nose, breathing in its scent. They didn't smell like pine as she expected them to. Instead, they smelled like plain fabric.

Concerned, Ash blinked harder, willing her vision to adjust to her surroundings as she forced herself to sit up in bed. Her muscles groaned as if they hadn't been used in ages. Her bones cracked as she shifted uncomfortably beneath the sheet, the cool temperature of the room bringing goosebumps to her flesh.

White-tiled walls and floors surrounded her. There was nothing in the room but her bed, one single chair, and a small counter with various forms of medical equipment and a sink atop it.

"There are no infirmaries in Crane," Ash whispered, her pulse pounding in her ears as she swung her legs over the edge of the bed. The sensation of the cold floors against the soles of her feet sent a chill skittering up her spine. She glanced down at herself only to find that she was wearing nothing more than a thin nightgown made of soft white cotton.

Ash fought to recall the events that led up to this moment, but all she could remember was vomiting blood on the East Cliff. Everything had gone dark after that, and now she hadn't the slightest clue as to where she was or how she had gotten there. Her mind began to race as she imagined every possibility, her stomach roiling as she thought of what might happen to her. What if she was in the Kingdom of Elves? Would she ever see the light of day again?

Snarling, Ash took a step toward the door, but something tugged painfully at her, pulling her backward. She winced, her eyes falling on a tube leading from her arm to a nearby machine, the source of the annoying beeping. A clear substance swam through the tube, pumping into her veins.

Ash's breath staggered as her fingers curled around the tube, ripping it out as quickly as she could. She cringed as blood began to trickle from the small wound left behind. The scent of it made her stomach growl, a burning hunger evolving in her gut.

Wrapping her arms around her stomach, Ash fought not to double over. Her eyes fell on the door once again, and she forced herself to step forward. *I could be anywhere,* she told herself as she approached the small window in the door, carefully peeking outside into a long white hall.

There was no one to be seen, but Ash knew that this place was likely crawling with some sort of Immortals. Whether they were Elves, Draconians, or Pandora, she didn't know. All she was sure of was that she needed to find a way out.

It wasn't so long ago that Ash had made the decision to go to Dracus. She'd even commissioned a stranger to lead her there, but that was supposed to be on *her* terms. Her grip curled around the doorknob, thoughts of Morghan swimming through her mind. The last time she'd seen him, they'd been surrounded by Pandora. He'd defended her, fighting the beasts as she fought to run to safety. What had happened to him?

Ash bit her lip as she prayed silently that the Werewolf hadn't died on her behalf. She slipped out into the hall, her gaze darting to the left and then to the right. Every door along the hall looked the same, giving her no inclination as to which way to go.

In the distance, Ash could hear footsteps and the chatter of healers. She cursed beneath her breath before racing down the hall in the opposite direction from which the voices had come. Her heart was pounding angrily against the walls of her chest as her bare feet slid upon the slippery floors, her gaze falling on a door unlike all the others.

A single button sat beside the door on the wall, displaying an arrow pointing up. Ash stared at it a moment, trembling with nerves as the voices grew closer. Her gaze drifted down the hall where she began to see the shadows of individuals as they prepared to turn the corner.

"Damn it," Ash grunted as she pushed the button. The doors slowly opened, and she didn't waste any time sliding into the small steel room that appeared.

The walls rumbled as Ash scanned a series of buttons

before her. Numbers one through four were displayed, and her head began to ache as she fought to decide which one to choose. Her fingers ran along the buttons for a moment before she decided on the first floor, her heart in her throat.

The room jolted, and Ash fell back against the wall. Her stomach dropped as she felt herself being lifted upward. She gripped the steel walls with all her might, her chest tightening as she pulled in deep breaths to calm herself.

Ash could feel the room slowing to a stop, and without warning, the doors opened. She was immediately met by a tall man clad in black and red, a black butterfly pin gleaming on his chest. His hair was cropped closely to his skull, his eyes the darkest blue she'd ever seen, his flesh radiant.

Noting the second badge on the man's chest, Ash began to panic. *General.* Without a second thought, she shoved the man as hard as she could and slid her grip down to the hilt of his sword, unsheathing it before darting toward the doors at the end of the hall.

"Hey! Stop!" the General called after her. "Guards!"

Ash gulped as she passed Healers, their mouths agape and their eyes wide with surprise. Alarms began to sound throughout the establishment as she pushed through a large set of glass doors, nearly falling down the stone steps in front of her.

Immortals stood everywhere that Ash looked, their gazes filled with curiosity and confusion. She was surrounded by a massive city, the sound of waterfalls rushing in the distance overwhelming her ears.

Fuck! Ash groaned at the sight of dozens of guards rushing her way, all dressed the same way the General had been. She gripped his sword harder, her knuckles turning white as she forced her shoulders back. Her hair blew in the bitter breeze, her eyes narrowing as the guards approached her, slowly and with caution.

The doors opened behind Ash, and she froze, the sensation of a man looming over her causing goosebumps to pebble along her flesh.

"Give me back my sword," the General ordered in a startlingly low tone.

Ash refused to move; her eyes glued to a man that approached her. He was as tall as the General, his hair the shade of dark chocolate. His eyes were a vivid green that Ash had never seen before. A scar was visible along his right brow, and his features were as sharp as the blade in Ash's grip.

Instinct led Ash to raise her sword, pointing it at the man's heart. He ceased his walking, slowly raising his hands above his head. Her mind raced as she thought of what to do. She knew she could fight, but she was surrounded. There was no way she would win.

"Don't do anything rash," another man directed from nearby. This one was dressed in a pale gray suit, a mop of sandy curls atop his head. His brown eyes were fixed on her, his expression stern.

I'm definitely in Dracus, Ash thought as she scanned the appearances of those around her. The red-and-black uniforms gave them away, as well as the sound of the nearby waterfalls. She swallowed hard against the lump forming in her throat, her mind drifting back to her conversation with Morghan and why she'd wanted to come to Dracus to begin with.

Lincoln.

As Ash lowered the sword, she wasn't surprised when the General snatched it from her grip. Her shoulders slumped as she sighed, her eyes closing for a moment as she thought of what to say.

"I need to see Marcus Bonaventure immediately," she announced.

The chocolate-haired man at the bottom of the steps blinked, his mouth falling open as his arms dropped to his sides. "That would be me," he told her, his voice catching slightly in his throat.

"Good." Ash descended the steps, holding out her hand to the man. She fought to remain stoic as Marcus took her hand in his own, though a sea of emotions were beginning to overwhelm her. She blinked against the tears beginning to well in her eyes. "I'm Ash VanCamp, and I need your help."

Subtle gasps sounded from the onlookers watching her, but Ash kept her eyes on Marcus. He opened his mouth to say something, but no words came out.

Ash bit her lip, wondering how she would be able to explain why she needed his help without making everyone believe that she'd lost her mind. "Malachai took my best friend," she continued. "I need you to help me get him back."

Loren rubbed his temples as he sank further into his seat at the round table. The rest of the Council had flooded in, and they were each barking at one another about what should be done with the feral patient Dracus had acquired.

"Missing VanCamp or not, she assaulted our *General* and stole his sword!" Ariel Manchester, the Air Clan leader, hissed from her seat.

"She was afraid," Shadow Daniels, the Earth Clan leader, came to the girl's defense. "How would you feel if you woke up in a kingdom when you'd never set foot outside of your home village?"

Shay Daniels, the Water Clan leader, nodded in agreement with her elder brother. "I would have done the same," she admitted with a wince. "Sorry, Axel."

The General scowled in his seat, his arms crossed before his chest. "Afraid or not, she's clearly off her rocker. Taming her will be like breaking a wild horse. She's insane. Do you honestly believe if her DNA matches Vincent's, that the Elves will let you put the bloody *Sectra* around her neck?" he asked his king, his brow wrinkling with worry.

"She's a person, not an animal!" Marcus thundered from beside the General. "Give her time to adjust to her surroundings. She still needs to heal and perform her elemental test. She'll be fine," he insisted.

Anastasia Volden snickered in her seat, rolling her gray eyes. "Maybe she's what we *need* as a Sectra Holder. She clearly has some fight in her. I'd much prefer someone with the guts of a warrior than a princess, like Mika," she announced with a huff, running her fingers through her long white hair.

Richard Anster cleared his throat from beside the king, drawing the attention of those around him. Loren glanced toward him, releasing a sigh of relief as he noted his advisor's calm demeanor. "We'll have her evaluated psychologically. It's evident she's been through trauma. We all heard what Vincent witnessed in that village," he explained slowly, his hands folded neatly on the table in front of him. "As Marcus said, we should give her time. The issue is, we don't have time. We came to an agreement with the Elves. If Ash VanCamp wasn't given the Sectra by the time she turned eighteen, the amulet would go to someone the Idonian Council agreed upon. And that deadline is tomorrow."

The Council remained silent, their eyes burning into Loren's flesh. The pressure that had fallen upon his shoulders throughout the last eighteen years was nearly too much to bear. And now, Idona had finally reached the end of their search for the Missing VanCamp. Loren was sure of it. He didn't need a DNA match to prove Ash was who she'd said she was. Yet this search had seemed to come to a bitter end.

"We should plan the ceremony." Valentina broke the painful silence as she tapped her fingers along the table. "The sooner the better. Ask for an extension if you must," she told the king. "We have the Missing VanCamp. That should be enough to get Thaddeus and Esmeralda to shut their mouths about the matter."

Loren stared at the Prophetess, wishing he was able to read her thoughts. Though, he didn't need to read her mind to know she was withholding something. His eyes narrowed as he watched her hold her breath. She was forcing herself to remain emotionless in order to hide the secret she wanted to keep.

"I want her to perform her elemental test first thing tomorrow," Loren announced, stiffening in his seat at the sight of his council's eyes growing wide. The King turned his gaze toward Marcus, noting how frazzled the Mentor appeared. "Do not leave her side. I want her under constant surveillance until we're sure she's stable."

"But she's still healing," Marcus warned.

"I think she's fine," Axel glowered.

17

The loss of both Ash and Lincoln weighed heavily upon the McBride household. The entire estate felt empty to Quinn, so much so that he could barely stand to be indoors. He hadn't slept a wink since they'd left the East Cliff, and while he knew Ash had likely been taken back to Dracus, he still had no idea of whether or not she was still living.

After they'd returned to the estate, Quinn and Cooper had searched endlessly through all of Eliza's old newspapers until they found one from when Marcus had been chosen as the High Queen's Guardian. He stared down at the image of one of Idona's four enchanted swords, White-fire, and was positive that it matched the imprint Sam had found in the snow.

Now, Quinn was surer than ever that Ash had been taken to the Kingdom of Dracus, and he was determined to make sure that she was alright.

"What if she *is* alive and doesn't *want* to come back?" Cooper asked, following Quinn through the fields behind their house.

Quinn shrugged, knowing that was likely a possibility.

He'd been preparing himself for a day Ash would leave Crane for years. But that didn't make it any easier. He'd never truly be ready for her to disappear from his life.

"That doesn't matter," Quinn retorted, his father's barn falling into view. The hairs began to rise on the back of his neck at the sight of it, well aware of what he and his brothers had been hiding inside it. "We still deserve a goodbye, and she would have given us one."

Cooper sighed, clearly distraught about the matter. "And how do you expect to get there? Not to mention, explain what we are when we do? If she is alive, Ash will be furious. Lincoln cornered her and ripped her a new one for keeping secrets. What'll happen when she finds out we were doing the same?"

Quinn's grimaced, his mind drifting back to all the times he'd explained why they shouldn't tell Ash about what they found. "Then we'll just tell her it would have only stressed her out more," he reminded Cooper. "At least she had *some* inclination as to what she was. We don't have the slightest clue."

"But we do," Cooper insisted, releasing an angry grunt. "We know exactly what we are. You just don't want to believe it."

Arriving at the barn, Quinn rushed to unlock it. The scent of hay and dust invaded his nostrils the second he opened the door. His nose wrinkled as he fought not to sneeze. He chose not to respond to his brother and instead headed toward the ladder that would lead him up into the hayloft.

Quinn ducked to avoid the loft's low, slanted ceiling. He shuffled through the hay, moving toward the southwest corner of the room before dropping to his knees. Cooper was right behind him as he pushed the hay away, revealing a small hatch door.

Quinn pulled the door open, his heart dropping into his stomach once he saw what remained within it. Two black uniforms with matching bows and quivers were there, as they should have been, but one set was missing. An Empty feeling evolved in the pit of Quinn's stomach as he looked over his shoulder at Cooper.

"Lincoln's bow is gone." Quinn's voice quavered.

Cooper turned ashen beneath the moonlight seeping through the cracks in the walls. "You don't think... that..." he trailed off, shaking his head.

"It's best not to jump to conclusions," Quinn assured Cooper, though he was really trying to convince himself. "Let's just get ready."

"You're sure about this?" Cooper asked softly.

"Now we have even *more* reason to go to Dracus," Quinn insisted as he tossed his brother his bow and uniform before pulling his shirt over his head. "If what that book said is true, and that bow falls into the wrong hands, there's no telling what could happen."

The two brothers rushed to put their uniforms on, pulling the dark hoods over their heads. Quinn stretched, having never been fond of how snug it was, but appreciated how fast it allowed him to run. The fact that they were clad in black would allow the brothers to blend in with the night and go unnoticed as they leaped through the trees. While he'd grown used to the fabric after a year of practicing in the shadows, he knew he'd never get used to it.

Quinn fastened his quiver around his thigh and took hold of his bow. He could feel it begin to vibrate in his grip, awakening at the sense of his touch. Engravings of Idonian knots began to glow blue, and Quinn's entire frame began to tingle as the weapons power ran through him.

Looking toward his brother, Quinn's breath hitched at

the sight of Cooper's glowing blue eyes. The floral pattern on his bow stood out against his dark uniform. "I'll never get used to this," he admitted, a chill running down his spine.

"So, what's your plan?" Cooper asked as he fastened his bow to his back.

Quinn's lips pursed as he thought of how his brother would react to the idea he had swimming around in his mind. "Find the Werewolf," he announced, making his way across the hayloft and down the ladder.

"You can't be serious," Cooper accused as he followed. "What makes you think even if you can find it, that it'll help us."

"We'll make it."

"And how do you expect to force a beast like that to do your bidding?" Cooper snapped.

Quinn released a long, audible breath as he locked the barn behind them, his gaze falling on the tall mountains that surrounded Crane. "If what that book said is correct, we shouldn't have a problem," he said as he started across the field.

WITH THEIR NEWFOUND ACUTE SENSES, IT HADN'T TAKEN Quinn very long to pick up on the Werewolf's scent. He fought against a sea of nerves racing through him as he followed it until he and Cooper came across a small cabin that looked like it was still in the process of being built.

Freshly cut trees were lined up along the property the beast had claimed for itself, ready to be used to complete the cabin. Piles of stone sat nearby, some having already been used to build a chimney.

While the cabin looked like it wasn't quite livable yet, it

had a roof, nonetheless. Quinn growled, wondering about the audacity the Werewolf had to think he could build a new home wherever he pleased.

"Technically, it's not in Crane," Cooper mentioned from the next tree over, as if he could read Quinn's thoughts. "Which explains why no one went out this far on our hunt for the thing."

"Even so, at least our father had the balls to walk up to Drake and announce his arrival," Quinn seethed as he dropped from the tree, retrieving a black arrow from his quiver and loading his bow. He pointed it at the front door as he approached the cabin, knowing the Immortal would likely sense his presence any minute now.

Cooper landed on the ground beside his brother, his bow already loaded as well. "Are you sure this is a good idea? We could find a map and take ourselves to Dracus," he said, his tone trembling with nerves.

"I can assure you it's *not* a good idea," a deep, husky voice chimed from within the cabin. "I suggest that whoever you are, you go back to that little village you came from."

Quinn hissed, baring his teeth as his bow string stretched further, taut against his fingers. "Well *I* suggest you come out here, like a man, and tell me that to my face."

Low, animalistic growls sounded from within the cabin, leading Quinn to stiffen. *These arrows don't miss,* he reminded himself as he waited for the front door to open. When it did, he forced himself to remain still. He turned every muscle in his body to stone, a glare like no other upon his face.

The Werewolf's arrogance quickly vanished, his eyes widening as his mouth fell open. "I'm not your enemy," he said slowly, his hands rising into the air.

"Not yet," Quinn retorted, gnashing his teeth.

"I don't plan on *ever* being your enemy, now lower your damn bow." The man's tone quickly changed from deep and husky to a startlingly low growl.

Cooper hesitantly obeyed, lowering his bow until his arrow was pointed at the snow beneath him. "Do as he asks, Quinn. Or he won't be doing us any favors," he whispered.

"How do I know you won't transition and shred us like you did those Pandora?" Quinn snapped, his stomach churning as he recalled how the beasts' remains appeared.

The Werewolf rolled his eyes, an annoyed grunt escaping him. "You know, I just can't stand violence," he sighed. "But I do what I have to do to protect innocents. If I hadn't intervened, someone else would have died."

Quinn held his stance for a moment longer as he considered what the Wolf had said. When he slowly lowered his bow, unloading it and placing his arrow back in his quiver, he watched as the beast relaxed. "Who would have died?" he asked, his eyes narrowing.

"A girl," the beast revealed.

"Ash," Cooper muttered.

"Yes! That was her name," the Wolf said. "I'd met her earlier that day. When I saw her surrounded like that, well, I had to act."

Quinn gawked at the beast. "You said you *met* her?"

"Yes, a few hours before I helped her with those beasts. We met near the cliffs," he admitted. "She asked me if I'd take her to Dracus, and I agreed. But, obviously that's not necessary now."

His heart breaking in his chest, Quinn fought to remain stoic. Had Ash really made a deal with this Werewolf? Exactly what had she been planning? "What's your name?" He changed the subject for his own sake.

"Morghan Henning," the Wolf said, pride shining in his eyes.

"Ah, that's right," Cooper mentioned, his lips curving into a smile. "I've seen your name in the papers."

Morghan frowned at the sound of his words. "Never mind the papers. Why are you here?" he asked, crossing his arms.

Quinn found himself at a loss for words. Of course, he knew why he was there. But he had a feeling this beast would outright laugh in his face once he revealed that. "I have a proposition for you."

"Let me guess." Morghan sighed as he descended the steps to his makeshift porch. "You want me to take you to that girl."

"Preferably," Cooper quipped, his gaze falling sheepishly to the snow.

Morghan was quiet for a moment, and Quinn watched as his facial expressions changed. The Werewolf began to pace in front of him, clearly deep in thought. "You know they'll lock you up, right?" he asked.

Quinn's heart faltered in his chest. "Why?"

Morghan snorted, now giving Quinn a disbelieving look. "Have you no knowledge of your history?" he mocked.

Rage began to coil deep within Quinn. His heart raced, his fists shaking at his sides. "We are *not* the same," he fumed.

"You're supposed to be extinct," Morghan countered, ceasing his pacing. "How do you think the Draconians are going to react to you showing up at their doorstep?"

Quinn bit back a hiss as he stared at the wolf, unable to hide how offended he truly was. "If we don't go to Dracus, we can't warn them about what happened to our brother. This isn't just about Ash anymore. The Dark Army has

Lincoln, or at least his bow, and Xavier is going to use that power against us all if we don't get him back."

Morghan's features softened, and Quinn could see in his eyes that the Wolf felt guilty about what he'd said. "Truth be told, I was considering going to King Loren about the same thing," he revealed, his voice so low it was nearly a whisper. "I saw what happened that night. Malachai, your brother, the entire attack they clearly used as one massive distraction. But I didn't know who your brother was, though I'll admit I was concerned. Malachai doesn't take people unless he can use them. Once your friend told me his name, it began to make sense."

Quinn's heart sank as he stared at the Wolf, blood pounding in his ears. At first, he was furious. How could this man have seen his brother be taken by the Prince of Darkness and say nothing? Why hadn't he tried to stop him? But, none of that mattered. It wasn't possible to change the past. What Quinn hoped he could do was change the future.

"Lead us there, then," Cooper surprisingly blurted. "Take us and we can tell the King together. If they want to lock us up, so be it. At least they can still try to get Lincoln back before Malachai uses him for whatever he's planning."

Morghan nodded slowly as his eyes drifted between the brothers. "Fine," he replied. "But we have to leave right now."

Quinn's breath caught in his throat, his mind drifting to Lilly. "We have to take care of something first," he told the Wolf. "Meet us at our estate in two hours. I'm sure since you know so much, you know where that is."

"As you wish." Morghan sighed, turning to head back into his cabin.

18

alentina trembled beneath her silk sheets, pain pulsating throughout her entire form like a beating drum. Goosebumps pebbled along her flesh as she pulled the sheet tightly around herself. Her head throbbed as she pulled in a series of deep breaths, hoping to calm herself before the sun arose and the day officially began.

Hints of orange were already visible in the sky as Valentina slowly opened her eyes. A groan escaped her, and she winced as it vibrated her tender throat.

Amelia, Valentina's predecessor, had always told her that being the Realm Prophetess was a blessing. The gift of prophecy was unlike any other in Si Realtra. The citizens of Idona all looked to Valentina for answers, relying on her to prevent any more devastation in the Realm.

On most days, Valentina took pride in her gift. She *wanted* to protect Idona, and all of Si Realtra. In the past, she'd done everything in her power to prevent anything that she could. In some cases, she'd done the unthinkable. Many people across the Realm still blamed the Prophetess for the High King's death. They likely always would.

"It's not a gift," Valentina rasped as she forced herself

to sit up in bed, sliding her legs over the edge. Her body ached, and she blinked against tears of agony pooling in her golden eyes as she stood, her legs wobbling. "On days like this, it's a bloody curse."

As Valentina made her way to her bathroom and turned on the shower, she caught a glimpse of herself in the mirror. She barely recognized the person staring back at her. Strands of hair were stuck to her sweaty forehead. Her complexion was pale, causing the dark circles beneath her puffy, swollen eyes to stand out even more than they usually would.

Many people wanted the answers Valentina could give them, but they weren't aware of the price she had to pay. Sometimes, the pain was so unbearable that she could barely focus on the visions she received. Her mind was jumbled; a puzzle broken into pieces.

Steam billowed in the air around Valentina as she stripped herself of her sweat-soaked nightgown, stepping into the shower. Her muscles tensed as the streams of hot water ran down her figure, washing the grime from her flesh. After a few moments, last night's pain began to wither away, leaving the Prophetess with a clear mind as she washed her hair, massaging her tender scalp.

The visions last night had been complicated, but Valentina was sure she could sort through them. She couldn't help but grow confused as she realized she'd seen the ballroom, and ten people standing upon the stage with gleaming pins on their chests.

Valentina's brow wrinkled as she rinsed her hair before reaching to shut off the shower. "That wasn't all." She clicked her tongue as she stepped out, wrapping a soft white towel around herself. She dried as quickly as she could before slipping into her bathrobe and making her way to her study.

An array of warm colors were spreading throughout the sky as Valentina rushed to write down everything she'd seen. Her wet hair dripped onto the paper, smearing some of the ink, but that didn't stop her. She was lost in her own mind as she attempted to piece everything together.

By the time Valentina finished, her hand ached from gripping her quill. The sunrise had already come and gone, and Dracus had awoken for the day. Through the glass walls, she could see Draconians as they walked to their daily jobs, smiling and laughing. Valentina wished that she could be so happy, but instead, she was filled with anxiety as she turned her attention back to her work.

Words and drawings were scribbled atop her parchment, and to most people, none of it would make any sense. But, to Valentina, it was beginning to. She shot to her feet, her hand rising to her mouth as she realized all she'd seen.

"It's happening," she breathed as she rushed from her study to her wardrobe where she snatched the first thing she saw. Valentina didn't care that it was the same, elegant dress she'd once worn to Princess Penelope's eighteenth-year ceremony. She didn't bother to comb out her hair and instead slipped into a pair of boots before rushing out of her apartment.

Marcus couldn't help but become curious about Ash as they waited for the Healer in her infirmary room. Occasionally, he spared the girl sidelong glances, his breath growing uneven as he noticed how much she looked like Vincent. Being in the same room as her was nothing short of surreal. Thousands of questions swarmed through his mind as he watched her fiddle with her fingers, her gaze fixed on the floor.

There were plenty of things Marcus wished to say to her. *Happy Birthday* had been the only thing to escape his mouth upon entering her infirmary room nearly twenty minutes ago. Now, the wait for Ebony had grown painful, and he thought it best to break their silence.

"How long did you know?" he asked softly, leaning against the small counter.

Ash didn't reply right away and grew visibly tense at the sound of the question. Marcus could hear her heartbeat falter as she sat at the end of the bed, her feet dangling over the floor. "Two years," she whispered.

Marcus's stomach dropped. Part of him wanted to be angry, but he knew he shouldn't be. He'd seen the village she'd grown up in. He knew how difficult it would have been for her to abandon it and head off to a kingdom with no clue as to what would happen.

"I was going to come here," Ash continued, finally turning to look at him. "I was going to leave the very morning after... what happened. I'd even convinced someone to bring me."

Marcus ran his fingers through his hair, biting his inner cheek as he thought of what she'd said to him yesterday. "But not because you knew you were the Missing VanCamp. For this friend of yours," he countered.

"I couldn't stay in Crane, anyway. The Villagers were starting to become suspicious of my mortality. They're not fond of people like us during times like these," Ash said, her shoulders dropping as her gaze returned to her empty hands. "But if I was going to walk into this kingdom, I wasn't just going to do it for me, or you. I want to try and save Lincoln."

Losing a friend was never an easy thing to endure.

Marcus knew this all too well. Waking up in Dracus so many years ago to find out that all of his fellow Black Knights had perished had changed him in ways that he would never understand. "How do you know that the Prince, *himself,* took your friend?" he questioned, his brows pulling together.

"A Werewolf witnessed it," Ash revealed. "The same one who was going to take me here, to Dracus, to try and help Lincoln."

Marcus stared at her, his expression blank. Of course, he and Craven had seen Morghan Henning in the mountains when they'd gone to retrieve Ash, but he hadn't expected that the two had known each other, or that the lone Wolf would be interested in helping her.

"The prince doesn't just kidnap people, Ash. He kills them. What interest would he have in a simple villager?" Marcus was having a difficult time wrapping his brain around what he was hearing. "It just doesn't make sense."

Ash bit at her lip, shaking her head slowly. "Morghan thought it was because his last name meant he *was* something. Some sort of Archer," she explained, her face flooding with confusion.

Marcus's nostrils flared at the sound of her words. "Why would Morghan think *that?*"

"He said something about the McBrides, and that if the Dragons were going to come back from extinction, the Archers might as well too," Ash replied in a placid tone. "But I told him he was wrong. The McBrides aren't Immortal. I've known them my entire life. They're as Mortal as could be."

Marcus began to pace, his hands becoming clammy as he thought of why Morghan Henning would assume such a thing. The Mentor wasn't daft. He knew the history of Si

Realtra. He knew about the Arebus Archers, and the McBride family that always led them.

"It's not possible," Marcus declared. "The Arebus Archers all perished at the end of the Five Realm War. When our Realm Sorceress opened the Underworld, they fell into it. Every last one of them."

A knock on the door pulled their attention, and shortly after, the Healer walked in with King Loren and Richard Anster at her heels. Marcus watched as a rosy blush arrived on Ash's cheeks, which amused him. How could the fiery girl he'd watched storm out of the infirmary yesterday and trigger every alarm in Dracus be so shy?

"Well, she's not lying," Ebony announced. "She is, in fact, a VanCamp."

"I'm not surprised," Loren said with a wry smile. "But this just means we have *much* to do. We need to plan the Sectra Ceremony, and we have less than two days now before our deadline."

Ash lifted a brow, her fingers curling around the bedsheet beneath her. "Ceremony?"

Marcus held his breath for a moment, wondering exactly what sort of Sectra Holder Ash would be. "It was in the High Queen's will that you would be given the Sectra when you came of age," he told her. "If we were unable to find you by the time you turned eighteen, we would have been forced to give it to someone else. And trust me, you're our best option."

The color drained from Ash's face, her lips pressing into a thin line. "There are far more deserving people," she told them all, gnashing her teeth. "I'm a walking abomination. A *Hybrid*. People aren't going to like that."

"She's correct," Ebony sighed. "I haven't completely deciphered every part of her DNA, but I can assure you, Marcus's extra venom definitely did something we've never seen before. So far, it only slightly compares to a single person that I can think of, but I'd need a sample of his to make sure."

Richard's brows raised, curiosity flashing in his eyes. "Who?"

"Hartford, the Berserker," Ebony replied, her tone rising an octave.

Silence spread about the room. As Marcus's eyes drifted from person to person, he found himself in awe of the possibility. His heartbeat began to quicken as he imagined what that would mean for Ash. He thought of the warrior she would become. A Berserker with a Sectra would surely be unstoppable.

"A Berserker?" Ash squeaked, her forest-green eyes wide with both fear and surprise.

"If that's true," Loren shook his head, amazed, "she'll regenerate. She won't die."

Richard nodded slowly. "Which means as far as the Realms are concerned, she won't be a Hybrid. She'll be a Berserker. A new form that depends on blood for nourishment."

"I don't want to lie," Ash snapped. "Just because I don't have wings doesn't mean people won't notice that I'm a Fae. I'm small, just like the female Fae, and my ears are pointed. People can either accept me for what I am or not."

"And Elf," Ebony whispered.

"Excuse me?" Ash blurted.

"Your eyes," Loren informed her. "You have Elven eyes."

Ash gave the king a disbelieving look, and at this point Marcus wasn't entirely sure of whether or not she knew Loren was the King at all. "And what next?" she asked.

"Will my eyes glow red when I'm angry? Am I a Pandora too?"

Marcus snorted, earning a glare from those around him. "What? She's funny. She sort of reminds me of Cedric," he admitted with a shrug.

"I'm sure we'll find out everything we need to know soon enough," Ebony told Ash kindly. "I'll summon Hartford to Dracus. Meanwhile, you're cleared for your elemental test. I say you go ahead and complete it. You can start getting acclimated with your Draconian parts and become a part of a Clan. I'm sure after that you'll feel right at home here."

"I'll prepare to reach out to the Elves," Richard announced. "I'm sure I can convince them to push our deadline forward a week, so we can properly plan the ceremony."

Loren quickly shook his head. "I'll tell them. After her elemental test," he revealed, visibly uncomfortable about this fact. "That way I have all the information we need."

"We'll do it now," Marcus told the king. "I'll fetch Alistair so he can complete his too. That way you can brag about him when you call them as well," he teased.

19

*A*sh eyed Alistair curiously, having never seen such strange markings upon someone's flesh. Then again, she hadn't seen much of anything outside of Crane up until now. Her heart was still racing from their journey to the Training Center, which had been filled with Draconians and their scrutinizing stares. Her skin crawled as she thought of how it felt to have so many eyes upon her. If anything, their stares only made Ash feel as if she'd been some sort of magnificent beast the Kingdom of Dracus had caught in the wild and claimed as their own.

Forcing the thoughts from her mind, Ash tried to focus on Marcus as he explained what she and Alistair needed to know about the elemental test.

"Benjamin Buttler, our current Head of Communications and the mind behind most of our tech and weaponry, designed the orbs himself," Marcus explained as he led Ash and Alistair into an empty arena. "They were meant to act as a much safer way to test elemental abilities. Before, the Clan Leaders would test each individual through a duel of sorts. For example, our Light Clan Leader, Blade, would throw beams of light at people to see if they could deflect them."

Ash shivered at the thought of having to endure a duel with the Draconian Clan Leaders as she watched Marcus approach a strange panel on the wall containing a series of buttons. Her brow wrinkled at the sight of them, her mind drifting back to the strange steel room in the infirmary. "Why does your Kingdom have so many buttons?"

Alistair laughed, clearly amused by her question. "Yeesh, Marcus," he shook his head. "Where did you find this one?"

Marcus released an annoyed grunt, pressing a few of the buttons. The room began to rumble around them, causing Ash to startle. She watched in awe as small platforms began to rise around the room, with shining glass orbs atop them. They were each different in various ways. Some seemed empty, while others were half filled with water or soil.

"All you two have to do is approach each set of orbs and place your palms upon them. You'll know within a matter of moments if you have an ability," Marcuse quipped. "I'll be retreating to the viewing room with the others. I'll direct you through the intercom."

"Others?" Ash's stomach churned, her eyes falling on a glass wall on the far side of the room. It was opaque, like many of the others that she'd seen in the Training Center. She'd imagined they were designed in such a way to give the trainees privacy as they worked to perfect their skills. But where was *her* privacy?

Marcus's gentle hand fell on her shoulder. "You're both rather... high profile. Of course, the Council is going to want to witness this test," he told her, his vivid green eyes smiling. "I'll be heading that way now. You two begin whenever you're ready."

Ash swallowed hard as she watched Marcus walk away, slipping into the room behind the glass. "High profile?" She looked toward Alistair, arching a brow. "What's that supposed to mean?"

Alistair's rolled his eyes. "It means we're special."

"I know what it means," Ash grumbled. "What I'm trying to figure out is what makes *you* so special."

"I'm a Dragon Rider," Alistair declared, a devilish smirk evolving on his lips. "And I've worked with the Draconians before, when I helped them rescue Penelope VanCamp from the Rebels."

Ash placed her hands on her hips, her eyes narrowed into slits. "Dragon, huh?" she pressed, clicking her tongue. "So, you mean to tell me that *you're* the Dragon Rider who kept our village from being obliterated by the Pandora?"

"I did happen to assist a village recently," Alistair replied slowly, tilting his head to the side. "But that doesn't explain who *you* are."

"Ash VanCamp," she admitted, a slight blush beginning to heat her cheeks.

Alistair's eyes bulged, his jaw dropping. He began to dip into a low bow, causing Ash to snarl. "I'm sorry, I didn't know," he apologized, his eyes on the floor.

"Get up!" Ash hissed, her blush intensifying as the seconds passed by. She was sure that by now, her entire face was the shade of a ripe strawberry.

Startled, Alistair did as she asked, straightening his spine. "But, it's custom to bow in the presence of royals, Princess," he reminded her, an inquisitive expression upon his handsome face.

"Listen, I'm no princess," she insisted, clearing her throat nervously. "Don't treat me like one."

"Don't *treat* you like one?" Alistair's brows raised.

"Let's just do this test." Ash glowered, nodding toward

the first set of orbs. He remained still, staring at her as if he was looking at some sort of ghost. Growling, Ash reached for him, curling her fingers around his shirt before dragging him off to begin the test.

CRAVEN LEANED AGAINST THE GLASS IN THE VIEWING ROOM, his arms crossed in front of his chest as he watched Ash and Alistair. His cheeks puffed as he fought to hold in a laugh at the sight of the Dragon Rider bowing. Failing, Craven laughed, imagining how much he'd tease his old friend for his later.

"I think he might be in shock," Shay mentioned. She moved to stand beside Craven, placing her palms against the glass.

Screens flickered to life around the room, the image upon them feeding from cameras placed on each of the pedestals around the arena. Craven's gaze drifted about them all, his heart fluttering nervously as the pair approached the first set of orbs.

"What ability do you think they'll have?" Shadow inquired from beside his sister Shay.

"It's impossible to tell," Richard insisted, his eyes glued to the screen that portrayed the feed from the first set. *Light.* "I suppose we're about to find out. If either of them has an elemental ability at all, that is."

Anastasia snorted from her place against the wall at the back of the room. "How ridiculous would it be if the VanCamp were one of the ten percent of Draconians that *don't* have some sort of elemental ability?"

"Quiet," Craven spat. "They're starting."

"Watch your tone, toddler," Anastasia barked.

In silence, Craven and the Council watched as Alistair

and Ash placed their palms on the Light orbs in unison. He held his breath, his heart quickening in his chest as he watched the orb beneath Ash's palm begin to glow abruptly. What was normally a yellow, sometimes gold light, was pure white, as if it had streamed straight from the Moons. A gasp escaped him, his eyes widening as he looked toward Marcus.

The color had drained from the Mentor's face. "Blade," he called to the Light Clan Leader. "Have you ever seen that before?"

Blade, a large man with brown hair that fell in twisted locks to his waist, grunted from behind Craven. "Can't say that I have," he replied.

"How peculiar," Ariel Manchester sighed dreamily, pressing herself against the glass as if to get a better look.

"I spoke too soon," Anastasia admitted.

It was clear that Ash was in shock herself. Craven could see her brow beginning to glisten with sweat. She was gaping at the light, watching as it faded before she shuffled, nearly stumbling toward the second set of orbs. *Earth.*

Alistair appeared excited for the VanCamp, his usual bright smile growing wider as they stopped at the next pedestal.

Craven squinted, his lips pursed as he watched the pair set their hands upon the orbs. He felt his breath escape him as he watched a pumpkin begin to sprout in the soil. It quickly grew from small and green to large and the perfect shade of orange. His heart nearly sprung straight out of his chest at the sight of the glass orb shattering, the pumpkin having grown too large for it.

"It's not uncommon for someone to have more than one ability," Marcus declared before anyone else could say a thing.

"That's bullshit and you know it," Craven accused.

"Just wait," King Loren ordered, holding up a single hand as he moved closer to the glass, arriving beside Craven. "Next is Water. Maybe Earth and Light will be the last for her, and Water the first for Alistair."

Craven nodded, his mind whirling as he watched the pair complete the third part of the test. The water in the orbs remained still for the Dragon Rider, but for Ash, they stirred instantly at the sense of her touch. She quickly retracted her hand, fear flashing through her eyes.

The viewing room remained silent, and Craven found himself to be awestruck as he watched Ash and Alistair move on to the fourth pedestal. *Air*. His palms were growing sweaty as he watched a funnel appear in Ash's orb, his heart now pounding against the walls of his chest.

"It's impossible," Richard gasped.

Craven shook his head as he watched Ash approach the last set of orbs. Alistair, at this point, was looking as discouraged as ever. He sulked, dragging his feet on his way to the pedestal while Ash moved slowly beside him, her feet dragging as well, but not out of defeat. Craven couldn't help but notice how sickly pale her complexion had become. His head tilted to the side, his brow furrowing as he watched her hold a shaky hand to the last orb.

This time, however, both orbs began to erupt with fire. Craven watched, a smile spreading across his lips as Alistair's eyes grew wide with surprise. "Finally," he muttered with a sigh, his gaze falling back to Ash.

"That's all five." Axel shook his head, his eyes portraying his disbelief.

Craven wasn't particularly concerned with Ash's abilities and was instead concerned about *her*. He watched as her knees wobbled, her head dipping slightly. "She's going to pass out," he growled as he flew to the door, bursting out into the arena.

Alistair had already noticed Ash faltering and had wrapped an arm around her to keep her from falling to the floor. Confusion and worry ran through Craven at full force as he reached for her, pulling her into his arms. His mind swam with ideas of what might have caused her to collapse.

The other Council members had flooded out of the viewing room and were now gathering around to stare curiously at Ash as she lay limp in Craven's arms.

"I thought Ebony cleared her for this test?" Craven snapped, his eyes set in a vicious glare that fell on Marcus.

"She did!" Marcus shouted.

The sensation of a rumbling stomach grew Craven's attention, and rage began to coil deep within his own gut. "Did you forget to feed her?"

Marcus's eye's bulged. "I assumed the Healers had!"

Growling, Craven hurried out of the arena, rushing toward the closest place that he knew had blood—the communications lab. Knowing they always kept a good stock in their fridge, Craven practically flew down the stairs into the Communications Center and approached the lab, kicking the door open due to his lack of free hands.

Benjamin looked up from the long glass table he'd been working at, his bright brown eyes widening with surprise. "What's all this about?"

"I need blood," Craven demanded, lowering Ash onto the table. "Now."

20

A cold sensation against Ash's lips pulled her back into a conscious state. She could feel a substance rushing into her mouth that tasted sweet, yet salty. Every cell in her form seemed to awaken, swelling and yearning for more. A slow sip quickly turned into a chug, her jaw aching as sharp fangs extracted in her mouth.

Ash shivered as the glass was pulled away from her, her entire body covered in a cold sweat. In a daze, she could hear voices nearby, but as her eyes fluttered open, all she could make out were shadowy figures.

A man hovered above her; his attention directed toward someone beside him. "They're all idiots, I swear!" he fumed, placing a palm against Ash's forehead. She flinched at the unexpected touch, but quickly relaxed as he began to run his hand over the top of her hair. The sensation reminded her of how her mother used to lull her to sleep, and she found herself smiling at the memory.

"What's wrong with her?" a familiar voice asked.

"Blood deprivation," one of the men replied. "Well, what could have been the beginning stages of it if Craven hadn't intervened."

Ash startled at the sound of the name, her heart skipping a beat. She'd read so much about a man named Craven in the papers her mother had collected throughout the years. Her breath caught in her throat as she considered the possibility that one of the shadowy figures around her might be the same warrior.

"Should we get her back to the infirmary?" one of the other shadows asked.

"Nah," the man above her replied. "Just give the juice a second to kick in and she'll be fine. Well, as long as Marcus remembers to feed her."

Ash's spotty vision began to clear, her muscles tensing as she took in the appearance of the man looming over her. *Yep, that's the one,* her mind whirled as she stared up at him. "You can stop petting me, I'm not a dog," she told him, watching as he quickly withdrew his hand from her hair.

"Okay, for the record," Marcus began, holding his hands up, "I was unaware that she hadn't been fed."

"As was I," another man said, and Ash recognized him from when he'd visited her earlier in the infirmary. "I'll have a conversation with Ebony."

"Don't you dare punish her!" Ash demanded, forcing herself into a sitting position. She winced, having not realized she was on such a hard surface. "Am I on a table?"

"Yes, my table," a man she'd first seen outside the infirmary replied. He was wearing a suit once again, his light curls combed away from his face. "It's not like I was working here, or anything."

Frowning, Ash swung her legs over the edge and pushed herself off the surface. She swayed slightly upon landing, the room spinning slowly. Placing a hand on the table to steady herself, Ash drew in a shuddery breath as she scanned her surroundings and the faces of the six men scattered about the large office.

A painful, awkward silence hung in the air as Ash shifted her weight uncomfortably beneath their stares. Her mind drifted back to the arena, and how it felt to have every orb awaken beneath her palm. Her chest grew tight at the thought of all the unwanted attention her abilities might bring her. Even now, curiosity filled the eyes of those around her.

"If you're all going to stare at me like I've got two heads, you can at least introduce yourselves," Ash barked.

Eyes widened around the room as the men looked toward each other, confusion flooding their faces. "You didn't introduce yourself?" The man in the suit chuckled, his eyes on the tall slender man across the table from him. The man set his sharp jaw, a strand of black hair falling out of place onto his forehead.

"Excuse me for being a little frazzled," the man snapped, his light gray eyes falling on Ash. "I'm Loren Mason."

Ash's stomach flipped at the sound of the name, her cheeks heating with an embarrassed blush as she realized she wasn't just in the presence of a Draconian Council Member. She was in the presence of the Draconian King, and she had been for most of the day, without realizing it.

"And I'm Benjamin Buttler," the man beside her revealed, straightening his tie. "Head of Communications."

Biting her lip, Ash gave them both a nod, her eyes falling on the man she was sure was the Electrical Immortal. "Craven Amsterdam," she mused, watching his violet eyes widen with surprise. He nodded quickly with a smile.

"I'm Richard Anster, the King's advisor and Second," said a man in the corner. She noticed how odd he appeared. While everyone around them appeared to be young, despite years of Immortality at their backs, Richard appeared to be much older—well into his forties. Streaks of silver ran through his brown locks, wrinkles in the form of crow's feet visible beside his dark eyes. He wore silk robes the color of red wine, a gleaming black butterfly pinned to his chest.

"Are we going to discuss what happened in that arena?" Richard inquired softly.

Benjamin leaned against the table beside Ash, his eyes narrowing in the advisor's direction. "Why, what happened in the arena?"

"You'd know if you were there like the rest of the Council," Richard chastised, baring his teeth.

"I'm sorry, did you not want me to continue gathering intel on that beast in the Forest of Fools?" Benjamin hissed in a challenging tone.

"You know," Marcus said, scratching at one of his temples, "Valentia wasn't there either. The fact that she'd miss such a thing is concerning."

"Speaking of Valentina," Alistair huffed, "she hasn't paid me a visit once since I've arrived here."

King Loren cleared his throat, drawing everyone's attention. "Valentina has been ill," he said matter-of-factly. "Visions can be really hard on her sometimes."

Shouting from upstairs in the Training Center peaked Ash's interest, her eyes flitting to the ceiling as it rumbled above her. "Where are they?" she heard a woman nearly shriek, clearly upset about something.

"You need to calm down!" a man growled.

Ash's gaze fell on the threshold, the sound of boots stomping down a set of stairs causing her stomach to knot. A woman with long, messy golden hair and wide, crazed eyes barreled into the office. She wore an evening gown, the same deep shade of red as Richard's robes, and boots fit for work in the fields. The woman looked as if she'd been kidnapped from a ball and forced to work on a farm for weeks until she finally made her grand escape.

The woman's chest rose and fell as she sucked in a series of deep breaths, her eyes on the king. Ash's demeanor grew still as she observed the frantic woman stride across the room, her unlaced boots clunking against the floor. She fought against a smile, unable to help but notice that the buttons on the back of the woman's dress had been left undone.

"Valentina," Loren greeted her warily, looking her up and down.

"We need to talk," Valentina replied urgently.

Loren blinked, and Ash could hear his heartbeat become uneven. Fear flashed in the king's eyes as he cleared his throat nervously. "Is it the Pandora?" he asked, his fists clenching at his sides.

"No," Valentina retorted, her eyes falling on Ash. "It's about *you.*"

Ash felt her heart drop into her stomach, her mouth falling open. "*M-me?*" she stammered.

"Yes," Valentina claimed.

"What about her?" Loren asked through clenched teeth.

Valentina bit her lip as her gaze flitted around the room, as if she were trying to discern whether the people around her were trustworthy. "I saw plenty of things last night," she said slowly. "But most importantly, I saw *her....* holding the Sovereign's Scepter."

Gasps sounded throughout the room, and Ash found herself shrinking beneath the stares that fell upon her. Alistair's eyes were bulging in her direction, and Craven's hand had risen to cover his mouth. Her heart skipped into a gallop as she looked toward Marcus, silently willing for him to insist that it wasn't true. That it was impossible. But all the Mentor did was stand in silence, his expression blank as he stared into nothing from his place in the corner of the office.

"Are you sure?" Loren fumbled with the question, his gaze flitting between Valentina and Ash, who was now shaking her head in denial.

"I'm sure," Valentina breathed. "I watched her rip it out of the soil."

Loren swallowed hard. "She has all five elemental abilities," he told Valentina, his voice trembling. "She's exactly how the Prophecy described her to be."

The Prophetess nodded slowly, a grave expression upon her face. "She's the Messenger."

he deadline had arrived.

After eighteen years of searching, praying, and waiting, the day had finally come. Vincent VanCamp's eighteenth birthday. *Ash* VanCamp's eighteenth birthday. And there was a strong possibility that she was in Dracus. Right this very moment.

Had Vincent not noticed that unopened letter in Cedric's files, they'd have been too late. By the time they'd realized their mistake, that the hidden village had *truly* existed, the Sectra would have hung from someone else's neck. *Anyone's* neck, but most likely Mika's.

Though it wasn't confirmed that the girl found in the hidden village was, indeed, Ash VanCamp, Vincent knew she was. His heart had told him so. Despite how ridiculous it sounded, he felt as if he'd found a missing piece of his soul, and he hadn't even *met* the girl yet. He simply couldn't bring himself to.

Vincent was filled to the brim with nerves as he entered the infirmary. His original intentions for heading there had been washed away by his churning stomach. The moment he set foot in the stark-white building, he felt a fever coming on. The tips of his pointed ears were red, his pulse thrumming in his temples as he fought to steady his breath. He wasn't ready to meet her. Not yet.

So, the Elf figured he'd visit Alistair. He traveled all the way up to the third floor, only to find that the Rider's room was empty.

"Excuse me, but do you know where Alistair Ward went?" Vincent asked a passing Healer.

"The Head Mentor took him for his elemental test, Prince," she replied before hurrying off to resume her duties.

Vincent stood in the hall for a few moments longer. *Perhaps it's a sign,* he huffed. *Maybe I should go visit her, then.*

Another hot flash swept over Vincent as he entered the elevator, slumping against the groaning steel walls. It dropped on its way to the basement floor. When the doors opened, his breath caught in his throat and his legs grew leaden. He couldn't move them, even if he tried.

The elevator doors eventually shut, the lights on the wall blinking rapidly, begging him to choose an option. But he *couldn't* choose. All he could do was stand there, frozen, as if he hadn't been the man to follow a Dragon all the way to the bloody Forest of Fools.

The elevator beeped, the sound ringing in Vincent's sensitive ears as the doors opened, revealing a Healer he'd come to know quite well standing on the other side.

"If I didn't know you were an Elf, I'd say you look ill," Ebony mentioned as she took her place beside him, reaching to press *one* on the panel before them. The elevator shifted before slowly beginning its ascent into the upper level. "Come to see your sister, have you?"

Vincent's eyes bulged. "I-uh…"

"I got the results back this morning. She is, indeed, your twin. Miraculous isn't it? Talk about impeccable timing." Ebony released a long whistle, shaking her head. "Marcus took her for her elemental test, with Alistair Ward I believe. He was released this morning, under Craven's care. Apparently, the two are great friends. Who would have thought?"

All Vincent could do was gape at the Healer.

"Happy birthday, by the way." Ebony offered him a bright smile as the doors opened and she disappeared into the hall, leaving him to his own devices.

The Elf stood there another moment, but as the doors began to close once again, he hurried out into the hall. Healers and patients walking back and forth hardly noticed him, standing as still as a statue.

VINCENT COULD HAVE GONE RIGHT TO THE TRAINING Center to meet Ash and watch her complete her elemental test with Alistair, but, he couldn't gather the guts. Instead, he found himself searching for someone he could talk to. While he would prefer to talk to Penelope about the matter, she was across the Realm in the Kingdom of Elves. So, he sought out the one person in Dracus that he knew would help him make sense of his thoughts.

Lucinda.

Vincent had found her in the library. Oddly enough, it was the perfect place. He'd always found peace by surrounding himself with books, though his current circumstances were far too stressful. He wouldn't find himself at ease any time soon.

The Sorceress was currently curled into a chair beside him, her nose deep into a spellbook he was sure she'd already memorized at some point.

"You know what sucks the most?" Vincent broke their

lingering silence, leaning back in his chair. "That if Malachai hadn't killed Cedric, he would have opened that letter from Aries and found Ash a lot sooner."

Lucinda looked up from her book, meeting his gaze. "Perhaps," she sighed. "But what matters is that you found the letter, and now she's here. And safe."

"What do you think she'll think of all this?" Vincent pressed, tapping his fingers on the table in front of him. "What if she prefers the family she grew up with over Penelope and me?"

The Sorceress shut her spellbook, setting it gently on the table before turning in her chair to face him completely. "Vincent," she began softly. "Don't make so many assumptions. Of course, she loves the people she's known throughout her life. But that doesn't mean she can't learn to love *new* people," she insisted, ruffling his hair.

"From what I've heard, she's not like us at all," Vincent said, smoothing his locks. "She's... wild. She attacked Axel! Pushed him right to the ground and stole his sword." He shook his head, clearing his throat nervously.

Lucinda snorted, clearly amused. "So, she hasn't been trained on how to act in court with the Elves. Maybe she knows how to handle a sword but doesn't know which fork to use with a salad. I don't think there is anything wrong with those qualities. If anything, I think she'll be relatable."

Vincent nodded, agreeing with what the Sorceress had said, yet, he couldn't help but worry about the moment he would meet Ash. He doubted he would have much time to mentally prepare himself, since it was evident that time would come incredibly soon.

"Lucinda!" a voice shouted just as the library doors were thrown open, and the Sorceress straightened in her seat. Vincent watched with curious eyes as Shadow approached their table with wide and frightened eyes.

"What is it?" Lucinda asked, her voice wavering.

"We need you in the Round Table room," Shadow revealed, his eyes falling on Vincent. "Would you like to come?"

Vincent's heart soared at the thought. "You want *me* to go to a Council meeting?" he asked, his jaw hanging open.

"Trust me, you won't want to miss this one." Shadow shivered as the words left his mouth.

ASH'S FIRST DAY IN DRACUS WAS TURNING OUT TO BE THE most stressful day she'd ever experienced. So stressful, in fact, that she'd nearly forgotten it was her own birthday.

As she was ushered into an elegant room centered by a large round table, her heart was racing the same way that it would if she were facing thousands of Pandora. A large, black chandelier dripped from the ceiling, casting a warm glow on the huge table surrounded by red velvet chairs. Paintings of past kings were hung along the walls beside black butterfly banners. Silver tassels hung from each banner, swaying with every slight movement in the large room.

Ash collapsed into a seat beside Marcus with the grace of an untamed bear, gazing out of the glass wall in front of her, in awe of the kingdom beyond. She scanned the tops of cathedrals and the roofs of shops and houses. Everything about Dracus was truly beautiful. Mist hung in the air from the waterfalls surrounding the kingdom. The ultimate form of protection *and* defense.

Valentina stood, hovering over what appeared to be an ancient book. The leather bindings were worn, and the pages yellow. The Prophetess had since combed her hair and changed into an outfit far less extravagant.

As more individuals flooded into the room, Ash found herself growing queasy. She wasn't sure exactly how large the Draconian Council was, but knew it was made up primarily of the Clan Leaders. The five warriors were so notorious that even the secluded villagers in Crane knew of them. A shiver ran down Ash's spine at the idea of being in the presence of such greatness.

"You know, just because it's my birthday, you didn't have to throw me such an elaborate party," she joked, jabbing Marcus in the ribs with her elbow in an attempt to lighten the mood.

The Mentor didn't respond and instead released a heavy sigh. But a man across the table with short brown hair and bright blue eyes chuckled. The sound brought a smile to her lips, despite her intensifying nerves.

Ash's gaze flitted throughout the room before lingering on a woman with waist-length crimson hair. Her amber eyes were nearly glowing beneath the chandelier light.

Beside the strange woman sat a young man. Ash's eyes fell on him, her breath escaping her. His wavy mahogany locks barely covered his pointed ears. Freckles dusted his cheeks and his small, narrow nose. His sage-colored eyes were wide, dancing about the room until they fell on Ash.

The pair stared at one another curiously, Ash arching a brow. She leaned forward in her chair, resting her elbows on the round table, hoping to hide how nervous she'd become. Staring at the man felt like staring into a mirror, and Ash's clammy hands began to tremble as she tore her gaze from his face and looked toward Marcus.

The Mentor was staring at Valentina, who was glaring at the empty seat behind him. "Where the hell is Axel?" she grumbled, tapping her foot impatiently.

"Maybe he's avoiding Ash," Richard teased from his place beside the king.

The comment only caused a blush to bloom on Ash's cheeks, her eyes falling to her lap as she fought to hide it.

The doors swung open once again, and Ash held her breath as she looked up to see the General striding to his seat, his red cape fluttering behind him. She caught sight of an axe strapped to his back and gulped, now thankful he hadn't taken hold of it to cut her down when she'd abruptly attacked him.

"Now that we're all here..." Valentina grinned as she scanned the faces of everyone seated at the round table. "It's best I explain why I've summoned you all so suddenly."

Ash listened to the Prophetess intently, forcing any thoughts of nervousness from her mind. She watched as Valentina turned the pages of her book, running her fingers along elegantly written script.

"We've always known that the Messenger would be a Draconian," Valentina began, her smile wavering as her lips trembled. "Specifically, a woman with unique skills. Ash's elemental test resulted in her having all five elemental abilities," she explained slowly, her tone's pitch rising with each word she said.

The sound of her pulse in her ears quickly became too distracting for Ash, her fingers curling into white-knuckled fists. She chewed at her lip, forcing herself to keep her eyes on the Prophetess, avoiding the expressions on the other faces around her.

"Last night, I received a string of visions." Valentina's voice shuddered. It was clear to Ash that she felt strongly about the prophecy she spoke of, which only made her feel guilty about wanting no part of it.

"I saw a group of ten on our dais in the ballroom," Valentina said, slowly shutting the book before her. "Warriors."

The King's brow furrowed as he leaned back in his chair, staring up at the Prophetess. "What warriors?"

"I can't reveal their identities," Valentina told him warily. "Not until I know who they are myself. All I know is that Ash was one of them."

Ash sulked in her chair, drawing her shoulders in. She could feel the Council's eyes burning into her flesh as she shivered. *Go where they will let you fight*, Eliza's voice rang in her mind. She shook her head, willing her words away.

"I saw vicious battles," Valentina continued, fear flashing in her golden eyes. "I saw blood, Magic, and pain. But most importantly, I saw Ash lift the Sovereign's Scepter from the spelled soil Amelia spoke of in this prophecy."

The room remained silent as everyone stared at the Prophetess. For the first time, Ash allowed her eyes to drop from Valentina's face and looked around the room. Some council members were staring at her, while others appeared dazed, staring into nothing.

"I'm certain," Valentina announced, straightening her spine, "that Ash VanCamp is the Messenger we've been waiting for. I can feel it in my bones."

Ash shook her head, disagreeing with the Prophetess. Marcus was as stiff as stone beside her, as if he was able to sense what she was about to say. "What will you have me do then?" she asked, her blood coming to a boil in her veins. "Storm into the Idonian Kingdom and *hope* I'm strong enough to face the Dark King himself?"

Valentina stared back at Ash, her golden eyes growing wide. "Not alone," she told her. "You have us. And the other warriors I saw."

Ash fought to stifle her anger, knowing it wouldn't do her any good. "What if I refuse?" she asked. Gasps sounded around the room. "Who would want the weight of Idona's fate on their shoulders?" she snapped, trembling beneath the judgment of the Council.

"We don't get to choose our fate." The General's sharp tone cut through the air around Ash like a knife. She looked over at him, her eyes meeting his deep blue orbs. "We play the hands we're dealt."

"Axel is right," the woman with the long red hair added, her tone much kinder. "We've always known that the Messenger will bear a weight unlike any other. Believe me when I say that every soul at this table prayed that it would be them. That every warrior in Idona would gladly take that burden. That we'd do anything to end this war."

Ash's heart dropped, her stomach roiling. She drew in a deep, painful breath as she thought of what to say. "And what happens if I fail?" she countered, crossing her arms.

"Don't fail," a man beside Richard told her. Ash's lips pressed together as she looked him over, noticing the scar running down his thick neck. Light brown hair fell in twisted locks down his back, adorned with gold and silver rings. His yellow eyes were narrowed in her direction, like daggers piercing her flesh.

Ash worked to master her evolving fear, her brows pulling in as she stared back at the man. It was impossible not to be intimidated by him, knowing if he were standing, he'd likely loom over her, his shadow large enough to swallow her whole. Her heartbeat grew sluggish as she realized that she had no choice in the matter. That this man would *make* her fulfill the prophecy.

"Ignore Blade's harsh comments." Richard waved the burly man off, scowling in his direction. "We'll ensure that you don't fail, is what he *meant* to say."

Valentina nodded quickly with a faint smile. "That's what the other nine warriors are for. I'm sure of it. The

Moons have their plan, and they've shown me how to execute it."

Beneath the table, Ash felt Marcus reach for her hand. She thought of pulling her hand away but felt his fingers weave with hers, holding it in place. "Just get the Scepter, Ash. I can assure you that if you fall, I'll pick it up and drive it straight through Xavier's heart myself."

22

Since the moment Quinn had left Crane, he hadn't stopped moving. Two days had gone by now, and he hadn't so much as stopped to take a breath. His uniform felt more like a second skin, and he appreciated it now more than ever. Blending into the night and concealing himself from the Pandora they'd encountered had been easy. Almost *too* easy.

Morghan had more of a difficult time hiding, so the Werewolf hadn't bothered. The Pandora seemed to fear him, and while some would attack and die shortly after, others simply fled. The shape-shifters might have the advantage, being able to transition into anything they wished, but that gift proved useless in the presence of an Immortal that rivaled them so severely.

Cooper had barely said a word since they'd begun their journey, and Quinn could see how tense he'd become. He was still young, though he'd deny it entirely. His eighteenth birthday was merely two weeks away, but that didn't mean Cooper was ready to leave the nest.

It was clear now, more than ever, that Quinn and his brothers should be afraid. Lincoln's capture was alarming in more ways than one. The bows they'd found clearly put targets on their backs, and from what Quinn heard from Morghan, the other Immortals weren't fond of Arebus Archers. But, what did the Dark Army want to use Lincoln for? And would the Prince of Darkness come back for Quinn and Cooper to use them as well?

Quinn's blood turned to ice in his veins at the thought. Now, the Strip sat in the distance behind him. They'd entered the Draconian jurisdiction, but still had two days left of travel before they made it to Dracus, unless they took advantage of their Immortal speed. Anything could happen in the time it took for him to arrive at his destination. And now, Quinn was beginning to think of thousands of ways he could die.

Whether it was the Draconians who killed him, or the prince himself, didn't matter. Leaving Crane and the safety of the Strip might have been the worst decision Quinn had ever made.

QUINN AND THE OTHERS HAD DECIDED TO USE IMMORTAL speed and ran as fast as they could toward the isle Dracus sat upon. The anticipation had begun to drive him mad. He wanted to get to Dracus and face his fate, whatever that may be. But, most importantly, he wanted to warn Dracus about Lincoln and make sure Ash was alright. And alive. Then, he'd be at peace.

"We're going to have to stop and rest soon," Morghan mentioned as they traveled through a thick forest. "We could set up camp near Redding. I could go and find us some food. The village knows me well."

Quinn frowned at the idea. "Why stop when we're so close to Dracus?" he asked, knowing that the Unity Bridge that connected Dracus to the rest of the Realm sat just off the village of Redding.

"You'll need your strength," Morghan insisted, plucking a twig from his golden locks. "And I need to freshen up."

"I have strength, and you can freshen up in Dracus," Quinn growled as he dropped from the trees, landing beside the wolf on the ground. Cooper quickly did the same, as silent as ever.

Morghan rolled his eyes as he changed directions, now heading northeast. "We've been walking and running at Immortal speed for days now. You might not like to admit it, but I certainly will. We're out of steam. You two won't stand a chance against the Draconians."

Glaring at the Werewolf's back, Quinn picked up his pace to walk alongside him. "You really think they're just going to put us down?" he asked, his heart quickening at the thought.

The Wolf didn't reply right away and instead kept his attention on the overgrown forest path before him. "Arebus Archers are too much of a threat," he admitted softly, driving his hands into the pockets of his jeans. "They were the original Immortals, created by the Sovereign to guard her. Their arrows don't miss, as long as the target isn't more than three miles away. They're faster than the other Immortals. Stronger. And after the Sovereign disappeared, they never picked a side."

Quinn's features softened as he listened to Morghan and what he had to say. It was clear the Werewolf knew far more about the Immortal communities across Si Realtra than he ever would. However, he wasn't sure he liked what he was hearing.

"What's that supposed to mean?" Cooper finally spoke, his tone harsh.

"It *means*," Morghan ceased his walking to face Cooper, who skidded to a stop, "that they can't be trusted. There have been times in the past where the Archers aided the Idonians. But there were also times where they aided the Amorians. Their last leader was more wicked than he was ever good. He spent his days at the side of Erim's Queen, Raina, who was beheaded at the end of the Five Realm War for the entire Galaxy to see. He committed countless crimes on her behalf before he finally came to Idona and swore loyalty to Gregor VanCamp. So, when our Realm Sorceress saw the Arebus Army on the battlefield with the Erminians, she did what she had to do. If the Arebus turned on the Idonian, Minorian, and Zerinian forces, we'd have lost the war. The existence of your ancestors was a risk Si Realtra couldn't take."

Cooper's mouth fell open, his teary eyes widening. Quinn watched his brother, his heart clenching. He knew what was running through his mind. They weren't ready to face a history they had nothing to do with.

"Let's camp." Quinn changed the subject. "We could use some time to gather our thoughts."

Morghan nodded slowly, turning to continue his walking. Cooper remained behind them, his feet dragging as he hung his head. Silence lingered between the three men as they searched for the perfect spot to sit down for a little while and perhaps get some rest.

While Quinn fought to maintain his stoic expression, he knew he would likely fail. His thoughts swam with ideas about what had happened in the past and what would happen next. Would he and Cooper wind up dead upon crossing the Unity Bridge? Or would they be the first Arebus Archers to finally pick a side?

Cooper had never been so afraid. He feared for Quinn's life, his own life, and Lincoln's as well. He worried about Ash in Dracus, and how she was fairing, or if she was still alive. His heart sank as he thought of the moment he'd watched her walk away from him. He shouldn't have let her go. And now, if she were dead, it was most certainly Cooper's fault.

Frowning, he looked up from the ground and watched as Morghan lit a small fire. The air was frigid and the ground frozen, but there was no snow to be seen yet in this part of Idona. Sighing, he leaned back against the trunk of a moss-covered tree while his stomach rumbled.

"I think I'll go on a hunt," Cooper announced softly as he pushed himself to his feet.

Quinn gave him a look that only made him feel daft. "Alone?"

"He'll be fine," Morghan mumbled as he blew on the fire, causing the flames to brighten and grow. "Besides, I'm starved. It's better to send one of you two to kill something quickly instead of walking all the way to Redding and drawing attention to myself."

"But it isn't safe," Quinn hissed.

Morghan snorted as he looked in the Archers direction, giving him a disbelieving look. "You really think he can't handle himself? I get that you're protective, but he's not a baby," he grunted, rolling onto his back before stretching out beside the fire.

Without waiting for his brother to protest further, Cooper pulled up his hood and took to the trees. He began moving from limb to limb, scanning his dark surroundings for any movement. He fought to drown out the sound of the fire crackling nearby, focusing all his senses on his hunt. His eyes tingled, the night around him glowing blue as he jumped to the next tree.

While being Immortal hadn't been Cooper's wish, he doubted now that he had experienced his heightened senses, he'd be able to live without them. Everything was easier. He moved faster, could see farther, and felt far too powerful for his own good.

The moonlight streaming down from the skies warmed Cooper's flesh and his entire body pulsated with its presence. He could feel it seeping into his pores, strengthening him. Walking and running constantly during the last few days had left Cooper with sore muscles and weak legs. But now, his fatigue seemed to vanish, and he felt like he could run for days if he'd wanted to.

High in a pine tree, Cooper slowed his pace. He realized that he'd been lost in his thoughts and wasn't sure how far he'd traveled from their makeshift campsite. The crackling of the fire was too far away for him to hear, and his mouth grew dry as he thought of how he'd find his way back to his brother and Morghan.

The sound of a squirrel scurrying up a tree drew his attention, and Cooper quickly drew his bow and loaded it. The bow vibrated in his grip as he released the black arrow. He followed it with his eyes as it curved in the air, flying toward his target. The sound of piercing flesh was quickly followed by a thump as the creature fell dead to the ground.

Cooper sighed, slowly descending the tree to fetch his kill. He frowned at the sight of it, knowing that while it was plump after preparing for Winter Solstice, it wouldn't be enough to feed three men. His stomach growled as he shoved the squirrel into his satchel, and he doubted the little beast would be enough to clench his hunger.

Turning to head back the way he came, Cooper leaped back into the trees. The scent of burning twigs and leaves wafted through the air, and a sigh of relief escaped him.

Knowing he'd be able to follow the scent back to his brother and Morghan, he listened for more squirrels scurrying in the surrounding trees.

Just two more squirrels and I'll head back, Cooper thought as he loaded his bow. He let the arrow loose, thoughts of another plump creature in his mind as he watched it curve through the air once again. He followed it, smirking as it pinned a second squirrel to the trunk of a nearby tree.

Cooper strapped his bow to his back before leaping over, gripping the rough bark with his gloved fingers as he slowly lowered himself down to where the squirrel was pinned. He snickered as he ripped the beast from the tree and shoved it into his pack. *Too easy,* he mused as he prepared to climb back up the tree.

The sound of distant voices in the forest led Cooper to freeze in place, his heart sinking. They were far, but still too close for comfort.

"There's a fire nearby," a man said curiously, his voice getting closer.

Cooper's pulse thrummed in his ears as one of the men stepped on a twig. It snapped, the sound echoing in the night. *They'll do the same thing to my neck if they see me.* He winced, debating whether he should attempt to move higher into the tree and hide behind the pine needles.

"It's close enough to check out while we wait," a second man said, and Cooper could hear the smirk in his sinister tone.

"I don't know Cade, if we're not where we're supposed to be, the Rat's errand boy will burn the message and head back to whatever hole he crawled out of," the first man grumbled.

"Stop being such a kiss ass," the man called Cade snapped. "Besides, I'm pretty sick of wasting my time coming all the way out here once a week just because

Ryole doesn't want to. Maybe if we fail to get the message, he won't make us anymore."

"Or he'll kill us," the second man countered.

"I'm not afraid of Ryole," Cade insisted.

"I doubt Ryole will be the problem. It's Xavier I'm worried about."

Cooper flinched at the sound of the name, his grip on the bark wavering. He slipped, but quickly caught himself. He shut his eyes, cursing beneath his breath.

"Did you hear that?" Cade growled, his voice so close that Cooper's limbs began to shake, his entire body now covered in a cold sweat.

"It was probably just a squirrel or something," the second man replied. "We should really be getting to the meeting place."

"But what if it's a spy?" Cade seethed.

Cooper's heart was beating so fast that he wondered if it might explode. His grip tightened around the bark, his hands growing clammy.

"If it makes you feel better, we can check out the fire *after* we get the message," the second man offered.

No. Cooper's mind whirled as he thought of who these men were, and how strong they might be. He refused to look at them, but it was clear that whatever they were, they were in their Mortal forms. It wasn't an unknown fact that only the men and women in with the highest ranks in the Dark Army maintained their Mortal forms, their faces often shielded by dark hoods and masks.

There was no doubt in Cooper's mind that these two men were of higher ranks, and that he wouldn't stand a chance if he had to face them on his own. *I need to get out of here and warn Quinn and Morghan.* He clenched his jaw, his muscles screaming from holding himself against the tree for so long. *But how?*

Images of what would happen if he was caught clinging to the tree flashed through Cooper's mind. His blood ran cold as he gulped down breaths to stay quiet. He could feel his knees weakening and his chest tightening. He needed to do something. *Anything.*

Cooper's lip quivered as a tingling sensation began to spread throughout his body. He felt as if he were being lifted into the air, floating toward the moons. A frigid breeze swam around him, ruffling his hair. At first, it was gentle, but the subtle breeze soon evolved into a rushing wind so harsh that Cooper choked, unable to breathe.

Crashing down to the earth, Cooper coughed, his breath completely escaping him. He kept his eyes squinted shut, fearful tears beginning to form behind his lids.

The warmth of a fire began to surround him, and Cooper's eyes slowly fluttered open. He winced at the sight of his brother standing over him, a look of pure shock upon his face.

"What the hell?" Quinn gasped.

Without uttering a word, Cooper sprung to his feet and began to stomp out the fire, ignoring Morghan's protests. "Xavier has men in this forest right now," he snapped as the Werewolf reached to stop him. "We need to move. *Now.*"

"Are you going to explain how you just appeared here so quickly?" Morghan asked as he thrust his arms into his jacket.

"I don't know." Cooper's voice wavered, the stress of this evening beginning to get the best of him. "I was clinging to a tree, listening to them talk, and suddenly *poof,* I was here."

The Werewolf abruptly reached for Cooper, placing his hands on his shoulders. "Did you just say you *poofed* here?" he asked, his caramel eyes widening.

"Yes," Cooper snapped, attempting to free himself from the Wolf's strong grip.

"Do you know how *rare* that is?" Morghan asked as he began to shake Cooper intensely. "You just transported! Only a handful of Archers throughout time have had that gift!" he claimed excitedly.

"Gifts?" Quinn arched a brow.

"You can explain later," Cooper snapped. "We need to get out of this forest before those men head this way. Or else they capture us just like they did Lincoln and use my *gift* against this Realm."

23

sh hadn't slept since the moment she'd learned that she was the Messenger. Her heart hadn't stopped racing. She'd lost her appetite completely for both food a*nd* blood. And while Marcus had tried to assure her that everything would be fine, she couldn't help but imagine what would happen if she failed.

While Dracus was buzzing, excited about the news, Ash was homesick. She wanted the McBrides. She wanted her own bed, back in Crane. She wanted nothing more than to find a way to turn back time, but that was impossible, and she had no choice but to get used to her new life in Dracus. So far, there had only been one thing in the Kingdom that she could do that felt normal.

Train.

Ash had been given a Mentor, and while she'd originally anticipated for it to be Marcus, seeing as he was tasked with the insufferable job of watching over her, she'd been wrong. However, she couldn't complain about who they'd chosen for her or what clan they'd put her in.

Now, Ash found herself for air as she dropped to her

knees. Craven did the same across from her, chugging a thermos of blood.

"I have to say, I'm impressed," he admitted as he leaned backward, bracing himself on his palms. "I don't know why they thought you needed training."

Ash shrugged, wiping her brow. "This is just a good way to keep my mind off of things," she told him, her stomach growling. The only way she found herself growing hungry was after an intense duel. "Pass that thermos."

Craven slid his thermos across the floor to her, and Ash quickly chugged what was left. "Maybe your time would be better spent actually *learning* about yourself as a Draconian." He sighed, pushing himself to his feet.

Ash's brow wrinkled. "What do you mean? I get hungry, I drink blood," she grumbled. "That's pretty much it, right?"

"You couldn't be more wrong." Craven sighed as he held out his hand. Hesitantly, Ash took it in hers and allowed him to help her to stand. Her legs wobbled for a moment, exhausted from overuse. "I say we shower and spend the rest of the day in the library."

Not fond of the idea, Ash frowned. "You're going to make me read things?"

"We have a week until the Sectra Ceremony," Craven reminded her as he ushered her toward the door. "By then, Valentina swears that she'll know the identities of all the warriors she saw. And that you'll all brief immediately afterward so you can leave and get the Scepter."

Ash's stomach churned at the thought. *Only a week?* A shiver swam down her spine. "And your point is?"

"That we should use the week wisely," Craven clarified as they walked down the hall. He stopped for a moment, gazing through one of the glass walls into another arena, where Alistair was currently training with the Fire Clan

Leader, Anastasia Volden. "I don't know what the Moons were thinking. He already has a Dragon. What the hell does he need *more* fire for?"

"Who knows?" Ash chuckled. "He looks happy enough."

"I suppose," Craven replied. "Even though I doubt he'll ever be as happy here in Dracus as he was in Mayfire."

Ash's heart sank at the thought. Marcus had told her very little about Alistair, and she suspected that was for good reason. Sometimes it was best to leave the past in the past, because some memories were just too painful to carry with you for the rest of your days.

Reluctantly, Ash had showered and dressed before meeting Craven in the library. He'd showed her to a table on the second floor, where countless books about Draconian history were scattered atop it.

"Sit," Craven ordered playfully, pointing to a chair.

Ash slumped down into the seat, crossing her arms in front of her chest. She watched as Craven took the seat across from her, folding his hands on the table. "What are we learning today, Teach?" she teased, her lips curling into a smirk.

"What to do and *not* do as a Draconian," Craven announced, blowing a strand of dark hair away from his eyes. "Well, mostly what *not* to do."

Intrigued, Ash leaned forward, resting her chin in her hand.

"Try to avoid drinking blood straight from the vein," Craven began to explain. "It'll trigger bloodlust, and you won't be able to stop yourself. It causes some sort of trance that's extremely difficult to break out of."

Nodding, Ash was beginning to wish she'd brought a notepad to write everything down with.

"If you bite a Mortal, they'll find the sensation to be incredibly painful," Craven continued. "If you bite another Immortal, they'll experience the exact opposite. It becomes rather sensual for them. So, I'd avoid it. Though, if you drink Immortal blood, it'll allow you to heal faster and spike your adrenaline. There are many benefits to doing this, but, it's best if a fellow Immortal donates the blood instead of you drinking it directly from them. Especially if you don't plan on following through with *that* act."

Ash could feel a vivid blush rushing to her cheeks. "I see," she replied shyly.

"*And*," Craven said excitedly, "if you *do* commit such an act with a fellow Draconian, you could risk creating a Lover's Bond."

"What's that?" Ash asked warily.

"I've heard that you can feel each other's emotions and pain." Craven shrugged, leaning back in his chair. "I don't personally have one with anybody, so I couldn't tell you how it feels. Normally, married people wind up with them. Although I've heard of it happening accidentally to battle companions. You know, rough battle, desperate need for blood. I'm sure you can imagine the rest."

Ash's blush grew hotter on her cheeks as she dropped her gaze. "Do you think I'll have a battle companion?" she questioned.

"That depends, really," Craven replied with a smile. "Battle companions are often trained together, and their fighting styles closely mimic one another, but, you'll be fighting with nine other people. The odds are, they'll all be your battle companions."

"I suppose that makes sense." Ash sighed, the sound of the library door opening grabbing her attention. She stood, glancing down to the lower level, only to find the one person she'd been avoiding walking in, his face shoved into a book.

Craven moved to her side, curious as well. "Oh." He shivered. "I suppose it's due time for you two to have a conversation, don't you think?"

Ash scowled, unsure of what she could even say to the man. "I doubt we'll bond as much as everyone wants us to," she retorted, her words laced with a sadness she'd hoped not to reveal.

The man looked up from his book, his eyes falling on Ash. Her posture grew rigid beneath his gaze, her heart halting in her chest. "Hello," he greeted her.

When she didn't respond, Craven elbowed Ash harshly in the ribs. "Hello," she squeaked, rubbing her sore side.

"Do you mind if I join you two?" he asked as he slowly ascended the staircase, arriving on the second floor. Ash pursed her lips as he approached, having not realized how tall he was before. How was she supposed to believe they'd shared a womb, when she likely needed to sit on a stack of books to eat at some of the tables in Dracus?

"Of course you can!" Craven quipped, returning to his seat at the table. "We were just discussing battle companions, but I think it's better if you two get to know one another."

Ash glared at her Mentor as she lowered back into her seat, her back as stiff as a board. She remained silent, watching as the man held his hand out to hers. She shook it, not willing to be rude to him, although she'd prefer to return to the apartment she was forced to share with Marcus and hide for a while.

"I'm Vincent," he said softly, slowly sitting in the chair beside her.

"I know," she replied, her gaze on the table.

"And you are?" Vincent asked, his brows raised.

"Ash VanCamp," she muttered, looking up into his sage eyes.

"No." Vincent shook his head with a crooked smile. "I mean who are you, *really?*"

Ash tilted her head to the side, arching a brow. "You saw our DNA results," she grunted.

"Yes." Vincent nodded, the waves in his messy hair bouncing slightly. "But that's not who you were for eighteen years."

"Oh." Ash's eyes widened, a faint smile now visible upon her lips. "Ashlyn Snow." She relaxed in her chair, watching as Craven shifted in his seat as if he were settling in for a long story. "My mother, Eliza Snow, found me in a forest, the same as the Chamberlains found you. We lived by ourselves in a cottage on Main Street until I was six when the McBride siblings were orphaned. After that we lived with them in their estate so that she could watch over them as well."

Vincent seemed enthralled with her words, his eyes filled with wonder. "I have so many questions about your village," he admitted, nearly trembling with anticipation. "We thought it didn't exist. Cedric and Marcus went to look for it, but said there was nothing in the Strip's swirl. Now I understand there was a barrier around it, one that made it appear invisible."

Ash nodded slowly, unsure of how much she should say about the village. "I'm afraid that it's meant to be a secret. There isn't much I should share," she explained sadly.

"I understand," Vincent assured her. "So, who are the McBrides?"

Having not expected the question, Ash fumbled with the right words to say. "My closest companions," she revealed, her heart clenching. "Quinn is the oldest. He was extremely helpful with trying to help me figure out what I was turning into. The second oldest is Lincoln, but he's no longer with us. He was captured by the Prince of Darkness last week, and we have no idea if he's alive." Her heart broke all over again as the words left her mouth. She watched as Vincent's smile faltered, shock and sadness now replacing the wonder in his eyes. "Cooper is the third brother. He was born two weeks after I arrived in Crane. Oddly enough, we were always referred to as the *twins*. And Lilly is the youngest. She's fourteen now, but well beyond her years. She's wonderfully bright and works as one of the teachers in the village when she's not home cooking for her brothers and me."

"They sound wonderful," Vincent told her, his smile returning. "But, what would the Prince of Darkness want to do with your friend Lincoln?"

"I was wondering the same thing." Craven glared.

Ash had grown weary of repeating what Morghan had said, but knew she'd have no choice but to tell Craven and Vincent what had happened as well. Although she doubted either one of them would be able to help her. While Marcus definitely seemed interested in looking for Lincoln, the Messenger Prophecy took precedence.

Just as Ash opened her mouth to speak, the alarms began to sound out in the Kingdom. She stiffened in her seat, her gaze darting to Craven.

"That's odd," he said, biting at his lip as he shot to his feet.

The buzz of the communications chip in Craven's pocket vibrated in Ash's ears. She watched him, her stomach flipping while he drove his hand into his pocket to retrieve it, his eyes bulging at the sight of whatever message he saw before him.

"Time to go," Craven yelped, rushing toward the library's exit at Immortal speed. Ash rushed to follow him, Vincent right beside her. She picked up her speed, fearing she'd lose the incredibly fast Draconian as they made their way through the castle.

The sirens wailed, vibrating in her sensitive ears as Ash followed Craven through the complicated city streets. "What's going on?" she asked, clenching her jaw as she reached for her boot. The absence of the dagger she thought was there made her curse beneath her breath.

"Someone's on the Unity Bridge." Craven gnashed his teeth. "The fact that they raised the alarms instead of letting them in means it's a visitor we *don't* want."

Curious, Ash wondered who it could be. They arrived in the city square to find King Loren standing beside the black butterfly fountain with his advisor. The Clan Leaders had already taken aim, each of them positioned strategically throughout the square.

Ash paled at the sight of Anastasia, who held two long chains in her hands. She watched them begin to glow red, sparking with evolving flames. *Oh, I'd hate to be on the other side of those.* She shivered.

Axel motioned for the Gatekeepers to raise the gate, and the sound of screeching metal rang in Ash's ears. Craven held out an arm in front of her, gesturing for her to move back. She frowned, wondering why the Draconians were so nervous about these visitors. Could people not come and visit the Kingdom as they pleased?

"I wonder who it is, if everyone's acting this way." Vincent sighed beside her, crossing his arms.

Shrugging, Ash hadn't the slightest clue. She watched, her fists clenching at her sides as the gate rose higher, revealing the boots of three men on the other side. Her brow creased as she squinted, her heart quickening in her chest.

The moment Ash saw who stood on the other side, her mouth fell open. "That's Morghan Henning!" She elbowed Vincent with a wide smile.

But, Morghan wasn't alone. Two tall men cloaked in black hoods stood at each of his sides. Ash's smile faded as she watched Marcus unsheathe his sword, white flames igniting around the magnificent blade.

"Get down on the ground!" Axel demanded, reaching for the axe on his back.

Archers perched on the rooftops began to load their bows, and Ash's heart sank as she realized they were preparing to *shoot* the Werewolf. "What are they doing?" She pulled on Craven's sleeve. "They're not going to shoot them, are they?"

"Do you not see who he's standing with?" Craven snapped over his shoulder. "Those are Arebus Archers. They're supposed to be extinct," he hissed.

Ash felt like the Realm suddenly stopped around her. *It can't be.* Her mind whirled as goosebumps prickled along her flesh. Her heart raced as she recalled the conversation she'd had with Morghan in the mountains. How he'd been sure Lincoln was an *Archer*. And now, he was standing beside *two* more.

Quinn and Cooper. Ash's breath escaped her as she fought to get past Craven. To her dismay, Benjamin had seen what she was trying to do and moved to contain her. She glared into his brown eyes, a vicious hiss rolling off her tongue. She reached for his tie, curling her fingers around it and pulling it hard, jerking his head forward. "They're my *family*," she whispered.

"Stop!" Valentina's voice suddenly rang as she rushed

into the square, her silk skirts in her fists as she fought not to trip on them. She moved quickly to Loren's side, the king glaring at her intensely. "They're the last of them," Ash heard her whisper in his ear.

"Last of them?" Vincent had clearly heard the Prophetess as well.

"Lower your weapons," Loren growled, his eyes on the three men who were lying with their bellies pressed against the icy cobblestone. "Morghan, you may rise."

The Werewolf pushed himself to his feet, scowling as he smoothed his jacket and jeans. "That was *no* way to greet an old friend," he huffed.

24

Ash paced the length of the quarters she'd been assigned, scowling through the glass walls as she watched Marcus speak with Benjamin and a small man she'd come to know as Grant in the lower level of the Mentor's apartment. She scowled as Benjamin's eyes darted in her direction, infuriated by his and his fellow council member's actions.

The glass was soundproof, which only increased Ash's level of frustration. At first, she'd pounded her fists against the walls, hoping they'd quickly become annoyed with her and let her out, but that hadn't worked. She'd considered sobbing but doubted either of them were soft enough to give in to a woman's tears.

"This is ridiculous," she seethed, flopping onto her silk-covered bed. Her mind swam with ideas as to what they'd done with the brothers. Were they in cells? Were they approaching gallows?

Frowning, Ash rolled onto her side and stared out at the setting sun. She wished she could say that she was surprised by today's stressful events, but at the end of the day, Dracus was just as crazy as it always was.

ASH HAD DRIFTED OFF, BUT WAS QUICKLY AWOKEN BY THE sound of her door unlocking. She sat up, watching as Marcus entered with a tray of wonderfully prepared food. The scent of baked chicken and fresh vegetables made her mouth water instantly.

"You think a simple meal is going to get me to forgive you for locking me in here?" she asked with narrowed eyes, ignoring her rumbling stomach.

"Yes." Marcus sighed as he set it on her nightstand. "It's not my fault you assaulted another council member."

"I barely touched him," Ash grunted as she reached for a slice of homemade bread smeared with melting butter. She took her first bite, chewing it gingerly, even though she had an intense urge to shove the entire piece in her mouth like the animal she truly was, but, Marcus was already disappointed in her enough for the day.

The Mentor stared at her, leaning against her vanity with a look that only made her feel as if she were about to be chastised and grounded from throwing knives in the yard. Memories of Eliza and her strange punishments flashed through her mind, a sudden sadness washing over her. Then again, while her mother's groundings might have been unusual, Ash had been a strange child.

"Stop looking at me like that," Ash growled, cutting her chicken with her fork. It broke apart easily, moist and perfectly cooked. "Where did you learn to cook?"

"Did you know?" Marcus changed the subject, his dark brows pulling together into two harsh lines. "That they were what they are?"

Ash shook her head, her mouth full of food.

"How could you live with them and *not* know?"

Swallowing, Ash reached for her glass of water to wash

her monstrous bite down. "I told you what Morghan *thought* they were. I didn't know that he was right," she said. "Matter of fact, I'm pretty pissed at them for *not* telling me, but that's besides the point. Your people were seconds away from killing them."

"Do you *know* what they're capable of?" Marcus gave her a look that only made her feel daft. "How are we supposed to believe that they don't share the same opinions their ancestors did? That their loyalty can't be bought? Clearly, Xavier has an interest in them already."

"They've killed just as many Pandora as I have!" Ash shouted at him, watching as he flinched. "They want this Dark War over as much as you or I. If anything, they're here to try and help their brother. To get him away from Xavier!"

Her blood beginning to boil, Ash blinked tears of anger away before they clouded her vision.

"Valentina seems to know something about them," Marcus added softly. "She's the one who's keeping them alive right now."

"And what about Morghan?" Ash scowled.

"He's with them."

Ash's cheeks puffed with air before she let out a long, painful breath. "Morghan shouldn't be in chains," she insisted, wishing she could say the same thing for the McBride brothers. But the truth was, she knew nothing about their Immortality or their abilities as Arebus Archers.

"I know," Marcus admitted, a muscle in his jaw twitching. "It won't be for long. We'll be having a council meeting about it in the morning. After they're interrogated."

Ash felt the color rush from her cheeks. "Interrogated by *who*?"

CRAVEN STOOD; HIS PALMS PRESSED AGAINST THE COLD glass table. His eyes were narrowed into violet slits, focusing on the younger brother who trembled beneath his gaze. His eyes were fixed on his shackled wrists, his lip quivering.

Do they really expect me to believe this practical child *is a threat?* Craven frowned, pursing his lips. Beside him, Axel stood with his arms crossed, his red cape standing out brightly against his dark uniform.

"How long have you known?" Axel's tone was nothing short of terrifying.

The elder brother glared up at the General, his cerulean eyes sharper than daggers. "No longer than a year," he replied spitefully.

"Have you recently been approached by any members of Xavier's Dark Army?" Craven was truly curious. The Dark King *had* to know there was more than just one brother for the taking.

"Not unless you count the destruction-level attack they issued on our village a week ago," he spat, tensing beneath his chains. "Do you think we would have come here if our loyalties were with Xavier or his piece of shit bitch of a son?"

Craven's eyes widened at the response, a smile quickly spreading across his lips as he rose to his full height. "What's your name again?" he inquired, arching a brow.

"Quinn, for the last damn time," he growled.

"Axel," Craven sighed, turning to face the General. "We've been at this for hours. Their story hasn't changed. They came here to see if Ash was alright."

The General scowled back at him. "Are you sure

they're not lying?" he sneered. "Maybe you should try shocking the little one at least *once* to be sure."

The younger brother winced at the thought, shrinking into his seat. "You're wasting your time," Morghan warned from his place in the corner. "And I'm starving. Can't you hear my stomach growling over here?"

Craven glanced toward the Werewolf, releasing an annoyed sigh. "You still owe me a thank you," he reminded him, his smirk transitioning into a frown. "Then, *maybe*, I'll give you some dinner."

Morghan rolled his eyes. "Thank you, Craven, for electrocuting some Pandora for me," he grumbled. "*Now*, can we eat? Poor Cooper over here is going to faint. I can smell it."

"Am not!" the younger brother snapped.

"This is serious." Axel's low, harsh tone, startled everyone in the room, including Craven. "Tomorrow, the Council will decide your fate here in Dracus. And being *in* Dracus is your only option. There's no way we can let you walk back across that bridge. You understand that, right?"

Craven could see how uncomfortable Quinn was with the idea. Sweat glistened along the Archer's brow, his muscles jumping under his skin. It was far too easy for the Draconian to tell that he was hiding something. "What is it?" he asked, his tone demanding.

Quinn was reluctant to answer. He drew in a deep breath, releasing it slowly before speaking. "Our younger sister," he said softly, his tone pained, "she's still in Crane."

"Is she safe?" Axel inquired, his brows pulling in.

"She's with the family of our Justice Keeper," Quinn replied, looking downward. "But she expects us to return to her, and we must."

Craven quickly recalled the conversation Ash and Vincent had had in the library earlier that day. From what he'd heard of the McBrides, he knew Lilly was a bright young woman with a promising future ahead of her, and she adored her brothers. "I see," he sighed, turning away from the brothers.

"She's better off where she is," Axel told them. "Dragging her into this mess would only interfere with the wonderful life she might have otherwise."

"But she could be just like them," Morghan countered. "Just because she's a girl does *not* mean if she picks up one of those bows, she won't become Immortal herself."

"It's best that she doesn't," Axel spat. "Let her have a normal life."

Craven swallowed hard, the idea of a young girl being left alone bothering him immensely. "She's safe where she is right now," he said, staring at his feet. "We have no idea what Valentina's seen, but it's clear she believes you're a part of what's to come. Bringing her here would only put her in harm's way."

"And it's best the rest of the Council doesn't know she exists." Axel's statement surprised Craven. "If they knew, they'd bring her in."

"That's…" Craven couldn't bear to finish his sentence.

"It's nothing," Morghan hissed from his corner. "Nothing other than keeping a young girl safe."

Craven's throat grew thick as he turned to face the Werewolf. What Axel and the Werewolf were asking him to do was unthinkable. *I can't lie to my king,* he thought, anxiety beginning to swallow him whole. *Not again.*

25

THE KINGDOM OF ELVES

Penelope VanCamp stared grudgingly at her opponent, flexing her sore fingers. She winced, her hands aching after gripping a spear for hours. She panted, her throat sore from sucking in breath after breath in an attempt to keep her mind calm. She was exhausted, there was no denying it.

"Battles can last for days," Aveo Calloway reminded the princess, his tone cold as he circled her, dragging his spear along the ground beside him. "You'll die if you burn out after only four hours."

The sun began to rise above the courtyard, and Penelope shuddered as it warmed her flesh. She glanced at the commander, her stomach churning. She despised him with every fiber of her being and always had. But, the way the sunlight fell on his tanned complexion made him glow in a deceiving way. He was truly beautiful. But only on the outside.

"Though I have to admit," Aveo sighed, his shoulder grazing hers, "you've improved."

Penelope nodded, pursing her chapped lips. "Does that mean we've finished for the day?"

"Not a chance," Aveo snickered, and Penelope felt a rush of wind ruffle her hair as he swung his spear at her from behind. She ducked, narrowly avoiding the strike. She reached for her own spear, spinning around just in time to block the commander's. She pushed as hard as she could against him, watching as his spear inched closer and closer to his chest. Her muscles screamed as she fought to hold him, the blisters on her palms stinging terribly. The white bandages wrapped around her hands were quickly soaked by her blood, causing her grip on her weapon to waver.

A hiss escaped the princess as she dropped the spear, the pain too much for her to bear. It fell to the ground smeared with blood. She took a step back, swallowing against the rage-fueled scream building in her throat.

A vicious smirk pulled at Aveo's lips as he drove his own spear into the earth. Penelope looked down at her bleeding hands, her face reddening. She looked up into the commander's bronze eyes, her nostrils flaring.

Without thought, Penelope launched herself at him. She struck him, her fist ramming into his jaw. Aveo staggered back, his eyes widening as she moved to kick him, thrusting her boot into his gut. He fell to his knees, and Penelope sneered as she listened to him struggle to catch his breath.

"Hand-to-hand combat was *not* the lesson today," Aveo growled, clutching his abdomen.

Penelope shrugged, ripping her bandages away to examine her wounds. She cringed at the sight of her ruptured blisters. "I just love the element of surprise," she told him, smiling despite her pain.

The commander rose to his feet, rubbing his sore jaw.

"You know, it's frowned upon to hit your betrothed in such a way."

The comment only made Penelope blush, but not with embarrassment. She fought the urge to spit in his face, her muscles and veins straining against her skin.

The Elves had thought if Penelope trained with Aveo, they'd develop a bond. That hadn't been the case. If anything, it had only led her to hate the commander *more*. The only difference was that now she had an excuse to hit him. That pleased her.

"I have to go," Penelope said, her tone less than kind. She straightened her spine and turned on her heels before storming into the castle. The cold, marble halls felt less than welcoming, but she knew that before long, she'd be able to leave them. Perhaps for good. If only Loren would reopen the portal to Dracus so she could make her grand escape.

As she climbed the stairs, blood dripped from her wounds onto the white floors. A servant gasped as they passed, the color draining from her face.

"Princess Penelope, you're injured!" she cried.

Penelope froze, glancing over her shoulder, having not realized she'd made such a mess. "It's fine," she insisted. "I'll stop by Prince Beck's chambers. I'm sure he has some bandages."

"Shouldn't you visit the healing waters?" the servant asked nervously as she kneeled to wipe the blood. "Those wounds will heal quickly if you do."

Frowning, Penelope examined her hands once again. "I'd rather not," was all she said before she continued down the hall, turning left into the royal corridor. Her eyes fell on the door to Beck's suite and she sighed through her nose.

Her frown deepened as she pounded her sore fist

against the door, listening as footsteps sounded within. Beck opened the door, rubbing his tired eyes.

Penelope pushed past the prince, shoving him aside as she entered his foyer. The scent of whiskey hung heavily in the air, and it was clear to her that Beck had likely been up most of the night either celebrating something or drinking his sorrows away.

"What are you doing here? It's barely sunrise," Beck groaned as he stumbled into his living room. "Why do you smell like blood and sweat?"

"I was training with Aveo," Penelope told him, her eyes falling on a liquor cart nearby. Most of the bottles were empty, but some were still half filled. She rolled eyes as she approached it, reaching for the only clean glass left and a bottle of brandy likely older than she was. She poured enough for a shot and drank it quickly, wincing as it burned down her throat and into her stomach.

"Do you know when the Draconians are going to reach out to the Elves?" Penelope asked as she approached the couch, falling down into it.

Beck ran his fingers through his messy golden hair, and Penelope could see the worry etched in his features. "They're going to have to do it soon, or else my parents will be knocking on their door," he sighed. "Axel said they were going to open the portals today, but more chaos has arrived in Dracus. Loren plans to be with his council all day."

"Great," Penelope snapped. "What exactly is going on over there? Benjamin said he was going to open the portals, but he never did. It's been two days now."

"You know," Beck smirked, reaching for a leftover drink on his end table, "I might know someone who can help."

"No, no, and *no*," Aries of the Fae crossed his arms, staring angrily at the Elven General. "And before you two think of pulling rank on me, I'll have you know that not only am I a Lord, I'm an Idonian Council Member, and Queen Cleo's *only* advisor. I win."

Penelope's brow knotted, her heart slowing to a calm and even pace as she stared back at the Fae. His burgundy eyes shone brightly in the light cast through windows, his black wings hanging limply at his back.

Aries had always been such an angry Fae. Whatever grudge he held against Si Realtra, he carried it with him always.

He would prove to be a wonderful ally one day.

"Don't *you* want to see her for yourself?" Penelope huffed, mimicking his stance. She pressed her fists into her ribs, summoning a glare strong enough to match his. "Aren't you at least a *little* curious about her? Or why the Draconians are being so secretive?"

Arie's features nearly softened, but his scowl quickly returned. "If they're being secretive about her, it's for good reason. Probably to keep the whispers from spreading through the halls of this very castle."

"But *we* won't whisper, will we?" Penelope took a step toward him, watching as he shifted his weight uncomfortably. "Besides, you know how long I've waited to meet my sister. Would you really keep me from her?"

"Just do it, Aries," Beck grumbled, leaning against the wall of his personal study which he rarely used. He'd since changed, appearing more like the general he truly was. His hair was combed, falling to his shoulders. His gold cape fluttered with every twitch of a muscle.

The Fae's gaze flitted rapidly between Penelope and

the General, the lump in his throat bobbing. He released an angry huff, a strand of dark hair flying away from his face. "Fine."

Penelope's smile widened, her heart leaping in her chest.

"What will you say to Thaddeus and Esmeralda?" Aries asked Beck, his eyes narrowing.

"I'll remind them that Penelope has the right to travel to and from each kingdom as she pleases," Beck declared with a crisp nod. "They can't argue with that."

"But they will," Aries warned him.

Penelope listened as the two Immortals began to bicker back and forth and was quickly lost in her thoughts. Her heart raced terribly in her chest, her entire body tingling. By this time next year, there was a large chance the princess would be nestled in the High Throne, her mother's crown of roses sitting above her brow. Xavier's reign would soon come to a painfully abrupt end, and eighteen years' worth of sorrow would fade away.

Glancing toward the two men, Penelope's stomach fluttered. She scanned them each one by one, chuckling beneath her breath. Both Lord Aries of the Black-winged Fae and General Beck Chamberlain would have a seat at her round table. She was sure of it.

26

Ash sat across from her brother Vincent, watching him survey the chessboard. It had only seemed logical to spend some time with him, though she couldn't keep her mind off of what might be happening in the Round Table Room today. Her stomach twisted at the thought of what the Draconian Council might decide.

Marcus had been with King Loren and the other council members all day, which had left Ash under Craven's supervision. She found it funny how they still felt the need to watch her closely, as if she might haul off and push another General.

Convincing her Mentor to take her to where they were holding the McBride brothers and Morghan hadn't been an easy task. If it hadn't been for Vincent, Ash doubted she'd have been able to pull it off. Now, the pair sat at a table in an empty cell on the bottom floor of Dracus's castle of glass.

The cell was nothing like what Ash had read in books. There were no iron bars across the windows of cold, closet-sized stone rooms. Her brow furrowed as she looked around, waiting for Vincent to decide what his next move was. There was a full kitchen, and a bathroom with both a tub *and* a shower. Comfortable furniture was placed around the living room. There were even activities for passing time, like chess.

"You've got me stumped," Vincent grumbled, rubbing his chin.

"Really?" Ash snorted. "I've never played. I'm just over here moving pieces around."

Vincent gawked at her, throwing up his hands in defeat.

Craven chuckled from his place across the room. He was lying on the couch, his hands folded atop his chest. "Beck and I played chess once, at a pub."

"How would you two play chess at a pub?" Vincent asked, lifting a single brow.

"I'm not sure," Craven sneered. "I don't remember much of that night."

Ash rolled her eyes, her grin widening. She found Craven's humor to be comforting in many ways, as he was beginning to remind her of Sam Waters. She'd known Sam her entire life, and a day hadn't gone by where he hadn't told her some ridiculous story or made her smile in some way. Her smile quickly faltered, her chest tightening as she recalled everything she was forced to leave behind in the hidden village.

A bright light erupted in the center of the room so quickly that Ash barely had a chance to react. She shielded her eyes with her arm, turning away from the source as Craven and Vincent shot to their feet.

The light faded quickly, and hesitantly, Ash lowered her arm to view what had happened. The first thing she saw were a set of large, black wings. Her breath caught in her throat, the blood rushing from her face. Her gaze darted to

Craven, who held a hand to his chest, sucking in deep breaths to calm himself.

"Not cool, Aries," Craven snapped.

PENELOPE'S HEART WAS THUNDERING AGAINST THE WALLS OF her chest, her breathing shallow as she took in the room around her. She loosened a sigh of relief at the sight of her brother. Had he grown even taller since she'd last seen him? A smile began to build upon her lips, yet it quickly faltered when her eyes fell on the young woman beside him.

Curiously, the Princess stared at her, watching as she rose to her feet with wide eyes, the shade of lush green meadows. She scanned her face, her heart breaking in another place as she took in each one of her features.

Looking at the girl felt like looking into the past.

Penelope was staring at Meera VanCamp's face.

"Princess Penelope," Craven greeted her from behind, though she paid him no mind. Her trembling hand rose to her mouth, her vision clouding as tears began to well in her eyes.

Everything Penelope had done to find this girl flashed before her eyes. Every law she had broken, every line she had crossed. Each time she conspired with Cedric and Abernathy in the darkest shadows of the Kingdom of Elves.

And here she was.

"Penelope." Vincent repeated her name. His voice sounded far away, as the princess's mind brought her back to a time where she watched her Guardian walk away from her for the last time. She'd sacrificed *so* much for this moment.

"Happy belated birthday" she heard herself say.

The twins looked at one another, each smiling. Penelope's heart swelled at the sight. They already looked how she'd always imagined them to be. Close. Inseparable. Bonded. All the things they should have been from the start of their lives.

"Do the Elves know you're here?" Craven asked, and Penelope pried her gaze away from the twins and looked toward the Draconian.

"I'm sure they do by now."

Craven's gulp was loud enough for Mortal ears to hear as the words left her mouth. But, Penelope no longer feared Thaddeus's wrath. Her time under their wings was finished. She'd removed her invisible chains, ripped them clear off. Soon, the Amulet would hang from Ash's neck, and it would be *her* will that was done. Not theirs.

"I'm sure they'll understand once Loren finally tells them about Ash and the Messenger," Penelope added, reaching to pat him softly on the shoulder. "Now that they're here, telling me to stay in the Kingdom of Elves would be a waste of breath."

"Loren planned to tell them today," Craven replied, growing visibly tense. Penelope eyed him curiously, never having spent enough time around him to learn how to read him.

"And?" Aries grumbled.

Craven scowled in the Fae's direction. "If you really *must* know, we received some unexpected visitors last night."

Penelope's curiosity piqued, her brow wrinkling. "And who might they have been?"

The room fell silent, and as the princess's eyes danced between Craven and the twins, she could see that they were reluctant to tell her anything.

"Morghan Henning led two Arebus Archers into Dracus," Vincent finally blurted. "Loren has been in the Round Table Room all day with his council trying to figure out what to do with them."

Penelope's mouth fell open, the hair on the back of her neck beginning to rise. Her hand rose to her chest, her fingers running along the smooth silk of her red blouse. "Well," she said breathlessly. "Isn't that something?"

"So *that's* what all the fuss is about?" Aries gave Craven a disbelieving look. "Do you think they would have willingly walked across the Unity Bridge if they had any cruel intentions?" he scoffed, his wings stiff at his back.

"The last time they were in Dracus, they saved the Kingdom," Vincent mentioned nervously.

"What happens to them isn't for us to decide," Craven announced, falling back onto the couch. "What I will say is when Axel and I interrogated them last night, they seemed more worried about Ash than anything else. Besides, I bet they'll be fine. The way Valentina intervened yesterday only makes me think she knows something we don't."

"Oh!" Vincent suddenly gasped, and Penelope stared at him, her eyes narrowing. "What if they're some of the warriors that are supposed to help Ash?"

"Help Ash?" Penelope's posture grew rigid, her chest tightening. "With what?"

A second painful silence lingered, and Penelope watched the twins spare each other worried glances.

"Spit it out."

Vincent's cheeks burned with an embarrassingly vivid blush, his gaze dropping to his boots. "Ash is the Messenger."

The words sent a wave of shock through Penelope so intense that it knocked the breath right out of her. "*What?*" she thundered, her heart in her throat.

Images of the Forest of Fools and the crack in the earth flashed before the princess's eyes. Her throat grew thick, her breathing impossible to control as a familiar fear swept over her. "No." She shook her head, reaching for Ash with a trembling hand. Her fingers curled around her blue knit sweater, pulling her forward. She stumbled against the princess, staring up at her with wide, surprised eyes.

Craven stepped forward, but Aries outstretched his left wing, blocking the Draconian from moving any further.

"What are you doing?" Ash asked softly, tense beneath Penelope's grasp.

Penelope wrapped her arms around her, blinking furiously against the tears threatening to spill from her eyes. Ash relaxed, but not completely. Her back was as straight as a board as she hesitantly raised her own arms to return the embrace.

For years, Penelope had waited for the Messenger. She'd prayed to the Moons every night, hoping when she awoke the next morning the nightmare she'd lived in would end. She wanted to lower herself into her parents' throne and restore order to Idona, but she didn't want her own sister risking her life to do it for her.

"It's a hard pill to swallow," Vincent said, his voice far away. "We thought Benjamin had told you."

Shaking her head, Penelope pulled in a breath to calm herself as she released Ash from her grip. She stared into her eyes for a moment longer, watching as shreds of silver faded from her meadow-shaded irises. Penelope's breath hitched at the sight, her skin crawling. They might share similar blood, but it was clear in that moment that they couldn't be more different.

"He only told me that the Dragon Rider, the Missing VanCamp, and the Messenger were all in Dracus," Penelope admitted, forcing the image of Ash's eyes from her mind. "He failed to mention that they were the same person."

"I'm not the Dragon Rider," Ash admitted sheepishly, her gaze dropping to the floor.

"That doesn't make it much better."

"It does," Vincent argued, suddenly sporting a smirk. "Wait until you find out who the Dragon Rider is."

"I'm not sure I can withstand any more surprises today," Penelope huffed, her mind whirling. "Something tells me I'm in for one hell of a lecture from Loren whenever he realizes I'm here. Perhaps we should get that over with before you shock me anymore."

Marcus found himself staring at the McBride brothers and the Werewolf, his heart racing at an unhealthy rate. He was sure they could all hear it, but would they know that it wasn't nervousness that was unraveling him, but anger? The Council meeting had been a nightmare at best. He'd never heard the Clan Leaders fight in such a way, nor had he seen Loren quite so infuriated. Richard had been the only one to remain calm, and the only time he'd said a word was to ask for another glass of whiskey or blood. Sometimes both.

The Council was at odds now, though Marcus hoped it wouldn't last long. He'd never seen Axel act the way he had. His ears were still ringing from when he'd shouted *Shut the hell up* right beside the Mentor.

And all of it was because of these two Archers, who seemed so calm despite the chaos they'd caused.

Valentina was all smiles, now that she'd won her fight to keep them alive and in Dracus, for now at least. She stood beside Marcus, her arm grazing his as she prepared to reveal to them all that had occurred.

"I'm Valentina." She introduced herself, her golden eyes twinkling.

The elder brother's brow furrowed as he peered in their direction. He seemed far less alarming without his hood shielding his face, but the power beneath his facade only led Marcus's skin to crawl. He could only imagine what the Prince of Darkness planned to do with the missing brother.

"These two idiots are Quinn and Cooper McBride," Morghan explained when the brothers remained silent, shooting chastising glares in their direction. "Forgive them for their silence, they're paranoid."

The comment amused Marcus, and he fought against a smile. *Rightfully so,* he thought, resting his hand on the hilt of Whitefire. He watched as Quinn's eyes fell on the sword, his face twisting into a scowl.

"I want to see her," Quinn blurted, his tone less than kind. "Then I'll do anything you want me to do."

Valentina's smile faltered, her eyes widening slightly before she asked, "May I explain a few things first?"

Marcus bit his inner cheek, easily recalling the fight they'd once shared in the Training Center. His groin hurt just thinking about it, and not in a good way. The Prophetess was far more than she seemed to be, and she would surely beat the brothers into pulps if they refused to comply.

Quinn gave her a nod, his tense shoulders relaxing.

"The three of you are to receive an apartment here in the castle," Valentina announced, gesturing to the three floors above them.

"The *three* of us?" Morghan asked with an icy stare.

Valentina matched his expression, and Marcus could hear the hiss roll off her tongue. "Yes, all three of you. The Sectra Ceremony will take place in five days, at the end of the week. After that, you will leave," she explained slowly. "What you do after Ash receives the Amulet is up to you. I only hope you'll make the right decision."

"What's *that* supposed to mean?" the Wolf fumed.

"It *means* that the Idonian people *need* you." Marcus jumped at the sound of Valentina's harsh tone. "You don't get to hide in the shadows forever, Henning. You knew this, or you wouldn't have led these two here."

"Or offered to bring Ash here," Marcus added for good measure.

"What are you going to do with Ash?" Cooper finally spoke. "Now that she'll have the Amulet, what are you planning? To throw a dress and a crown on her and dangle her in front of the Realm?"

Marcus wasn't surprised by the Archer's words, though he hated that he'd said them. Is that how the people in Crane and the nobles saw the Immortals throughout the Realm? He'd known people had felt that way before. Rather recently. *Rebels*.

"No," Marcus told him, his gaze flitting between the brothers. He internally cursed himself for not realizing it sooner, or at least, the possibility of it. The symbol the Rebels had once given was the same symbol pertaining to the hidden village legend, the mountains, the Strip. Even though it had turned out that the Rebel stronghold hadn't been in the hidden village, but directly beneath it, it wouldn't be idiotic to assume that the villagers in Crane would have been Rebels.

"Then what?" Quinn snapped.

"Ash will be leaving Dracus," Valentina told the brothers, and Marcus watched as their brows raised in surprise. "She'll be leading a team of ten warriors to complete a series of tasks."

"Tasks?" Cooper asked curiously. "What sort of tasks?"

Valentina gulped loud enough for Marcus to hear, and he himself felt uneasy about the Prophecy. He hadn't yet managed to swallow the truth. He didn't want to believe that Ash, as vicious as she was, would have to face such darkness. And he doubted the McBride brothers, and even Morghan, would be pleased about it either.

"Three tasks," Valentina continued, her voice dangerously low. "Tasks that will surely not only test her strength, but her patience as well."

"You're being very vague," Quinn told the Prophetess. "Why would she have to complete *any* tasks? What are these? Trials for her to prove who she is and what she's capable of?"

"No!" Valentina growled. "Ash is the Messenger. These tasks she needs to complete are a part of the Prophecy. After she completes them, she'll be able to retrieve the Sovereign's Scepter. And she'll use that to kill the Dark King."

Marcus watched the brothers as their faces began to portray their shock. Their mouths fell open in unison, their eyes bulging as they looked toward one another. He wondered how they must feel, learning that the girl they'd grown up alongside was the very woman the Realm had been waiting for.

"I find it quite funny," Morghan sighed, leaning against the wall, "that all of these species are coming back to life, right around the same time the Messenger surfaces." The wolf rubbed his chin, deep in thought about the matter. "It's like Si Realtra is coming back from the dead."

QUINN'S HEART WAS IN HIS THROAT AS HE WAITED FOR Marcus to track down Ash. He and Valentina had left the door to their strange cell open, and he could see their shadows in the hall weakening as they walked away.

"Well, that was unexpected," Cooper said, his face blank.

Nodding, Quinn felt as if he were in a dream. No, a nightmare—a sick and twisted one, at that. His limbs felt heavy as he sulked into the couch, his mind drifting to places he wished that it wouldn't. Part of him felt like he should be happy. Isn't this what everyone in Idona had been waiting for? Both Rebels and Immortals alike? Even the Dark King himself had been waiting for the Messenger, even though he would be less than thrilled she'd finally surfaced. But, Quinn wouldn't be able to escape his nerves about Ash embarking on such a difficult journey. He didn't want her to.

"You know," Morghan grumbled as he began to pace. "That little friend of yours said absolutely nothing about being a VanCamp. Now, I feel like a fool. I should have realized."

"I lived with her and didn't know," Cooper told the Wolf as he rose to his feet, beginning to pace himself. "You're not the only fool."

The sound of shouting down the hall drew Quinn's attention, his brow wrinkling as he made his way to the open door. He peeked out into the hall, noticing another open door at the very end of it. If it weren't for all the people shouting at once, he might have been able to make out what they were saying.

"I wonder what that's all about," Cooper said nervously as he joined his brother in the threshold.

"I'll go see," Morghan offered, pushing past the pair with a devilish grin upon his face. But before the Wolf could make it a few steps down the hall, people began to flow out of the other room.

Quinn's mouth fell open when he watched Marcus stomp out into the hall, a woman with long brown hair and bright eyes in tow. He recognized her immediately. *Princess Penelope.* He debated whether he should return to the couch and ignore them, since they were clearly dealing with a matter he had no business meddling in. But he couldn't stop himself from staring at her for a moment. Not because he found her beautiful, even though she undoubtedly was quite pretty, but because she was Ash's sister and seeing her in the flesh seemed surreal.

Cooper gulped beside him, having realized who the princess was as well. "It's strange," he whispered in Quinn's ear. "They seem so different, yet they look so much alike."

Nodding, Quinn's breath staggered as more people left the room. His eyes widened out of both fear and awe at the sight of a Fae. *Immortals. Immortals everywhere.*

"Morghan," the Fae quickly noticed the Wolf standing in the hall, "I've heard you've lost your damn mind."

"Was it ever really there to begin with?" Morghan countered.

Quinn felt his throat tightening as Penelope and Marcus's arguing intensified while more people moved past them in the hall. Many faces he'd seen in the papers Eliza had collected—Craven Amsterdam, in particular. A living legend of sorts. Vincent VanCamp, who he'd half expected to be shorter given his twin's size. But then he saw her. His heart quickened, his stomach fluttering with nerves as he found himself bursting out into the hall.

Ash was smiling, staring at Marcus and Penelope as they bickered. While she appeared to be the same, it was clear she'd transitioned completely now. The last time Quinn had seen her, she'd still appeared to be somewhat Mortal. But not now. She was radiant, and her hair longer.

Her eyes were an intense shade that reminded him of a vibrant forest in the spring.

When her eyes fell on him, Quinn's heart jumped into his throat. He saw an onslaught of different emotions flash through her eyes as she pushed past the crowd in the hall, her pace increasing from a walk to a run. He moved out of the threshold to meet her, the bickering in the hall silencing as she crashed into him. He wrapped his arms around her, burying his face into her silky hair. Silently, he wondered how, despite everything that had happened, she could still smell so much like home.

Ash's tears began to dampen his shirt, and he could feel her trembling against him. "You lied to me," she whispered against his chest, and he felt the Realm shatter around him.

PENELOPE FOUND HERSELF ROAMING THE CASTLE HALLS, hoping to clear her mind now that night had fallen. The Elves were furious with her, but their fury would fade over time. It always did.

Now that the communication lines were open once again between the two kingdoms, Penelope would reach out to them tomorrow and politely tell them to postpone her wedding to Aveo until the Messenger fulfilled her prophecy.

Ash. The Messenger.

Penelope's mouth grew dry as she thought of what might become of her sister. Another part of her heart would break the moment she left to undo the damage Xavier had caused to their Realm. She felt selfish, wishing that she wouldn't go. Not so soon.

Complaining wasn't something Penelope did, but she

wanted to. She wanted to scream at the top of her lungs and ask the Moons why it was that everyone she cared about had either disappeared or died? Was it so wrong of her to want her family to be *whole* for a change?

The need for a slice of chocolate cake and a stifling hot cup of tea led Penelope down to the kitchens. She wanted to indulge in sweets and force every negative thought from her mind. Perhaps she would head to the library and lose herself in a good book after she'd had her fill of delicious things.

Guards were positioned throughout every castle hall, likely more so than usual considering Penelope's presence there. She gave each of them nods as she passed, slipping into the Great Hall. It was empty. Not a soul in sight as she approached the kitchens beyond. Light seeped through the crack beneath the door, causing the Princess to stop dead in her tracks. Who else had been in the mood for a midnight snack?

Pushing the door open, Penelope found a man sitting on the center island in the room, his back to her. If he sensed her presence, he didn't acknowledge it right away. Instead he sat, dipping his spoon into a tub of ice cream.

Tattoos swam down the man's arms in delicate patterns, the sight enthralling to the princess. She'd seen men and women who'd mark themselves with ink after battle, but nothing quite like what she was seeing now.

He had a head of pale waves that fell nearly to his jaw, but he'd pushed them away from his face, which allowed Penelope to see the hint of a sharp jawline from where she stood. There was a certain familiarity about him, the way he sat, and the way he ate. The boyish lack of manners, yet the regal appearance of a noble.

Penelope cleared her throat.

The man looked over his shoulder, his eyes widening as

he hopped off the counter, his silver spoon still in his mouth. Penelope stared at him, fighting against the scream begging to escape her. Whether it would be from excitement or sheer shock, she did not know.

Neither of them said a thing. Penelope's pulse thrummed in her ears, her heart pounding angrily in her chest. She stared at him, her eyes as wide and teary as the day she'd heard about his death. She wanted to know everything. Where had he gone? How long had he been here in Dracus? But, she bit back her questions. He'd likely had enough of those over recent days.

"I still have that glass dragon," was what she told him.

28

Four days had passed since Ash had met Princess Penelope and Aries of the Fae. Four days spent training from dawn until dusk, in hopes that she might be able to perfect her abilities before she left on her journey. At first, she'd fought not to cower as Craven escorted each of the Clan Leaders to the front door of Marcus's apartment each morning, the sun just barely beginning to creep above the mountains. Now, on the last day of training before the Sectra Ceremony, Ash was nearly shaking in her boots.

Craven had warned her that it would only get more difficult before he'd left her to have her dinner with Marcus every night. She could only imagine what the *last* day might mean for her. And now, she knew.

Ash found herself outside, behind the castle of glass, where snow-covered fields stretched out to the edge of the Realm—the very end of Idona's existence. Cold air bit at her cheeks as her long braid blew in the wind, her heart pumping unevenly as she forced her gaze to remain on the Draconian General, and not the other spectators who had come to watch her.

The King stood beside Axel, his gray eyes sparkling with kindness as he flashed her a toothy smile. "Tell me, Ash, what do you think you've spent your time so far in Dracus training for?" he asked her, cocking his head as he shivered beneath his thick robes.

"To fulfill the prophecy," Ash muttered, her cheeks burning with embarrassment.

Snow was falling in chunks from the skies above, covering the armored shoulders of the uniform Marcus had given to her earlier that morning. It felt foreign upon her flesh. And despite how hard she worked, she felt as if she hadn't earned it yet. But the Draconian uniform meant she was cleared for the field, and that she wouldn't complain about.

"You're not wrong," Richard informed her from beside the King. "But there is much more to it. In the past, people who were chosen to receive one of the five Sectras were tested by the other Sectra Holders. Your mother was the last to wear it, and she endured a harsh test conducted by the holder of the Sword of Erim, Daveus Richmond.

"Unfortunately, the Galactic Gates are closed. Daveus can't test you, and neither can Ellaria, the holder of Zerin's Bracelet. But with your Sectra Ceremony taking place tomorrow evening, it's crucial that you're found worthy," Richard finished, his lips twitching toward a smirk.

Ash's heart raced as she allowed herself to glance around at the spectators who surrounded her on the field. *Everyone* seemed to be there, including the McBride brothers, whom she'd tried to avoid. She wasn't sure what to say to them and was still trying to figure out why they'd lied to her about their Immortality. But still, she met Quinn's gaze and held it for a moment, watching as he gave her a nod.

You can handle whatever they throw at you. She knew what he was trying to tell her.

Pulling in a deep breath, Ash's gaze darted back to the King. She'd endured grueling tests from each of the Clan Leaders. She'd worked day and night, training with Craven and Marcus, and even Alistair. He may be as new here as she was, but he knew his way around a sword. Anyone who was anyone had stepped in to help her hone her skills. They *wanted* her to succeed.

"Who will it be then?" Ash had a feeling it would be a stranger. Someone she hadn't faced yet.

"Warriors from our own Realm, across the three remaining kingdoms," Axel revealed, and Ash could see how much he was enjoying this. He wanted to see her meet her match. This was her punishment for humiliating him. "You won't face a Draconian, as we've already cleared you for the field."

"That's a shame," Ash teased. "I would *love* to fight you."

Richard snorted, clearly amused by her comment. "One day, I'm sure you'll get the opportunity," he told her. "But for now, we'll start with Aries of the Fae."

Ash's heart fell into her stomach, and her mind whirled as she tried to recall her elemental lessons from throughout the week. Vincent had told her about the Fae, but she didn't know enough to feel comfortable *fighting* one. She cursed beneath her breath as she watched him approach, clad in midnight blue armor. His dark wings fluttered as he took his place. The only weapon he carried was a bow on his back, and a quiver at his thigh.

He levitated above the earth, and Ash knew she was at a *serious* disadvantage. She quickly recalled a day, not long ago, when she was sure it had been a Fae she was turning into, and how she feared what would happen when wings sprouted at her back. While she *had* become Fae, she'd been unlucky. This would likely be the *only* moment she wished for wings.

"You may begin," Richard announced, now standing at a safe distance with the other spectators.

Aries held Ash's gaze for a moment, which gave her the opportunity to think about what she might do with him. This wouldn't be an easy fight, as she'd never be able to get close enough to him to use the sword Marcus had provided for her. But she wouldn't need it. A devious grin began to spread on her lips as she readied her herself, her fists clenching as she braced for impact.

In an instant, Aries plunged up into the air, wings flapping in a fury. Snow whooshed around Ash, clouding her vision. She bit at her inner cheek, watching him as he darted through the sky, loading his bow. He was fast. *Too* fast.

The second she lost track of him, she heard the familiar sound of an arrow sailing through the wind.

He was going straight for the kill.

Frowning, Ash recalled what she'd learned from Ariel earlier that week, and summoned the air around her. The arrow flew off track, flying toward the crowd of spectators. Ash watched as it sailed right toward Cooper, her heart in her throat, but before the Archer could blink, he'd caught it in his grip. The other spectators clapped around him as he snapped it in two.

Ash's brow raised at the sight, but she knew that wouldn't be the only arrow Aries sent her way. Only now, she had no idea where he'd gone. She clicked her tongue as she focused yet again on air, knowing that would be the only element strong enough to bring him down. She'd sweep the current straight from beneath his wings.

But she'd need to find him first.

Growling, Ash focused on every sense she had. Sight,

sound, smell, and even taste. *There you are,* she chuckled, finding him above the clouds with her Elven eyes. He was smiling, ready to set his second arrow free. She raised her hands, reaching and *reaching* for the air around him. It was far, nearly an impossible stretch of her abilities. It felt like it took hours to feel him, but the second she did she gathered the air around the Fae, trapping his wings in her angry gusts and ripping him from the sky.

The ground shook as Aries crashed, surrounded by his thick feathered wings. Clouds of snow billowed into the air, and for a moment, Ash smiled. She'd brought the Fae down in a matter of minutes. She was certain now—air was his weakness—and she would surely use it against him if he dared to take flight again.

Sporting a cocky smile, Ash approached the clouds of snow, walking through them until she found him lying on the ground. Aries smiled up at her, his stark-white teeth gleaming.

In a second, he dove upward, wrapping his fingers around Ash's braid. He pulled hard, and in a quick flash of pain and shock, she fell into the snow beside him. He rolled on top of her, pinning her wrists above her head with one strong hand while the other found its way to her throat.

Ash cursed, loud enough for every spectator to hear.

She'd underestimated him.

Struggling to breathe against the pressure on her windpipe, Ash brought her knee up with all the strength she could muster. She drove it into him so hard that it knocked the wind straight from Arie's lungs. He curled on top of her, hissing, barring his sharp canines. His grip around her throat faltered, and she gasped, filling her lungs with the frigid air.

Aries moved to hold her wrists with both hands, but

Ash couldn't allow him to get a decent hold on her again. If she remained pinned like this for too long, they would call the fight and she would lose. She couldn't bear to let the last four *brutal* days of training she'd endured to be for nothing.

Though a voice in the back of her mind told her not to, Ash's pride quickly drowned it out. She summoned fire, and the air heated around her. She could feel it burning, deep within her gut as it manifested around her hands.

"Fuck!" Aries released her wrists to escape her flames, his leather gloves singing.

Now with free hands, Ash could beat the Fae to a pulp if she wanted to. She *hated* being held down, and she certainly wanted to repay the favor. A snarl escaped her as she lunged upward, slamming her skull into his nose and knocking him backward. He fell into the snow, his hands raising to protect his bleeding nose as she shot to her feet and drew her sword. The tip of it arrived at the base of his neck.

"Not bad, for a Fae with no wings," Aries drawled as he stared up at her, his burgundy eyes shining like red wine in the bright winter light.

The spectators roared with applause from the perimeters of the field as Ash reached to help the Fae to his feet. He gave her a nod of approval before leaving her to join the others. Ash sighed, rolling her shoulders as she turned to view the King approaching with an Elf at his side. Her breath hitched at the sight of him, and the General's badge fastened atop his chest. Everything about the man shined, from his golden hair and eyes to his chest plate and the gauntlets around his forearms.

Ash's eyes lingered on the claymore sheathed at his side. The hilt was made of glistening white gold, smooth as bone. She held her breath a moment, silently wondering how she'd be able to fight this Elf and win.

"May I introduce to you, General Beck Chamberlain." King Loren patted the General on his armored shoulder.

While the King spoke, every element flashed through Ash's mind. Which one would weaken him? *Maybe I should bury him, just far enough to where only his head is sticking above the snow.*

"It's a pleasure to meet you." Ash forced the words out. *Not under these circumstances.*

Beck held his stoic facade, but his eyes betrayed him. They were smiling.

The spectators remained silent. Deathly silent. Every one of them watched, wondering how this fight would unfold. Craven, Alistair, and Morghan were whispering amongst themselves. The Realm Sorceress, and even the Healer who'd been working with Ash since her arrival in Dracus were there, yearning to see what happened next. She could even hear someone biting their nails.

The General closed the distance between them, slowly and carefully until he was standing right in front of her. Loren remained behind them, still in the field, watching them excitedly as they stared each other down.

Ash peered up at him. He towered over her, and she fought not to shrink into his shadow. She could see in his eyes that he was struggling. With what, she didn't know.

The urge to yield, to toss her sword into the snow, was extreme. She'd heard of Beck, and his victories. She knew what sort of warrior he was. Surely, she'd want him to aid her on her journey. She hoped he would be one of the nine people whose names Valentina would reveal tomorrow, but she did not want to fight him.

Beck continued with his stony stare, and Ash fought not to move a muscle. Her mouth fell open as a sudden smile stretched across his lips. He backed away from her then, laughing a musical laugh that only led her blood to boil, burning through her veins.

"I'm sorry, Loren," Beck announced, shaking his head. "I can't do this."

"Excuse me?" Ash gawked at the General, her grip tightening around the hilt of her sword. "Are you *mocking* me?"

"No!" Beck quickly attempted to redeem himself. "You don't have to prove your worth to me."

A slow clap sounded throughout the fields as snow began to rush down harder in thicker flakes from the skies above. Ash frowned, unsure of whether to be appreciative or offended by the Elven General. She ground her teeth together, watching as Beck dipped into a low bow before turning on his heels, his gold cape blowing in the breeze behind him.

29

Today was the day. This evening, Ash would receive the Sectra that had once hung around the High Queen's neck. She'd proven herself worthy. She'd trained, honed every skill, and had faced Aries of the Fae and won. And while the Fae was normally angry, last night at the feast King Loren had held, he seemed pleased with her at best.

This morning had been nothing more than a blur. She'd planned to sneak away to the Training Center for a time, but was intercepted by Marcus and the platter of pancakes he'd prepared. Afterward, she'd been summoned by Penelope. Hesitantly, she'd trudged her way to the Princess's suite only to find a group of women waiting for her.

Anastasia, Shay, Lucinda, and Ciara, a friend Penelope had apparently made during the time she'd spent in Dracus. They'd planned a day to pamper themselves before the ceremony later, which Loren had planned around recreating her parents Mortal tradition—the Fire and Ice Ball.

Ash had been *more* than uncomfortable as her nails

were painted a shimmering color that reminded her of midnight, by Shay. She'd sat frozen in her chair the entire time the hairdresser fussed over her long locks. After an hour of trying to fasten it in a braided bun atop her head, it was decided that her hair had a life of its own and wanted to be free for the evening. Now, half of it was braided while the rest of it curled, falling freely down her back.

"You're not very talkative," Lucinda mentioned as she sipped on her wine. "Nervous?"

Nodding, Ash knew she couldn't deny it. The clock was ticking, and in a short while she'd need to slip into the dress the castle designer, Henry, had made for her. She spared it a glance now, the blood rushing from her cheeks as she viewed it hanging in front of the closet. The train was longer than she was tall, and it was made of black silk fabric with a matching lace overlay. The black feathers coating the train, shoulders, and bodice reminded her of Aries' wings. Or worse, Pandora feathers. She gulped.

"Meera was the same way," Lucinda revealed, reclining in her chair. She was already wearing her dress, lost in a sea of deep green satin. "It didn't matter that just the day before, she'd defeated Daveus Richmond in a duel."

"And I was just as nervous at my first ball. Even more so at my eighteenth-year ceremony. Be thankful they didn't give you one and are giving you the Sectra instead." Penelope visibly shivered as the words left her mouth. "At least you have a wonderful escort."

The color returned to Ash's face in the form of a vicious blush. "I didn't ask for an escort."

"Well, you have one," Anastasia grunted as she paced, her bathrobe wrapped tightly around her. "And if you ask me, he's quite yummy."

Ciara giggled from beside the princess, nodding in agreement.

Ash sighed in her seat, crossing her arms. When Loren had asked who she wanted to escort her to the ball, and who'd she would make her grand entrance into society with, she'd been shocked. She hadn't expected to need an escort. So, she'd looked at those who'd been seated around the dinner table last night, and in a rush of embarrassment and anxiety, she'd said the first name that came to her mind.

"I only chose Craven because I've spent the most time with him." Ash defended her decision. "And I couldn't suggest one of the McBride's or Morghan because they're too controversial right now. I suppose it's a blessing they're even allowed to the ceremony to begin with."

"Oh, so you *would* have chosen a McBride?" Lucinda teased lightly. "What, is one of them your love or something?"

Ash's heart ceased to beat for a moment. "No," she answered, perhaps too quickly. But, the truth was, there had only been one man she would have ever wished to escort her to a ball. And he was gone. Most likely forever.

THE DRESS WAS SUFFOCATING, AT BEST. ASH WRITHED beneath it, longing for a pair of pants. The lace sleeves were itchy, and the heart-shaped neckline too low for her liking. She felt exposed, and she hated every bit of it.

The other girls fawned over her. Penelope had even told her she looked like a midnight queen, but Ash was not a queen. She hadn't worn a dress since Pat McBride's funeral many, many years ago. She made a mental note to never wear one again, as long as she could help it.

Looking at herself in the mirror felt like staring at a stranger. Wasn't it just weeks ago that she'd trudged home after a battle with the Pandora, covered in blood from head to toe? She frowned, and the Sorceress scowled at her expression.

"You're stunning," Lucinda insisted, though she looked far more extravagant. She'd curled her poker straight hair, and it fell around her in gracious waves. The strange shade of red stood out against her porcelain skin. Even her eyes seemed brighter beneath her thick lashes and gold-shaded eye makeup.

Ash had never worn a sliver of what Cooper had once called *face paint*, but now, her lips were as red as the blood in her veins. Her eyes were lined, and her lashes nearly as thick as Constance's were every day.

"Your escort is here." Anastasia sighed from the threshold, her silver gown shining in the chandelier light.

Ash's stomach dropped. Seeing herself looking such a way was bad enough, but she'd nearly forgotten *everyone* would see her as well. She watched herself blanch in the looking glass.

"I wasn't aware being your Mentor meant that I was courting you," Craven teased, examining her dress. Ash felt her cheeks heat with a vivid blush, strong enough to shine through the *face paint* Lucinda had so delicately applied to her face. "You clean up nice though, I will admit."

Ash pursed her painted lips, her fists clenching around her skirts. "This is *not* a date," she growled as she pushed past him, entering the long hall.

Lucinda snickered from behind as she passed them, her arm linked with Humphrey Adam's. Ash watched as they disappeared down the long hall before sucking in a shuddering breath and following.

ASH CLUTCHED CRAVEN'S ARM SO TIGHTLY THAT IT FELT AS if her lace sleeves had been sewn to his black velvet tuxedo jacket. They stood at the top of a set of grand stairs, watching as Penelope and Loren made their prestigious entrance. She barely heard the announcer as he'd introduced them to the flock of Immortals who'd come to witness her accept the Sectra.

Ash Snow-VanCamp, is what he'd said. She made a mental note to thank Loren later, for not allowing the person she was before she'd arrived in Dracus to fade away so easily.

Barely able to hear the sound of her own heartbeat over the cheering and applause, Ash forced a smile. She scanned the thick crowd of people covering the black-and-white marble floors and surrounding the red-clothed tables scattered about the ballroom. Loren approached the dais, smiling as he greeted his following. She focused on him for a moment, her legs trembling beneath her skirts as she descended the staircase.

"You're going to snap my arm in two," Craven muttered in her ear.

Quickly, she released her grip on him as they melted into the crowd. Ash released a sigh of relief as she arrived before a set of familiar faces. Marcus grinned at her, his vivid eyes sparkling, likely from a few pre-ball drinks. She imagined she'd return to his apartment later to find that he and his fellow council members had cleared out the liquor cabinet.

"Words can't describe how relieved I am that this event

is taking place," Marcus admitted, taking her hand in his own for a moment, squeezing it reassuringly.

The Mentor had told Ash many things about the sacrifices people had made to find her. Over dinner every night, he'd told her stories of Cedric, Abernathy, and even Beck. How they'd all prayed every night for this evening to arrive. She smiled, thankful that at least Beck, Penelope, and Vincent were here to witness it.

"You look like a dream," Morghan told her, his voice startling her from behind. "Far from the brat I met in the woods."

Ash's smile quickly transitioned into a frown. "That's the shittiest compliment I've ever received," she replied, crossing her arms.

Quinn grunted, announcing his presence at the Wolf's side. Ash spared him a sidelong glance, straightening her spine. He looked about as uncomfortable in his suit as she was in her dress. A costume for the role she now had to play.

"Far cry from the harvest festival," he mused.

Ash nearly smiled but steeled herself. She couldn't avoid him, especially when he was one of the few pieces of home in Dracus. But they had much to sort out. "Where's your brother?" she asked, scanning the crowd. The moment she caught sight of Cooper taking a shot of something with Alistair, her stomach flipped. "Oh, don't let him drink!"

"Why?" Craven gave her a disapproving look. "He's a man, isn't he?"

"You don't understand," Quinn sighed, his cerulean eyes revealing the slightest glint of worry. "He's rather... exciting when he's a bit tipsy."

Morghan chuckled, clearly fond of the idea. "I'll go warn him that it won't take much for Loren to change his mind about his presence here." He sighed before trotting off.

Ash wasn't surprised when Alistair offered the Wolf a shot too, or when he took it.

"We should find our table," Craven suggested.

Nodding, Ash wasn't opposed to sitting for a time. It sounded far more pleasing than having to prance around, pretending that she knew how to walk in heels.

Their table, of course, was beside the dais, next to where the council members were all sitting, aside from Marcus, who was now mingling with Grant and a few other communications officers.

Ash lowered into her seat, scanning the other names around the table. A faint smile appeared on her lips when she spotted Cooper's name plate beside her own.

"If the king shows faith in them, his following will too," Craven told her as he waived down a woman carrying a tray of champagne. He stole two glasses, setting one in front of Ash. "Drink. It'll get rid of the nerves."

Normally, Ash would refuse. She'd rather be clear-headed. But one glance at the dais, and knowing she would soon have to stand upon it, and the glass was at her lips.

Vincent walked over to join them, plopping into his assigned seat across from her. "So, how do you feel?"

Ash arched a brow, fighting the urge to chug the champagne. "Like I've been thrown into a den of wolves."

"Lions would be better suited," Craven pointed out matter-of-factly.

Ash had watched the festivities unfold, while Craven remained at her side. Others came to visit their table, taking breaks from their dancing. Penelope made her rounds throughout the room, bidding hello to every Draconian noble she could find before she returned to her seat beside the king for dinner.

Dinner was called and the guests all found their places at their tables. Ash smirked at the sight of Cooper rushing toward her, nearly sliding into his seat.

"I see you're taking to Dracus quite well," she chuckled.

"They really know how to throw a party here." Cooper whistled as Quinn took his seat beside him. "It's just a bit crazy that it's all for you."

Vincent eyed the two brothers warily. Ash's gaze flitted between him and the McBride brothers, her heart suddenly feeling a bit warm in her chest. The rest of their tablemates quickly arrived, including Alistair Ward, Humphrey, and Lucinda.

Over dinner, Ash listened, her eyes wide, as Lucinda and Humphrey recalled the night they'd worked with Marcus to save them from the Idonian Kingdom's fall. The Mentor was currently seated with the rest of the Council, but his eyes were upon them. He smiled, as if to hide the sadness brought upon by the memories of that evening.

Ash silently vowed to find a way to thank all three of them for what they'd risked to save her and Vincent, and she wondered if her twin felt the same. She looked toward Quinn, who seemed in awe of the story. These were the answers they'd always wanted to hear. Now that they had them, Ash wondered what they would do with themselves. Two years of a complicated search for the truth had come to an abrupt end, and a small voice in her mind told her she'd long for the days when she'd once known nothing.

AFTER DINNER WAS THROUGH, ASH'S HEART QUICKENED into a steady gallop. She found herself clutching her glass of wine as she watched Loren return to the dais. The room fell silent. The sudden absence of constant music and chattering left her ears ringing as she fought to calm herself.

"There it is," Craven whispered in her ear. He gestured to a silver coated box that Richard held in his hands. The advisor remained behind the king, his eyes bright as they fell on Ash. Her breath hitched.

As if he could feel her sudden panic, Craven placed a calming hand on her shoulder. She wondered if it were meant for comfort, or to keep her from fleeing.

Frightened, Ash looked toward Quinn, as if he'd be able to tell her how to act when she approached that dais. All he did was stare back at her, nodding slowly.

"We've gathered here this evening to lay our past to rest," Loren announced, his hands folded behind his back. "A mission that lasted eighteen years has finally come to an end, and with pride, we can now fulfill our late High Queen's last will and testament. It was her wish that Idona's Sectra go to her daughter, Ash VanCamp, upon turning the age of eighteen. For a *very* long time, we weren't sure if that would happen. We only have the Moons to thank that it will happen this evening."

Loren's eyes fell on Ash, and in that moment, she felt the Realm stop around her. She held his gaze, her stomach fluttering as he gestured for her to rise. She hesitated, but a quick kick from Craven beneath the table had her jumping to her feet.

Penelope rose as well, swaying with grace as she moved around her own table to greet Ash. Her arm linked in hers, the princess's gentle hand falling over her own, Penelope guided her to the dais, stopping only when they reached the steps.

Loren held his hand out to her, and Ash took it, immediately embarrassed by how sweaty her hands were. She climbed the steps, one at a time, fearing she'd roll an ankle for the entire kingdom to see. Once she arrived at the top, Richard moved to her side and took hold of her other hand. She sighed through her nose, hoping the onlookers wouldn't notice the calming breaths she kept pulling in.

"The Idonian Amulet was the first Sectra to be forged," Loren began again. "It has been worn by Everly Cavanaugh, heir to Si Realtra's first High King. It has been worn by Alexi Grimm, our Realms fiercest Mortal Warrior. Upon his death, it was given to his sister, Blair Grimm, who later married Graham VanCamp. Her widowed husband wore it himself until the day he died of old age. It was his will that it be given to his grandson, High King Gregor VanCamp. And it was when he died during the Five Realm War that his son Gideon VanCamp decided it was to go to his wife, Meera VanCamp. His exact words were '*It would look much better on her.*'"

The crowd laughed as Loren quoted Ash's father. He spoke more about the history of the Sectra's, and about the history of the main Realm. He spoke of how these past eighteen years of darkness, of Immortal Silence, would come to an end. That the darkness had begun with a ball, and it would end with one now. Once he finished his speech, she heard the sound of the silver box opening beside her. An invisible, ancient power filled the air.

All of Ash's senses tingled as she looked toward the amulet. A shiver swam down her spine, like a spider on her back. She held her breath as Richard released her hand to lift the Sectra from the box, gasps sounding throughout the room. Without another word, he stepped behind her and gently placed it around her neck. The second it grazed her skin, like icy fire, she felt its power seep into her pores.

Richard clasped the chain and released the amulet, stepping back to her side to reclaim her hand. The entire kingdom trembled as the crowd applauded. The crystal chandeliers swayed, the glasses filled with wine and blood alike rattled on each table.

Ash caught sight of Valentina approaching the dais in a dress of shimmering gold. The Prophetess was a stiff reminder that while the amulet might now lay around her neck, this night was far from over. She held her breath, her eyes dancing about the ballroom. Exactly who would she fight alongside through Idona's darkest hours?

NEW FIRE

30

Marcus watched Valentina step onto the dais, a moving picture of grace, arriving beside Ash as Loren and Richard released both of her hands. Seeing her wear the amulet had struck a nerve, one that nearly brought tears to his eyes. The last time he'd seen the beautiful weapon, it had been forced into his hands. A symbol of the High Queen's impending death. He shivered, hoping no one would notice.

Loren and Richard stepped back, opening up the dais for the warriors Marcus knew Valentina was about to announce. His heart quickened as he glanced toward the table beside him, where Craven sat, as pale as a ghost.

There wasn't a doubt in Marcus's mind that Craven would walk toward that dais at some point in the next few minutes. With his power, and his abilities, there was no way the Moons wouldn't have chosen him.

Valentina cleared her throat, preparing to begin her speech. Marcus's attention fell back on the Prophetess, and he reached for his glass of whiskey. He knew he'd need it.

"We have not only gathered here today to watch our beloved Idonian Princess, Ash Snow-VanCamp, accept our

Realm's sacred Sectra, we've come to see her rise as the Messenger as well. We've truly been blessed to receive all we were waiting for in one person, who stands beside me today, ready to fulfill her prophecy."

Ash was as frozen as the ice in Ryiah beside the Prophetess as she spoke, which Marcus found quite endearing. Who knew the great warrior capable of killing the Dark King had such stage fright?

"But," Valentina continued, a devilish smirk upon her face, "we cannot send our Messenger off alone. The Moons have shown me the best people to aid her."

Gasps sounded throughout the room, and for a moment, Marcus's grip around his glass tightened. He wondered who they would be, and if he would trust them. He didn't just spend eighteen years trying to fulfill a promise to Meera, only for Ash to walk off into the Realm and perish.

Frowning, Marcus fought against his negative thoughts and focused on Valentina. He knew she'd chastise him publicly if she noticed he wasn't paying attention.

"A second prophecy was born," Valentina revealed, and a chill ran down Marcus's spine. "Visions overran my mind with such unspeakable force, it took me a moment to realize what it was. A Prophecy indeed. One where a team of warriors will aid our Galaxy and rid it of Darkness. Idona's Allies."

Ash noticeably jumped at the sound of the title, a faint smile spreading across her red-painted lips. Marcus pulled in a deep breath, his heart growing heavy. He wondered if it was truly possible. Could a team of only ten undo the damage Xavier's Dark Army had inflicted on this Realm? He hoped it was.

"Nine warriors will join Ash here on this dais, and tomorrow they will begin their preparations. Each of them has a story of their own, and different backgrounds. Some you'd never expect, and some have proven their right to call themselves an Idonian Ally through acts of bravery that could never be mirrored," Valentina explained, her voice stern, yet tainted by the hope she was spreading throughout the ballroom.

Goosebumps pebbled along Marcus's flesh as he took another sip of his whiskey. The warriors could be anyone. *Anyone* in this room.

"I wasn't very surprised when the Moons revealed to me who the first warrior would be," Valentina admitted. "The moment I met him, some time ago now, I could see in his eyes, the will to fight. The need to redeem his fallen. All he needed was a little push in the right direction."

Spit it out, Marcus nearly allowed himself to groan.

"Morghan Henning." The name sent a wave of pure shock through the ballroom. Marcus's mouth fell open as he turned to the table beside him, watching as the Wolf rose from his seat. If he was surprised, he didn't show it as he approached the dais and took his place beside Ash. However, the Messenger hadn't done such a good job of hiding her surprise. She gawked at the Werewolf, and he did nothing but smirk at her.

The ballroom shook once again with applause, and what was left of the whiskey in Marcus's glass swayed from the ruckus.

Axel, who Marcus could have sworn was just standing beside him, approached the dais with a set of nine boxes in his arms. Loren took one, opening it gently and lifting a silver badge from within. Marcus's eyes narrowed curiously at the sight of it—two Dragons curved upward, shaping a heart, while a claymore drove down the center. It was truly captivating. Marcus was sure it was a symbol of unity.

"The second warrior wasn't very surprising either,"

Valentina continued, silencing the applause with the sound of her voice. "A woman of pure strength, whom we fear as much as we admire. While Dracus and her clan will surely miss her while she's away, Anastasia Volden will surely prove to be the asset our Messenger needs to succeed."

Marcus looked down the table where Anastasia stood, her eyes wide with surprise. The expression was quickly replaced by her usual, stony facade as she approached the dais and allowed Loren to pin one of the badges to her dress.

The members of the Fire Clan throughout the room, including Alistair Ward, their newest addition, cheered louder than anyone else.

"The third warrior has no doubt earned their position on this team," Valentina grinned. "Over and over again, he has surprised our kingdom with his bravery, and his sheer will to succeed in anything he chooses to do. Craven Amsterdam."

Marcus breathed a sigh of relief as he watched his violet-eyed comrade walk toward the dais. Craven showed no emotion as he took his place beside Anastasia. He'd likely been expecting his name to be called.

"The fourth warrior was a stranger to me in my visions. But those visions kept coming, and before long, he didn't seem like a stranger at all. He seemed like a man, hell-bent on saving his fellow Idonian citizens. That man is Cooper McBride."

The look on Cooper's face was priceless. Marcus couldn't help but understand now, why the Prophetess had fought tooth and nail for those brothers to stay in Dracus. She'd seen them prove the council wrong. She had already known they would.

Cooper rose from the table. To say he was momentarily trembling would have been an understatement, but the

Realm Sorceress quickly came to his aid and gave him a gentle push toward the dais where the other warriors were waiting for him with welcoming smiles.

Sighing, Marcus finished off his drink. He wouldn't dare flag down a waiter for another one right now, so he scanned the table. His brows rose once he noticed Axel's nearly full glass, left unattended. He swiped it, only to find Benjamin glaring at him from across the table.

"The fifth warrior is not a stranger at all. She's protected our Realm viciously, for centuries. And I was not the slightest bit surprised when the Moons chose her to walk this new path." Valentina shivered as the words left her mouth, her eyes falling on the Sorceress before she could bring herself to say her name. "Realm Sorceress, Lucinda Cross."

Lucinda stood, bowing before she left her place at the table. She sauntered up to the dais, her green skirts swirling around her as she practically skipped up the steps and slid into her spot beside Craven. Loren placed the pin on her dress, and she scowled at the king, likely for piercing a hole through the fabric.

"The sixth and seventh warriors…" Valentina sucked in an audible breath, her eyes now wet with tears. Marcus wondered exactly how long she'd known about these people, and what they would do. Had she been waiting years for everything to fall together the way she'd needed them to? "Are both men we thought we'd lost, yet they've come back from the dead. Despite the horrors they had faced, they weren't shaken. They haven't lost their will to avenge our fallen High Queen, and the fallen villages and cities in our Realm. Marcus Bonaventure and Alistair Ward."

Marcus's eyes darted to Alistair, who rose from his seat. As he watched him approach the dais, he quickly realized he'd forgotten that she'd said his own name as well.

She said my name. His mind whirled for a moment. *Wait.*

"What are you doing?" Benjamin snapped from across the table. "Get up there."

Stunned, Marcus rushed from the table so quickly that he nearly tripped. He steadied himself, his heart pounding against the walls of his chest. As he climbed the steps, moving to stand beside Lucinda, he sighed with relief. Loren arrived in front of him to pin the badge to his chest, patting Marcus's shoulder before returning to his place to wait for the next warrior to be announced.

"Our eighth warrior is a natural born leader," Valentina announced proudly. "He may be a stranger now, but he won't be for long. I've seen the powerhouse he will become, and while some might fear him, it should only be our enemies that do. Quinn McBride."

Quinn seemed less than surprised. If anything, he seemed uncomfortable as he climbed the steps to the dais. He stood beside Marcus as stiff as a board as Loren pinned the badge to his chest. If he wanted a chance to prove everyone wrong about the Arebus Archers, he certainly got one.

"And our last warrior," Valentina beamed, stepping down from the dais as if she were going to walk to the crowd and pluck the poor soul out herself, "has an incredibly bright mind, but shouldn't be doubted on the battlefield. He's been trained by the best and has the blood of our greatest past warriors running through his veins."

The Prophetess paced the front tables, her eyes scanning the faces of each clan leader. She stopped for a moment in front of Blade and then began moving again. Marcus's cheeks puffed with the breath he was holding as she ran a finger along General Beck's shoulder, but then she stopped, her gold eyes smiling as she stared down at the startled prince in front of her.

"Vincent VanCamp," Valentina mused as she took his hand. Marcus's breath hitched as the prince gaped at the Prophetess. It hadn't been so long ago that he was just a newborn, being rushed to safety as his family's kingdom fell off in the distance. It hadn't been so long ago that he was just thirteen, pacing halls in the Kingdom of Elves, praying that his older sister was still alive. And now, he'd grown to be the *opposite* of what he'd thought he would be.

The sight of the Draconian King placing the badge on Vincent's chest would never leave Marcus's mind. He'd never forget what it felt like to join hands with everyone upon that dais. When they bowed, and the kingdom erupted in applause once again, Marcus's eyes burned with coming tears. He hoped that somewhere, Meera was watching him proudly. That she knew he'd received this chance to redeem himself.

31

Ash watched from afar as Craven and Alistair celebrated with the other pronounced Allies. Each of the warriors were excited beyond belief, but, she wasn't in the mood for celebrating. In fact, she dreaded the days to come.

Sighing, Ash snatched a tall glass of blood from a silver tray as a waiter passed her by. She rose it to her lips, savoring the taste for a moment. Her stomach churned as she watched the attendees dance, swirling in gentle circles in tune to a song she knew was likely ancient. One she'd never heard and didn't know the steps too.

A tinge of jealousy sprang through her at the sight of a man, dipping his beautiful date as they lost themselves in the music. They stared at each other with such loving eyes it made her stomach churn.

"I could teach you, if you'd like." A voice startled her from behind. Ash swirled to see who it was, only to find that the Elven General had snuck up behind her.

A faint smile played at her lips. "I'd rather dance with swords, General," she replied, silently wondering if she'd had too much wine and blood.

Beck smirked, leaning against her table. "You aren't too happy that I declined to kick your ass in a duel, are you?"

"Infuriated, actually."

"Oh, I'm sure we'll have much time in the future to duel all we like. Once this is all over." Beck sighed, crossing his arms. He'd shed his tuxedo jacket and his tie the moment Ash and the others had vacated the dais. "My parents send their apologies for not being here," he added, his voice little more than a whisper.

"I'm sure leaving the safety of their kingdom is too much of a risk this time of year." Ash fought against the disgust that overwhelmed her at the thought of the Elven King and Queen. She'd heard the stories. She knew they wanted the Sectra hanging around her neck to go to their daughter, Princess Mika Chamberlain. She'd also known what Beck had done to try and stop it. He'd offered help to people he shouldn't have. He'd disobeyed his father's orders. In fact, he'd committed treason.

Beck nodded slowly; his expression grim. "I have to say, I'd have loved to have been one of your Allies. Stay out of the golden walls for a time."

"You're an Ally," Ash told him abruptly, and he looked over at her, his brow wrinkling. "In your own way. Sure, the nine people over there taking shots and dancing will help me directly, but don't think for a second I won't need you when the time comes to take back that Kingdom."

"Talking like a true politician now," Beck sneered.

"Well, you want to help, don't you?" Ash lifted a brow.

"Yes."

"Then ready your army, General."

"As you wish, Princess," Beck replied, his smirk returning.

For a moment, Ash looked at him without uttering a word. She looked into his golden eyes, nearly shielded by his golden hair, and silently wondered if his heart was made of gold as well.

"If you're up to it," she inched closer, whispering into his ear, "I have a special job for you."

"And what might that be?" he inquired, his eyes narrowing.

"Rumor has it," Ash whispered, "you have a score to settle with the Dark Prince."

QUINN WATCHED FROM HIS PLACE BESIDE MORGHAN AS ASH spoke with the Elven General across the ballroom. He barely recognized her, but that wasn't what surprised him. It was the way she spoke to him. They were close enough for even the Werewolf to notice.

"Interesting choice," Morghan muttered. "But then again, it's hard to resist us alluring Immortals."

"That's not what's happening." Quinn was sure of it. He knew Ash better than he'd like to admit some days. He knew that the four chambers of her heart were made of steel. *Impenetrable* steel. If she felt love at all, it was for her family, and her village. "I think she's up to something."

"Like what? Bedding the Elven General, and a prince, of all people," Morghan snorted. "Have you seen your brother? He's dancing with the Realm Sorceress."

Quinn spared Cooper a look and practically bristled. Cooper *was* dancing with Lucinda. He was swirling her around as if he'd been dancing all his life. "I told you not to let him drink."

"I'd stop focusing on him when your beloved is about four centimeters from Beck," Morghan warned, and Quinn's attention snapped back to Ash. He cursed beneath his breath as he took in what was such an unsettling sight. Where was her damn escort?

"She's not my beloved. I'm betrothed."

Morghan sighed heavily. "You're all such a complicated lot of people," he groaned. "Didn't your betrothed sleep with your brother?"

"That's none of your concern," Quinn growled.

"Let me guess." Morghan pressed on despite Quinn's very clear warning not to. "It's a setup, between your parents. And you wouldn't dare defy your father."

It took Quinn everything he had not to haul off and deck his fellow *ally* right in the snout he knew was hiding beneath his mortal facade. Instead, he found himself striding across the ballroom, unsure of what he was doing at all. He arrived before Ash and the General, far more quickly than he had intended too, and found himself at a loss for words as the pair stared at him with curious eyes.

"Quinn." Ash greeted the Archer, her tone uncertain. "Are you enjoying yourself?"

Quinn's gaze darted between herself and Beck, who abruptly backed away, creating as much space between them as he could. "Am I imposing?" he asked, clearly having noticed the general's immediate withdrawal.

"Not at all," Beck replied quickly. "In fact, I was just leaving. I have... things to attend to at home. I hope you both enjoy the rest of this evening. If either you need anything, I'm a portal away," he chimed before vacating the ballroom.

Ash scowled at the place the General had been sitting, her blood now boiling in her veins. "What the hell was *that*?" she snapped.

"I would like to speak with you," Quinn announced, crossing his arms. "Alone."

ASH ASCENDED THE STEPS TO THE BALLROOM, AFTER bidding goodbye to Loren, the council, and her siblings. She'd left Craven with Alistair, as they were so clearly having a wonderful time with no sign of stopping any time soon. Cooper was left under the watchful eye of Morghan, who promised to pry him from Lucinda's grip and return him to their shared apartment unscathed.

She frowned at the sensation of Quinn's eyes on her back as she kicked off her heels, kneeling to pick them up. The silence in the castle halls was unbearable compared to the noisy ballroom she'd just endured. Her ears rung terribly as they turned various corners, wandering aimlessly.

"First and foremost," Quinn finally spoke, as if he'd spent all their time in silence trying to find the right words, "I owe you an apology."

"You *all* do," Ash growled before she'd had a chance to tame the slew of emotions running so angrily within her. "You let Lincoln nearly *rip* me apart for keeping my Immortality a secret when you had all been doing the same thing!"

"For good reason," Quinn argued. "You saw the way they reacted to us when we arrived here. You saw the way they all looked at us this evening."

"And you thought I, of all people, would have looked at you in such a way?"

"We didn't know what was coming to us," Quinn told her. "We didn't want anyone, including *you*, caught in the crossfire. Surely, you can understand *that*?"

His words hit her like a wall of pure, impenetrable stone. She knew that fear, all too well. She'd prayed every night since she'd read Meera's letter that the Immortals wouldn't come for her and harm the McBrides in the process.

"We had our reasons." His voice broke, filled with the remnants of pain and regret. "And you had yours. But no matter what we kept from one another, or how we tried to protect each other, it all came crashing down, anyway."

"Tell me about it." Ash blinked against the tears stinging her eyes. "You want to know why I asked Morghan to take me to Dracus?" She pulled in a deep, shaky breath to calm herself. "So you wouldn't follow me here and wind up caught up in whatever I was thrown into. And now, here you are. An Idonian Ally. Following me into the Lion's den, anyway."

"Valentina saw what she saw," Quinn reminded her. "But even if this hadn't been the fate the Moons chose for me, you're damn right. We'd have followed you anyway. *Especially* once we learned of what and *who* you are."

Ash cursed loud enough for it to bounce off the castle walls. This wasn't what she'd wanted. She wanted them all safe in Crane, far away from the dangers lurking ahead.

"What were you talking to the General about?" Quinn's question was so soft she'd hardly heard it, even with her Fae ears.

Frowning, Ash turned to face him. She took in his appearance for a moment. His tie was out of place, his jacket wrinkled. His hair now dangled in front of his eyes. "Since he wasn't named an Idonian Ally and he isn't going with us," she began, though she wondered if she'd regret telling him a thing, "I gave him a different job. While we're off doing whatever it is Valentina has planned for us, he's going to be tracking Malachai. He's going to find Lincoln."

Quinn's eyes bulged then, his jaw clenching.

"What?" Ash spat. "Did you think I'd forget about him once they gave me this Sectra and named me Messenger? I want him back just as much as you do. I know that everyone else thinks it's impossible, but I don't believe it is. If I can't go out and look for him myself, there's no better person I could have picked. Especially since Marcus is now wrapped up in all of this too."

Silence spread between the pair, and Ash huffed as she turned to walk further down the hall. They rounded a corner, one lined with paintings of people she knew she would never live up to. The Great Lion Mason, Loren's father, was the first face she saw. And after him, a long line of kings and queens were portrayed, immortalized by the work of extremely talented artists.

Quinn remained quiet beside her, entranced by the paintings as well.

They'd made it halfway down the hall when Ash spotted a painting of Valentina, and beside it, the former High King and Queen. Her breath caught in her throat, her heart skipping a beat as she stared up at their faces.

While she may have seen Gideon and Meera VanCamp's features in the papers, she'd never seen them in such detail. Vibrant eyes stared back at her, both different shades of pretty greens. Gideon bore an olive skin tone, much like Ash and Vincent's, while Meera was fair, pale in comparison to her husband. She was truly stunning. Her dark auburn hair fell to her waist in waves. The crown upon her head was littered with diamonds, sparking above her brow.

As Ash stared at the painting, she knew this was as close as she would ever get to her parents. She wasn't sure what was worse. Losing Eliza Snow, who was undoubtedly the best mother she could have ever asked for, or having no memories of the parents to whom she truly belonged.

"They look so happy." Ash's lip quivered as she surveyed the surrounding paintings. There was one of her siblings with the Chamberlains. And then, her eyes fell on a vacant spot. She could see the marks in the wall from where a painting once hung, but now, it was nothing but a blank space.

"I wonder who used to be there," she thought out loud.

"Xavier."

Ash looked toward Quinn; her eyes wide. "Really? How do you know?"

"Benjamin told me when he gave me a tour," he revealed. "We all knew that he was Gideon's advisor, but, I wasn't aware how much he was cherished. He must have earned the trust of everyone to be immortalized in this hall."

Ash shivered at the thought of the betrayal.

"Now, your painting will hang there," Quinn added with a faint smile. "Fitting, seeing as you'll put an end to the rancid bastard."

A wave of shock swept through Ash, her fists clenching at her sides. "They should wait," she whispered. "Until I earn my place in this hall."

"Messenger or not, Ash, you're still an Idonian Princess," Quinn reminded her softly. "You were born having earned your place."

She swirled to face him, her face set in her best glare. "No," she argued. "Even if I had been raised in the Kingdom of Elves with Penelope and Vincent, I would still feel the same now. You earn respect. You aren't born with it."

"I suppose you're right." Quinn sighed. "I'm in that

position myself. I will never be respected, or even trusted, unless I earn it. Maybe we'll earn it together."

"I'd rather like that," Ash replied, her features softening. "I wouldn't have it any other way."

Quinn reached for her hand, squeezing it gently. They stood in silence once again, their eyes drifting from face to face. They roamed the hall, walking back and forth, examining every painting.

For a while, Ash felt like nothing had changed. Whether they were in Crane, or Dracus, she and Quinn were still snooping around, trying to find answers to questions and learning about the parts of Immortal history that Crane couldn't teach them.

"Do you really think that General will stick his own neck out to try and find Lincoln?" Quinn asked as they passed the painting of the Chamberlain family for the third time that evening.

"I do," Ash told him. "He's not what he appears to be."

"Well, I'll owe him the biggest debt imaginable if he can pull it off," Quinn grumbled.

"As will I."

Quinn nodded, and Ash watched him glance down at their hands, still intertwined. "I have something for you," he announced, reaching into the pocket of his dress shirt, beneath the Ally Badge. "I thought you might appreciate this on our long journey ahead," he said as he revealed the pocket watch in his grip.

Ash stifled a gasp at the sight of it. "I'm surprised you thought to bring it," she beamed, taking it in her free hand. She immediately opened the watch, her heart warming at the sight of the picture.

"Maybe they'll use that picture, for that blank space on the wall," he chuckled. "Wouldn't Sam be thrilled?"

"He'd brag about it until his dying breath." She rolled her eyes at the thought.

Quinn gave her a crooked smile and said, "That's not the only thing I thought to bring. I'd have given you your daggers a lot sooner, had you not avoided me as if I were some sort of evil plague the last week."

Her stomach fluttered at the thought of her enchanted daggers. She'd tried to fill the void she'd been left without them, but no dagger in Dracus could compare to the set the old bookkeeper had given her. "Why must you be so kind to me?"

"I will never be unkind to you," he replied with a sigh as they resumed their walking. "We aren't children in the mountains anymore. We have no true idea about what will happen to us on this journey. We've met plenty of people, and will meet many more. But we won't forget where we came from, or who loved us first."

32

Marcus awoke the next morning to Ash clattering in the kitchen. Normally, he was up long before her, but after a few too many drinks last night, he'd stumbled into bed past three in the morning. The sun was already high enough in the sky for the Mentor to realize he'd slept far too late in the day for his liking, so he rolled out of his bed and rushed into his bathroom to freshen up.

The scent of muffins invaded his nostrils as Marcus quickly showered and dressed. His mouth watered as he walked down the stairs into the lower level of his apartment, catching sight of a set of daggers and a whetstone on his coffee table in the living room. They were beautiful enough for him to stop dead in his tracks to admire them. He could practically smell the power radiating from them.

"Admiring my daggers?" Ash chimed as she approached from the kitchen, two mugs of coffee in her hands. She handed him one and gingerly sipped her own. "Quinn brought them for me."

Marcus took a long sip of his coffee, hoping the energizing substance would be enough to get him out the door and through the long day that was awaiting him.

He took his eyes off the daggers and looked toward Ash for a moment. The amulet was hidden beneath her red sweater, but the chain was visible around her neck. An enchanted chain. One she could only remove herself.

Something about the girl had seemed to change, compared to how she'd been the last week. She seemed softer, and less on edge. Happy, even. She'd made muffins. In fact, Marcus was sure she'd transitioned into an entirely different person overnight.

"Where did you get them?"

Ash smiled, and for once, it reached her eyes. "A book-keeper in Crane gave them to me one day when Quinn and I visited his shop. He'd said someone had left them for me."

"Who?"

"I have no idea," she admitted with a sigh. "The book-keeper said it had been nearly fifty years ago. All I know is that it had been a man, whose name the keeper had forgotten. Quinn was convinced he'd gone mad with old age. He died shortly after, so I couldn't ask him any more questions. I thought about approaching his son but decided against it. I doubt he knows anything. Sometimes, some mysteries are better left as just that—mysteries."

Marcus couldn't disagree with her, and before he had a chance to reply, his stomach growled loud enough for his neighbors to hear.

Ash laughed, her emerald eyes sparkling. "Lucky for you, I woke up with the itch to bake. I made berry muffins."

The Mentor didn't need to hear anything more before he ventured to the kitchen and snatched one off the platter in the center of his dark granite island.

He took a bite, his taste buds nearly exploding with flavor. He fought not to demolish the muffin in one bite. "Remind me to let you cook more often. It appears I'm not the only one in this apartment with that gift."

"I can bake, but I'm not much of a cook," she replied, jabbing him in the ribs with her elbow on the way to the sink where she quickly rinsed her mug. "But if you want eggs, I'm your girl. Now, we have a meeting to get to."

Valentina and Benjamin were the only people waiting for them when Ash and Marcus arrived in the communications center. They'd found them in a conference room, seated along a long glass table. The glass walls were left clear instead of their usual opaque so that the others could find them, but so far it appeared none of them had.

"I imagined we'd have a late start considering last night's festivities," Benjamin chuckled as Ash lowered into a seat across from him. "But another minute longer, and I'm going to send Blade to snatch them all from their beds."

"Now that would be a sight to be seen," Marcus snorted.

"I'll rip them from their beds myself," Valentina grumbled, her arms crossed over her plain white t-shirt. Ash was surprised to see her dressed so casually, but then again, she imagined they'd be sitting at this table for quite a while. Comfort was certainly the key to surviving such a long meeting. She herself was glad she'd worn a set of comfortable boots opposed to her usual leathers, though she was quick to kick them off under the table.

Voices and laughter down the hall drew her attention, and Ash's eyes fell on the threshold just as Lucinda and

Vincent walked in. They were each bright eyed, and Vincent had even brought a notepad. He was prepared, which wasn't unlike him in the slightest.

Humphrey and Grant, the Communications Officer, came to join them with trays of coffee in their arms. They set one on the table in front of everyone who'd arrived so far and then Grant took a seat for himself beside Benjamin while Humphrey lingered in the back of the room.

Before long, Morghan led the McBride brothers into the conference room. Quinn appeared annoyed, likely with Cooper, who was evidently hungover.

Anastasia flowed in next, taking her seat beside Valentina and reclining in her chair. She seemed refreshed, without even a hint that she'd been so tipsy last night she'd hit on Morghan in front of *everyone*.

Craven and Alistair were last, both of them rubbing their tired eyes as they lowered into their seats.

Lastly, Loren arrived. He smiled at everyone as he took a seat beside Grant, appearing to be less than a king in his casual wear. His hair was still damp from a shower, and if Ash didn't know any better, she would have thought him to be a run-of-the-mill Draconian with no title to his name.

"Now that you've all thought to join us," Benjamin sneered as he rose to his feet, "it's time we explain to you *exactly* what the Messenger Prophecy entails. And what you'll have to do to fulfill it."

Ash shrunk into her seat, her eyes on the Head of Communications as he reached for his information tablet on the table. "The ten of you are Allies, but you won't be working alone. Here in Dracus, Valentina, Loren, Grant, Humphrey, and I will work to aid you. We're your task force."

"You'll be provided with a plethora of equipment that will allow you to communicate with us throughout your journey," Grant added. "We'll help in any way that we can. The more people the merrier."

Valentina grinned as she took hold of Benjamin's tablet and pressed something that turned one of the glass walls into a large screen. Upon it was a map, displaying all of Idona. Ash's eyes lingered on the Strip, and it's intricate swirl. Her heart lurched at the sight, and she wondered if one day she might return to Crane.

"To fulfill the prophecy, Ash must complete three tasks. Tasks that you will all aid her with. The first task involves cutting down Xavier's numbers. You'll split into three divisions and head to different parts of the Realm," Valentina explained, highlighting three locations on the map. "There are three Pandora bases. They *used* to be bases containing Gideon's Mortal Army. Each team will take them down, preferably at the same time, to prevent Xavier from sending any reinforcements."

Ash's palms grew sweaty at the thought of how difficult that would be, especially if they were to split into three teams. How could such a small number of Allies defeat thousands of Pandora per base?

As if the Prophetess could hear what Ash was thinking, she said, "You'll each be provided with explosive arrows. And one of the bases, the one closest to the Forest of Fools, holds explosives. You can thank Aries for that information, as he's smelled them. What they planned on using them for, we don't know. But the team that heads to the Forest of Fools will only have to set off the explosives, and that should do the trick. As for the other teams, you'll have to rely on different methods. Long-range fighting will be better suited, I can assure you."

A shiver skittered down Ash's spine as she recalled how it felt to be attacked by thousands of Pandora. At least then, Drake had had a small army.

"For the second task, the teams will unite and approach Veda the Red Witch. She holds a particular serum that will be needed to replenish the power on the Sovereign's Scepter's blade," Valentina told them, and Lucinda's gasp from down the table hadn't gone unnoticed. "The serum goes by the name of Moonshade. It has the ability to paralyze individuals while also penetrating different forms of Darkness and Black Magic."

Lucinda shook her head furiously and said, "It's far too dangerous to approach Veda and expect to get anything out of her. Especially a serum as rare as Moonshade. She'll do something awful. Place a curse on Ash, or worse."

Ash's breath hitched at the thought. "Do I even want to know exactly who this Witch is?"

"Veda and I go way back." Lucinda shivered as she spoke. "She's my nemesis. And I don't just mean that we have an undying hatred for one another. She's as strong as I am in the ways of Magic. I wouldn't trust her anywhere near any of you. She's a ruthless, conniving bitch."

"Well, can we *make* the serum ourselves?" Alistair asked, scratching at his temple.

"Most of the ingredients hail from other Realms," Lucinda replied, her expression dark. "We wouldn't be able to obtain them. Not as long as the Galactic Gates are shut."

Marcus let loose a long whistle, reclining in his chair. "Well, we're just going to have to hope we approach Veda on one of her good days."

"One of her good days involves corrupting the minds of those around her to will them into doing her bidding," Lucinda barked.

"I'm sure between all ten of us, the bitch won't stand a chance," Anastasia drawled as she reached for her coffee.

"We'll see." The Sorceress didn't sound confident about the matter. Not in the slightest.

Valentina cleared her throat, drawing everyone's attention once again. "Once you obtain Moonshade from Veda, you'll head to the Forest of Fools. You'll need to carefully, and I mean *carefully* approach the cavern in which the Sovereign's Scepter sits. A beast guards it."

Ash watched the color drain from Alistair's face. "That *beast?*" he gaped.

"*That* beast," the Prophetess confirmed sadly. "There's no doubt in my mind that it was Xavier who put him there to slaughter the Messenger before they had a chance to spill their blood on the soil surrounding it, which would release the first Sorceress, Siobhan's, spell."

Ash swallowed hard, her mind racing. All three tasks were dangerous enough, and to think once she'd finished with them, she'd need to march to Solaris City in the Idonian Kingdom and *hope* she cut down the Dark King. She began to tremble at the thought, goosebumps evolving on every part of her flesh.

"And that's it?" Quinn, to Ash's surprise, asked.

"No." Valentina shook her head. "After Ash finishes with the three tasks and obtains the Scepter, she'll need to take it to the center of the Realm where moonlight shines the brightest. If she can do this during a three full moon cycle, the weapon will be at its most powerful state when she approaches Xavier. After that, you are all to report back to Dracus so we can begin planning for battle."

"And as for the teams?" Marcus inquired.

Grant rose from his seat, a grin spreading across his lips. "That's where I come in," the Communications Officer chirped, fiddling with his own information tablet.

The maps disappeared from the screen, and another image appeared, displaying three columns. Each of them was labeled with a different color—*Sapphire*, *Green*, and *Black*.

Ash leaned forward, resting her elbows on the table. Her gaze flit curiously between Grant and Valentina as she wondered who they'd chosen for her to fight alongside.

"These divisions will continue throughout your journey as Allies," Valentina told them all as she paced before the screen. "I imagine that even after the war ends, the Idonian Allies will always be needed. Each division will specialize in a specific thing."

"We decided who would be on each division by using a software program Grant created for the matter," Benjamin added. "We took everything from personalities to fighting styles into consideration. The people in your division will be the people you're most compatible with."

Loren nodded, rising from his seat. "Think of your fellow division members as battle companions. You will not only fight alongside these people, but camp with them as well. Essentially, you're stuck together."

Valentina elbowed the king playfully, likely recalling the days where they fought as battle companions together. She chuckled beneath her breath and said, "Each division will have a leader to guide and direct the others. We chose our leaders based on personality."

Brows raised, Ash bit at her inner cheek. Hopefully whoever they'd chosen as leaders wouldn't cause any rifts in the Ally bonding process.

"We'll start with the Sapphire division," Benjamin began, fiddling with his information tablet. The first name appeared on the screen. Ash's name. "Ash will lead this division, and it's members will be Morghan Henning, Alistair Ward, and Cooper McBride."

Ash fought not to gawk at the names as they appeared on the screen one by one. She wondered what sort of software would decide that she and Morghan, of all people, were compatible to work together to whatever ends they would need to as Allies. But, she found herself smirking at them all. She wouldn't argue with the fact that she'd managed to snag herself the Wolf, the Dragon Rider, and an Arebus Archer.

"That division will be the biggest," Valentina sighed. "For now. I'm not certain, but I have a feeling more Allies will join you all in the future."

Each Ally turned their curious gazes toward the Prophetess as the words left her mouth, and Ash found her stomach fluttering at the thought of expanding their team. But *who* would be the next Ally? She imagined that she would likely lay awake at night pondering who it could be, or who *they* would be.

"I do know for certain that there *will* be an eleventh Ally," Valentina announced, and Loren's mouth fell open. "I don't know who they are, so don't bother asking," she told the king before he had a chance to say a word.

"As for the Green division," Benjamin steered the conversation back in the right direction, "it will be led by Quinn McBride."

The Archer jumped at the announcement, his eyes widening with shock. "You want *me* to lead a division?" He shook his head, shooting the Prophetess a disbelieving look.

"The software chose you," Grant told him. "You've got great leadership qualities."

Quinn stared at the Draconian, clearly stunned, but said nothing more.

"The other members of the Green division are Lucinda Cross and Craven Amsterdam," Benjamin added quickly, confusion flooding his face.

"You chose *me* over the Realm Sorceress and *Craven?*" Quinn gawked at them.

"The *software* chose you," Grant clarified.

"I'm a *horrible* leader," Craven told Quinn.

"And I'm already leading a league of Sorcerers," Lucinda added with a bright smile. "The last thing I need to do is lead you two."

Defeated, Quinn sulked in his chair.

"And the Black division," Benjamin sighed through his nostrils, clearly having had enough of being interrupted, "will be led by Marcus Bonaventure. The remaining members are Vincent VanCamp and Anastasia Volden."

Anastasia's grin stretched from ear to ear as she stuck her tongue out toward Marcus. "Somehow I had a feeling we'd get stuck together."

"Great," Marcus huffed.

"Well, the software has spoken." Morghan sighed. Grant gave the Wolf an appreciative nod. "What happens now? We leave?"

"We'll brief throughout the rest of the weekend, while Henry finishes up with your uniforms," Loren replied. "It gives you all some more time to get acquainted with your divisions, and your team as a whole. I suggest you maybe have a nice meal together."

Ash fought not to frown. She wondered how the King thought anyone of them would be hungry after learning what they would have to do.

33

*L*incoln found himself standing in a study, surrounded by people he didn't know. But he couldn't care less about who they were. The only person he cared about was the king sitting behind the desk beside him.

The Archer stood in silence, the familiar weight of his bow on his back. The weight was comforting, as if without the weapon, he wasn't whole.

While Lincoln might feel complete in his uniform, and as he ran a hand over the feathers of the arrows in his quiver, he felt empty all the same. The only desire he had was to obey. To earn the favor of the king beside him.

And perhaps another desire, for the magnificent woman standing on his other side.

Soroya.

She spared him a sidelong glance, her red-painted lips spreading into a devilish smirk. Lincoln remained still, unwilling to portray any emotions in front of the others in the room. Though he was sure she'd enjoy watching him endure any punishment the king might give him. This was all a game to her. A wicked, sinful game. And Lincoln was willing to play.

When they were alone.

"Where is he?" the king barked, tensing in his oversized chair.

"Shall I go fetch him, Your Highness?" Lincoln offered.

"No, wait," Alrich directed, his eyes squinting as they met the Archer's. Lincoln held the Pandora's stare, his blood chilling in his veins. Every time he looked in Alrich's eerie red eyes, he felt the pain of the injections he'd given him. The burning. The begging to make it stop, even if that meant death.

The door to the study was flung open, and a man clad in black passed through before shutting it behind him. The Prince. He scanned the room, his nose wrinkling as his eyes fell on Lincoln. The Archer bit back a hiss.

"Good of you to join us," Xavier snapped sarcastically.

"What's all this about?" The Prince matched his father's tone without even a hint of kindness in his eyes.

The king frowned deeply, thrumming his fingers atop his large oak desk. Lincoln could see that he was restraining himself but wished he wouldn't. He wished he would stand up and make his unruly son bow before him. Or better yet, allow Lincoln to do it for him. But he knew why Xavier was patient with Malachai. Without the Prince, he'd have no Pandora, or weapons, or an army. If it hadn't been for the Prince, the King wouldn't have won his throne.

If he needed to play nice with him, then so be it.

"We've received word from the Rat," Xavier announced, lifting a letter with a broken red seal. The Prince crossed the study in quick strides, his black robes swaying around him. He took the letter from his father's hand and read it quickly. He appeared to be unmoved by the letter's contents, but Lincoln could see the shock and worry flash through the Prince's eyes for a fraction of a second before it vanished.

"And what do you plan to do about this?" Malachai asked through clenched teeth.

"We've been preparing for this day for a long time, Malachai," Xavier reminded his son softly. "However, we didn't anticipate for the Messenger to be a VanCamp. Especially not this wilding they've snatched from the Strip. Now, the stakes are higher. Ash wears the Sectra, which means we need to intercept her before she finishes those three tasks. There's no doubt in my mind that if she invades Solaris City and our Kingdom, with the amulet and the Scepter she will destroy it all."

Malachai nodded, his expression grim. "What will you have me do?"

"We're getting there," Xavier growled. "To start, we must protect our bases. I'll be sending Ryole and his second and third to oversee them. Ryole will go to the Regal Mountains, Savron to the Lakelands, and Cade to the Forest of Fools."

"What about Storm?" Malachai pressed, his brows pulling together.

"I've sent Storm to the Regal Mountains as well, but to protect the Coven and aid Veda if she needs it," Xavier replied, reaching for his glass of water. He took a long sip before he continued. "Lincoln and Alrich will recruit Mortals affected by the energy we've been sending out into the Realm to add to our numbers."

For a moment, the Prince stared at Lincoln. The Archer didn't move, and instead held his gaze, unblinkingly. "You think he's ready for that?"

"Whether he's ready or not is none of your concern," Xavier snarled. "You focus on your own task."

"And that is?"

"Dispatch Ash VanCamp. I don't care how you do it. But the sooner, the better. That way, we avoid her invasion of this kingdom altogether. And, once you bring me that sweet Sectra around her neck, the Immortal Kingdoms will have no other choice than to take a knee. With their armies, we'll have no trouble taking Erim. I still don't understand why she hasn't used the Sectra herself to name herself High Queen, as she could. The only odds are that she hasn't realized the position she now holds, or that the Immortal Kingdoms are refraining from telling her what she's capable of doing. Either way, it doesn't matter. If we can get our hands on the Sectra, we'll do what she hasn't done. Take the Realm. Take the Armies. Move forward."

The Prince said nothing and instead stood as still as a statue. Lincoln watched him, attempting to read him. He wondered if the task he was given frightened him. Was it possible? Had the man who'd destroyed Death Valley and drove the Werewolves into near extinction gone soft?

"How do you want her? Flayed?" The Prince arched a brow.

"Maybe cut her into pieces and send each of her limbs to the other kingdoms?" Ryole chuckled from his place in the corner. "Maybe we should keep her head, put it in a shadow box and keep it on display."

Ryole's minions, Cade and Savron, chuckled beside their commander. Lincoln's eyes rolled.

"And what of Soroya?" Malachai changed the subject.

"I'll remain here," Lincoln's temptress sighed. "One of us has to remain at father's side. Besides, someone needs to prepare Solaris in the event that you fail."

For the first time, the Prince smiled. Lincoln could see, just by watching the pair as they gave each other dirty looks, how close they were. Sibling rivalry, at its best. Even in the midst of a war.

Siblings.

Lincoln's brow furrowed at the thought. Did he have siblings? He took a moment to wonder. *No.* He shrugged. He supposed he didn't.

It had taken Malachai every ounce of energy to keep his composure during his meeting with his father. He'd completed difficult missions before. But this. *This?*

After carefully exiting his father's study, Malachai kept his chin high as he closed the door behind him. The others remained within, discussing the details of their gruesome tasks. Every soul in that study played a wicked part in this next masochistic phase of his father's game of war.

Malachai swallowed hard as he imagined the Mortals Lincoln was tasked to recruit. The portal evolving in the skies above the Idonian Kingdom was at fault for their changes. At first, the Prince had been skeptical about the entire idea. Rerouting ancient Fae Magic from the portals that used to thrive across the Realm seemed like a surefire way to piss of Queen Cleo. But either she hadn't noticed, or she'd decided the stolen Magic wasn't worth approaching the Dark King.

Xavier had planned to use the Magic to create a *new* portal. One strong enough to bring him to other Realms, bypassing the Galactic Gates. But, of course, he'd conjured a second devilish plan. Veda had laced the Magic with her own *Black* Magic, including a spell that would give Mortals throughout the Realm abilities and strengths they hadn't had before. Perfect new assets to the Dark Army. It was Lincoln's job to fetch them all.

Thankfully, Alrich would be with him. That thought was comforting to Malachai, seeing as he wasn't sure exactly how horrid the Archer was now. He'd known the injections would wipe away his memories, but whatever Soroya had done to the Archer had turned him into an obedient, angry dog, and Xavier was about to let him off his leash.

Malachai had certainly drawn the short stick. His stomach churned as he stormed down hall after hall, seeking the safety of his own quarters. He was to dispatch the Messenger. Slay her before she made her way to the Sovereign's Scepter. Rip the Sectra from her neck and give it to his father. He would hand Si Realtra over to Xavier.

Malachai barreled into his quarters, slamming his front door behind him before he placed his hands on his knees and doubled over, forcing himself to breathe.

Ash VanCamp. Malachai's dirty little secret. But now, she was no longer in the little haven Crane had become for her. She was in Dracus. She was the Messenger.

What sort of sick and twisted reality was Malachai now facing? How could he keep the only promise he'd ever made when Ash was the very being destined to destroy his father's growing empire?

There wasn't much Malachai could do about anything now. He knew, as he fought the urge to wretch on his foyer floor, that all bets were off. He needed to bury what was left of his mortality and do what needed to be done. He no longer had a choice.

"Sorry, Pat," he muttered.

34

*A*sh refused to allow herself to feel. She'd forced any inkling of fear from her mind as she and her fellow Allies endured the endless meetings regarding what was to come. They'd prepared, as much as they could. And tomorrow, the journey would begin. Though she tried, she couldn't escape the feeling that some of her Allies wouldn't return to Dracus.

Now, they'd all gathered in Marcus's apartment. She'd helped him all day to prepare a meal big enough to feed them all. Some members of the council would join them, and she'd needed to count the settings at his large dining table at least fifty times to make sure there were enough.

Richard had arrived early, likely drawn in by the alluring scent of roasting chicken. He stood beside Ash now, looking over her table settings. At first, she wasn't thrilled to have King Loren's Second breathing down her neck. But, without him, all the silverware would have been on the wrong side of the plates.

"Are you ready?" Richard asked softly.

"Nope," Ash replied. "But that doesn't matter."

"I'm sure you'll do just fine," he told her, patting her shoulder.

"Did you two want to help pour wine or are you just going to stand there staring at your reflections in the silver spoons?" Marcus grumbled from the kitchen. Ash released a heavy sigh before stalking off to pour wine.

Marcus watched as Ash and the other Allies crowded around his living room table. Alistair had found a deck of cards, and he was beginning to believe that Lucinda might have placed a spell on them. The Sorceress hadn't lost a game of *Bullshit* yet.

It was either that, or she'd developed the talent of reading minds.

"You're a filthy liar," Lucinda accused Morghan, who picked up the pile of discarded cards in defeat. His hand was now thicker than all the rest, and he wore a glare unlike any other the Mentor had seen.

"Quite an interesting troop," Valentina mused from beside him.

"I'm not sure what the Moons were thinking." Benjamin winced.

"Did you notice," Loren mentioned thoughtfully, "that three of you were also a part of the mission to rescue Penelope? That the Moons chose the warriors with enchanted swords?"

Penelope gasped from beside the king. "How strange!"

"I'd say it's a coincidence," Benjamin said.

"Or," Valentina chimed, "it wasn't a coincidence at all. We'll never know."

Dinner was eventful. Laughter filled the apartment, bouncing off the glass walls. Ash feasted upon all the delicious foods she and Marcus had slaved over all day and washed it all down with blood and wine.

There was no mention of the tasks, which she was grateful for. For one last night, she wanted to relax. The others seemed to have the same idea, and Ash smiled at the sight of Cooper and Quinn falling into conversation with the others so easily. Looking at them all now, you wouldn't have known they were seconds away from being slaughtered if Valentina hadn't intervened.

Ash felt her communications chip buzz in her pocket, and she fished it out to see who had messaged her. Ebony. The Healer. "Oh!" she gasped as she read the message.

"What is it?" Vincent asked curiously.

"Hartford, the Berserker, is here," Ash replied, her heart quickening in her chest. "She's comparing our blood samples and will summon me later to discuss them."

"He has impeccable timing," Loren said sarcastically.

"At least he showed up at all," Lucinda mentioned. "Getting that Berserker to leave the mountains is like telling a Mermaid in Minora to leave the water."

"Ah," Anastasia sighed dreamily. "What I would give to be on a white, sandy beach in Minora with some beverage with an umbrella in my hand. I don't care what it is, as long as it's strong."

"One day," Craven told her soothingly, patting the Fire Clan Leader's shoulder.

Later that evening, Ash and Cooper helped Marcus clear the table and serve dessert. Richard opened a bottle of champagne and passed it around the table so everyone could fill their glasses for a toast. They toasted to the future, and the Dark War's inevitable end.

The clock struck ten, and Penelope rose from her seat. The Princess cleared her throat, drawing everyone's attention. Ash eyed her with a wrinkling brow, wondering what it was that she was about to say.

"I have an announcement," Penelope beamed, her bright smile nearly glowing. "I'll remain here in Dracus until Xavier is thrown off my throne."

Vincent had grown rigid in his seat beside Ash, and she could sense the tension thickening in the air. "You're supposed to be married to Aveo this spring," he reminded their sister nervously. "He'll be expecting you to return to him."

Penelope's smile faltered at the sound of her brother's words, and everyone around the table maintained their silence. Ash wasn't completely aware of how things worked in the Kingdom of Elves, but she didn't doubt for a moment that Vincent was loyal to the Chamberlains. While they'd certainly conspired against Penelope, and Ash herself, it wouldn't change all the Elves had done for the VanCamp children that had grown inside their city of gold.

Ash looked toward Marcus as if he might know what Penelope would say next. But the Mentor appeared just surprised as Vincent.

"I won't be marrying Aveo." The kindness faded from Penelope's eyes as she spoke.

The sound of someone choking on their drink was the only sound to be heard. Ash looked over to see Morghan patting Lucinda's back and fought against a smile.

Vincent was quiet. So quiet that Ash's stomach churned. She wasn't even sure if he was breathing.

A silent, cold war seemed to evolve between Ash's

siblings. She shrunk in her chair, unsure of what was about to occur.

"The Idonian Council decided it," Vincent reminded his sister, and Ash could see a subtle fear flash through his eyes. He looked toward Loren, as if to beg the king to say something that would change her mind.

"No," Valentina mentioned. "We had no say in who the Chamberlains chose to betroth her to. They merely informed us who they'd decided upon."

"We just didn't argue with them," Richard added.

"You'll sever your ties with them," Vincent warned. "You'll righteously piss them off."

"I will not allow the Elves to manipulate me, especially once I ascend to my throne. I love Thaddeus and Esmeralda dearly. I love their children even more. I loved their nephew." Penelope's voice strained, her eyes growing misty. "But I know how they will try to use me. I will not rule Idona and Si Realtra. They will."

Every Ally around the table sucked in a nervous breath in unison. Even Ash went still, her eyes growing wide as she pondered what Penelope had said. She may not know how to act in court, or anything about how these kingdoms worked, but she knew the line Penelope had just crossed.

The accusation on the Elves was more than just a shock to every soul around the table. Penelope's words were strong enough to start a war.

"So, what will you do then?" Vincent snarled. "Hide in Dracus? Hide from them? Create tension on our ties with them until they *snap?*"

"I will not hide," Penelope growled, her grip tightening around her glass of champagne.

"Then what will you do? Send them a letter and apologize for betraying them?" Vincent rose from his seat, and

Ash winced beside him. "You may eventually become High Queen, but if you're not in their favor you're going to make *all* of our lives a living hell. What if they refuse to help us now? What if they won't allow the Elven Army to come to our aid when we attempt to take our kingdom back?"

Ash felt herself blanch. Would the Elves do that? Would they deny helping them if Penelope refused to marry Aveo?

"You have no idea what you're risking," Vincent accused. "You might *enjoy* the fact that you don't have to marry Aveo. You might *love* the idea of no longer being a puppet beneath their strings. But you've royally fucked *us*." He gestured to the Allies. "Who could you marry now? Who would be willing to betray the Elves as well? You've failed to realize that while we might be VanCamps, we have *nothing*. Our father's army is *gone*. We need that alliance and you know it."

When Loren stood from his seat, Ash's throat grew dry. She looked toward Marcus once again, only to find that his head was in his hands. Craven was as pale as a ghost. Morghan simply sipped his champagne. The McBrides looked toward one another, likely as confused as ever. Lucinda and Alistair were stiff in their seats, their backs as straight as boards. And, Anastasia appeared enthralled with the drama.

"If the Elves decide that Penelope's unwillingness to marry the Commander is cause enough for them to selfishly keep their army from joining the rest of us on the battlefield, then they'll be making a grave mistake." Loren seemed unfazed by the idea, and Ash could see that he wasn't afraid of the Elves in the slightest.

"So, you're willing to start another war?" Vincent shook his head in disbelief.

"If it comes to that," Loren replied. "I surely hope it doesn't."

"We've endured thirty years of war already," Vincent spat. "And you're going to keep Idona from the peace it deserves over a betrothal?"

Penelope's nostrils flared.

"It's selfish," Vincent declared. "You're selfish."

"Vincent," Lucinda barked, her amber eyes narrowed in warning.

Vincent paid the Sorceress no mind and instead continued with his harsh words. "You're not even a queen yet. You're no different from Ash and me. You have no title, no army, no court, and no kingdom. Even if the Draconians are willing to help you, if you start a war with the Elves you won't win. You'll damn us all."

"The Draconians *will* help." Loren's tone remained remarkably calm despite Vincent's hateful words. "And Penelope *will* be Queen."

"Only after Ash wins her throne back *for* her!" Vincent thundered.

Ash's heart was in her throat as her gaze darted between her siblings.

Loren shook his head and said, "She will be Queen no matter what happens in the Idonian Kingdom."

Whatever reply Vincent had vanished from the tip of his tongue. Ash stared up at him, her heart thundering against the walls of her chest. A deafening silence spread throughout the room once again, one tainted with the aftermath of her brother's harsh words and Penelope's evolving rage.

"What are you saying?" Vincent asked the king, his tone so soft it was startling.

"That I will be the one marrying Penelope."

Ash's breath hitched as she watched her brother shake

his head before storming out of Marcus's apartment. The sound of the front door slamming startled everyone, and even though she'd been expecting it, Ash still jumped in her seat.

Everyone around the table stared at one another as Penelope and Loren took their seats, now hand in hand. Ash chugged the rest of her champagne, as many others did. No one said a word as they digested all that had just occurred.

The Werewolf was the first to speak, amusement flickering in his caramel eyes. "Well, congratulations."

35

Ash was still unnerved by her siblings' fight, though she tried to push thoughts of it from her mind as she approached the infirmary. Sleep had escaped her, and she'd found herself staring at the ceiling for most of the night. Though she wanted to understand Vincent and his fear, she couldn't help but feel bad for Penelope. It was no secret that she'd loved Cedric, and that if he were alive, none of this would have happened. But, if she loved Loren too, why shouldn't they be together?

Frowning, Ash walked through the empty streets of Dracus, watching as the sun began to rise. She had an hour before she was supposed to meet the other Allies in the square, beside the black butterfly fountain. From there, each division would head to their designated Pandora base.

The Ally uniform felt far more comfortable than Ash had imagined. It wasn't far off from the original Draconian uniform she'd been given. The design was the same. The impenetrable fabric, new-aged chain mail, or so Benjamin called it, was snug against her skin. The jacket bore a hood to shield her face as they traveled throughout the realm. A sapphire-colored diagonal stripe ran from her left shoulder down to her right hip. The same color lined the inside of her jacket, where she held a small arsenal of daggers.

Last night, before everyone had dispersed, Loren had given her one of his father's swords. *Lionheart.* It wasn't an enchanted weapon, but the king told her it was made of the strongest steel in the Realms. King Sampson of Zerin had given it to the great Lion Mason after he'd aided him in the second Zerinian civil war a hundred years ago.

Ash ran her hand over the gold hilt as she glanced down at it. The base of the hilt was in the shape of a roaring lion, and the cross-guard flowed as if it were the beast's mane blowing in the breeze. The grip was wrapped with gold intertwining with silver, and a single diamond the size of a strawberry adorned the pommel. It truly *was* a beautiful sword, and Ash was grateful for the gift. She only wished she could find a way to properly thank the king.

The walk to the infirmary felt like an eternity, but Ash appreciated the silence. It was calming. But, once she arrived in the infirmary's empty stark-white tiled halls, her nerves spiked. She pulled in a deep breath as she approached Ebony's office, passing the elevator where she'd pushed Axel to the ground on the way. At least now she had a name for the moving steel room.

Ebony was waiting inside her office with the tallest man Ash had ever seen. His hair fell in light brown waves to his waist, his skin speckled with scars. Lucinda had said he hailed from the Regal Mountains, yet it appeared Hartford was a mountain himself.

"Ah, so this is the lass," Hartford mused as Ash closed the office door behind her. He looked her over, his brows pulling together. "You mean to tell me this tiny thing is my kin?"

Ash's head tilted slightly to the side. "Kin?"

"All Berserkers are my kin," Hartford clarified. "But I have none other than you, as my brothers and sisters were torn limb from limb during the Age of Monsters. They were set aflame, so their bodies would never knit back together."

The sudden horror took Ash aback, her mouth falling open.

"By who?" Ash fought not to gawk at him. "I thought the Age of Monsters was a time of unity for Idona. Where everyone pulled together to defeat them. It was what brought peace between the Draconians and the other kingdoms."

"Witches." Hartford shrugged.

"Yet you remain in the Regal Mountains where they also live," Ebony glared. "What makes you think they won't eventually come after you?"

"I can handle myself, milady."

Ash snorted as she watched the silent exchange between the Healer and the Berserker. She waited patiently for them to speak but didn't miss the tension rising. But not the bad sort of tension. Ash's couldn't help but cringe the moment Ebony batted her thick lashes. Ash cleared her throat to draw their attention and hopefully put an end to their silent flirtation.

"So, am I a Berserker then?" She lifted a brow.

"Indeed." Hartford gave her a nod. "Strange sort, though. I imagine you won't be as strong as I. Poisons would likely be able to do you harm, as well as some enchanted weapons, depending on the type."

Ash nodded, having expected as much.

"But blows on the battlefield won't put you down," Hartford added with a cheerful smile. "I bet you'd endure the knitting process."

Ash cringed at the thought. "Sounds pleasant."

"It is when you wake and realize you didn't die, even when your opponent cut your head clean off."

"But what *sort* of Berserker might she be?" Ebony chewed on the end of her pen.

"There have been other kinds before," Hartford explained. "We're divided by the color of our eyes. My sort was the first, created by the Moons themselves. Some sort of being manifested before us and left us golden crystals. I know, it sounds foolish, but it's true. I was just a boy then, four hundred years ago. But despite my mother's wariness, my father did as the being had asked. We brought those crystals to our lips and breathed in the power. Our eyes began to burn golden. My clan was known as the Golden Berserkers of Dairth."

"And the others?" Ash pressed, sliding into a chair.

"The others were created by a Sorcerer in Minora who desired to replicate us. The Blue Berserkers. But they were deemed abominations by their fellow Minorians and were hunted down and tossed into the Underworld." Hartford's expression turned grim, and a chill swam down Ash's spine. "There have been no others until you, lass," he told her. "Though I sense another presence. Something has awakened in the Idonian Kingdom."

Ash felt the color drain from her face, her heart stuttering to a stop. "What sort of something?"

"I'm not sure. I'd investigate, but I don't particularly have a death wish," Hartford replied. "I wonder what color of Berserker you'll be."

"How would we find out?" Ebony chirped.

"Piss her off."

"Excuse me?" Ash rasped.

"Berserkers all have a rage we can't control. It's like a box chained shut deep within our gut. When we're angry or threatened it unlocks, and we become stronger." Hartford began to pace as he spoke. "I'd love to teach you more, but a little birdie tells me you're to leave and complete some tasks."

Frowning, Ash wished for a moment she could stay in Dracus for another day and pick Hartford's brain.

"I'll be in Dracus for a while," he said, as if he had heard her thoughts. "When you get back, I'd be happy to tell you everything I know and teach you about your inner-Berserker. I can't tell you how happy I am to have kin again."

"So, what was the verdict?" Craven asked as Ash approached the square. She was happy the other's hadn't arrived yet and lowered herself onto the stone edge of the fountain.

"I'm a Berserker, alright," Ash sighed. "Though not as strong as Hartford. He said poison and enchanted weapons could still harm me."

Craven sulked at the sound of her words, crossing his arms across his chest. His uniform was nearly identical, aside from the green stripe running across him. It was odd, in Ash's opinion, to see that stripe be anything other than red.

"Why the long face?" Ash kicked at his boot with her own.

"I wouldn't want my only clan mate to die," he admitted easily. "So, stay away from poisons and enchanted weapons. On second thought, hand over your daggers."

Ash chuckled. "Not a chance."

The pair remained silent for a moment, watching as the sun began to rise above the mountains. Icy mist from the waterfalls flew toward them as the wind changed directions. Ash used her air abilities to keep it away, unwilling to freeze before they'd even crossed the Unity Bridge.

"I'm surprised we're not on the same division," Craven mentioned, his eyes falling on her sapphire stripe. "We fight well together. For a moment, I wondered if we'd be battle companions."

Ash's eyes grew wide at the thought. "I figured you were destined to be companionless, since you've gone so long without one."

Craven glanced toward her, his violet orbs meeting hers for a moment. "When you're as strange as I am, that's how it seems. But then you came along, with all of your own strangeness."

"Perhaps we should name our two-person clan *the misfits*," she suggested, watching as a faint smile finally appeared on his lips. "And just because we're not on the same division, it doesn't mean we're not battle companions. It just means that we have to share our strangeness with the others, is all."

THE OTHER ALLIES ARRIVED, AND AFTER A LAST-MINUTE briefing about where each division was supposed to go and what they were supposed to do, the gate between them and the Unity Bridge began to creak open.

The other Draconians had gathered to see them off, and each stood with a fisted hand over their heart. A symbol of respect shared throughout each of the five Realms.

Tears dripped from Valentina's eyes as they passed her by, one by one. Loren inclined his head to each of them, including Vincent, despite their spat last night. Benjamin,

Grant, and Humphrey pressed their fists against the fist of every Ally as the line passed them by. Penelope took Ash's hand for a moment, and though they shared no words, she could see the begging in her eyes. To win. To come back.

Ash swallowed hard against the lump forming in her throat as she set foot on the glass bridge. The heights made her stomach flutter, and she pulled in a breath before forcing herself to walk. She kept her eyes on the forest ahead, the waterfalls so loud she could barely head the Draconians cheering.

She didn't dare look over her shoulder to view the kingdom for what could be the last time.

Behind her, Morghan whistled a merry tune. The soothing sound was calming as she cleared the second half of the bridge. Icy snow crunched beneath her boots as she arrived on land, releasing a heavy sigh of relief.

The Allies would travel to the village of Redding and then head their separate ways. Ash and her division would head to the Lakelands, while Quinn and his division would head toward the Forest of Fools. The Black division would head to the Pandora base near Lorcan, just outside of the Regal Mountains. Their journey would be the shortest, and since it was crucial they attack each base in unison, Marcus had vowed to travel slowly, though he wasn't happy about dragging things on.

Mindless chatter took place between the Allies as they trekked toward Redding. Ash found herself unable to speak and lost in her thoughts instead. Quinn walked beside her, baring no expression upon his handsome face. She occasionally glanced toward him, and their eyes would meet. They really didn't need to speak to know what the other was thinking.

Oh how far we've come from home, Ash thought.

IT TOOK NO LONGER THAN AN HOUR AND A HALF TO GET TO Redding. The Draconian village was buzzing with life, as if they weren't in the midst of a Red Winter. The villagers took notice of the Allies and stopped dead in their tracks then bowed before offering the symbol of respect. Ash felt her cheeks heat with a vivid blush as she glanced toward the Sectra hanging around her neck.

A barkeep waved, offering for them to step into his tavern. Ash looked toward Quinn, and then toward Marcus. The two men shrugged before taking him up on the offer.

While Ash would rather get to work, she didn't mind the idea of a refreshing glass of ale before she said her goodbyes to the other divisions.

They gathered around the bar, each of them taking a tall cold glass in their hands. The barkeep asked to take their picture and said he was an aspiring photographer. Ash looked toward the other Allies who nodded, and they each held up their glasses and grinned from ear to ear. Ash fought not to blink at the flash as she thought of whether this would be the only picture she'd have of all her fellow Allies.

36

Goodbyes were hard enough, so the green division hadn't said any before Quinn and the others began their journey toward the Forest of Fools. He led the way, though he had no idea where he was going. Thankfully, Benjamin had thought to sew miniature information chips into the sleeves of their jackets, and whenever any of them wished, they could use them to view a holographic map of Idona. Every once in a while, he would check to make sure they were on the right track.

"You know, you could just ask me," Lucinda reminded him softly.

Quinn's cheeks heated with embarrassment as he glanced over his shoulder at the two Immortals following behind him. "I'll admit, I have much to learn about this Realm. He sighed, turning his attention toward Endurion Lake, which sat on his right. He admired the ice-covered waters, watching as the surface sparkled in the early afternoon sun.

"Before long, we'll pass through the village of Witherow," Lucinda explained as she moved to walk beside him, leaving Craven by his lonesome.

"I know of Witherow," Quinn told her. "They're the only other village our Justice Keeper, Drake, trusts. They know of Crane's existence and aid us by providing us with the weekly paper, clothing, and whatever else they can offer."

The Sorceress gasped softly beside him. "I have so many questions about your village," she revealed sheepishly. "Ash once said the secrets aren't hers to tell. But surely you can at *least* tell me about that invisibility barrier surrounding it."

"I don't know how it got there," Quinn told her sadly, wishing he could tell her more about the matter.

Lucinda frowned slightly. "Well, there aren't many people who can perform an eternal spell like that," she informed him, her hands clasped behind her back. "I can, and our prior Realm Sorceress, Amethyst, could as well. I imagine she might have placed it there, which interests me. What sort of connection could she have had to Crane?"

"What makes you think *she* did it?" Craven asked from behind. "What if a Witch did?"

"The only one strong enough to do something like that would be Veda." Lucinda shot the Draconian a dirty look over her shoulder. Quinn chuckled, having found the Sorceress's expressions to be quite entertaining. "And why would *she* do something kind enough to protect a village in that way?"

"Is she really *that* bad?" Quinn asked, though one look from the Sorceress made him wish he'd never asked the question.

Lucinda hung her head for a moment, and while Quinn expected for her to appear angry, her shoulders slumped with sadness. "Veda was my mother's dearest friend," she admitted. "We lived in the city of Aren, in the Regal Mountains. I wasn't old enough to remember what their friendship was like before I became ill. I was six at the time. I recall them fighting about something once, and the next morning I woke up unable to breathe. My lungs had filled with fluid, and my temperature was high enough to kill me. None of the Witches in Aren knew what to do for me, so my mother rushed me to the Elders Estate in Ryiah. I died there."

Quinn was struck silent. He fought not to gape at the Witch, his heart clenching in his chest.

"They brought me back. When I awoke, my hair was this strange shade. I asked for my mother, but she had left. The Elders told me she'd gone back to Idona to fetch my things, including my favorite stuffed animal. A rabbit. One my father had given to me before he'd gone missing." Lucinda released a shuddering breath, her lip quivering as she continued. "My mother never returned. Eventually, when I grew older and graduated as a Sorcerer, I returned to Idona. Our home was filled with cobwebs. The wood floors in my bedroom were stained with blood. My mother's blood. My stuffed rabbit was still on the bed, stained with blood as well, as if she'd been holding it when Veda came to kill her."

Quinn's mouth was dry as he looked toward Craven, wondering if he had known. The Draconian appeared to be just as shocked as he was, his nose wrinkling with a coming rage.

"That's why I don't want Ash anywhere near Veda." Lucinda straightened, holding her chin high. "She's as wicked as they come. And, while I've fought her plenty of times over the years, I have not yet defeated her. Even with my scythe, which is undoubtedly one of the deadliest weapons in this Galaxy that isn't a Sectra. One day I'll succeed. I'll finish her."

THE GREEN DIVISION WAS STILL CLOSE ENOUGH FOR ASH to smell as she led her own division along the Strip. Another crack appeared in her heart as she thought of Quinn, Craven, and Lucinda facing a Pandora Base on their own. At least their base contained explosives, and one spark of Craven's electricity would set them off. Lucinda was powerful enough to take on the camp on her own, but that didn't mean she wouldn't worry. She couldn't help herself.

Morghan walked beside Ash, having combed this Realm enough times to lead them anywhere. He was like a walking map, and his senses were strong enough to keep them out of danger.

The air was cold, despite how early into Winter Solstice they were. Ash wasn't even sure what day it was. She imagined that Giving Day was quickly approaching, but that she'd likely still be in the field when it took place.

"So, Messenger," Morghan drawled. "How are you feeling?"

Ash glanced up at the Wolf, noting how strange he appeared in his uniform. He'd been so adamant, once, on the fact that he'd never set foot in an Immortal Kingdom. That he wouldn't be a puppet. That everyone wanted a piece of him.

She cleared her throat and said, "Fine, I suppose."

"It doesn't sound like it," he replied with narrowed eyes.

"I'll live." Ash hoped. "But what about you? How angry are you with the McBrides for dragging you into this mess?"

"We did no such thing," Cooper nearly shrieked from behind her.

"I have a feeling that had they not dragged me from my comfortable home, Valentina would have hunted me down, anyway. Perhaps herself." Morghan sighed through his nostrils, driving his hands into his pockets. "It appears this is my destiny, or so she says."

Ash nodded, having been told a similar thing by the Prophetess once upon a time. "Funny," she mused. "We met that day in the forest with no clue as to what was coming, yet here we are now. Marching toward our impending death."

"Our fate has intertwined, or so it seems."

"We are *not* marching toward our impending death," Alistair declared, and Ash could feel his eyes burning on her back. "We will *shred* this Pandora Camp and defeat the Red Witch, and then I'll steer clear while you approach that… beast."

Cooper snorted, and Ash glanced over her shoulder to see him shake his head. "One Arebus arrow and that thing is down for good." He patted the Dragon Rider's shoulder. "Don't worry, Ward, I'll protect you."

"Says the man who let Ash walk off on her own on those mountains." Morghan gestured toward the Strip that stretched for miles beside them.

Ash peered off into the distance and realized her Elven eyes couldn't find the end of the mountain range. She gulped. They had a long journey ahead of them—at least a week until they made it to their destination. She hoped that Benjamin had packed enough blood.

"It was *one* time," Cooper snapped.

"Your brother will never forgive you if it happens a *second* time," Morghan warned. "Don't think I didn't hear that conversation you two had this morning."

"I can handle myself." Ash held up a hand to silence Cooper from saying another word.

"And now I'm here," Alistair added. "She'll be fine."

"Well, you have a Dragon," Cooper said softly.

"Speaking of the beast," Morghan grumbled. "We could really use its assistance in the Lakelands."

Alistair was silent for a moment before he said, "She's laying eggs, so I intend to leave her alone."

"Perfect timing." Morghan frowned.

"Eggs?" Ash ceased her walking for a moment to turn and look at the Rider.

The smile on Alistair's face was revealing enough for him not to say anything. "From what I've read of Dragons, they lay eggs every five hundred years. It appears now is the time. She isn't the only mare who's laid them, at least four more have. They typically lay twenty eggs each. This is what they've been waiting for to rebuild their forces."

"Exactly how many Dragons *are* there?" Morghan gawked.

"Thirty-four."

"That's a blood army!" Ash gasped.

"Before you ask," Alistair frowned at her, "I am only the Rider of *one* Dragon. Willa. I can't speak to the others; therefore I have no control over what they do. I don't even have control over what Willa does. She just helps me."

Ash's smile widened at the thought of thirty-four Dragons overtaking the skies. "Do you think others will choose Riders?" she inquired, her heart quickening at the thought.

"Hopefully," Alistair sighed. "What a dream that would be. Another Dragon Age at the end of the Dark Age. Idona reborn."

Night had fallen, and Marcus directed his division to cease their walking for the evening. They set up camp just outside of Lorcan, while Anastasia headed into the village to gather information about the base they would approach.

Vincent remained silent as he helped Marcus pitch the tent. Benjamin had only packed one, for the sake of traveling light. While this at first seemed like a great idea, now that Marcus was staring at the size, he cringed.

"At least it comes with an invisibility cloak," Marcus mentioned from his place atop a fallen tree-trunk.

The Elf nodded but didn't utter a word as he roasted the rabbits, they'd hunted on the way there, over the fire Anastasia had so graciously created.

"You can't keep silent during this entire journey," Marcus told him, sipping his thermos of blood.

"Yes, I can," Vincent finally spoke.

"I understand why you're worried." Marcus frowned, worried himself. "But truly, Penelope marrying Loren isn't a horrible idea. The Elves should have considered him to begin with."

"They chose Cedric because it was obvious that they loved each other," Vincent explained, his tone laced with pain over the Elf's loss. "They chose Aveo after because aside from Beck, he's the most powerful Elf in the Realm. His family is incredibly prestigious. They're house is large. They complete a large portion of the Elven Army."

Nodding, Marcus was incredibly familiar with the Calloway's. "But would you rather your sister marries a Commander, or a *King*?"

"I'd rather her not start a war."

"Well, you should know that after you left last night, they told us they wouldn't be saying anything about the matter until *after* we seize the Idonian Kingdom," Marcus explained, his lips twitching toward a smirk. "Their excuse for keeping Penelope in Dracus is that it's too dangerous for her to travel, since there's no doubt that Xavier knows the Messenger has surfaced. It's likely that he'll try to strike her."

Vincent glanced up from the rabbits, his eyes meeting Marcus's for a moment. "While that's great and all," the Elf frowned, "it doesn't mean there won't be any bad blood between the Draconians and the Elves afterward. In case you haven't noticed," he gestured to his pointed ears, "I'm an Elf. What side am I supposed to stand on?"

Before Marcus could reply, Anastasia came rushing through the trees. She was furious. Flames practically flickered in her eyes.

The Mentor rose to his feet, reaching for Whitefire. "What is it?"

"They moved the fucking base."

37

"What do you mean they *moved* it?" Vincent snapped, rising to his feet as well. The rabbits began to char, but he paid them no mind. "It's practically an entire village. City, even. How could they just get up and move it?"

Anastasia shook her head, now pacing before the fire that intensified with her every step. "The Innkeeper said that it was sudden. That one day, the base was in the valley, and the next, it was gone. She said she sensed Magic was at play, which means some Witch-bitch transported an entire *city*."

"Where is it now?" Marcus's heart was beating so viciously against the walls of his chest that his vision grew spotty. "*Tell* me they didn't combine two of them."

"She had no idea. I asked around a bit more, and some say they believe the Dark Army moved it closer to the Regal Mountains. Maybe ten miles past Dairth, right on the edge of the range," Anastasia spat, her clenched fists trembling at her sides. "Which means we're going to have to find the damn thing. Let's hope we do it in the bloody week it takes for the others to get to their assigned bases. If they haven't moved those as well."

Marcus's blood turned to ice in his veins as he stared at the Fire Clan Leader. "What Witch is powerful enough to do that?" He wasn't sure he wanted to know the answer.

"Veda." Vincent's eyes were wide, his complexion pale.

"Which means she's working with the Dark Army." Anastasia's head was in her hands as she ceased her pacing, dropping into a squat. "Someone should probably call Ash and tell her that her first task might have just combined with her second."

ASH WAS GRATEFUL FOR VIDEO CALL, THOUGH SHE FOUND it quite strange to see Marcus's face on the screen of her chip. The device filled the palm of her hand but was light enough for her to hold up without her arm aching over time. She'd been speaking to Marcus for nearly an hour while the others sat nearby, watching with grim expressions.

"It's been twelve hours since we left, and everything has already gone to shit," Anastasia barked from behind the Mentor.

"Just find the base," Ash directed through clenched teeth. "If Veda's there, don't proceed. Wait for us."

"What about Lucinda? They're going to be farther away. Once news of the other bases going down spreads to the Pandora near the mountains, others could show up. Bigger enemies." Marcus shivered, his brow wrinkling with worry.

"Then we call for aid," Ash said, though she wasn't sure who would dare to come.

Marcus nodded, the worry vanishing from his face.

"We'll find the base," he said before bidding her goodbye and ending their call.

Ash tossed her chip onto the ground as a frustrated growl escaped her. She fought the urge to bang her head against the tree she was leaning against. "I have a feeling the Dark Army is much larger than we anticipated," she admitted, her eyes falling on the others.

"What do you mean?" Cooper squirmed in front of the fire.

"The Pandora were created in the Regal Mountains," Morghan nearly whispered. "It's not wrong to assume they would have friends there. Friends who were exiled by the Idonian Council and would wish to do it harm. Witches, Giants, Trolls." His nose wrinkled with disgust.

Ash reached for her thermos, glad for once that blood often had the same effect as alcohol. "Are you sure your Dragons are busy?" She looked toward Alistair.

"Dragon," Alistair pointed out matter-of-factly. "Not *Dragons*."

Ash's frown deepened as she looked toward the tent they'd pitched. The single tent. She sighed as she pushed herself to her feet. "Let's just sleep while we can," she suggested.

Alistair snuffed out the fire as she pushed into the tent, claiming the cot in the middle. He climbed in after her, and Cooper after him. It took a few moments for the Archer to settle, and Ash was only a second away from snapping at him when he finally grew still.

Morghan enabled the tent's invisibility cloak before he transitioned into his Wolf form outside, since it was decided he would keep watch. She heard the Wolf yawn, though it sounded more like a howl. While sleeping outdoors, in the middle of nowhere, during a Red Winter made her uneasy, she knew nothing would get past

Morghan. Even if he chose to slumber, he would wake at the slightest sound.

Ash found herself staring at the ceiling while the two men on each of her sides did the same. They remained silent as she pulled her blanket tighter around herself and kicked off her boots. For a moment, she felt strange sleeping beside a near stranger, but Cooper's presence was comforting. They'd pitched tents outside behind the McBride Estate in the summer, enough for her to get used to his snoring. The only difference now was that they weren't camping for fun, and it wasn't summer. It was a Red Winter. And it would likely be the bloodiest one yet.

Lucinda shook so viciously beside Quinn that the entire tent rattled. He glanced toward her, a deep frown upon his face. He felt bad for her. He truly did. Knowing her nemesis was turning out to be a bigger threat than they'd anticipated was likely infuriating for her. And they were the farthest away.

"It'll be fine, Lucinda," Craven assured the Sorceress from her other side.

"Marcus and Anastasia might have proven to be strong warriors, but Vincent…" Lucinda's voice trembled. "She'll know who he is. She'll target him."

"Vincent is a man," Craven added. "He can hold his own."

Quinn wanted to agree with the Draconian, but the hiss that escaped the Sorceress told him to remain silent.

"He's Gideon's only son," Lucinda seethed.

"Marcus won't let anything happen to him," Quinn finally intervened. "Neither will Anastasia. He'll be safe. You read the message both Marcus and Ash sent us. You know what her directions were. They're not to approach the base if the Witch is there. The Sapphire division will race toward them. Which means Vincent will have even more protection."

Lucinda seemed to calm beside him, and the Archer released a subtle sigh of relief.

"You don't know what it was like," she whispered in the dark. "To race from that Kingdom with him in my arms. So small. So fragile. So close to death if I made even *one* wrong move. I was afraid to run with him, scared that I would trip. I understand now that he's grown," she said solemnly. "But I will never forget falling to my knees and thanking the Moons the moment I heard that Mika Chamberlain found that baby."

Though he barely knew her, Quinn reached for her hand. He took it in his own and squeezed it the same way he squeezed Ash's hand the day her mother died. These people were strangers to him. But grief and fear were some things they all had in common. And if they wanted him, *him*, to lead them, this was the best he could do.

"What was it like?" Lucinda asked him. "When Ash was found?"

Quinn's heart skipped a beat as he recalled the memory. "I was upstairs in my room, not sleeping, though I should have been. My mother was pregnant with Cooper. When I heard a baby crying downstairs, I thought my baby brother had been born. So, I crept past Lincoln's crib and made my way down the stairs.

"I found them in the family room. My father and Eliza Snow were huddled in front of a fire, rocking a newborn. They were crying. Afraid. She was nearly blue from the cold." He shuddered, tears welling in his own eyes. "Eliza saw me and told me to go back up the stairs. She said everything was fine. The next morning, Eliza was gone with the baby. I didn't see them until the next week, when Cooper was born. When I saw her again, she was pink and healthy. I watched Eliza put Ash in the bassinet beside my brother, and she and my mother joked that they were twins. They spent every day as babies together."

A sniffling sound came from across the tent, and Quinn's brow furrowed.

"Craven, are you crying?" Lucinda asked.

"No!" he snapped.

38

*E*ach day, the temperature grew colder, even beneath the earth. The tunnels beneath Idona were vast, stretching from every corner of the massive Realm, creating a deadly labyrinth. Lincoln gripped his torch and sighed, longing to fill his lungs with fresh air, no matter how frigid it might be.

The shadows of the thirty Pandora following him stretched before Lincoln in the tunnels. They remained in their Mortal forms, carrying whips and various weapons to keep the sixteen Mortals they'd obtained so far in line. Every once in a while, a whip would crack, and a cry would pierce through the air. Lincoln would always glance over his shoulder and give the Pandora a nod of appreciation.

The Archer didn't have the time to deal with the Mortal's disobedience, or their tears. The sooner he delivered the small army of Mortals he would collect, the better. He grinned at the thought of the praise he would get for delivering such rarities to his king.

Their abilities were fascinating. So far, at least. One

man could cause earthquakes but had no control over his gift. The earth trembled every time he became angry, or afraid, and Alrich would have to knock him out before the tunnels collapsed around them.

They'd been to two villages in two days—Blackbay and Witherow. By morning, they would reach the tunnel's intersection where more of Xavier's favored men were waiting for him. They would take the sixteen Mortals back to the Idonian Kingdom, while Lincoln moved on to collect more.

"We'll be heading to Crane next," Alrich told the Archer as he walked beside him.

Lincoln grunted, flexing his fingers at his sides. "How many are there?"

"Just one."

"Just one?" He gave Alrich a long look, his eyes narrowing. "Seems like a massive waste of time."

"I don't think so," his comrade said, handing him the long list of names. He gestured to the name of the girl they'd retrieve tomorrow and Lincoln found himself staring at it, confused by its familiarity. "She's not like the Mortals we've been collecting."

"What is she?"

"A Witch," Alrich replied, his tone flat as usual.

"Interesting," Lincoln mused, running his tongue over his teeth. "But, why would a Witch be hiding on the Strip? I thought they'd all joined Xavier's forces."

The Pandora didn't respond and instead continued to walk beside Lincoln in silence as they approached the intersection. The Archer decided not to press him about the matter, respecting the fact that there were some things that even the King's precious Dark Recruiter shouldn't know.

TRACKING DOWN THE MESSENGER WOULD LIKELY BE harder than killing her. At first, Malachai had flown to Dracus in the form of a hawk with the two Pandora he'd chosen to aid him. He didn't know their names. He didn't care. He was too busy hiding in his own mind, mentally restacking walls against his feelings brick by brick.

The Prince wasn't surprised when her scent vanished just after the Unity Bridge. She'd likely learned a few tricks from the Draconians, specifically their notorious tracker.

However, there was one scent Malachai was familiar with that lingered in the air. *Morghan Henning*. He scowled as he perched on a tree in the forest that stretched all the way to Redding. He and his two followers were high enough to avoid the eyes of the guards that patrolled the area, and he watched them eerily, debating whether he should use them to practice all he'd do to the Messenger.

It took the Prince a while to debate about what he should do. The Rat had told them who the Allies were, but he'd said nothing about who was accompanying who as they departed for the Messenger's three tasks.

If he followed Morghan's scent, it might indeed lead him to the Messenger. But what if it led him to one of the Archers, or the Realm Sorceress? His feathers ruffled at the thought. Their arrows didn't miss, and Lucinda Cross's spells were far-reaching. She was powerful. Malachai was sure he could take her but fighting her now would be a waste. Not when there were bigger enemies for him to play with.

His followers watched him, waiting expectantly for the Prince to decide his next move. His anger intensified as his patience wore thin, and he ultimately decided to follow the

Wolf's scent. If the Messenger wasn't with him, well, he'd torture everyone that was until they told him her location.

Malachai took flight, pushing through the air with a vengeance. He rushed toward the Wolf, unwilling to waste more time. He wanted this task over so he could live to hate himself another day.

39

It had been three days since Ash had left Dracus, and she hadn't slept a wink since the first night. They hadn't bothered to set up camp again, and she and Alistair both avoided using their abilities to conserve their energy for the coming battle. With the black division in far more danger than they'd anticipated, it was crucial they destroyed their base immediately so they could rush to aid them. Time was of the essence.

Ash felt her chip buzz in her pocket, and she slowed her pace as she reached for it. "Take a small break," she told the others as she stepped behind a tree to read the message.

Her stomach fluttered nervously when she saw Beck's name flash across her screen. She swallowed hard against the lump forming in her throat as she opened the message. Her eyes widened more with each word that she read, and she debated whether she should call Quinn.

"What's wrong?" Cooper must have taken notice of her paling complexion. She looked up at him, her breath catching in her throat.

One look toward Alistair and Morghan told them to back away and give the pair a few minutes of privacy.

"We'll find something to eat," Alistair offered as he and Morghan slipped further into the trees.

Ash glanced toward her surroundings. They were still beside the Strip, and the towering buildings of Mayfire were visible off in the distance. Her blood chilled at the sight, knowing that while the city still stood, it was no more than a shred of what it used to be.

"Well?" Cooper pressed.

"Read it." Ash handed him her chip and watched as his face twisted with disgust.

Cooper shook his head, handing her chip back. "They're kidnapping Mortals now. Great," he groaned. "But why would Beck tell *you* that?"

"Because…" Ash's words tangled in her throat as she stared up at the Archer. Her eyes lingered on his black bow for a moment too long, a shiver running down her spine. "I asked Beck to help me find out what happened to Lincoln. He's been tracking him by scent. And where the scent has led him, people have disappeared. He believes Lincoln is at fault for the disappearances."

Pain flashed in Cooper's eyes, his mouth falling open and then closing quickly. She knew he didn't want to believe her. She didn't want to believe Beck, either.

"Lincoln wouldn't do that," Cooper insisted. "He wouldn't work for them willingly. Morghan said he was *dragged* from Crane. If he's doing anything, it's because they're forcing him to."

Every fiber in Ash's body *wanted* to believe what he said, but she'd seen Lincoln change over time. He'd become angry and distant. He'd wanted to re-establish the Rebels, to ascend to a position of power over them all. He'd wanted to punish the Immortals for their silence, and their failure to protect the Mortals in this Realm. Was this his way of doing that? Joining the Dark Army? She nearly choked on her own breath as the thought swam through her mind.

A rustling in the trees surrounding them led Ash to bite back her reply, unwilling to allow Morghan and Alistair to hear her thoughts about the matter. But it wasn't the Rider or the Wolf who jumped from the trees. It was three large Pandora wolves, teeth bared and claws ready to strike.

Ash sprang into action as Cooper loaded his bow with three arrows beside her. The Pandora took one look at the Archer and his glowing blue eyes and hesitated long enough for her to summon the earth around her.

The ground shook as roots pierced through the earth, wrapping around the wolves. She could hear their breath constrict as the roots tightened around their necks.

Ash snarled, debating whether or not to steal the air from their lungs as she drew two of her enchanted daggers. Their red eyes bulged at the sight of them.

"Shall I kill them, or should you?" Cooper arched a brow.

The Pandora struggled against the roots, slowly but surely smothering beneath their weight. Ash debated taking a seat, reaching for her thermos, and refreshing herself with blood while she watched them die.

"Maybe we should put that amulet to use," Cooper added with a smirk. "See exactly how powerful the Sectra is."

Ash's heart soared at the thought, but the Pandora began to transition in front of her. She blinked against a flash of light, summoning earth once again to keep them restrained. She fought the urge to stagger backward as she took in their Mortal forms. Her blood ran cold as she stared at the Pandora in the middle, her dagger's immediately flying toward the unfortunate souls on his sides.

Blood splattered on the snowy ground as the Pandora faded to black mist. She didn't dare take her eyes off the man she'd left alive to watch the mist seep into the Underworld.

Ash had seen his face before. In the papers Eliza had collected. Her chest grew tight as she scanned his face, and his all too familiar features. Long black hair fell past his shoulders, shining in the sun's fading light. His red eyes were narrowed into slits, a hiss sailing past his clenched teeth. Her pulse thrummed in her ears as her eyes fell on the symbol on his black-hooded cloak. Three intersecting swords embroidered with shimmering crimson-red thread.

The roots tightened around the man's throat as Ash felt that box Hartford had mentioned unlock deep inside her gut. Her blood heated, rage coiling in her stomach.

Cooper took one look at her and stepped back, his face flooding with confusion.

"Malachai," Ash snarled, tightening the roots even more.

MALACHAI COULDN'T BREATHE. THE ROOTS WERE SHARP, digging into the flesh of his neck. The scent of his own blood flooded his nostrils. His face grew numb, likely turning blue. His head throbbed, the blood vessels in his eyes threatening to burst as he stared at the woman in front of him.

She was beautiful, and it disgusted him. Her eyes were burning silver, glowing more and more as the seconds passed by. He could smell her strength and her power. He watched as shreds of sapphire began to invade her irises, swimming toward her pupils in thin, swirling lines.

Panic began to set in. *The amulet,* he inwardly cursed, for he couldn't speak even if he tried. If she set it off, she'd obliterate their surroundings. Her Allies. The forest. The animals hiding in the trees. He doubted she had any idea on how to control the weapon.

And those daggers. Malachai's eyes fell on them, on the earth beside him. They'd killed his subordinates so fast; they were gone before he'd had a chance to blink.

"What have you done with Lincoln?" Her voice rattled in his ears like thunder.

Malachai shook his head, unable to answer her, though he didn't want to. She'd kill him. He cursed himself. He'd fallen into this trap so easily. What sort of Prince of Darkness was he?

"He can't answer you, Ash," the Archer spoke softly, though his eyes portrayed the same sort of disgust the Prince had seen in Meera VanCamp's eyes.

The Messenger growled, the sound animalistic, as she reluctantly loosened the roots around his neck. Air filled Malachai's lungs. He pulled it in, nearly choking on it as the spots in his vision faded away.

"What have you done with Lincoln?" she asked again, her eyes shining as her connection to the amulet intensified.

If Malachai answered, and he told the Messenger the truth, she'd kill him. Part of him wasn't afraid of death. In fact, he'd welcome it.

"He has no memory of you," the Prince rasped. "I created a series of injections to erase his mind. He remembers nothing."

"Why?" she roared.

Malachai held his tongue. He pushed his mortality

even further down, reminding himself that feeling nothing was better than enduring the pain of breaking the hearts of others. Princess Penelope's scream still rang in his ears from when she'd found her betrothed's body pinned to his headboard by the lance Malachai had thrown.

"Tell me," she ordered, reaching for another dagger in her boot.

The Prince stiffened, wincing in pain as the roots dragged against his flesh once again.

"Or I'll slit your throat and drag your corpse across the Realm for everyone to see the same why you dragged Lincoln from those mountains," she declared, pointing toward the mountains with her dagger.

"Even if I tell you, it won't do you any good," Malachai warned, his voice coarse. "He's lost to you. Even if you managed to capture him, and good luck with that, he'd fight you tooth and nail. He's here physically, but he's gone all the same."

The Messenger stared at him, all emotion vanishing from her beautiful face. He stared back, waiting for her to strike. The dagger in her hand would end him quickly. Before he knew it, he'd be standing in the Underworld beside his ancestors, leaving this war for his father and his new pet to finish. He might relax, enjoy the heat of flames.

"Well?" Malachai asked. "What are you waiting for? Just kill me and be done with it."

She blinked, the blue fading from her eyes and only leaving the silver behind.

"No," she said with a shrug.

"What?" the Archer gawked at her.

Malachai's mouth opened to speak, but before any words rolled off his tongue, she hit him. Her nails dragged across his cheek, drawing lines of scarlet blood. He fell backward, his eyes wide with shock.

"I'm not going to provide you the satisfaction of killing you." She stared down at him, nothing but humor in her eyes, her lips set in a vicious smirk. "I'm going to make you suffer. I'm going to take you on an adventure. You can watch me while I destroy *everything* that you love. And maybe, just *maybe*, I'll kill you, eventually. But I won't make it quick. I'll drag it out. And I can't wait for the day where you beg me to make it stop. *Beg* me."

Malachai swallowed. Twice.

The scent of the Wolf hit the Prince like a wall as he approached, none other than Alistair Ward at his side. Their gazes drifted from him, to the Messenger, and to Cooper before landing on him once again.

Ward held his shirt in his hands, and after a moment, he released it. Berries fell onto the earth beside the Prince, some bouncing off his head.

"What the hell, Ash?" Morghan snapped.

"Don't curse in front of our guests, Morghan," the Messenger snapped. "Be polite. Don't you know you're in the company of a prince?"

40

Quinn stared at his brother's solemn face, his heart pumping rapidly in his chest as he fought the urge to chuck his chip into the forest. He wondered, silently, if he would prefer how he'd felt when he'd thought Lincoln was dead.

Lucinda and Craven sat nearby, staring vacantly at their hands.

"She's truly going to keep him?" Quinn asked, pushing thoughts of Lincoln from his mind. He couldn't think of him. Not when Ash was dragging the Prince of Darkness behind her like a dog on a leash.

Cooper nodded, his expression grave. "She wants to make him suffer," he whispered, as if he were afraid Ash might overhear. "I do too, of course. But this is dangerous. Too dangerous. Who's to say he won't break free and kill her? Even with the enchanted chain Morghan used."

"I'm sure she could trap him again, if she did it so easily the first time," Craven said warily. "But Marcus is going to lose his shit when he finds out."

"We shouldn't tell him," Cooper blurted, and Quinn could see that his brother immediately regretted the words.

His frown deepened, sadness and worry written in the creases of his brow. "It's just... it'll only complicate things. And, while she hasn't said it, I think that Ash believes if the Prince ruined Lincoln the way that he did, that he can fix him too."

Lucinda snorted, raking a hand through her long hair. "That man has never done anything kind. Why would he help the woman destined to turn his father's growing empire to ash?"

Quinn knew she was right. But he knew Ash, likely more than anyone else. More than even Lincoln. She was sick with grief over him, so much so that it was heartbreaking. She wouldn't give up on him, even if he didn't remember her or any of them. She'd make a deal with the Prince of Darkness to save him if she could.

"I say Cooper kills him," Craven grumbled. "Her anger toward him would be far easier to deal with than the entire sapphire division lying dead on the ground while that *Prince*," he said the name with such disgust that Quinn cringed, "runs back to his father with the amulet."

"If he makes one wrong move, I will. No questions asked," Cooper declared before ending their connection.

ASH FELT NUMB. SHE STARED AT THE FIRE, PLAYING WITH the flames, watching as they danced. Some swirled up into the air, others took the shape of horses, running in circles.

The sound of twigs snapping made her aware that Cooper was returning from ratting her out to the green division. She made sure to give him a good, long glare as he took a seat beside the fire.

"Don't look at me like that," Cooper growled.

She ceased her playing with the flames, her eyes narrowing as she said, "I'll look at you however I please."

Malachai's snort from across their small campsite was enough to make her eyes burn silver again. She wondered if she'd ever experienced pure *hate* until now. Just looking at him made her blood boil. She found herself needing to constantly fight against the urge to summon more roots to strangle him once again.

If it hadn't been for the Wolf and his small collection of useful tools that he carried in his pockets, Ash would have drained all her energy dragging the Prince around. Now, his wrists were bound together by an enchanted chain. The same sort that cradled her amulet. The chain could only be removed by the same hands who'd put it on.

While Richard had originally placed the amulet around her neck, for theatrics, he'd made sure to find her later that evening and remove it so she could replace it herself. Now, she was the only one who could remove the chain.

And she was the only one who could remove Malachai's chains, too.

"Permission to hit him?" Morghan lifted a brow.

"If you do, avoid his eyes. If they're swollen, he won't be able to see what we're about to do to his precious Pandora," Ash replied, reaching for her thermos. She took a long sip, her eyes falling on Alistair, who sat as silent as could be, staring into the fire. He'd barely said a word since he'd returned to them to find the Prince in Ash's grasp.

The Prince was watching him too, as if he were waiting for him to say something. For a moment, she wondered if he was going to pester the Rider, but instead he turned his gaze on Cooper.

"You must be the baby McBride," Malachai crooned. "What a shame, for you to have to live in the shadow of your elder brothers."

Cooper grew rigid across from the fire. Ash watched a muscle twitch in his clenched jaw and drew in a nervous breath.

"You know, the Arebus only cherish their firstborn sons. Those that come after mean nothing to them, or *meant* nothing to them," the Prince continued, sporting a sinister smile. "A second son is usually bad enough. But a third?" He clicked his tongue. "Those are just a waste of life."

Ash gave Morghan a warning glare, to hold the Archer back if needed. The Wolf gave her a nod before inching closer to the Prince, blocking Cooper's path if he chose to strike.

"My father considered you, though," Malachai mentioned. "But Lincoln was the better choice. I'm sure you understand. After all, he's stronger, smarter, and even more handsome, or so my sister thinks so."

Ash bit back a snarl as her gaze darted between Cooper and the Prince.

"I'm surprised that the Moons thought you were worthy enough to join the Messenger," the Prince pressed further, searching for a reaction. "But who am I to judge their bad decisions?"

The sound of Cooper's heart racing flooded Ash's ears, and she was sure that the others could hear it too.

"Shut your mouth," Alistair growled.

"Oh." Malachai perked, straightening his spine. "The Rider speaks. For a moment, I was beginning to think you were maimed like the rest of your family."

And that was it.

Cooper barreled past Morghan so quickly that Ash was sure he'd vanished and reappeared right at the Prince's throat. His fingers were wrapped around his windpipe, his grip so tight that his knuckles were turning white.

Morghan, clearly stunned, rushed to stop him. Ash held her breath as she watched the Wolf throw the Archer off the Prince, Cooper wincing as he hit the ground. She rushed to him, helping him up before dragging him away from Malachai, who was pinned beneath a snarling, massive gray wolf.

As she passed the fire, she took a hold of Alistair's uniform jacket and trudged him along as well. She waited until they were far enough away from the crackling fire before she released them both.

Cooper was trembling so viciously she'd wondered if he'd load his bow and fire an arrow that wouldn't miss the Prince's heart. She'd been so focused on the Archer that she hadn't realized the angry tears flowing from Alistair's eyes.

Another crack seared through Ash's heart as she looked at him, the pain of the Rider's past written all over his face. She hugged him without thought, bringing him as close to her as she could. Her head only rose to his chest, but that hadn't stopped her from squeezing him, hoping she could somehow make him feel even the slightest bit better. No, she didn't know the details of what had happened to his family, and she'd never ask. She didn't want to know.

It took him a moment, but Alistair hugged her back, his breathing ragged.

"I don't know what you think you're doing," Cooper told her. "But I want Lincoln back as much as you. And the second we get him, and fix him, I want to watch one of *his* arrows rip through that bastard's dark heart."

The other two divisions had been strangely silent, and while Marcus wondered why, he had other things to worry about. They'd found the base in the early morning on the fifth day since they'd left Dracus. The sun had just begun to rise when Marcus picked up on their scent. He and the others had trailed it, carefully and quietly, until they found the base—not near the Regal Mountains, but within them.

They'd needed to retreat. For now. The others were still two days away from their locations, unless they wasted their energy using Immortal speed. Marcus frowned. He wished they would, seeing as if that were the case, he wouldn't have to hide on a mountain range crawling with Idona's finest criminals.

Anastasia had gone to scout the base, and though he worried for her, she was lighter on her feet than he or Vincent. He'd only agreed to send her alone because the Pandora slept during the day. As long as she could avoid the beasts that stayed awake to patrol, she shouldn't run into any trouble.

"You let her go rather easily," Vincent mentioned as he

reclined against a tree. He didn't appear uneasy about their surroundings, not in the slightest.

"She knows the terrain," Marcus told him. "Before she became the Fire Clan Leader, shortly before I arrived in Dracus, she was stationed here. For years, she aided Gideon's Mortal Army in monitoring the range's inhabitants. That base these bastards moved had once been her home."

Vincent spared the Mentor a glance, his sage eyes filled with curiosity. "I hadn't known that."

"She and Humphrey worked together closely in these mountains," Marcus added. "Back when I was a toddler. Before he moved to the Idonian Kingdom."

"Wasn't it Humphrey who found you?" Vincent seemed fearful as he asked, and Marcus didn't blame him. It was indeed a sensitive topic. One he didn't often allow himself to think about.

The Mentor nodded, clenching his jaw at the memory.

"You don't have to talk about it if you don't want to," Vincent told him, his voice soft and kind.

"There isn't much you don't already know," he replied, his stomach churning as memories of his childhood, and lack thereof, began to overwhelm him. "I awoke one morning when I was ten. Alone. My family had vanished without a trace. I became a pickpocket to survive, but eventually Gideon's Royal Guard caught on. The King sent Humphrey to seek me out. One day, he followed me home, straight into my pile of treasure. He threw me over his shoulder and walked me through Solaris City, all the way up to the castle."

"And that was that?" Vincent smiled.

"And that was that."

The rest of Marcus's story was no secret. Everyone knew of the twelve-year-old boy Gideon and Meera

VanCamp had taken under their wing. Some even considered Marcus to be their first son, though there was never an official adoption. But still, Meera was the mother he'd never had. And if he had memories of his *real* mother, he'd buried them so far deep within himself, he doubted he'd ever recall what had happened to her.

LATER THAT DAY, ANASTASIA RETURNED, COVERED IN DIRT from head to toe. Marcus wasn't sure he *wanted* to know where she'd been, and how close she might have come to getting caught. He simply turned the other way as she dove into the tent to clean herself and swap her filthy uniform.

When she joined them, she stole Marcus's chrome thermos and nearly chugged its entire contents. He frowned, knowing there wasn't much left between them. Vincent held the remaining thermoses in his own pack, and he'd likely be hesitant about giving either of them some until *after* they'd obliterated the base.

Soon, they would need to hunt the old-fashioned way. Marcus just hoped the deer on these mountains weren't diseased.

"So?" Vincent urged Ana to speak, nearly trembling with anticipation.

"Veda isn't there," Anastasia breathed, her lips stained with blood. "But I watched reinforcements arrive. Some large, scarred Pandora in his mortal form with two massive broadswords on his back. I heard them call him Ryole."

Marcus blanched. "Why would they call for reinforcements if they don't know we're coming?"

Ana shrugged, though he didn't miss the shred of fear in her charcoal gaze. "Maybe they do. Maybe waiting for the others to strike is a waste of time."

"How would they know? It's not in the papers, Loren made sure of it." Vincent rubbed his temples, his face wrinkling with worry.

"We should tell the others, just in case Xavier sent his other minions to the other bases," Marcus suggested, reaching for his chip in his pocket.

ASH FELT HER CHIP BUZZ ONCE AGAIN AND GROANED THE second she saw Marcus's name. She'd known he'd call eventually, but she'd been dreading it all the same. One sharp glare toward Morghan told him to push Malachai into the brush and keep him there.

Once they were in the clear, Ash accepted his call, only to find both Marcus *and* Quinn staring back at her. Her heart halted, and she silently prayed this wasn't an intervention.

"What's going on?" Quinn asked, and Ash caught a glimpse of Craven walking behind him. She smirked at her Mentor, who smirked right back.

"We've found the camp. There's no sign of Veda, but Anastasia watched reinforcements arrive. Someone named Ryole. It appears they might already know we're coming."

Ash had never seen Marcus appear quite so spooked, and the sight was enough to give her goosebumps. She bit at her lip, cursing beneath her breath as she glanced toward Morghan. The Wolf stood, half in the brush and half out, his left foot likely crushing Malachai's windpipe to keep him from speaking.

"Any idea who Ryole is?" she asked, her eyes narrowing.

Morghan looked down at the Prince beneath his feet. She watched him snarl, baring his sharp canines. After a moment, he looked up at her and said, "I think Ryole might be a commander in the Dark Army. Undefeated from what I hear."

"What should we do? Sack it now?" Ana asked, and Ash could have sworn she heard the Fire Clan Leader crack her knuckles.

"If they already know we're coming, why not?" Quinn asked. "We're half a day away from our location. I've been dreading this enough. I'd like to get it over with."

"We can make it to the Lakelands in a few hours if we use Immortal speed," Alistair mentioned. "Right now, we're beside Mayfire. The base sits on the north side of Ardon Lake. If we hurry, we can get there by nightfall."

"Before, preferably," Ash muttered. "I'd rather catch them while they're sleeping."

"Then it's a plan." Marcus loosened a nervous sigh. "We'll ready ourselves and hit the base now."

"Watch out for Ryole," Ash told him. "And be careful."

Marcus gave her a nod before severing their connection, and Quinn bid her goodbye before severing his as well. Ash imagined the next time she spoke to either of them, they'd have finished with the first task. At least she hoped she spoke to them again.

Morghan released Malachai, and the Prince struggled to his feet sporting a wicked scowl. Dusty boot imprints were visible on his cloak, the entirety of his black uniform ruffled.

"I assume you can use Immortal speed? Or did you accidentally leave that out during your little science experiment?" The Wolf glowered at the Prince.

"It would be easier if I could shift, but it seems your chains prevent me from doing such a thing," Malachai snapped.

Morghan chuckled, clearly pleased with himself. "I'm

glad you're enjoying them. Though, I didn't take you for the submissive type."

Ash winced at the dark, long look the Prince gave the Wolf. "We don't have a lot of time to waste here," she intervened, stalking over to them before taking a hold of the Prince's dirtied cloak. "You'll run, or I'll drag you. Your choice."

ON THE WAY TO THE BASE, MALACHAI HAD RELUCTANTLY informed Ash about what was waiting for her there. She hoped he couldn't see how pale she'd become. *Savron.* Her stomach churned as the sun set over Ardon Lake. A Sorcerer, one with a specialty in illusions. *Wonderful.* She groaned.

While Malachai had given up Savron's name and what he was capable of, he'd said nothing about how Xavier had known they were coming. She supposed it didn't matter how they knew, since no matter what, she was still approaching the most difficult battle she would face to date.

Though Malachai's attack on Crane was surely a contender.

"You look a little sick, Princess," he mused as she dragged him beside her. "Worried?"

"Not one bit." She swallowed against the lump forming in her throat. "Are you excited for the show?"

"Will there be fireworks?" Malachai inquired, his eyes falling on her quiver. Ash glanced down at it herself, noting the red feathered arrows.

"As many as your heart desires."

"How sweet of you," he drawled.

Storm clouds hung in the sky, threatening yet another blizzard as Ryole left the only tavern throughout the base and stumbled toward the barracks, his legs wobbling. He supposed he'd had one too many glasses of ale, but a man his size could withstand much more than he'd downed. He reached into his pocket, withdrawing a roll of tobacco and a lighter. He drew the roll to his lip and flicked the lighter aflame, bringing it to its very end as he inhaled the smoke sharply.

The Commander's guilty pleasure, one that he'd never quit. He rather enjoyed how it felt to inhale and then exhale. He loved the way the tendrils of smoke fluttered into the air before dissipating. He loved the scent, so alluring for him yet deterring for so many others.

As Ryole walked, trudging along the snowy ravine the base now sat upon, he scanned his surroundings. Yet another bad habit. His gaze fell on a nearby cliff, narrowing as he searched for any watching eyes. But there was nothing. No sign of the Allies the Rat had reported heading their way.

The barracks were a mere few feet away when he

heard it. The familiar sound of a bow string being pulled. He stiffened, his eyes darting toward the cliff once again, just in time to watch a red feathered arrow sail through the wind, flying straight toward him. He hit the ground before he had a chance to suck in a breath of preparation or shout a warning, covering his head with his arms.

MARCUS HELD HIS BREATH, REFUSING TO TAKE HIS GAZE OFF the Commander as he waited for the blast he knew was coming. "Don't tell me that was a fucking dud," he growled, his fingers gripping the rocky earth he was perched upon.

"Give it a second," Anastasia hissed, her palms out and ready to control the flames once they appeared.

Vincent clicked his tongue on the other side of the Fire Clan Leader. He loaded his bow a second time, and the moment he let his arrow fly, the first one erupted. Marcus watched as flames shot toward the stormy gray sky. The Realm shook around him, trembling as the second arrow exploded no more than a mile south of where the first had landed.

Pandora began to flood out from the barracks and various buildings scattered throughout the base. Over a thousand of them, ready for the fight of their lives.

Anastasia strained beside Marcus, sweat dripping along her brow as she worked to spread the flames. Screams began to pierce through her fire's angry roar, echoing off the mountains surrounding the black division.

As the Fire Clan Leader worked, the Mentor loaded his own bow. He pointed the deadly arrows toward the clusters of Pandora forming in the ravine below. The flames burned bright, heating his surroundings, swallowing those that had transitioned into birds in their fiery grasps.

Explosion after explosion shook the mountains, and Marcus was beginning to wonder if the cliff they'd positioned upon was growing unstable. He swallowed against the lump in his throat as he watched the Pandora burn.

Marcus's jaw clenched as he watched the chaos unfold. He stared down at the ravine in disbelief, his stomach churning. There were only three Allies. They were outnumbered. Severely. Yet, Anastasia's fire and Vincent's perfect aim was enough to turn the tides of any battle.

The mountains continued to rumble, and the Mentor scanned the fiery ravine, searching for any runners. His eyes fell on the Commander, on his feet now, directing his following, half his face red and swollen. Marcus's breath caught in his throat.

"What the hell is *that?*" Ana gasped.

Ryole gritted his teeth against the pain radiating up his right side. He could feel his flesh melting. He could *smell* his flesh burning. He didn't dare raise a hand to touch his face, or even look at his right arm. He'd survey the damage when the enemy was dead.

The Commander had to commend the Allies for their stealth and surprise. "What a waste," he growled as he peered toward the cliff, hissing as smoke stung his eyes. He fought not to choke on the air around him, his lungs burning every time he dared to take a breath.

With no other option, Ryole waved the catapult forward and watched the small unity of Pandora struggle to push the massive machine through the flames. Normally, he'd have barked at them before pushing them aside and loading the machine himself. But his options were limited. He didn't dare move a muscle as he watched them load the bucket with one of their cherished Prince's recent creations.

Just a normal boulder, or so it seemed. Ryole smirked, his heart nearly leaping out of his chest. *Finally,* he breathed, trembling with excitement. He'd been waiting for the perfect excuse to use the newest trick up his sleeve.

"WE NEED TO MOVE, *NOW!*" MARCUS THUNDERED AS HE backed away from the cliff's edge. The sound of a rope snapping sent him into a deep panic, and he watched as Anastasia unraveled one of her favored chains with no more than a flick of her wrist. She flung it toward a barren pine tree, wrapping it around its trunk. She pulled it tight, making sure it was sturdy before she took hold of Vincent and reached for Marcus as well.

On any other day, Marcus would have admired her skill and told her so. He reached for her outstretched hand, his fingers just barely grazing hers when a massive boulder crashed into the cliff. It crumbled beneath him, falling into the ravine below.

The scent of smoke hit the Mentor as he fought to gain his footing. His nose wrinkled, the cliff caving beneath his feet bit by bit. He was falling, he had no doubt about that. He would fall into the ravine below, like a lamb to the slaughter.

But that smoke. He glanced toward Anastasia, her lip quivering as he fell further from her grip. She could smell it too.

"Get off this cliff, *right now!*" he ordered, his voice lost in the cracking of stone and the roaring of the flames below.

Marcus felt his nail beds splitting, the scent of his own blood wafting through the air as he fought to get a grip. It was no use. He pulled in a breath and surveyed the drop. The smoke was far too thick for him to see where he'd land, but he let go anyway. He fought not to cry out as he slid against the sharp edges and rubble. He knew what was waiting for him at the bottom, and he had mere seconds to find a way to leap, hoping he could gather enough distance before he splattered on the rocks below.

Growling, and silently praying to the Moons, Marcus pushed himself off the cliff, reaching to draw Whitefire.

ANASTASIA KNEW SHE NEEDED TO *MOVE*. SHE COULD HEAR the cliff beginning to sizzle around her, the strange smoke filling her nostrils and coating her throat, leaving an awful, ashy taste upon her tongue. She didn't need to know what it was. She didn't *want* to know what it was. All she wanted was to get away from it, as quickly as she could.

Knowing she had no choice, Ana yanked her chain free from the tree, cursing beneath her breath as she and Vincent nearly lost their footing and began to slide on the now slanted terrain.

Sparks began to ignite around them, and Ana yanked Vincent to his feet. She was sure they were a blur as they raced away, fire beginning to bloom behind them. Black flames, growing larger by the second, pummeling toward the two Allies as they rushed for safety.

"We need to get down there," Ana snapped. It was their only option. Whatever this fire was would devour everything in its path, and the raging battle below them was undoubtedly the safest place.

She led Vincent further down the mountain, the distance to the ground below growing shorter with each step they took.

"Now," Ana demanded, taking Vincent's hand before leaping into the ravine below.

They landed, concealed by the smoke billowing around them. Ana could hardly see through it as she scanned her surroundings. Hints of glowing red eyes, black fur, and flames were all that surrounded them.

Ana drew her second chain, summoning her fire to ignite the chains in her grip. She began to whip her way through the crowds of Pandora, their yelps filling her ears. Vincent remained at her side, picking off any beasts that she missed with his broadsword. She fought to remain calm as she searched for any sign of Marcus.

A bright white light began to shine through the thick fields of smoke. Ana released a sigh of relief. *Whitefire.* Marcus was fine. They were fine. They would win.

Marcus was sure he'd broken a few bones, but he pushed anyway. He fought through the crowds, igniting the night around him. The scent of blood and smoke likely drifted throughout the entire mountain range, but if the beasts had any alliances with the Witches or any of other species crawling around the Regal Mountains, they didn't come to aid them.

There was no sign of Veda, even as the smoke eventually cleared and revealed the horror they'd inflicted upon the base. Burned corpses lay across the ravine, some still smoldering. A wicked, unusual fire burned on the destroyed cliff above them, sailing through the mountains at unstoppable speeds.

Marcus recalled what had once happened to the Grimm Estate, many years ago. Cedric Chamberlain's home was destroyed by Amorian fire.

The Mentor's blood chilled at how close he and the other Allies had come to losing their lives to the fire. He'd never seen anything like it. He walked through the carnage, over to where Vincent was counting the dead and making sure that they were, in fact, dead.

Anastasia lingered nearby, panting and pale. Marcus knew she'd used most of her energy, was likely parched and in desperate need of blood. He'd never seen her unleash so much fire, especially in the form of a massive wall that swept through the base and swallowed any remaining Pandora in its path.

"Well," Marcus sighed as he took one last look at the destroyed base, "that was chaotic."

43

Quinn hadn't heard from the other two divisions, and he wondered silently if Ash and the others had made it to the Lakelands, and how they were fairing with the Prince of Darkness as a prisoner. He cringed at the thought as he peered out at his assigned base. It was dawn, and he was tired, but the time to strike was now.

After firing Arebus arrows to dispatch the guards on the four watchtowers that sat in the corners of the base, the trio concealed themselves in the valley between sets of rolling, snow-covered hills. They'd picked the spot with the best view of the base and began examining it—every disgusting inch.

"Review the plan," Quinn ordered one last time, glancing toward Lucinda and Craven.

"I sneak in," the Draconian began with a weary expression. "Find the explosives and set them off with a shock."

"It should be enough to take out more than half of the base," Lucinda added. "Whatever is left, Quinn and I will take care of."

The Archer eyed the scythe in her hand and swallowed hard. It gleamed silver in the early morning light, the crescent-shaped blade sharp enough to slice through rock. A strange, glowing orange orb was positioned in the center of the blade. He'd never seen anything like it and wasn't sure that he wanted to know what sort of Magic pulsed through the weapon.

"I'll use *Inceptstatis* to freeze their movements," Lucinda continued. "Then we'll use Immortal speed to move through the base, picking them off. It should take us no more than forty minutes. Every time the spell weakens, I'll replenish it."

It seemed easy enough, or so Quinn thought. But Craven's task made him uneasy. There was no room for error, and the risks were high. One shock. That was all it would take. But should that shock be too large, or too intense, the man beside him could lose his life.

The electricity that made Craven so unique, and so feared by his fellow Immortals, could bring him to his end.

"I've dealt with worse," Craven huffed, as if he'd read the Archer's mind, had seen his darkening thoughts.

"There's a well over there," Lucinda mentioned softly, gesturing to the stone well that sat on the north side of the base. "If I were you, I'd send the shock from there and then jump in."

"Any clue on where they're holding the explosives?" Quinn asked, his eyes dancing about the various buildings. The barracks, the mess hall, the training centers, he wouldn't know where to begin looking, having never seen such an establishment.

Craven and Lucinda were both silent as they searched, and before long the Draconian snickered. "There," he said, pointing to an older building on the southern side of the base that looked as if it would crumble any second.

"But I don't think I could stand by that well and reach the building with my shock."

Silently, the Draconian rose to his feet. There wasn't a sound to be heard as he began his approach. The snow didn't crunch beneath his boots, and Quinn admired him for his stealth, all while holding his breath as Craven picked up speed, no more than a haze as he ran toward the crumbling building.

CRAVEN COULD SMELL THE POWDER AS HE RAN. HE KNEW, and wasn't surprised, that he'd been right. Though, he still needed to be sure before he sent off the wave of shock that would ultimately take out most of the base.

The explosives were the very reason the green division had been sent to this base, instead of the Regal Mountains or the Lakelands. Because *he* was on the green division. And *he* was the one who could set the explosives off from a hopefully, decent range.

Frowning, Craven wished for a moment that he'd been blessed with normal gifts. Perhaps if he'd been born with the ability to manipulate the earth, he'd find himself less in danger of blowing to bits.

After a peek through one of the broken windows along the backside of the building, Craven confirmed his suspicion. There they were, stacked in crates piled so high they brushed the ceiling. He gulped at the sight of them all, counting each crate swiftly. There were one hundred and ten, and though he wasn't sure exactly how many explosives were in each crate, he imagined there were plenty.

This blast wouldn't just take out half the base, it might swallow the entire thing whole.

He pursed his lips, slowly backing away from the

building as he glanced to where Quinn and Lucinda waited out in the field. Running back to warn them would waste time, and before long, the other Pandora might notice that the guards assigned to the watchtowers were missing. An annoyed grunt escaped him as he drove a hand into his pocket and retrieved his chip.

Craven sent a message to Quinn, letting him know about what he'd discovered. He hoped his comrades were smart enough to back further away, perhaps to even leave him. But, he knew they wouldn't. The thought angered him, as he wasn't worth them risking their lives. Ash needed as many of them alive as possible, if she were to complete the other tasks and face Xavier.

He didn't wait for Quinn to reply and drew Shadow-strike. The obsidian blade shone brightly in the light of the rising sun. Craven glanced toward the sky, taking a moment to view the streaks of oranges and pinks before he turned his back on the beautiful sight. The shadows dancing on the snowy terrain as the sun ascended further into the sky flocked toward the enchanted sword, and he gathered as many of them as he could.

Biting his lip, Craven moved to a safer distance. He didn't care if any Pandora lurking within the buildings noticed his presence. Once he deemed the distance between him and the explosives acceptable, though still too close for comfort, he drove his sword into the earth.

Shadows began to stretch from the blade, and Craven watched them eerily as they traveled toward his target, obeying his will. He could feel the electricity, thrumming throughout his form. He trembled, summoning as much as his body could handle after days of travel with little to no sleep.

One shock.

That's all it would take.

Pulling in a deep, shuddering breath, Craven allowed his electricity to surround his palms. It wrapped around the silver hilt of his sword, swirling in purple streaks as it moved down the blade and into the line of shadows below. It whined, popping in his ears as he pushed it forward, watching as it sailed toward his target.

Seconds.

The entire ordeal had taken seconds, and Craven was ripping his sword from the ground and turning to run for the well as the shock he'd sent barreled into the crates. The entire building imploded as he ran, shrapnel flying toward him as he fixed his gaze on the well, refusing to look over his shoulder.

Bang after bang, building after building. Each boom sounded like an angry crack of thunder, the electricity he'd released flying toward the air like violet streaks of lightning. Still, Craven refused to look over his shoulder. He refused to see the wall of flame rushing toward him but could feel it nearing. Sweat dripped from his brow, stinging his eyes as he blinked. Each breath he took felt like red hot flames, and the scent of his own hair burning made him nearly scream.

Craven dove into the well as if it were a pond on a hot summer's day. He fell at least ten feet into icy water. He was submerged in it, peering down into the dark depths as he pushed himself up, swimming toward the surface. He'd gone from sweating to teeth chattering in a matter of seconds, and his heart felt as if it might explode from fear.

Fires raged ahead, covering the top of the well and Craven's view of the sky. He hissed, the water beginning to warm around him. He wasn't sure if his body had just gotten used to the frigid temperature, or if the water was heating, slowly coming to a boil.

After a few moments, Craven realized it was the latter.

Quinn had never seen anything like it. Even the explosive arrows they'd used to nearly destroy their own village didn't compare to the amount of fire and shrapnel he saw flying through the air. His mouth grew dry as the Pandora's screams ended as quickly as they'd begun.

The outright shock of the entire deal nearly left Quinn trembling, but then he thought of what it was like to grow up in a village in central Idona, where the fight was always the thickest. How many times had Crane been ambushed while the villagers slept? A smirk pulled at his lips. Finally, the Pandora were getting what they deserved.

However, while Quinn wanted to celebrate their clear victory, he wouldn't dare. Not until he was sure Craven was alright. And at that moment, the only thing that could be seen in the base was a large funnel of swirling, glowing orange flame.

"Where is he?" Lucinda whispered; her face struck with horror.

For a moment, they'd been able to see him run. They'd watched as a sea of shrapnel flew at his back. If he'd realized he'd been hit by any of it, Craven hadn't shown it. Instead, he'd run until the raging storm of fire seemed to swallow him whole.

"Can you stop the fire?" Quinn asked, his heart in his throat.

Lucinda shook her head slowly. "I wouldn't dare until the entire base is nothing but ash and bone. But I can walk *through* the fire," she admitted as a wand slid out from her sleeve, landing perfectly in her grasp.

Quinn blinked, admiring the diamonds encrusted upon the white marble wand. It was truly beautiful. A wand fit for the Queen of Sorceresses.

Lucinda whispered a spell that he hadn't heard, but he watched as a strange silver mist began to envelope her. Quinn stifled a gasp, the mist fading away as Lucinda bit on her wand, using her free hands to quickly braid her hair back. She tucked the long plait of blood-red hair into her jacket, pulling her hood over her head.

"Use your mask," he directed, having learned a thing or two back home when the fires used to fight against the Pandora got a bit too out of hand. The less smoke she breathed in, the better.

The Sorceress nodded, handing him her wand so she could fasten the mask around her face. It covered her nose and mouth, nearly rising to her amber eyes, which shone brightly against the black fabric. She took her wand from his hand and rolled her shoulders, giving him a nod before she darted into the flaming base.

CRAVEN HAD NEVER SEEN SUCH ICY WATER BOIL SO QUICKLY and was now beginning to regret every time he had grown frustrated when the stove in his apartment failed to boil his pasta water in a timely manner. He cursed over and over again as he began his ascent, placing his feet against one side of the stone well while his back leaned against the other.

It would be risky, but Craven was out of options. He wouldn't be able to grip the damp stone. Even the rubber tread of his boots had difficulty gaining traction. But, if he didn't move quickly, he'd become Draconian stew. His stomach churned at the thought.

Water was beginning to bubble beneath him, steam surrounding Craven as he braced himself between the well's walls. His back ached as he pushed it against the harsh stone, his legs screaming in agony as they held most of his weight. If he survived this, he'd likely sleep for days.

The flames still raged above, their heat nearly suffocating as Craven inched upward. He found himself in the middle of two horrid options for death. He could try and hold out until the flames died down above, or the water settled below. But as of now, he could either go up further and burn alive, or fall down the well and boil alive. Neither scenario was pleasing to think about.

Growling, Craven held his position. He wasn't sure how much time had passed, but he doubted he could stay this way for much longer. He murmured a prayer to the Moons, the Sovereign, and whoever else might be listening as searing pain shot through his back. His jaw clenched; his teeth bared as he stifled a scream. He wasn't sure what the pain was. A burn? A broken bone? He paled at the thought of a broken spine and how that might affect him during the rest of the tasks, should he survive his current predicament.

The water continued to sizzle below, nearly whispering in Craven's ear as his body weakened. His boots slipped on the stone walls, his injured back barking in agony as he slid down.

A gasp escaped the Draconian as he prepared himself. Perhaps he would see Queen Meera in the afterlife, if there was one at all. Then maybe he could tell her how he'd tried that night the kingdom fell. How he'd tried to get to her in time. That he, a Draconian Lord who'd joined the Draconian Army because he'd simply had nothing left, might have been able to save her from the Dark King.

"Craven!" He heard someone shout his name.

The water was too close now, so much so that he feared that if he even spoke a word, he would be distracted from holding himself up. Tears of agony welled in his eyes. The pain in his back, his aching legs, burns scattered throughout his body, and the heat—it was terrible. So hot that every breath he took seemed to light his lungs aflame.

"Craven!" the voice shouted again, closer now.

His heart soared, though he doubted he'd be saved. He was too close. Too close to the death that awaited him. The slow, painful death waiting in that boiling water below.

But then she was there—Lucinda, peering down into the well with wide, frightful eyes. Half her face was covered in a black mask, but a strand of her strange hair fell free from beneath her hood.

"Can you climb?" It was a stupid question, but he shook his head.

Craven recalled a moment, one that seemed like so long ago now, where a certain Sorcerer had used a spell to lift Alistair Ward into the air above a raging battle. To cast shadows that Craven himself could use against the enemy. *Abernathy.*

"That spell!" he gasped. "Lev-"

The Sorceress had clearly known what he was about to say already, and Craven sighed with relief as he lifted from his spot perched between the stone walls. For a moment, he feared the flames awaiting him above, but it seemed Lucinda had taken care of that as well. No spark of flame grazed his flesh as he landed on the ground beside the well with a thud, the pain roaring in his back once again.

He bit his lip to keep himself from crying out.

"Your head is bleeding," Lucinda mentioned as she stared down at him, her hands on her narrow hips.

"I was just blown up," Craven snarled.

"Can you walk?" She lifted a perfect brow.

"I can manage."

QUINN PACED THE FIELDS IN FRONT OF THE BASE, SWEATING from the heat radiating from it. He wiped his brow, his gaze darting throughout the wall of fire. It wasn't until he watched Lucinda emerge, Craven limping and leaning on her side, that he was finally able to take an even breathe.

"How bad is he?" he asked warily as the Sorceress approached, gently lowering the Draconian to the ground. Quinn tried not to gawk at him. He was bleeding from his head, and there were burns on bits of flesh visible on parts his Ally uniform didn't cover. But, he'd expected him to appear far worse after all he'd just witnessed.

Lucinda shook her head. "He needs a healer," she declared, releasing a heavy sigh.

"Don't you have some sort of... healing spell?"

"There isn't much I can do for his burns, or his internal injuries," she admitted, her frown deepening. "Healing isn't something Sorcerers specialize in. Some Witches, perhaps, but those are gifts that they are born with. And even at that, it's a rare gift to be had."

"So, what should we do?" Quinn asked. "Where is the closest Healer?"

Lucinda's eyes flashed to the forest that sat off in the distance, her brow furrowing. "Technically, Cleo's Safe Haven. But we wouldn't make it there easily. We would only injure ourselves trying to get through the Forest of Fools. It's best we take him to the Kingdom of Elves, where they have immaculate healing springs beneath their castle."

"Then that's where we'll go," Quinn declared, reaching to throw the Draconian over his shoulder. He expected Craven to yelp at the very least, but he remained unconscious, his breathing shallow. *Smoke inhalation.* The

Archer cringed, watching the Sorceress as she retrieved the scythe she'd left on the ground. Once in her grip, the weapon vanished. Quinn blinked, his jaw dropping.

"I'll explain that trick later," Lucinda grumbled before leading the way to the Kingdom of Elves.

44

The Lakelands were truly beautiful. Flat plains with tall grass were adorned with lakes of all shapes and sizes. Ardon Lake, one of the largest bodies of water in the main Realm, sat less than a mile from where Ash stood, admiring them all. Thick layers of ice covered each lake, sparkling in the midday sun, nearly blinding her as the rays of sunlight bounced off the shiny surfaces.

The base sat nuzzled between Ardon Lake and its much smaller sister, Lake Dornear. Ash wasn't surprised to see the size of it, though she'd silently hoped it would be smaller. It was boarded by high stone walls, but she could sense the amount of heartbeats within—enough to make her breathing stagger.

"Nervous?" the Prince inquired, leaning against the tree she'd chained him to just a few minutes before.

"Not a chance," she lied, knowing he could probably tell.

"Don't forget, you promised me fireworks," Malachai sneered.

Ash fought to ignore him and turned to her Allies instead. They were lingering nearby, waiting for her command. She swallowed hard as she approached them, her eyes on Cooper. His black bow was already glowing the same blue as his eyes, revealing a floral pattern that reminded Ash of Spring Solstice. He was ready, or so it seemed. But was she?

"Are we clear on our plan?" she asked, fighting to master her nerves and hoping her tone hadn't betrayed her.

"I still think it's a bad idea." Alistair glowered. "Craven and Anastasia both told us that using our abilities to that extent will drain us. It could cause you to faint, or worse, blood deprivation."

"Well that's what's going to have to happen then." She shrugged. "Unless you know another way through those stone walls."

Morghan eyed the Rider, his brow wrinkling. "A Dragon would certainly be able to fly *over* the walls and incinerate everything within. But, that's just an idea."

"For the last time," Alistair grumbled, "I will not be summoning Willa. Now come off it."

Eyes rolling, Ash pulled in a deep, calming breath. She looked toward Malachai one more time, only to find him lying against the tree with his head tilted back, as if he planned to nap throughout the entire ordeal. Her blood began to boil at the sight, but she forced her attention toward the base. She'd deal with him later.

WHAT HAD HAPPENED IN CRANE mere weeks ago now seemed impossible at the time. A few hundred Mortal villagers against thousands of Pandora hell-bent on wiping their village from existence.

Now, Ash realized, worse could have happened. Now,

there were only four of them against thousands of Pandora, and it was she who had come to destroy them.

The tables had turned.

Her stomach fluttered with rage, that box holding her inner-Berserker having unlocked the second she placed her palms against the earth and summoned a quake that sent the stone walls flying toward the ground, splitting the base in two. The event should have weakened her. She should be on her knees, begging for blood, but the rage kept her moving, fueling her and strengthening her.

It would be Pandora blood staining the snow this Red Winter.

The base, now a heaping pile of splintered wood and stone, was soiled with blood. Piles of black mist blew in the breeze from every Pandora struck by one of Cooper's Arebus arrows or grazed by the blade of one of Ash's daggers.

Dagger after dagger flew from her hands. She drew Lionheart to sustain her each time she needed to retrieve them, driving the blade into beast after beast.

The ground was unstable, the ice having broken upon the nearby lakes, shattering like glass. Icy water flowed into the base, flooding it. It almost appeared as if the lakes were joining, creating one massive body that froze Ash's toes in her boots as she worked to slay the beasts.

Their constant shifting into various animals no longer fazed her. She anticipated it, refusing to tremble as wolves transitioned into bears right before her eyes. She only continued to move forward, her blades against their claws and teeth. Her will against theirs.

The temperature control fabric of her uniform was barely able to keep the chill from sinking into her bones, but the heat of battle kept Ash pushing forward. She wasn't sure how many Pandora were left, but she kept throwing daggers and swinging her sword. She wouldn't stop until there was nothing left, even if she needed to fight until the remnants of the base were deep beneath the water of the conjoining lakes.

Morghan barreled past her in a blur of gray fur, sinking his teeth into the enemy with swift and deadly precision. It wasn't the first time she'd seen him fight, though she was still in awe of him. She imagined how free it felt to run on four legs.

Fire swam through the tall grass around the water's edge, creating a border, keeping any of the beasts from attempting to escape. The flames were left by Alistair's sword, Dragons Breath. It trailed him wherever he went, his sword glowing like an ember in the fading sunlight, the only presence of warmth in this damned frozen land.

Ash's gaze lingered on him for a moment as she took a much-needed deep breath. On the battlefield, he was far from the stammering man who'd bowed and called her princess at the start of their shared elemental test. She smirked at the thought, laughing at the memory before a pair of strong hands gripped her shoulders and thrust her into the icy water.

Ash surfaced, gasping for air. She stared up at a man whose blank, dark eyes were shielded by locks of silver hair. He stared at her as if he'd hated her all his miserable life. As if he'd been waiting for the moment to execute her since he'd crawled out of his mother's womb.

Fear crept up Ash's spine as she watched mist that matched his silver hair seep from his fingers, weaving around them, thickening as the moments passed by.

Magic. She clenched her jaw.

"Savron Phantom," she greeted him, recalling what little Malachai had said about the man Xavier had sent to guard this base. She was surprised this was the first she was seeing of him—the prestigious Warlock turned Pandora. The combination made her stomach churn. Warlocks were perhaps as rare as Berserkers, and just as frightening. Savron had added the ability to shape-shift to his arsenal of tricks.

She hoped he didn't notice her throat bob as she gulped.

"Bitch," he retorted, his eyes falling on the dagger in Ash's tight grip. "What are you doing to do with that? Pinch me?"

Before she could reply, a black arrow flew through Savron's back, dripping with dark blood as it exited his chest, right through his heart.

"I'm sure *that* felt like a pinch," she told him as he dropped to his knees in front of her, revealing one angry Archer standing behind him.

"That's no way to talk to a woman," Cooper growled, kicking the Warlock hard in the back. The arrow snapped beneath his boot as Savron fell face first into the water. Cooper then outstretched his hand and Ash took it gratefully, allowing him to pull her to her feet. She patted his shoulder, breathing a sigh of relief.

MALACHAI STARED WIDE EYED AT THE BASE, HAVING BEEN unable to take his eyes off the entire ordeal since the moment the battle had begun. He'd saved this camp once —from the Rebels. And now, he'd watched it crumble to the ground in a matter of minutes by the hands of *one* woman. She hadn't even bothered to use the Sectra and instead relied purely on her Draconian abilities and her skills with the weapons she was used to wielding.

What was left of the buildings burned, thanks to the

Dragon Rider's fire. Whether he'd used his own abilities or his enchanted sword, that didn't matter. It still burned either way.

Cooper had indeed been underestimated. Nothing got past the Archer, or his deadly arrows. It had been a long time since Malachai had seen a member of the Arebus in action, and he'd nearly forgotten how skilled they were. He was fast. *Impossibly* fast. Whether he was loading his bow, releasing an arrow, or drawing his sword, anything he did was in a blur.

Fireworks. Fireworks indeed.

Cursing beneath his breath, Malachai began to realize exactly what his father and the Dark Army were facing. He'd only had the pleasure of meeting *four* Allies. And the other six, he didn't want to think about them. Not about the Realm Sorceress, the other Archer, or the Electric Immortal. He doubted that Valentina could have put together a more powerful team. Even if they were Mortal instead, between them, they still had three out of four enchanted swords and a Sectra.

Malachai groaned.

The Sectra.

He'd nearly forgotten about the blasted thing, and what he was supposed to do with it.

The enchanted chains still bound the Pandora Prince to the tree, and he pulled against them, cursing beneath his breath. It had been far too long since he'd needed to break free of chains similar to these. Truthfully, he was surprised the Wolf had even had them, and was curious to know *how* he'd gotten his hands on a set.

Then again, he'd put nothing past Morghan Henning. Nothing.

Now, if only the Wolf hadn't underestimated *him*.

ASH WAS FROZEN TO THE BONE AND EXHAUSTED BEYOND belief. But they'd done it. They'd taken down the base in a matter of hours, using everything from earth abilities to fire abilities, to the jaws and claws of Werewolves, and arrows that never missed their targets. Ash might not have been able to see it before, but it was clear now. The sapphire division was indeed a force to be reckoned with.

Sighing, she crossed her arms and surveyed the wreckage. They'd planned, endlessly, on the way here to come up with the perfect approach. They'd foregone sleep to talk about *every* possible outcome. When they'd first learned that so few of them would be taking down complete *bases*, they'd all been uneasy. But late nights filled with ideas and plans had led them to this moment. To success. And now, once Ash figured out what to do with Malachai, she could move on to the next task.

"Oh, we've got a runner!" Cooper announced, loading his bow. He let his arrow fly, and Ash watched as it flew through the air, curving around bends and sailing above the carnage as it found its way to the Pandora's heart. In an instant, black mist was once again seeping into the Underworld. "Oops," he chuckled.

Ash rolled her eyes before she turned her attention to the tree line, her stomach churning. "I should go check on our noble guest," she said. "You three make sure we didn't forget anyone. Wouldn't want any of them to miss out on the fun."

"Aye Capitan." Alistair saluted her, gleaming sword still in hand.

Shaking her head, Ash waved the fire boarder away as she passed through, her legs barking as she ascended a slight incline. As she glanced over her shoulder, she could confirm that during her reckless attempt at sinking the base into the earth, she'd unintentionally joined Ardon Lake with Lake Dornear. She supposed that now, Ardon Lake surpassed Lake Endurion in size. Cringing, she whispered an apology to the cartographers throughout the Realm.

Malachai was still leaning against the tree, a look of pure amusement on his face as his eyes met hers. She forced a grin, her teeth chattering from hours in the freezing water as she arrived before him.

"Did you enjoy the show, Prince?" She lifted a brow.

"More than you'll ever know," he replied dryly.

Ash turned to look toward the mess once more, her heart warming as she watched her fellow Allies walk through the water, using Alistair's glowing ember-like sword as a flashlight to lead their way through the darkness. "I'm pretty sure that's not what that sword was intended for," she pointed out matter-of-factly.

She could have sworn she heard the Prince chuckle beneath his breath, but the sensation of movement behind her had her spinning around so quickly her head swam. She stared at him, hands free from the chains and instantly around her throat and mouth to keep her from screaming for help. She fought to bite his palm and failed as he pulled her against him, releasing her throat. The cool sensation of a dagger running up her side beneath her uniform jacket and shirt made her squirm, panic setting in.

Staring into his eyes, Ash foolishly hoped he'd see her. How badly she was begging for him to stop. But as he stared back at her, she saw nothing in his red orbs, now glowing again furiously, as if he'd realigned with the hateful parts of himself.

The scent of her own blood overwhelmed her senses as the dagger plunged into her side. She slumped against him, tears spilling from her eyes, hot against her frozen flesh as they rolled down her cheeks.

The Prince pushed her away, and she fell on her knees into the snow. He stared down at her with nothing but fury and what, for a moment, seemed like regret. A silent apology. His gaze dropped from her own and fell to the Sectra, hanging around her neck. He reached out for it, his fingers grazing the glowing sapphire in its center, but quickly pulled his hand away and ran.

Ash watched him as he transitioned into a hawk and fled into the snowy night sky. Her breathing was ragged. She wanted to scream, but no sound came out. Not even when her eyes dropped to the dagger in her side. One of *her* enchanted daggers. She cursed, darkness creeping along the edges of her vision as blood pooled in her mouth.

As she fell on her back, she stared up at the now vacant sky. Nothing but snow was there, swirling as it fell to the ground in heaps. Falling harder, faster, covering her uniform and face. It would bury her, as she lay there dying. She could feel the serum, Moonshade, coursing through her veins, racing to her heart. It slowed as she pulled in what was likely her last breath and allowed herself to slip into a state of unconsciousness from which she'd never wake.

45

listair was relieved, now that it was over. He'd been unable to rid himself of the anxiety welling deep in his gut about the attack. Now that it all was said and done, he felt like he could breathe again, and he could think about the next task. Veda the Red Witch. Between all ten Allies, he was sure they wouldn't have much of an issue, no matter how much Lucinda seemed to think so.

He'd rather deal with the Red Witch than the beast in the Forest of Fools any day. His heart sank at the thought of that wretched *thing*. Scars now decorated his flesh because of it. Without Vincent, he would surely be dead. Dead, and not rejoicing in this moment, celebrating that they'd finally finished the first task after a near week of traveling and nerves.

Along with unanticipated surprises.

Maimed like the rest of your family. The Prince's words rang in Alistair's ears as he waded through the water, now up to his waist. He shivered, either from the chill or the memories he'd fought to bury. He'd watched it all. *Seen* what they'd done with his own eyes. The way his six year-old sister's shrieks sent the birds leaping from their branches out of fear, fleeing to the sky for safety.

He swallowed hard against the memory. It hadn't been Malachai who'd done it, but another man with a scarred face. But the Prince had been there. He'd watched from afar, turning his back before one of his Pandora bastards moved on to the child. They'd saved her for last. They'd made Aislynn watch their parents die.

Shivering, Alistair climbed out of the water and onto what he wished was dry land. The snow had begun to fall, hard and fast, covering the tall grass in a blanket of thick white. He scanned the tree line, searching for Ash and that blasted Prince. His heart sank as he realized they weren't in sight, quickening his pace.

The scent of blood lingered in the air, but not leftover from the attack. No. This was something different. Something sweet. Something that made his mouth water instantly. His stomach churned as he approached the tree where they'd left the Prince. His chains dangled around the trunk, swaying in the winter breeze.

"No," Alistair whispered as he turned to view Morghan and Cooper approaching, laughing. As his eyes met theirs, their smiles vanished.

They rushed up to him, eyes wide with fear as they spotted the chains. At first glance, it appeared that both Malachai *and* Ash had vanished. But what the Wolf revealed was much, much worse.

"I hear it," he breathed. "Her heartbeat." His eyes drifted to the ground, just a few feet from where Alistair stood. He followed the Wolf's gaze, his eyes bulging as they fell on the mound of snow.

Alistair dove onto his knees, sliding through snow and slush as he reached for her, pulling her out from beneath the thick layer and onto his lap. He stared down at the dagger, his heart racing as bile crept up his throat. One of *her* daggers. Her *enchanted* daggers.

Cooper was silent behind the Rider, and Alistair didn't dare look up at him as he ripped open her uniform. "Shit, shit, *shit!*" he roared at the sight of black spreading through her veins, racing toward her heart.

"She's a Berserker." Morghan sounded more like he was trying to convince himself of this fact. "This can't harm her. It *shouldn't* harm her."

"We need to move," Alistair demanded. "*Fast.*"

"Move to where?" Cooper was in a daze, his complexion turning green. Alistair finally spared him a glance, his heart breaking at the sight of the tears filling the Archer's wide eyes. Alistair knew that look. He'd *worn* that look.

And *oh* what Quinn would do to his brother if he found out Cooper let Ash out of his sight and she wound up gravely injured. Again.

Alistair had heard the pair argue enough about the matter for his mouth to grow dry at the thought. He didn't want to be anywhere near the McBrides when news of this got out.

"Healer," was all the Rider could manage to say through his sea of horrifying thoughts. "Ebony."

"We won't make it on foot," Morghan barked. "It's too far. A week away."

"Should we remove it?" Cooper looked as if he was about to wretch into the snow. "She's so pale. Are you sure she's breathing?"

"Not for fucking long," Alistair growled, his hand wrapping around the daggers hilt. "Hold her down. She might wake, and this is going to hurt," he warned.

Cooper did as he asked, lowering to sit beside the Rider. He placed shaking hands on Ash's frozen shoulders, a tear dripping from his eye and landing on her cheek.

A hiss rolled off Alistair's tongue as he ripped the dagger from Ash's side. She didn't stir. Fighting the urge to scream, he tossed it onto the ground. Blood began to seep from the wound, rushing in a thick stream on to the snow. "Pressure." His mind whirled as he slipped out of his uniform jacket, wadding it in his fists and pushing it down against the wound. For a moment, he thought of cauterizing it with his fire, or perhaps the hot blade of his sword, but decided it was best to leave that decision to a trained Healer.

Morghan raked a hand through his golden hair, releasing a long breath. "Ward," he said softly. "I think it's time you summon that Dragon."

A frustrated growl escaped Alistair as he gently transferred Ash from his own lap to Cooper's, taking his hand and applying it to his wadded-up uniform jacket atop her wound. "Push," he ordered as he shot to his feet. The cold air nipped at his bare arms, though it was the least of his worries as he walked a few feet away, staring up into the black night.

Silently, he called for her. Willa would hear him. Hear him begging for her help. Hear his apology for tearing her away from her eggs. But he had no choice. Not with the damned *Messenger* dying in the snow, her blood staining his fingers.

It took a few moments, but lucky enough for him, the Skyward Range sat just a few miles west from where he was standing. It wouldn't take Willa long to arrive, and the moment he saw her sapphire eyes flicker, piercing through the night off in the distance, he released a shuddered sigh of relief.

The Dragon landed, causing the already unstable

ground to shift even more. What was left of the base sank beneath the depths of water as Ardon Lake and Lake Dornear meshed even further.

It didn't matter how often Alistair saw his Dragon, or how long they lived together in the Dragons Den, he would never fail to gape at her size. Or how her long, spiked tail wagged whenever she saw him. Though it wasn't wagging now, not when Morghan and Cooper gawked behind the Rider.

Willa's massive nostrils flared.

"No, no," Alistair warned, his gaze darting between his beloved beast and his Allies. "They're friends."

He could see understanding in her eyes as he turned to face the others once again. "Help me get her up. Now." He hoped he didn't sound too harsh, but if he had, neither Morghan nor Cooper said a thing. The Wolf lifted Ash into his arms while Alistair returned to his Dragon. He walked up her outstretched wing, eyeing Morghan warily as he approached with a *very* limp Messenger in his arms.

"She won't eat you," Alistair told him as the Wolf hesitated just before Willa's wing.

Morghan gave him a look that said otherwise as he stepped up the wing and handed Ash over to the Rider. "Be quick," he warned as he scaled back down. "Update us when you get there, and every second afterward."

Alistair nodded, clicking his tongue. Willa perched, readying herself for flight. He sucked in a nervous breath, pulling Ash tightly against him while he held his bloodied jacket to her wound. He'd yearned to be on his Dragon, to feel the air rush past him as he looked upon Idona from the skies above. He'd laid awake at night, thinking about how his stomach dropped whenever she dipped, flying down to the earth. How his eyelids fluttered whenever she went too fast, though he loved it. Loved every second.

This was not how he wanted to take flight again. Not after so much time had passed since that dreadful night where he'd last seen Willa, flying in circles above the Forest of Fools. Roaring. Roaring for *him*.

"Dracus," he told her before she dove into the air. Alistair gripped Ash for dear life, now wishing for a saddle of sorts. He would have loved to take Ash for a ride on the Dragon one day. Show her what it was like to fly. After all was said and done, a way to celebrate their victory. Those two strangers, dying one day in Dracus and living the next. He cursed beneath his breath. This was *not* how he wanted to share his first ride on Willa with another. Especially a woman.

The Realm passed below him in a blur, and as the bright twinkling lights of Mayfire began to sparkle below him, he allowed himself to look for the millisecond it took for them to pass it by.

"No more death," he said. "Not while I'm around."

MORGHAN WATCHED AS WILLA DOVE INTO THE AIR AND took off, as fast as the speed of light. He allowed himself to breathe, though it was painful to do so. His fists trembled at his sides, rage coiling in his stomach. He'd expected it. He'd known Malachai would loosen from those chains eventually. He'd just hoped the Prince would run. Leave the killing for another day.

It was foolish to hope. Especially for the Pandora Prince to come to his senses and *stop*. Just once.

"We should call the others." Cooper's lip quivered as he said the words. Normally, the Wolf would chastise him. Grown men didn't cry. But he'd seen how much these strange people from Crane cared for one another. He'd seen it the day they'd shown up at his cabin on a whim. They'd hoped he would help them. They were foolish, too. But Morghan had helped them, anyway.

Now, he'd helped the McBrides get to Dracus. It had nearly killed them all, but they'd gotten their wish. They were able to see Ash and make sure she was alright. Even he had been curious about the girl he'd fought to save on that cold, winter's night. He wanted to see how she fared as well. However, none of them knew what they were truly getting themselves into. And now, here the Wolf stood, trembling with rage because he'd *allowed* himself to *care* about these people.

Foolish. He was foolish.

Morghan's pocket began to vibrate, and despite himself, he winced, startled by it. Growling, he retrieved the chip. Anastasia's name flashed across the screen, and he pulled in an unsteady breath. Bad news. It had to be bad news.

He answered the call anyway.

"Hello." The Wolf fought to keep his tone even, as if the Prince of Darkness himself hadn't just impaled the Messenger with her own blasted dagger.

"Oh, thank the *Moons*." Ana's face flickered on the screen. The connection wasn't great, but it would do. "Do *any* of you answer your calls? I've been trying to get a hold of Alistair all damned day."

"Not in the middle of battle," Morghan replied, his tone flat.

"Understandable," Ana quipped. "Anyway, we're in the Kingdom of Elves."

"Why?" Morghan's heart faltered.

"Well." Ana bit her bloodied lip. She looked *rough*, covered in ash and blood, likely none of it her own, if Morghan knew her as well as he thought he did.

"Marcus fell off a cliff, and apparently Craven blew himself up."

Eyes widening, Morghan looked toward Cooper, who was even paler beside him than he'd been when they'd found Ash's body.

"He's alive," Ana mentioned. "Both of them. But, the healing springs beneath the Kingdom of Elves are their best bet for healing quickly. So, if you're all finished there, I'd be on your way here. So we can regroup. Wait…" her voice trailed. "Where *is* Alistair? And Ash?"

Morghan gulped. "She was also injured. Alistair summoned his Dragon to take her to Dracus."

"She's a Berserker," Ana countered, giving the Wolf a disbelieving look. "She should just heal over the course of a few hours. Why send her all the way back there?"

A long silence occurred, one where Morghan looked toward Cooper once again, as if he might be able to answer the question without revealing to the black division that they'd been holding the Prince captive. And that it had backfired. Badly.

"Malachai stabbed her with one of her enchanted daggers," Cooper blurted.

Anastasia's eternal smirk faltered in that moment, her gray eyes darkening as she stared at Morghan. "How?" she asked in a whisper, as if she feared Vincent or Marcus would overhear. "I mean, I knew it was a possibility, but I didn't expect for him to show up at any of the bases. I figured he'd save himself for when we try to take back the Idonian Kingdom."

She assumed he showed up to the base. Morghan's brow raised. Perhaps this would work in their favor.

"Yeah, we were shocked," he lied, wiping his sweaty brow.

"Well, what are you two going to do?" Ana asked softly. "Go to Dracus, or come here?"

Morghan shared a look with Cooper. He'd much rather head back to Dracus to make sure Ash was alright. That way, the sapphire division could go meet with the others *together*. But, he knew, despite what he wanted, that they should join the other Allies. Represent their division. Hold down the fort for the Messenger, in a sense.

"We'll head there, so we have a plan in place for the second task when Ash is healed," Morghan announced.

Ana gave him a curt nod. "I'll let the Elves know you're on the way," she said before severing their connection.

"It'll take us days," Cooped groaned. "And we're both too drained to use Immortal speed."

Morghan remained still for a moment, pulling in a series of deep breaths as he thought of what the fastest route to the Elves might be. Cooper was correct. It would take them days. He wasn't sure how the others had managed to get there so quickly, but imagined they'd completely drained themselves doing so.

Just as Morghan was going to begin trekking around the massive lake and toward the Kingdom of Elves beyond, a thought occurred to him. He paused, turning to give Cooper a long look.

"You can teleport," Morghan reminded the Archer, crossing his arms.

Cooper's eyes widened, but he shook his head. "I don't know how," he told the Wolf. "It happened one time and was essentially an accident."

Morghan's brow furrowed, his eyes narrowing. "Try."

"I told you, I don't know how."

"How did you do it before?" he pressed.

"Well…" Cooper pursed his lips. "I was in a tree and I heard those two men talking. They were clearly Xavier's men, and they'd noticed the fire. I'm not sure what happened after that. All I know is that I panicked and thought of how I might be able to warn you. The next thing I knew, I was back at our campsite."

"So," Morghan sighed, "close your eyes and think of Quinn, and how you want to go to him."

Cooper scowled, shifting uncomfortably on his feet. "I would rather not go to him," he said, glancing over his shoulder toward the blood staining the snow.

"Just think of your brother," Morghan demanded. "We can deal with it when we get there."

"I have more than one brother, you know."

"Do *not* think of Lincoln," the Wolf spat, taking hold of Cooper's shoulder. "Now focus."

Cooper squirmed beneath Morghan's hand; his eyes squinting shut. His face twisted with determination, his chest rising and falling as he took breaths to calm himself. Silently, the Wolf pondered how wonderful his gift might become. He didn't doubt for a moment that over time, Cooper would exceed his brothers in strength and power. The thought excited him. He couldn't wait to see the Immortal this Arebus Archer became.

"This is the worst birthday of my life," Cooper muttered.

46

he Kingdom of Elves. Quinn's chest tightened as he looked around. Craven had immediately been rushed to the healing springs, deep beneath the white marble and gold castle that towered over the massive city. The Elven Guard held him by the gates, their eyes upon him, their hands hovering over the hilts of their swords.

Lucinda remained at his side, scowling at the guards as they waited for direction. They were both tired, filthy, and worried about Craven. The *last* thing Quinn wanted to do was be dragged into another Round Table Room to fight for his life.

The Guards had summoned a Commander, one named Aveo Calloway. Quinn recognized the name the second it came out of the tall, red-haired Elf that oversaw the gates. He steeled himself, his thoughts drifting to Princess Penelope and King Loren.

The Commander approached them, clad in silver and gold armor atop a dark gray uniform. The silver cape flowing behind him signified his title, though without it, Quinn would surely be able to tell that he was in a position of power in this Kingdom.

The Elf's long sandy hair was braided at his temples, and from what Quin knew of the Elves, he knew the style to be a warrior's tradition.

"Aveo." Lucinda gave the commander a half-hearted nod. "Can you please tell your guards to let us pass so we can make sure Craven isn't dead?"

The Commander's bronze gaze flashed from the Realm Sorceress to Quinn. The Archer remained still, well aware of the weight of his bow upon his back. He held his gaze, revealing no emotion. The Draconians themselves had been wary of his presence in their kingdom. He doubted the Elves would be any kinder, if not more hateful.

Aveo's eyes lingered on Quinn's bow before dropping to his quiver. His nose wrinkled as if he were smelling him, perhaps trying to figure out if he was real or not.

"Well?" Lucinda growled.

"I cannot allow him to pass," Aveo said, his tone flat.

"You're kidding." The Sorceress glared.

"I am not."

Silence spread throughout them, and Quinn's blood quickly began to boil. *Ridiculous.* He fought to stifle his anger. *Absolutely fucking ridiculous.*

"He's under the Draconian King's orders," Lucinda reminded the Commander, her tone so low it was startling. "He's an Idonian Ally."

"Pat McBride swore loyalty to High King Gregor VanCamp once," Aveo spat.

Quinn's heart fell into his stomach, his eyes widening at the sound of his father's name sailing past the Commander's lips. Lucinda's gaze darted over to him; her face having gone pale.

"He is not Pat McBride," the Sorceress said through clenched teeth.

"But he is a McBride, is he not?" Aveo crossed his arms. "I've read King Loren's messages to the Elves. I know their names."

What had his father done to make the Immortals in this Realm hate him so much? What secrets had Pat kept? Hadn't he just been a farmer, a loyal villager in Crane? Bile crept up the Archer's throat as he thought of a way to defend himself for something he had no idea about.

"I am an Idonian Ally," Quinn finally spoke, gesturing to his uniform. The green stripe ran from his right shoulder to his left side, the silver badge on his chest. "I am loyal to the Messenger. I command this division, and one of *my* Allies is in *your* healing springs. You're a Commander. Would you not be there for one of your men when they fall?"

Lucinda stiffened beside the Archer, a small sound comparable to a squeak escaping her.

"My last name and my lineage do not matter at this moment," Quinn added, forcing his tone to remain even. Apparently, he hadn't the slightest clue about his lineage. The last thing he wanted was to lose his temper, though it was extremely difficult not to.

Aveo's face twisted, something like disgust flashing through his eyes. "It'll always matter."

"Not to me," Lucinda hissed. "Now let us pass, give Quinn clearance, or I'll *make* you. In case you failed to recall, I am your Realm Sorceress and a member of the Idonian Council. You can't defy me."

The Commander grew rigid, and Quinn bit back a laugh.

"Fine," Aveo reluctantly agreed, a muscle twitching in his jaw. "But he must be registered."

"Registered?" Quinn's brow raised.

"We'll handle that later," Lucinda insisted. "You can

deliver the forms to the springs," she directed the Commander, sauntering past him.

Quinn spared Aveo another glance before following her, giving the Commander a nod that he knew would drive him mad. He followed the Sorceress through the massive city, keeping his gaze fixed on her back. He would thank her later for standing up for him, but that didn't change the fact that she knew his father. That Aveo knew his father. There was no doubt in his mind that the Sorceress had known whatever Quinn and his family didn't know. The entire time. She'd likely put the pieces together the moment he'd crossed the Unity Bridge. She knew so much that he didn't, but was she withholding the truth for his own sake? His stomach churned at the thought. The way the Commander said his father's name made Quinn wonder if he wanted to know the truth at all.

THE HEALING SPRINGS WERE MAGNIFICENT. FORMED DEEP beneath the golden castle, the granite walls surrounding the place sparkled in the candlelight flickering throughout the vast area. Pools, dozens of them, were filled with hot water containing healing properties Quinn would never understand. All he could do was appreciate their wondrous nature as Craven lay within one, floating on his back.

The Draconian was in a deep sleep, his burns already showing signs of improvement. Quinn nearly sighed with relief until he remembered he still hadn't heard from the Sapphire division. Anxiety welled deep within his gut once again as he thought of Ash, Cooper, and the others. They *had* to have defeated their base by now. If they'd defeated it at all.

Quinn had been lost in his thoughts about all the

different ways Ash's part of the task could have gone wrong, especially with the Prince of Darkness in her midst, when the Elven Princess led the black division into the healing springs. She hadn't looked at him, only the bow that lay beside him on the ground.

Marcus looked terrible as he discarded his weapons and uniform jacket before practically falling into the water. Anastasia did the same, something haunting in her gaze as she slipped into the water.

Vincent spoke with the princess, a smile on his face as he told her about all they'd done. She seemed enthralled by every word he said, and it was easy for Quinn to see that the Elf was at home here.

"That's Mika Chamberlain," Lucinda mentioned beside him. "Beck's older sister."

Quinn nodded, having seen her picture portrayed in the paper. "I know."

"She's not as unkind as Aveo," the Sorceress added. "He just takes his job very, *very* seriously."

"Clearly."

"I know you're probably curious." She winced as she said the words.

Quinn's heart faltered, his jaw clenching. "I only want to know one thing," he told her.

"And what's that?"

"How long have you known?" He finally looked toward her, his breath staggering. Her lips curled into a frown, her gaze dropping from his and falling on the warm water their feet dangled in.

"Since the moment I learned your names," Lucinda whispered.

"Do I even *want* to know what he did?" Quinn tried his best to whisper as well but failed. He knew by the way Anastasia was looking at them, now frowning as she nervously glanced toward Marcus, who kept his attention on the water surrounding him.

If Vincent and Mika were staring at him too, Quinn didn't know. He refused to look at them and find out.

"No, you don't want to know," Lucinda admitted. "But you'll find out, eventually."

"Great," Quinn groused, fighting not to tremble with rage. He shut his eyes, steeling himself.

Footsteps approached him from behind, and he could feel someone standing behind him, looming over where he sat. He opened his eyes to find Mika staring down at him, wearing a kind smile.

"These springs are meant for healing," she mentioned softly. "Many forms of healing. Not just physical." The Princess gestured toward where Craven floated nearby. "It can fix whatever ails you if you let it."

Stunned by her words, Quinn found himself staring back at her. Her golden eyes were warm, her matching braid falling over her shoulder. Her hands were folded in front of her deep blue dress. Her demeanor was far kinder than the Commander's, and for a moment Quinn thought that maybe he'd come across a few Immortals who didn't treat him like their enemy.

"I think you could all use a drink," Mika added before he had a chance to reply. "Vincent, why don't you help me fetch some?"

The Princess left him, linking her arm with Vincent's and laughing musically as they exited the springs and began their ascension up into the castle above.

"Well," Ana grunted. "That was weird."

"How so?" Quinn frowned.

"Mika is… complicated," was all the Fire Clan Leader said before dipping beneath the water.

Before Quinn had a chance to demand more answers

from the Draconian, a flash of blinding light surrounded the springs before something crashed into the water right in front of him. He was instantly drenched, dripping from head to toe along with the Sorceress beside him. He wiped the water from his eyes, only to find Morghan and Cooper floating in the hot spring in front of him.

The Wolf was scowling at the cowering Archer, his golden hair limp and wet in front of his eyes.

Quinn was instantly on his feet, scanning the water for Ash and Alistair. "Where are they?" he asked, his temper rising once again.

Cooper stared up at him, his eyes wide with fear. Something was wrong. *Very* wrong.

"Calm down," Morghan insisted the moment his eyes met Quinn's, as if he could see the eternal rage burning in his irises. "Give us a chance to explain, please."

"Where *are they*?" Quinn demanded.

"Dracus," Cooper revealed. "They're both in Dracus."

"And, where is *he*?" Quinn's mind drifted to Malachai, no longer caring that the members of the black division, including Marcus, were in earshot. Their eyes were all upon them, the Mentor now leaping out of the pool to approach them, his brows pulling together.

"Who?" Marcus's eyes narrowed.

"Malachai," Quinn snapped. "What did he *do?*"

"He stabbed her with an enchanted dagger," Morghan told him calmly. "But Alistair took her back to Dracus on his Dragon, and I'm sure she's doing just fine."

Quinn's breath hitched, his heart dropping into his stomach.

"He showed up at the base?" Marcus gaped at them.

"No." Quinn shook his head, his blood boiling in his veins. He should have stopped her. He should have made her let the Prince go. Morghan should have as well. None of them should have let her even *attempt* to convince the Prince to lead them to Lincoln. To undo whatever it was that he did to him. "He was already with them."

"What?" Anastasia asked softly.

"She thought she could get him to lead her to Lincoln." Quinn shook his head again, fighting the urge to scream. "Or tell her where he was and how she could fix him."

"*Fix* him?" Marcus growled.

"Malachai made a series of injections to erase Lincoln's memories," Morghan explained with a grave expression. "We're not sure about all the details. We just know that he's not the same. Xavier is using him."

"For what?" Lucinda nearly whispered.

"I don't think you want to know," Morghan told her.

Silence spread throughout the spring, each Ally staring at one another, all eyes filled with shock and fury. Mika eventually returned with Vincent, where Morghan regretfully told him the awful news he and Cooper brought. But they all took wine and blood from the Elven Princess and listened as the Wolf explained all that had occurred throughout their journey to the Lakelands. How the Prince had managed to break free from enchanted chains, and how even though he'd stabbed Ash, he hadn't gone after her Amulet. He hadn't killed her when he could have, and likely should have, seeing as there was no doubt in Quinn's mind that it was what Xavier had sent him to do.

Later that evening, they were each assigned suites in the castle. As Mika led Quinn and Marcus to theirs, she was silent most of the way. It wasn't until they arrived at the suite that she finally spoke.

"I hope your brother turns out to be alright," she said as she unlocked the suite and ushered the two men inside. "I have watched this war tear too many families apart."

With that, the Princess left, likely retiring to her own chambers for the evening. Marcus shut the door before sliding a hand through his damp hair. For a man that had fallen off a cliff, Quinn was surprised to not see a mark anywhere on him.

On a table in the foyer sat a stack of papers. Quinn's brow furrowed at the sight of them.

"Ah," the Mentor snorted as he skimmed them, "registration forms."

"What should I do with them?" Quinn asked, feeling awfully daft.

Marcus took one look at Quinn and another look at the forms before he snatched the pile from the table and tore the papers in two. "Tell them you'll fill out registration papers when you can do so in the Idonian Jurisdiction *after* Penelope is High Queen of Si Realtra."

47

There was a time, not so long ago, when Loren would be on the front lines. When his father would look at him and say, *You are of no use to our people here, on this isle.* And he'd been right. Loren and Valentina had fought together, leading the Draconian army alongside Axel as they worked to defend Idona as the Five Realm War raged on.

Now, another war gripped the main Realm in a deadly vice, and all Loren could do was remain in Dracus, on the isle surrounded by waterfalls. It was one of the safest places in the entire Realm.

He was sick with worry and had a desire to be out on the battlefield with the Allies. The odds were not in their favor. Three enemy bases filled to the brim with Pandora and whatever else Xavier had commissioned to do his bidding. By now, they should have defeated them, but there was no word. Not from any of the three divisions.

As Loren stood before the glass walls of his study, gazing out into the kingdom beyond, he wondered what had come of the ten individuals he'd sent out into the Realm. His stomach churned as he imagined what they'd already endured, and whether they had survived it. The weight of the Realm had fallen on their shoulders, and while they were each powerful indeed, the king couldn't escape the idea that he'd sent them to their deaths.

Thick storm clouds rolled in from the north, hovering above Dracus, blocking Loren's view of the starry night sky. Snow began to fall in thick flurries, quickly covering the kingdom in a thick blanket of shimmering white. He admired it for a moment, knowing it was the first heavy snowfall since Winter Solstice had arrived. Tomorrow, children would likely be in their front yards, building snowmen while their parents strung lights on their front porches, preparing for Giving Day.

Loren doubted he'd celebrate Giving Day at all this year. It was still a month away now, but he doubted he'd be in a joyful mood. Not when the end of the Dark War was in view, and a far bigger storm brewed on the horizon.

A knock on his study door pulled Loren from his thoughts, and he turned from his glass wall to watch Penelope enter. His breath staggered at the sight of her, his hands growing clammy. The skirts of her silky lavender dress swayed with her every movement as she dipped into a slight bow, her chestnut hair slipping over her shoulder, so long that it nearly grazed the decorative carpet.

Penelope straightened, her porcelain complexion pale. She was worried as well. He doubted she'd slept much in the week since Vincent and Ash had left.

Yet there was joy in the Princess's eyes when she looked at him. A spark of happiness that Loren felt as well.

"I missed you at dinner," she mentioned softly.

Loren glanced toward the large grandfather clock in the corner of his study and frowned. He hadn't realized so much time had passed since he'd come here earlier this morning to sift through messages on his information tablet.

"I apologize for my absence," he replied, his mouth growing dry as his gaze fell on Penelope again. She was approaching him now but remained on the other side of the desk, maintaining a respectable distance. A distance the King had yet to close between them.

"Are you alright?" she asked softly.

Loren swallowed hard as he stared at her. When he wasn't worrying about the Allies, his mind was trapped in the moment he'd asked her to marry him. It had been sudden, and while Loren had thought of it on nights where sleep escaped him, he'd always kept those thoughts to himself. His desire had gotten the best of him as he'd escorted her back to her suite after the Fire and Ice Ball.

The King had taken her hand to keep her from walking into her suite, where she would have begun to pack her things to return to the Kingdom of Elves. It had been a shot in the dark, truly.

You don't have to go, Loren had told her. *Marry me instead.*

Loren hadn't expected for her to love him. He thought that at the very least, they'd develop an alliance that would better for *both* of their kingdoms. One that would prevent Penelope from being used by the Elves. He thought he'd do Gideon an honor by helping his daughter to a throne and allowing her to stand on her own two feet. To rule, even if just from Dracus. To give hope to the Mortals throughout Idona and let them know that the VanCamps were *here*, and they weren't going anywhere.

To his surprise, she'd cried tears of joy. At first, he wasn't sure if it was just because she wouldn't have to marry Aveo, or have his children, or because she truly *wanted* to marry Loren. Upon further conversation, it had turned out she'd cried for both reasons.

"I'm fine," Loren finally replied. "Are you alright?"

Penelope blinked as if she hadn't expected the question. Loren silently wondered if anyone had bothered to ask her that at all. Had the Elves considered her feelings when they'd buried Cedric, only to begin discussing who would replace him as her betrothed? Had anyone asked her how it felt to watch both of her siblings leave Dracus, knowing the chances were high that they would never return?

Loren's blood began to boil at the thought. Had anyone ever bothered to ask the Princess how she felt about *anything*?

"I'm fine," Penelope insisted. "Despite the circumstances, I'm happy. Actually, I think I might have found a way to solve our problems." She beamed. "I was thinking about my mother's will. She made it clear that she wanted *me* to ascend to the throne, and that the Sectra was to go to Ash. But we never considered the chain of command. Perhaps we need to look at it more closely."

"What are you getting at?" Loren's chest grew tight.

"Ash can change Idona and mold it however she wishes. That is what it means to be the Sectra Holder for the main Realm," Penelope explained slowly. "When the Sectras were created in the wake of the great Six Realm War, and at the Dawn of the New Age, they were given to six warriors from each of the Realms. But the Amulet... that was declared by the Sovereign to be a symbol of unity and peace. Whoever wore it afterward would bear the responsibility of maintaining the peace won after the Great War. It is why Xavier wanted the Amulet so badly. Because wearing it meant he would gain that respect from the other Realms. That they would *have* to listen to him. But he would not have used that power to maintain the peace. He would have used it for complete control."

Loren was silent as he listened to Penelope's every word, his heart pounding against the walls of his chest.

"Ash has that respect now," Penelope continued, straightening her spine. "She surpasses me as the rightful heir. Every soul in this Realm has no choice but to follow her lead, which means, she may decide who rises to the High Throne."

The King's eyes widened, his stomach twisting into knots. "What are you saying?"

"Xavier may have won control over the Idonian Kingdom, but he was never crowned as High King. With no High King or Queen on the throne, it is the Sectra Holder who leads the Realm, per the chain of command. Which means, Ash could be High Queen. It's been done before, where the Sectra Holder takes the Realm for themselves. King Sampson Ivanenko of the Zerinian Empire did it."

Loren shook his head, unable to stomach the idea that Penelope might be shoved off her throne.

"And, if Ash becomes High Queen, the Elves will not be able to withhold their army," Penelope added, her lips twitching toward a smirk. "She can be the bridge between all communities in this Realm. She can unite us all. And, she can put a stop to my betrothal to Aveo as well."

"But you've waited your entire *life* for that throne," Loren gaped at her.

"It doesn't matter." The Princess shrugged. "I don't care who sits on that throne, as long as this Realm is rid of Xavier and his Dark Army. No matter what happens, we'll still be married." She winked.

The King's heart was in his throat as he rounded the desk, arriving in front of her. He was at a loss for words, his mind racing as he thought of how brilliant Penelope had become. How selfless her words had just been.

Loren's pulse pounded in his ears as he reached for Penelope, wrapping his arms around her waist, pulling her against him. He could feel her heart thundering against his ribcage as his gaze lingered on her lips. He reveled in how it felt to have her melt against him, her hot breath on his face lighting a flame of desire he'd fought to bury for too long.

Penelope's bright eyes sparkled with the same desire as she reached up, placing her warm hands on his face before pulling him down. Her lips brushed against his before she deepened their kiss, his heart now threatening to explode entirely.

It would be far too easy for the king to lose himself in their kiss. He willed time to stop completely, his tongue just barely grazing hers as she lowered her hands from his face, her fingers running down the buttons of his white shirt.

Loren's breath caught in his throat as she loosened his tie, his hands roaming down her sides. He fought against the urge to back her against his desk and failed. The jar of ink for his quill splattered on the carpet as he pushed everything on the oak surface aside. Papers and framed pictures fell to the floor with a crash as the buttons to his shirt came undone.

He nearly growled as his hands ran up the soft, bare flesh beneath Penelope's dress. She writhed beneath him, her hands reaching for his belt when the castle shook around them.

Loren broke their kiss, panting as he hovered over her. "What the hell was *that?*"

For a moment, Alistair felt as if he were standing back in Mayfire, watching the city of Dragons burn, as he stood in silence. Helpless. Useless.

The second he'd walked into the infirmary, a massive mountain man had snatched Ash right from the Rider's arms and rushed her into the first empty room he could find. More Healers, perhaps *dozens* of Healers, followed suit. And all Alistair could do was stand outside the door, listening to the chaos raging on the other side of it.

Growling, Alistair paced the halls for a while, occasionally trying to peer past the bodies within the room to view Ash as she lay lifelessly on the bed. His chip buzzed endlessly in his pocket, but he paid it no mind. Instead, he pushed his back against the cold tiled wall and slid down into a crouch, his head falling into his hands.

Willa was still waiting in the square. Alistair could sense her and tried to reach out to her via their mental link, but she wouldn't budge from her place. He doubted the Dragon would leave until she deemed everything alright. He hoped the Draconians weren't giving her too much trouble, as he couldn't muster the energy to walk out of the infirmary to give her any commands. Especially since it was clear, she wasn't in the mood to listen to him at all.

The sound of rushing footsteps pulled Alistair's attention, and he lifted his head from his hands, only to find Loren and Penelope round the corner. He stiffened at the sight of the king's appearance. Loren's hair was ruffled, the buttons to his shirt half undone while his tie sat loose and crooked around his neck. Penelope seemed less frazzled, though her dress was certainly wrinkled and her cheeks flushed.

"Ward!" Loren bellowed as he arrived in front of the Rider. "Why the hell is there a Dragon in my city square!"

Alistair hadn't thought of what he would say to Loren or the Council, or anyone for that matter. He debated telling a lie, to protect Ash from being ridiculed for her clearly *bad* decision but knew that the truth would come out eventually. So, he told Loren and Penelope to take a seat and explained everything. From the beginning.

The King was silent as he sat beside Alistair in the hall, slouching against the wall. "Well…" he shook his head, a muscle twitching in his jaw. "What Ash did was brave. It sounds like Xavier did what we all silently expected him to do. He sent out his best to dispatch her. By entrapping the Prince in those chains, Ash bought herself enough time to finish her first task."

Alistair stared at the king, his mouth falling open. He hadn't thought of it that way.

"It still doesn't make sense," Penelope mentioned from the Rider's other side. She sat with her knees pulled to her chest while her skirts fell around her, like a blanket of silk. Her eyes were bright, her brow creased. "Malachai doesn't leave people alive."

Silence spread between them as they remained seated in the hall. Alistair rubbed his temples, knowing what the Princess said was true. Once Malachai had a target in mind, the unfortunate soul inevitably perished.

Ebony continued to bark orders inside the room behind the Rider, and though he hoped all would be well soon, he couldn't escape the idea that she might fail. That Malachai's track record wouldn't be broken today.

"I should step in," Loren said as he rose to his feet, stretching. He fixed his buttons and smoothed his hair, sucking in an audible breath before he opened the door to the healing room and entered.

Silence fell inside, and Alistair cringed. His eyes burned, tears threatening to flow freely down his cheeks. His chest was unbearably tight, and every breath he took felt like a shard of glass invading his lungs as he waited for Loren to return.

Alistair's chip buzzed in his pocket once again, the sound bouncing off the tiled walls. Penelope looked toward him, shadows dancing in her eyes.

"Are you going to get that?"

Reaching into his pocket, Alistair cursed at the sight of the name. "It's Marcus," he told the Princess. "I don't know what to tell him yet."

"Give it to me," Penelope urged. "I'll let him know."

Nodding, Alistair did as she asked and watched as the Princess rose to her feet and walked down the hall where she took the call. He couldn't hear her over the sound of his pulse pounding in his ears as Loren exited the room, with a very exhausted Healer at his side.

"She will be fine," Ebony announced. "We gave her a blood transfusion using Hartford's blood to rid the Moon-shade from her system. You got here just in time."

Alistair trembled with relief as he pushed himself to his feet, his legs wobbling. Loren placed a calming hand on his shoulder, and the Rider pulled in a breath to rid himself of the nerves overwhelming him.

"Hartford the Berserker." Alistair said the name, a shred of hope igniting deep within his churning gut. "What will his blood do to her?"

"We're lucky he was still here," Ebony breathed, wiping her brow with the back of her hand. "Ash was a Berserker *before* this transfusion, but I imagine Hartford's blood will rid her of any weaknesses she might have had. She could be a full-fledged Berserker now, but I'll need to get more samples from her over time to confirm. I'd still suggest that she stay away from poisons and enchanted weapons."

"I'll make sure of it." Alistair grumbled at the thought of the daggers Ash decorated her uniform with.

Ebony offered him a smile, though it quickly faltered. "I'd like to ask a favor of you," she told him softly. "Ash needs blood. Immortal blood to quicken her healing process. She's in dire need of it now. If we don't get some in her soon, she could face signs of blood deprivation which will only lengthen your time here in Dracus."

"She can have mine," Alistair blurted without thought. "Just get me a cup, and I'll empty some for you."

Loren paled at the sound of his words, his pale gray eyes darting between the Rider and the Healer. "Did Anastasia not explain this to you?" he asked warily.

"She did." Alistair gave the king a nod. "But she advised against letting any other Draconians drink straight from the vein."

"Normally, I would agree with her," Ebony told him, her lips pressed into a thin line. "But in this scenario, the healing properties in our Immortal blood are far more potent when the blood is taken straight from the vein."

Alistair felt the blood rush from his cheeks and cleared his throat nervously. "I thought that practice was reserved for lovers."

"And you'll soon understand why," Loren said.

Ebony gave the King a long look, her dark eyes like daggers. "I will monitor everything. There won't be any activity of *that* nature in one of my healing rooms."

Loren gave the Healer a sharp nod, his eyes falling on Penelope, who paced farther down the hall, still on a call with Marcus. "I'll escort Penelope back to the castle," he offered and then vacated Alistair's presence without another word.

"I'd like my chip back at some point," the Rider muttered as Ebony ushered him into the healing room. She quickly rid the room of any extra bodies, and for that he was thankful. The last thing he wanted was an audience. However, Hartford remained, still hooked up to a machine, his blood continuously running into Ash's veins through tubes.

Alistair eyed the mountain man, having never seen anyone quite so large.

"So this is the lad you chose to feed my kin?" Hartford's golden gaze flashed with amusement. "You smell strange."

"I *smell* strange?" Alistair kept his eyes on the Berserker, fearing what he would find if he glanced toward the bed.

"What are you?" Hartford asked, his intense eyes squinting.

"A Hybrid," Ebony clarified. "Much like your kin. Now let him do what he has to do and keep your mouth shut."

The Berserker bristled, but Alistair ignored him as he moved closer to the bed. He finally allowed his gaze to fall upon her, his heart dropping at the sight of how pale she'd become. Her complexion was comparable to the stark-white bedsheets surrounding her. Her lips bore a blush tint, her veins still tinted black beneath her nearly transparent flesh.

Alistair pulled in a deep, calming breath as he prepared himself. At least he could do something to help. For once in his miserable life.

Alistair had never seen nor *felt* anything like it. His mind was still whirling as Ebony and Hartford left the room and sent in maids to clean up the blood. *The blood.* There was so much of it. Most of it was Ash's, some of it Hartford's. The scent of it nearly drove the Rider mad, the hunger he'd ignored throughout the base take-down and the chaos that evolved afterward weighing heavily upon him.

As he settled into a chair beside Ash's bed, his pulse still pounding in his ears, the wound on his wrist still a fresh reminder of all that had occurred, he debated whether he should leave her to fetch some blood for himself. But as he stared at her, watching as the color returned to her cheeks, he couldn't bring himself to. What if something went wrong while he was away? He swallowed hard at the thought.

Stomach rumbling, Alistair leaned back in the chair. He watched her pulse throb and listened to the blood rush through her veins. His mouth watered, his heart quickening in his chest. Oh, he'd *wanted* to bite her. He'd wanted to do *more* than just bite her.

He'd suffered through the desire and pushed thoughts he knew he wouldn't normally have otherwise from his mind. Now, he bit his tongue, willing those thoughts of Ash and *her* blood to fade.

The door to the healing room creaked open, and Alistair tore his gaze away from Ash's throbbing pulse to view who entered. Shadow approached him, a thermos and a bouquet of roses in both of his hands.

"I figured you would need this, after your long day." The Earth Clan leader sighed as he offered the thermos. Alistair took it without question, twisting off the cap and chugging the contents within.

They stood in silence for a moment, Alistair embarrassingly twisting his wrist so the wound lay against his black uniform pants.

"They'll be sending more people out into the field now," Shadow said, approaching the end of bed. His frown deepened as he surveyed Ash, his nose wrinkling. "To investigate why Mortals are being stolen from villages by a certain Arebus Archer our Messenger wants to save from Xavier so badly."

Alistair's heart sank, his grip on his thermos wavering. He stared at the Clan leader as he thought of all Malachai had said about Lincoln. The pain in Cooper's eyes during those harsh moments was nearly too much to handle. But to know Xavier was using Lincoln in such a way... he wasn't sure how the McBride brothers would recover from that.

"They suspect it has something to do with why the ancient Fae Magic was drained from the portal caverns across the Realm," Shadow continued warily. "Aries suspects that they're trying to compile the energy in the Idonian Kingdom. To create a portal strong enough to rival the Galactic Gates themselves. Grant has found evidence of such a thing hovering above the Idonian Kingdom, like an evolving black hole. They plan on sending Humphrey to investigate. To try and shut it down."

"Alone?" Alistair's eyes bulged.

"Humphrey knows the Idonian Kingdom better than anyone else in Dracus," Shadow insisted as he crossed the room, setting his bouquet of roses in an empty vase. "His mission will be to find out who precisely is controlling that portal, kill them, and shut it down."

"And what does this have to do with Lincoln?" Alistair pressed, his heart hammering against the walls of his chest.

"The portal..." Shadow shook his head, as if he refused to believe what he was about to say. "It's laced with something else. Magic, or something stronger. Grant suspects that if Lincoln is fetching Mortals throughout the Realm, they've been affected by it. That Xavier is sending out surges of energy to *change* people. People that he can use against us."

Alistair was sure he'd gone as pale as a ghost, his throat now so dry that he felt as if it were swelling shut.

"If Humphrey can shut it down," Shadow added, lifting his chin slightly as he crossed his arms, "it'll prevent Xavier from fleeing into another Realm and stop whatever changes it's causing in Mortals across the Realm."

"That's one awfully large job for just one man," Alistair warned.

Shadow nodded slowly, pursing his lips. "It's a good thing that our *one* man is the only one capable of pulling it off."

ASH'S HEAVY EYELIDS FLUTTERED OPEN TO THE SIGHT OF familiar white-tiled walls. Her chest immediately tightened as something weighed her legs down. She fought to lift her head to see what it was, but the pain in her side caused her to cry out in agony. She trembled beneath the thick blanket atop her, her gaze drifting about the room.

There was nothing but a single vase filled with red roses in full bloom, with a note beside it. She skimmed the delicate script upon it with her Elven eyes. *Get well soon, Ash - Shadow.*

Cursing beneath her breath, Ash fought to move her legs. Something stirred at the end of her bed, and she gathered enough strength to lift her head.

Alistair was sitting in a chair beside her, his arms draped over her legs. He was in a deep slumber, his eyelids twitching as he endured whatever dream his subconscious had brought upon him.

"Alistair," Ash whispered, her voice hoarse. She sounded like she hadn't had a sip of water in days, though a sweet taste of blood lingered upon her tongue. Her heart surged as she noticed it, her mouth immediately watering for more. She doubted she'd ever had anything quite so delicious and wondered what it was they'd given her as she watched the Rider stir more, his eyes drifting open.

"Get off my legs," she barked softly.

Alistair straightened, his eyes widening as he stared at her. "How do you feel?"

"Like I was stabbed by a demented Prince," she snarled.

"You took it like a champ," Alistair clearly lied.

"Sure," Ash drawled. "That's why I'm here. In Dracus. While the other Allies are Moons know where."

"They're in the Kingdom of Elves," he revealed as he lowered back down into his chair, raking a hand through his messy pale hair. "You weren't the only one who ran into trouble."

Ash's heart sank, and despite the pain, she forced herself to sit up in bed. "Who else?" She wasn't sure she wanted to know the answer to her question, but held the Rider's gaze, willing her lip not to quiver in his presence.

"From what I've gathered, Craven nearly blew himself up, and was the first to be rushed to the Kingdom of Elves. They have healing springs there, beneath their castle," Alistair explained. "Marcus was next. He fell off a cliff. Lucky enough for him, us Immortals are harder to kill. He was brought to heal there as well. But you—" he cut off his words, his eyes drifting to where he knew her wound was hidden beneath the blankets. "You needed to come here. To Ebony and Hartford."

Nodding, Ash blinked against her forming tears. "How soon can we leave to meet them?"

"As soon as you're healed."

"How long will that take?" Her eyes narrowed.

"As long as it does." Alistair gave her a warning look. "We will not rush the process. We need you to be at your best before we approach Veda."

Ash couldn't argue with him. "I should be dead, but he didn't kill me. He could have. But he didn't."

Alistair's brow raised, his eyes widening. "What exactly happened, Ash?"

"I'm not sure." Her lip trembled as she spoke. She wanted to remember but couldn't bring herself to. She couldn't bear to relive that moment. "Perhaps we'll never know."

49

Constance Waters had prepared herself for the inevitable. She knew they would come for her. Since the moment she'd watched the silver mist flow from her shaking fingertips, she'd known.

Rumors had sailed throughout the Strip. Mortals in the surrounding villages were being taken by an extinct Archer with glowing red eyes. A small army traveled behind him; whips always ready in their hands. It hadn't taken Constance more than a fraction of a second to realize that her time had come. So, she'd taken a long, hot bath. She smelled the delicious breakfast Lilly had cooked in their kitchen. She'd listened to the girl laugh with Sam, despite the absence of her own family.

Constance had allowed them to leave that morning, to go and tend to the McBride Estate and the many animals living on it. She'd kept her fists in the pockets of her blue velvet cloak to keep herself from reaching out to Sam, to keep him from leaving her. She'd cried hopelessly as she watched her brother and Lilly walk through the fields, disappearing into the mountains beyond.

The shouting came soon after, and Constance had held

her breath as she walked out onto her front porch. It was then that she saw him, clad in black. The ancient bow was strapped to his back, his matching quiver strapped to his thigh. His eyes met hers and Constance's heart shattered in her chest. Whoever this man was, he was certainly not Lincoln McBride.

"Constance Waters." He said her name, yet his voice was hardly his own.

The villagers each stared at her with wide, fearful eyes as she descended the steps of her porch. She kept her spine straight, her chin high as she approached him.

"Lincoln," she greeted him, playing on a useless hope that he might recognize her. But there was no recognition in those glowing eyes. Not a shred of it as he motioned for one of his men to come forward, shackles in his hands.

"You've been summoned by His Majesty the King," Lincoln informed her. "You will report to the Idonian Kingdom where you will complete your registration and take your oath to him."

"Xavier is not my king," Constance assured him as she allowed the man beside the Archer to shackle her wrists, and then her ankles. "You may march me to the Idonian Kingdom, leash me, bind me, gag me, torture me, but I will swear no oath."

"As you wish."

"Constance." The baker, Jeremy, stepped forward, as if to stop the Archer and his men from leading her from the village.

"Stand back," she ordered. "Tell my father when he returns that I left this place with honor. To atone for our family's sins."

The baker nodded, casting his damp gaze to the cobblestone beneath him. Constance knew that he was aware. Of who, precisely, she was. Who Sam was. What they meant to Xavier's Dark reign. Who Xavier was to *them*. It wasn't Constance's past that she was running from. No, everything her family was hiding from had occurred before she'd even left her mother's womb. But in this Galaxy, you carried the mistakes of your ancestors. In this case, proudly.

Lilly couldn't bear to see the estate so filthy and covered with dust. So, after she and Sam finished with tending to the animals, she'd entered her family home and gathered all her cleaning supplies. As she dusted every surface, her mind drifted to the rumors she'd heard. Her heart quickened at the thought of what was happening to the Mortals stolen from their homes. She silently prayed that that horror wouldn't arrive in Crane.

As she made her way into the kitchen, Lilly's gaze fell on the block of knives she favored while cooking. They had been her mother's, and she'd sharpened and polished them endlessly throughout the years since her death to keep them pristine. Since Sam was still working in the barn, she decided she'd retrieve each of them, and wash, sharpen, and polish them.

Lilly scrubbed at a knife, her hands lost in suds that smelled of eucalyptus and pine. She breathed in the scent, as it reminded her of long nights washing up after dinner with her brothers and Ash at her sides. Everyone had a job. She would wash, Quinn would dry, Ash would set the clean dishes in their places, Cooper would wipe down the counters, and Lincoln would sweep and mop the floors. For a moment, she could feel them there. Doing the same tasks they'd always done before the war struck their home and tore her family apart.

Anger began to bloom deep in Lilly's gut. Too much. She'd lost too much in a matter of weeks, and her heart was broken. The organ that fueled her was in pieces. The blood that sailed through her veins as hot as the fire blooming in the Underworld. She wanted them back. She wanted every one of them home. She never wanted to lose another soul again.

Out of the corner of her eye, Lilly watched as a knife lifted from its place in the wooden block. She stared at it, her fists trembling beneath the sudsy water. The knife hovered in the air, drifting toward her as if it was carried by gusts of wind she couldn't feel.

A sneeze crept along Lilly's sinuses, and though she tried to will it away, it escaped her. The knife crashed to the floor below, the sound of metal against tile ringing in her ears.

Lilly stifled a gasp as she stared at it, focusing all her energy on the knife once again. She watched, her eyes wide with amazement, as it lifted from the ground and sailed above her shoulder, before gently falling into the water.

Staggering backward, Lilly stared at the water, the knives hidden by the thick layer of soap. Her lip quivered as she glanced toward the window. It opened swiftly, allowing a frigid winter's breeze to rush into the kitchen. Lilly gripped her arms, working to warm herself as she imagined the window slamming shut. It did as her mind asked it to. Perhaps too hard, since the windowpane cracked upon impact. She cursed beneath her breath, a word her brothers would have chastised her for.

The Mortals who had been stolen from the villages had also been rumored to have strange abilities. Lilly's eyes watered as she approached the sink, retrieving her mother's knives from the water. She dried them quickly and then put them back in their places. She drained the water in the sink and then rushed for her cloak, wrapping it tightly around herself.

Lilly swallowed hard as her eyes fell on a book lying on the kitchen table. The same one Cooper had gifted Ash on her birthday. It had remained there since the moment Ash had set it down.

Reaching for the book, Lilly shoved it beneath her cloak and rushed out the back door, locking it behind her. She ran for the barn, her boots nearly catching on muddy slush as she fought to slide to a stop before the open doors.

"We need to go," Lilly called to Sam. "Now."

"What's wrong?" he asked as he appeared in the threshold, slipping his arms into his wool coat, his cheeks flushed from hours working in the stalls.

"I-" she wasn't at all sure how to explain what she'd just experienced. "Something is wrong with me."

Sam's brow wrinkled, his eyes flickering with concern. "What do you mean?" His eyes narrowed in her direction as he shut the barn doors. "Did you get your first bleed or something?"

Lilly's cheeks flared at the sound of the question. "No!" she shouted through clenched teeth. "I accidentally moved one of my mother's knives. With my mind."

Sam's eyes widened. He'd heard the rumors too. They'd discussed the matter last night at dinner. The strange abilities the Mortals supposedly had. Allegedly, one of the men from Witherow had been able to summon earthquakes depending on his moods. The idea was unbelievable. *Not now...* Lilly shook her head, her chest rising and falling with each breath she took.

"We need to go to Dracus," she announced. "If we don't, they'll find me and use me."

Nodding, Sam took her arm in his hand and guided her through the fields. "We'll fetch Constance and be on our way," he assured her, his wary gaze meeting her own. "I won't let any harm come to you."

Lilly believed him. She trusted Sam as much as she trusted her own brothers. But would he be enough to keep her from Xavier and his Dark Army? She gulped at the thought, refusing to entertain the idea as they began their trek toward the village. She kept a hand to her chest, holding her father's book against her heart. Perhaps when they had a chance to stop, she might flip through it. Maybe somewhere on the many pages, she would find an answer as to what was happening to her and why.

BY THE TIME SAM AND LILLY MADE IT BACK TO THE village, he could feel that something had gone wrong. Terribly wrong. The hairs on the back of his neck raised as he approached his family home. His fellow villagers watched him, their expressions grave. Just as he was about to reach for the handle to the front door, something deep inside him told him to stop. His hand fell to his side as he turned to face Lilly, whose eyes were still wide with fear.

"She isn't there," Jeremy announced sadly from across the street.

Sam stiffened at the sound of the baker's words. "Where is she, then?" he asked, his tone less than kind. His father was in Blackbay to refresh their stock of explosive arrows. His absence left Jeremy in charge, but that didn't ease the terror rising in Sam.

"There was nothing we could do," Jeremy told him as he stepped across the street, arriving at the bottom of the steps to the porch. "She told me to stand down."

"What the hell happened?" Sam thundered, and the

villagers crowding the streets winced at the sound of his tone.

"Lincoln." Jeremy shook his head, tears brimming his pale eyes. "He arrived here leading an army at his back. They put her in shackles."

Lilly's hand reached for Sam's, and he took it without a second thought, squeezing it gently. He didn't dare look at her face. No part of him wanted to see the sorrow that lurked there.

"She told me to stand down," Jeremey added again, his voice weak as he hung his head. "She said she was to atone for your family's sins."

"Fuck," Sam growled, his stomach churning.

"What do we do?" Lilly's voice wavered.

"Go," Jeremy directed. "Warn the Immortal Kingdoms. Raise an Army. Call upon our fellow Rebels in hiding. Do whatever you have to, to get her back. End the entire war, if that's what you have to do."

Nodding, Sam pulled in a calming breath. "Alert them. Tell them to prepare. I'll send word when it's time."

Jeremy placed a fist over his heart. "Wipe any memory of that bastard Walsh from their minds, Sam. Lead us. In honor of our fallen leader."

"I will," Sam replied. "I will."

It would take far too long for Marcus to come to the realization that his time being a Guardian had come to an end. Now over eighteen years ago. But that didn't stray from the fact that he'd made Meera a final promise to protect her children, and he wouldn't break that promise. Not willingly. Yet, somehow, he had.

Memories, long and buried, tried to break through the surface of Marcus's mind as he had fled to the healing springs beneath the castle, for peace more than healing now. His body felt normal, despite its atrocious fall. He hadn't anticipated to live through it, yet he had. By the grace of the Moons, or perhaps the Sovereign herself, he supposed.

Something gnawed in the back of Marcus's mind as he allowed the water to surround him once again. Something that told him that not everything was as it seemed. But he buried the thoughts. Whatever havoc his memory wanted to release upon him, he didn't want to know.

The sound of bare feet padding along the granite floors pulled Marcus from his misery. He glanced up, only to see Lucinda staring back at him. She wore nothing more than a thin nightgown, the same shade of her amber eyes.

"The sun hasn't risen," she told him as she arrived beside his chosen pool of steaming water. "What brings you here at this hour?"

"I couldn't sleep," Marcus admitted. "I imagine you couldn't either."

"Not a wink." Lucinda sighed as she slipped into the pool, sinking beneath the water. Her hair billowed around her, and Marcus watched her with an evolving smile as bubbles streamed to the surface.

How the Realm Sorceress felt about Veda the Red Witch was no secret, and Marcus knew a thing or two about unfinished business. He imagined that it was taking all of Lucinda's strength to keep herself from striking Veda alone, to finish the Witch for good and steal the Moonshade on Ash's behalf. To save them from any impending danger.

Lucinda rose above the water, sucking in the steaming air around them.

"The worry is eating you alive, isn't it?" he asked.

"They do not understand what she's capable of," Lucinda insisted, keeping her eyes shut as she floated through the water. "Her power has kept her alive for half a millennium. She's undefeated. Even by me. She has the worst of tricks up her sleeve, and there's no doubt in my mind that she might hand over the Moonshade. But not without cost."

Marcus eyed the Sorceress, his mouth growing dry as he thought of all the Witch might do to Ash, or any of the Allies for that matter.

"With Magic, there is always consequence," Lucinda told him, her eyes drifting open to reveal the sincerity flickering within them. "Whether the consequence is a price you must pay for what you seek, or a punishment for whatever Magic you wielded on your own, there is always a downside. For me, I am drained. My spells weaken me. For Veda, she demands payment. She doesn't need to, but it amuses her when people fail to pay their debts. She uses their worst fears to kill them."

Marcus felt a chill, even in the eternally warm spring surrounding him. "What price do you think Ash will have to pay for that Moonshade?"

"There's no way of knowing," Lucinda said softly. "It depends on the mood she's in. Perhaps she'll steal Ash's fertility and prevent her from growing any children in her womb. Perhaps she'll place a curse on her."

"Ash has the Amulet," Marcus breathed. "It'll protect her."

"Not from a curse." Lucinda sighed as she sat up in the water. "And whether she can use it to defeat Veda depends on timing. Even with the most powerful Sectra, Veda is fast. Unpredictable."

There wasn't much that Marcus knew about Veda the Red Witch. Like most Witches, she was banished to the Regal Mountains by Gregor VanCamp. There were few occasions where the former Guardian had needed to venture out to the estranged, desolate mountain range. Up until recently, he could count the number of times he'd set foot on the territory on one hand, even throughout his search for the Missing VanCamp. He would openly admit that he didn't know a great deal about the potential enemies that lurked there, but he figured he would find out soon enough.

THE SUN WAS HANGING HIGH IN THE SKY BY THE TIME Ebony and Hartford came to visit Ash. The Healer examined her while the Berserker practically fawned over her. His big hand ran over her hair as if he were a father assuring his child that everything was alright.

As the pair worked, taking blood samples and vitals, Ash watched them. She didn't miss the slight *looks* they gave one another, Ebony's giggling, blushing, or the batting of her eyelashes. By the end of it all, she was smirking from ear to ear.

"You're in love," she accused, propped against a mountain of pillows.

Alistair nearly spat out the blood he'd been drinking at the table across the room.

Ebony gawked at her, her blush returning in a particularly vivid color. "What makes you say that?"

"You didn't deny it," Ash teased.

"That's enough lass," Hartford grumbled. "Teasing us is no way to thank us for saving your wee life."

Ash's brow perked, her smile widening. "You know," she gestured to Alistair and herself, "Hybrids don't seem to be much of an issue anymore. If that's what you're worried about."

"That's nonsense." Ebony waved her off, casting her gaze downward as she pretended to fiddle with her information tablet.

"Well, last time I checked," Ash sighed as she grasped the enchanted chain around her neck, lifting the Sectra into the air, "I can make certain decisions regarding our Realms way of life. Perhaps the law against Hybrids could be revoked."

"You'll have plenty of other more important decisions to deal with," Ebony told her flatly. "Worrying about Hartford and I would be a waste of time."

"Call it repayment for saving my *wee* life." Ash grinned.

CADE FLETCHER WAS FURIOUS.

And a failure.

Not only had he failed to defend the base his king had chosen him to protect, he hadn't even made it there in time. He'd arrived a mere few hours after the entire base imploded. The Pandora that had lived there were now piles of ash and bone. There were no survivors. Not a soul in sight.

The Sorcerer stood there in silence, his stallion grazing in the valley behind him. Perhaps now he should run, rather than admit his defeat. He wondered what might come of him. If he'd be reduced in rank or slaughtered for all of Solaris City to see.

No matter what direction Cade ran in, he would never run far enough. There was no sense in even attempting it.

Frowning, Cade turned to retrieve his horse. He supposed there was still a chance the other bases were under siege and needed his assistance. If he helped Ryole or Savron, he might be able to redeem himself.

Before the Sorcerer could reach for the stallion's reins, a flash of light appeared behind him. Cade stiffened, his wand slipping from his sleeve and arriving in his grip as he slowly turned to see who now stood behind him.

Storm.

Cade's fellow Sorcerer stood before him, arms crossed in front of his black wool cloak. His shoulder-length brown hair was nearly frozen with ice, his bright eyes narrowed.

"You're alive," Storm mused, turning to view the base behind them. "They're clearly not."

"Not all of us have teleportation spheres and the ability

to shift into beings that can fly," Cade snapped. "Why are you here? To mock me? And why do you look like you just spent four days in Ryiah's wilderness?"

"To fetch you. And, because I just finished fetching Savron from a freezing lake," Storm revealed, slipping his hands into his pockets. "We're regrouping then?"

"So, it's done then?" Cade hissed. "The Allies have won? Just like that?"

"Just like that."

"Did Savron survive the freezing lake? Is Ryole alive?" He wasn't sure he wanted to know the answer to his questions. It was difficult enough to stomach the fact that the Allies had obliterated a quarter of their forces in a matter of days. Perhaps hours.

"Come with me and find out for yourself," Storm directed, kneeling to retrieve the chrome sphere he used to travel so easily.

Cade's jaw clenched as he turned toward his stallion, tapping its backside. He watched as it barreled off into the surrounding valley, and for a moment, he wished he was atop it, fleeing from whatever punishment was on the horizon.

"Tell me," Storm said as he tossed the chrome sphere into the snow, a portal to the Regal Mountains flickering to life. "Do you still *hate* retrieving those messages from the Draconian jurisdiction?"

Growling, Cade's face twisted into a scowl. "I'd give anything to just be Ryole's errand boy again."

It had taken two days' worth of healing in the infirmary for Ebony to deem Ash well enough to be discharged. She'd have been happier if that had meant she could leave Dracus and regroup with the other Allies in the Kingdom of Elves. However, she was forbidden from leaving the Kingdom for another week at least, perhaps two, to allow her wound to heal completely.

Ash hadn't known her daggers had been blessed with Moonshade. That it was the same serum her second task revolved around that made the enchanted set so powerful. She smiled at the coincidence, though she had grown a small hatred for the substance. The Moonshade was the very reason she was healing slowly, while as a Berserker her wound should have healed within a few hours.

"A few weeks ago, an injury like that would have killed me," Ash told Penelope, who led her gently through the Council's corridor. While she'd been released into Alistair's care, seeing as Ebony had commanded him to watch over her and keep her from doing anything rash, the Rider had needed to handle his Dragon for a time, and he'd enlisted the princess's help in keeping her from rushing off into the Realm.

"It nearly killed you now," Penelope reminded her softly as they arrived before the king's suite. "You had us scared half to death, you know."

Ash bit her lip as she watched Penelope place her palm against the identification pad beside the door. It began to glow from red to green, and the sound of it unlocking led her brow to raise.

"He gave you access to his personal quarters?"

Penelope gave her a small smile as they entered the extravagant foyer. "He plans to make us dinner today," she told her, leading her gently into the sitting room beyond. Black velvet couches sat atop a decorative carpet woven with red and gold thread. Paintings and black butterfly banners adorned the walls, flowers and books piled on every surface.

"Any particular reason for that?" Ash glowered at her older sister as she gently lowered herself onto one of the couches. A dull ache still reverberated down her side, a constant reminder of what Malachai had done to her. Once the pain faded, she'd still have the scar. A symbol of her own stupidity in thinking she might have found a way to get Lincoln back.

"We just want to make sure you're well," Penelope insisted as a maid drifted into the room, a silver tray of tea in her hands. "Thank you, miss," the Princess said as she took a cup for herself.

The maid approached Ash, and she hesitantly took a cup for herself. Normally, she'd have insisted fetching her tea herself, as she didn't believe in commanding others to do the things she could so easily do on her own. But, the pain in her side told her to keep her mouth shut and accept the assistance. For once.

"Richard will also be joining us," Penelope added with a bright smile. "Valentina as well."

Ash's jaw clenched. "Are you sure this is just a friendly dinner?"

LATER THAT EVENING, ASH SAT UNCOMFORTABLY AT Loren's dining room table with Alistair at her side. He appeared rather awkward himself, his spine as straight as a board as he examined the meal before him.

The King and his fellow Council members sat in silence, eyeing both Ash and her fellow Ally over their tall glasses of blood. Penelope chewed softly, as a princess should. The only sound to be heard were the quick gulps of drinks and the swallowing of roasted chicken.

Ash kept her gaze on her plate, still nearly full. She hadn't had much of an appetite since she'd awoken in the infirmary. The only thing she cared to consume was blood. Preferably Immortal blood, which she'd learned had been the delicious taste coating her mouth when she'd first awoken.

"Well," Loren began, his gray eyes smiling. "Congratulations on completing your first task."

Nodding, Ash offered him a smile. "What an adventure it was."

"If that's what you want to call it." Alistair sighed.

Richard cleared his throat, and Ash's gaze darted toward the man who sat beside the Prophetess across the table from her. "There are some things we'd like to discuss with you, Princess."

Ash stiffened at the word, her fingers curling around the fabric of the napkin in her lap.

A trap. Not a dinner.

"And what are those things?" Ash inquired as sweetly as she could manage.

"In regard to your Sectra, and your position in this Realm," Valentina added. "You are aware that you hold a particularly high standing in Idona now, correct?"

Nodding slowly, Ash hadn't thought much about it. Sure, she'd told Ebony she now had the power to revoke laws, if she chose to, but she hadn't bothered to consider what else she might do, or the politics surrounding her current status.

"The Sectra Holders throughout our Galaxy are warriors chosen to defend their Realms. They're as respected as the kings and queens that rule the population," Loren told her, folding his hands on the table in front of him. "Long ago, when Zerin broke out in a vicious civil war, the royal family perished, their entire court with them. There was no heir, and because of this, as Sectra Holder, Sampson Ivanenko, was named King. He is still king to this day, as he chose not to appoint another."

Ash looked toward Alistair, as if he might know exactly what the King was trying to say. All the Rider did was stare back at her, his eyes dropping to the Sectra that hung around her neck.

"You, as the Sectra Holder to the main Realm, have the power to choose our way of life here in Idona, and hold a higher status than your fellow Sectra Holders throughout Si Realtra," Valentina told her softly. "When the Idonian Kingdom fell, with no Sectra Holder to take Meera's place immediately, it was decided that the Elves and Draconians would rule Idona together. But now that we *do* have a Sectra Holder, that agreement is void. The Elves and the Draconians are no longer in charge of what occurs in our Realm."

Ash gawked at the Prophetess. What little she'd eaten

of her dinner threatened to make another appearance. "Why are you telling me this *now* and not before I received the Sectra?" she asked, her heart rate growing sluggish.

"The Amulet has remained with the royal family since it was first blessed by the Great Sovereign herself," Loren told her warily. "*We*," he gestured to those around the table, "have never had anything to do with it. There was no question of rule because the Sectra has always been worn by a High King, High Queen, or one of their heirs."

"I *am* one of their heirs," Ash reminded him, her tone less than kind.

"When Xavier seized the Idonian Kingdom and took your parents' throne," Richard told her, his expression grave, "it caused a rift in the chain or ruling Idona has experienced since the Dawn of the New Age. This is the first time in history that the Idonian Sectra has been held by someone *outside* of the Idonian Kingdom. The first time any of *us* have to worry about it. Forgive us if it took us some time to realize exactly what it all means."

Ash's heart sank in her chest, her features softening. "I apologize," she whispered. "So, what am I to do now, then?"

"You're interim High Queen," Valentina told her, her words causing Ash to jump in her chair, which only resulted in her wincing from pain shooting up her side. "I know, it's not what you want, and by no means to do you have to *keep* that title once you've defeated Xavier. But, the title will give you enough pull to bring our Realm's armies together. Whether it be by force or not."

It was then that Ash realized what this was *really* about. The realization hit her so hard that she nearly choked on her own breath, her eyes darting down the table to where Penelope and Loren sat with blank stares in her direction.

The silence spreading about the room spoke a million

words. It told a story, one of love and one of war. One of rivals and one of Allies. Inwardly, Ash felt that she had no *true* place at this table, with these people. She may be a VanCamp by blood, but her heart was not in Dracus, or the Idonian Kingdom. It was in Crane.

Yet, if what Richard and Valentina said was true, Ash could be the bridge between the Elves and the Draconians. She could keep the peace throughout the Realm, as every Sectra Holder was meant to do.

"I'll be your interim High Queen. For now," Ash offered with a sigh.

"You already are," Richard reminded her kindly.

"And when the war is through," Valentina added. "you'll be able to choose someone to take your place. As High King or Queen."

Ash blinked, surprised by her words. "But Penelope is the direct heir."

"I *was*," Penelope revealed, her voice revealing a tinge of sadness. "But now that you wear the Sectra, it is your decision who ascends to our parents' throne. Which means you could pick anyone."

Swallowing hard, all Ash could do was stare at her. She didn't say a word, though her mind was racing. She watched as her sister took Loren's hand in hers, and though love seemed to matter far less than the war raging around them, it was a miracle to find it in the midst of the darkness that had swallowed their Realm. One would think that after such loss, it would be impossible to experience any love at all. Yet there it was, for Ash to see, right in front of her eyes.

Smiling softly, Ash knew exactly what she would do as interim High Queen.

"I'm going to need a coronation."

wo days waiting in the Kingdom of Elves had been long enough for Quinn. He found the Golden City to be enthralling, though it wasn't enough to distract him from the stares he and Cooper received everywhere that they went. If it weren't for the message they'd received from Alistair last night, that Ash was being released from the infirmary, he might have lost his mind by now.

He'd been furious with his brother for allowing Ash to slip into such danger, but in the end, the only person that could be blamed was Malachai himself. One day, Quinn would make the bastard pay for what he'd done to not only Lincoln, but now Ash as well. The pain he'd inflicted upon this Realm had gone on long enough. And though the Archer desperately wanted to be the man who would one day behead the Prince, he knew he'd need to get in line, for there were *many* people who wanted to get their vengeance.

Every citizen in Idona, to be exact.

"You look lost in thought," Craven mentioned as he took a seat beside Quinn in the massive Great Hall. The Elves certainly took pride in every room in their castle, and it showed everywhere that the Archer dared to look. Every floor was made of white marble, speckled with silver and gold. The walls were pale yet adorned with massive banners portraying the Chamberlain family symbol—the tree of life.

"There's nothing else to do here for us right now but think," Quinn grumbled as he pushed his food around his plate with his fork. "No matter how much I dreaded that first task, I'd pay any amount of coin to get out of here and complete the second. Waiting for Ash and Alistair is pure agony."

Cooped gave his brother a nod of agreement. "I bet Loren will let them use the portal rooms as soon as she's cleared to leave Dracus."

"In another bloody week," Craven growled.

"As long as she's healed, that's all that matters," Cooper insisted, optimistic as usual, despite the dreary circumstances.

Sighing, Craven focused on his meal, still trying to regain his strength from his near-death experience in a boiling well. Only a few minutes of silence between them had passed when the screens throughout the Great Hall flickered on, revealing King Loren's face. He wore his crown, which only told the Draconian that whatever he was about to say would be some sort of royal decree.

"A Realm-wide broadcast!" an Elf gasped at the table beside them.

As if they'd been summoned, the other Allies rushed into the Great Hall, striding toward their table. "Have any of you checked your messages?" Marcus asked with a glare.

Quinn paled, his heart skipping a beat in his chest. "No," he admitted. "Why? Did something happen to Ash?"

"Just watch. Valentina said Ash is about to address the Realm," Lucinda said as she patted his shoulder, her eyes finding the closest screen. Quinn followed her gaze, his throat growing dry.

"Greetings my fellow Idonian citizens," Loren began with a wide smile. "So far, this Red Winter has been chaotic at best. And I appreciate each and every one of you, Mortal and Immortal, for your patience with us. It's been a long eighteen years without our beloved VanCamp's holding the High Throne. But all of that changes. Today."

Quinn's eyes bulged as the king stepped aside to reveal the room he'd been standing in. The Draconian throne room. The black marble floors were nearly covered completely by Draconians, while Loren joined his fellow Council members on the dais. Everyone but Anastasia, who now sat beside Quinn, her eyes wide with shock.

"What the hell does he mean?" Morghan shook his head in disbelief. "It's impossible. Xavier still holds the High Throne."

"It's not impossible," Lucinda told him. "Not as long as the Sectra hangs around Ash's neck. Something tells me all of this has something to do with *that*."

An orchestra began to play music, and each body in the throne room turned to face whoever approached from the door. It was Penelope VanCamp holding a sparkling silver crown atop a velvet pillow.

Quinn gulped as he watched Ash follow behind her, dressed in nothing other than her Ally uniform. She appeared well, though slightly pale. Her movements were rough, clearly forced. He could tell she was in pain, though she held her head high as she fought to hide it.

He shook his head, unwilling to believe what he was about to see. Unwilling to believe that it was *real*.

The moment Lincoln returned to the Idonian Kingdom, having chosen to deliver Constance to Xavier personally, every screen in Solaris City flickered on. He ceased his walking, his grip still around the Witch's arm. Alrich stood behind him, gaping up at the screens as well.

"What's going on?" Lincoln asked him, watching as a woman in a black uniform with a sapphire stripe across her jacket approached the dais.

"I'm not sure I want to know," Alrich hissed.

Everyone in the city had paused to watch the screens as well, their eyes wide and their mouths open. Not a word was spoken as they watched the woman kneel before the Draconian King, an amulet hanging from her neck. The sight of it led many people in the city to gasp and some to growl.

"Ash Snow - VanCamp," The Draconian King began, every word he said laced with strength and sincerity. "Do you swear to protect our Realm, and the entire Galaxy of Si Realtra, with your life?"

"I do," the woman answered, still kneeling before the king.

"Do you swear to rid our Galaxy of any evil that may arise?

"I do."

"Do you swear to lay down your life for your Idonian people if need be?"

Lincoln grew more and more rigid with each word the King said, and each *I do* the woman replied with.

"Will you guide this Realm until your dying breath?" The King shuddered as the question sailed past his lips. He stared down at the woman, his black crown gleaming in the lights above them.

"I do."

The King's smile stretched from ear to ear as he turned to face the Princess beside him, gently lifting the crown from the pillow she held. Lincoln held his breath as he watched it lower until it was nestled onto the woman's forehead. She rose to her feet then, a silver badge gleaming on her chest in the center of the sapphire stripe running across her jacket. Two Dragons forming the shape of a heart, separated by a shining claymore. He released his breath, his grip around the Witch's arm tightening.

She cringed, yelping from the pain he inflicted.

"On behalf of the Draconian Council and the Idonian Council, I proclaim you Interim High Queen of Si Realtra," the King announced, and Lincoln could have sworn a single tear slipped from his eyes.

"This is bad," Alrich huffed from beside the Archer. "Really fucking bad."

MALACHAI STARED UP AT THE SCREEN WITH WIDE EYES, HIS knees weakening. He found himself lowering to sit on the edge of the fountain in the Solaris City square, his stomach twisting into knots. He'd failed. And now, the entire Realm knew. His father included. There wasn't a doubt in his mind that the Dark King was watching her right now as she stood with that crown of diamonds atop her head. The Sectra gleamed brightly around her throat.

Malachai had failed. Ash had lived. And now she was High Queen.

Interim High Queen. Malachai frowned at the title. He wondered exactly what the Messenger was planning as he watched her turn to face whatever camera was broadcasting her coronation for the entire Realm to see.

Her green eyes were shining brighter, speckled with silver as she stared into the camera. She stood there as if he hadn't stabbed her just a few days ago. As if she wasn't fazed by that attack at all.

"I am no queen," were Ash's first words to the Realm she'd just sworn to protect with her life. "But I am your Messenger. And let what I'm about to say be a message to the Dark King living on borrowed time, his Prince of Darkness, and the Pandora who have terrorized our Realm for three decades. Your reign has now come to an end. Xavier, you are now just a man in a castle you have no right to. And I will *personally* come to take it back. Every army in this Realm will be at your doorstep by winter's end. This is Idona's *last* Red Winter.

"And to my fellow citizens of Idona, if you have held on to the VanCamp family flag all these years, fly it now. If you were once a member of my father's Mortal army, sharpen your sword and polish your armor. If you were once a Rebel, join us when we call. We will not just take back our Kingdom, but our entire Realm. Together."

The connection was lost, either on purpose, or on accident. Malachai didn't care either way. No longer having to look at her face was a relief.

The entire city was cloaked in a thick, tension-filled silence around the Prince as he rose from his seat on the fountain's edge and turned toward the castle looming off in the distance. His father was there. Likely screaming. And he would have to face him.

He should have killed her, and though he still had no clue as to why he didn't, Malachai would pay the price for his failure. He pulled in a breath, the frigid air turning to sharp shards of ice in his lungs, and pushed through Solaris City. The people he passed bowed, though they had no idea what he'd done and what he would now face, or that they may never see him again.

Whatever Malachai had done to get his father to the throne he now sat on would not matter the moment he walked through those castle doors. His creation of the Pandora wouldn't matter. His beautiful mind wouldn't matter. He'd failed when he was needed most, to dispatch the woman who was designed by the Moons *specifically* to kill his father. His ultimate match. The only person capable of defeating a man possessed by the purest form of darkness.

Nothing mattered. Not anymore. And soon enough, Malachai was certain he would be reduced to nothing himself.

Craven was in shock.

For a long moment, the Great Hall remained silent as if everyone else was in shock as well. But then the roaring began, from his fellow Allies, as they shouted for joy and jumped up and down. Ash was High Queen.

The Draconian shook his head as if this was all a dream and he was willing it away. But it was not a dream. The heir to the Idonian throne had carried the crown down that aisle in the throne room herself. Penelope had handed over her throne to *Ash*. For whatever reason, Craven was unsure.

The VanCamps had taken back their throne.

There was no doubt in Craven's mind that in Dracus, they'd discovered some sort of loophole. But then again, it wasn't a loophole at all. The chain of command in each Realm had always been clear, and with no High Queen or King to stand above Ash as the Sectra Holder, that left her in control of Idona with the option to take the throne for herself, as King Sampson of Zerin had once done.

Interim High Queen. Craven's brow furrowed. It was clear, by that title alone, that Ash didn't intend to remain High Queen. So, was this all a ruse to keep the Elves from striking against Penelope when they found out what she'd done? To stop them from punishing the Draconians and Loren by keeping their army behind these golden walls?

"This is insane," Vincent insisted. "Absolutely insane."

"Insane indeed," Marcus agreed. "But the best thing I've ever seen."

"Finally." Morghan reclined in his chair.

"We should celebrate," Anastasia suggested.

"We can," Lucinda said. "*After* we all finish the remaining two tasks. You all seem to forget there is still a prophecy to fulfill. Ash needs that Scepter if she expects the words she just said to ever ring true."

Esmeralda stared at the screen in her personal quarters, though it was black now. As black as the blackest night. The girl's face had disappeared, leaving the Elven Queen to her thoughts.

"What do you make of this, Mother?" Mika asked from her spot on the soft white couch.

All the Queen could do was shake her head, her eyes growing dry as she'd failed to blink in minutes.

"Does this upset you?" her daughter asked softly.

"No," Esmeralda told her truthfully. "It's just... surreal."

"Yes, it is," Mika breathed. "But our Realm will finally be safe."

"Your father won't be happy about this," Esmeralda

blurted, regretting her words as soon as she said them. "Loren never reached out to us to inform us of what he was doing. We prepared Penelope all her life for *her* to ascend to her parents' throne. The Draconian King should have included us in this decision. After all, he did say on behalf of the Idonian Council. He did not include the Elves in that statement. Your father will be offended."

Mika nodded slowly, having gone pale. "What do you suppose he'll do about it?"

"Moons only know, dear."

53

The second the connection was severed, Ash excused her from the throne room and found the nearest washroom to wretch in. Her sore side screamed at her as she emptied the contents of her stomach, wiping her mouth with the back of her hand. She could only hope the people of Idona had listened to her. That maybe, somewhere, Lincoln had seen her face and remembered her.

"Ash?" Alistair's voice sounded further away than it truly was. "Are you alright?" he asked.

The only sound to greet the Rider as he entered the washroom was the sound of more vomiting. He sighed, moving to stand behind her.

"Let's hope that broadcast doesn't blow up in my face," Ash said between gasps of air.

"I'm sure it will," Alistair told her, though she could hear the smile in his voice. She turned to look at him, her eyes watering. "Why don't we go somewhere and try to relax and just not think of it?"

Nodding, Ash pushed herself to her feet with wobbly legs and followed the Rider out of the washroom. They returned to Marcus's apartment, where they'd stayed last night, instead of the apartment Alistair shared with Craven. Apparently, the pair had rekindled their friendship so quickly that the Electric Immortal had offered Alistair a bedroom.

Though they'd brought Craven's cat, Luna, to stay with them in Marcus's apartment. Valentina had been looking after the fluffy black feline while her owner was away, but Alistair had grown rather fond of her, and decided he'd rather have her for now.

By the time they made it back to the Councilor's Corridor, and to its very end where Marcus's apartment lay, the cat was already meowing for her dinner. Now that Ash had emptied the contents of her stomach, she was starving as well.

"Should I call and have someone bring up dinner?" Alistair asked as he shed his uniform jacket, hanging it over one of the barstool chairs beside the large island in the center of the kitchen.

Ash shook her head and opened the fridge. It was nearly empty, as Marcus had donated all the perishable food to the castle kitchens. But, there were still a few chicken breasts in the freezer, and some broth in the cupboard.

"If we can get someone to fetch us some carrots, celery, and pasta, we might be able to make some homemade chicken soup," she told him, her stomach rumbling at the idea.

"I'll send a message to Shadow then." Alistair grinned. "I'll let him know that Her Majesty would like him to personally grow her some vegetables."

Ash bristled. "Don't you dare!"

"Too late."

"Alistair!" she snarled.

"What? I'm just being a loyal subject." The Rider shrugged.

"You do realize that this is temporary, right? Only until I slaughter Xavier and give the throne to someone far more deserving and qualified," Ash reminded him as she pulled on one of the cabinets, revealing the small wine rack hiding within. She smirked at the full bottles of red, white, and blush wines. "Dry or sweet?" she asked with a smirk.

"Got any whiskey?" Alistair frowned.

"Not a fan of wine?"

"Oh, I am," he assured her. "It's just I could use a shot more than anything right now."

SHADOW ARRIVED AT THE APARTMENT A SHORT WHILE later, sporting a deep frown with a canvas bag filled with Ash's requested vegetables.

"It's been two hours and you're *already* throwing out demands?" Shadow chastised as he dropped the bag on the counter.

"That was Alistair," Ash assured him as she offered him an empty wine glass and poured enough wine to fill it to its brim. "Want to stay for dinner? Consider it payment for your vegetables."

Shadow's brows perked as he raised the glass to his lips. "I have no other plans," he quipped, his pale eyes flashing with amusement. "What's on the menu?"

"Homemade chicken soup," Alistair announced in the middle of thawing the frozen chicken with his fire abilities.

"Perfect." Shadow beamed. "Shay and I always used to make chicken soup on the eve of a big storm."

"Big storm?" Ash's eyes drifted to the glass walls. Her smile quickly transitioned into a frown as she noted the heavy storm clouds rolling in from central Idona. "Fantastic. Just what we need."

"It's not like you're going anywhere," Shadow reminded her, which only led her frown to deepen. "For now," he added to redeem himself.

Sighing, Ash sank into one of the barstools and finished off her glass. She eyed the canvas bag in front of her on the island and bit her lip. "Since you grow vegetables, can you cut them too?" she asked Shadow with her best, dashing smile.

THE EVENING HAD BEEN PLEASANT. SHAY HAD EVENTUALLY joined them, finishing off the rest of their soup in a manner of seconds as they watched the snow begin to fall through the glass walls. Even though the Daniels siblings were curious to know about Ash's childhood, she had pressed them about their own, and indulged in their adventurous stories.

Shay and Shadow were an interesting pair. Two siblings orphaned due to the Five Realm War, who possessed two different elemental abilities strong enough to rival everyone in their separate clans. Shadow had become the Earth Clan Leader when he turned thirty, the youngest age any Draconian had been to earn the position. Shay had followed soon after, at twenty-seven, and broke his record.

That had been twenty years ago, and both siblings still held their positions proudly with no intentions of giving them up. Their sibling rivalry to best each other at everything is what had driven them all the way to their seats on the Council. As Ash fought to sleep, she wondered if she and her siblings would have been the same way, though she and Lincoln had always had a slight rivalry of their own. The only difference was that what they usually fought about was who would kill the most Pandora, or who could hit a bullseye first with a bow and arrow. Whoever lost would muck the horse stalls. Alone.

Smiling at the memory, Ash allowed herself to laugh, likely for the first time, perhaps in weeks. The sensation felt strange in her throat, the sound nearly foreign.

Turning in bed, onto the side that didn't inflict any agony upon her, Ash found herself catching sight of the storm. The snow was falling so hard she could barely make out the view of the Training Center she usually had. In fact, all she saw was pure white.

The storm was unnerving, as if it was unnatural. Ash hadn't seen anything like it in all her life. Perhaps the isle Dracus sat upon saw more snow? She shook her head, doubting that was the case.

Anxiety began to grip Ash once again as she thought of the enemy, and what they might be capable of. Upon meeting Savron, it was clear that Xavier's Dark Army was more than just the Pandora. He had at least one Warlock, but did he have more? Were there Sorcerers working with him? Sorcerers capable of summoning storms such as the one raging outside?

Ash's breathing grew ragged as she thought of what they would face at winter's end, when she and every available army would march on the Idonian Kingdom. What exactly would be waiting for them at the gates to Solaris City? She wasn't sure she wanted to know, but knew she needed to end it. As soon as she could, so that she could hand off her crown to someone else and fade back into the shadows, where she belonged. Out of sight. Out of mind.

Growling, Ash couldn't wait another second. She needed to get back out into the field and get that Moonshade from the Red Witch. She needed to feel that Scepter in her hands and then feel Xavier's chest cave beneath its blade.

She dressed as quickly as she could, slipping into her uniform pants and jacket. Her side screamed at her once again as she bent over to tie her boots and armed herself with her daggers. One of them was still missing. She hoped Morghan and Cooper had retrieved it for her, or else Malachai might return to the scene of the crime, snatch it, and use it on her once again.

Ash's mouth grew dry at the thought.

She would not survive him a second time. Not if he had one of her daggers.

Pulling in a deep breath, Ash left the oasis of her room and shut the door behind her before turning down the hall. She passed the master bedroom. Marcus had left the opaque function of his walls turned off, and she was able to see through the walls. His bed was neatly made, every surface in his room cleared of all objects but one. A photo of him with the late High King and Queen when he was little more than a boy. Ash frowned at the sight and silently prayed Marcus wouldn't be furious with her for what she was about to do.

Knocking on the glass door to the guest bedroom, Ash listened to bare feet padding across the hardwood floors as Alistair moved to answer her. He opened the door, clad in only a pair sleeping pants, a glare upon his face.

"Why are you in uniform?"

"Get dressed." Ash kept her eyes on his face, though this was the first she was seeing of the tattoos sprawling across his chest in the same elegant, knot-like patterns that swam down his arms. "We're leaving. Now."

"You aren't cleared for the field yet," Alistair reminded her with a growl.

"The war won't wait for me to heal."

"It's been going on for almost thirty years," he reminded her. "I'm sure it'll be okay with an extra week."

"Get dressed," she repeated her command. "Or I'll leave without you."

Reluctantly, Alistair abandoned his place in the threshold and rushed to put his uniform on. While he was doing that, Ash fetched her pack and headed down to the kitchen where she piled chrome thermoses filled with blood inside. Enough to sustain her and Alistair, even if her body relied on it now more than it usually did. A healing Draconian was a *hungry* Draconian.

As she strapped Lionheart's scabbard to her back, knowing it would be easier for travel opposed to its usual place on her hip, Alistair approached her. He was still scowling, even as he slipped a pair of black gloves onto his hands.

"It's blizzarding out there," he grumbled.

"I'm aware," Ash told him as she slipped gloves onto her own hands and wrapped her black mask around the lower half of her face. "We'll need to find someone willing to open the gates to the Unity Bridge."

"You mean the glass bridge that will be impossible to see in this snow?" Alistair's brows pulled together. "The really *slippery* glass bridge?"

Ash released a frustrated growl. "We'll go slow."

"You've lost your mind, Princess," Alistair accused as he abandoned her side, and headed for the front door. "And just so you know, no one is going to open that gate for you. Not now. For more than one reason. You're still healing, and the weather conditions are less than ideal for travel on foot."

"We could always break into the portal room," Ash suggested.

"How many rules did you want to break today?"

"As little as possible," she sighed, "which is why we're going to walk. To the Kingdom of Elves."

Alistair shook his head in disbelief. "That's a week and a half away from here. We'll be crossing the entire Realm. Whereas if we waited the week until you were healed, Loren would *let* us use the portal room."

"Then we'll go to the Regal Mountains," Ash countered. "That's only five days away. We can reach out to the other Allies and tell them to meet us there."

"And risk encountering Veda on our own?" Alistair scoffed.

"I am not going to sit in this kingdom and wait any longer," Ash declared, her fists clenching at her sides. "Not when we've already finished one task. I bet you that storm outside is Xavier's doing. Something to slow us down, to keep us from getting that Moonshade he knows will kill him."

Alistair's eyes widened above his mask. "I hadn't thought of that."

"Well, I did," Ash snapped, looking toward the glass walls once again. She stiffened at the sight of the wall of white before her. This would not be an easy journey. Not in the slightest. "That storm looks like it was made for Ryiah. Not Idona."

"Who could do that?"

"A Sorcerer." It was a guess. "One that specializes in summoning storms."

"There's only one Sorcerer I know of that is capable of such things," Alistair said softly. "Abernathy. But he wouldn't work with Xavier. He'd slit his own throat before he'd do that."

"I don't care *who* it is," Ash insisted. "They're trying to deter us and it won't work. Now, let's go. I'm sure Benjamin will open the gate for us."

"Are you sure about that?" Alistair asked warily.

"If he doesn't, I'll strangle him with his tie."

BENJAMIN WASN'T WEARING A TIE; THEREFORE, ASH couldn't choke him with it when he said no. But she still had her bare hands, and the temptation to use them was certainly there.

"Please." Ash debated whether or not sticking out her bottom lip would work, but the look in Benjamin's brassy eyes told her otherwise.

"No." Benjamin crossed his arms in front of his plain white t-shirt.

Sighing, Ash glanced around the long corridor as if there might be someone listening. The only other souls in sight where the guards, and last she knew, they were forbidden from speaking of council member interactions.

"Listen…" she fought not to growl and failed. "There is someone out there, somewhere, generating that storm outside. They're trying to hold us back, and right now, they're succeeding."

Benjamin's features softened, his brow furrowing. "I thought it looked off. How'd you come to the conclusion that someone might be causing it?"

"Savron Phantom," Ash admitted. "If Xavier had a Warlock working for him, he probably has more. And Sorcerers, too. He has an entire host in the Regal Mountains. Malachai said so himself. And from what I've heard about Hans of the Mist, plenty of powerful beings lurk there. Who's to say Xavier wouldn't use one of them to conjure up a storm like this? One powerful enough to get us to hunker down and try to wait it out. But it won't end. I'm sure of it."

"Not until he needs to pull everyone in to defend the Idonian Kingdom," Alistair added.

Benjamin sucked on his teeth, his eyes darting between the two Allies. "Where will you go?"

"The Kingdom of Elves. So we can proceed with our fellow Allies," Ash replied. She wouldn't dare approach Veda without all nine of them.

"That's a long walk for someone in recovery from a serious wound," Benjamin warned, his eyes narrowing. "I doubt your stitches have even dissolved yet."

"I won't push myself. Alistair can kill for me for the time being."

"And if you're intercepted?" Benjamin lifted a brow.

"I have abilities. I won't lift my sword."

"What if it's Malachai that intercepts you?"

Alistair stiffened beside Ash, and she could hear his breath catching in his throat. "Then I'll summon my Dragon and let her shred that prick to ribbons."

"Why not summon your Dragon now?" Benjamin countered. "Surely she can fly *above* the storm."

"It's too risky," Alistair replied. "Even above the storm, the winds will be harsh. Too harsh to fly in."

"Then at least let me get you guys some gear," Benjamin insisted, and Ash's heart leaped in her chest. "Grant and I have recently developed something new with Vincent's help. It's a force field of sorts. It'll protect you from the storm. We'll have to retrieve it from the Communications Center."

"Thank you." Ash released a breath of relief.

"Long live the Queen." Benjamin winked.

Constance shook terribly as she was led through the Idonian Castle. Under different circumstances, she might have been in awe of the place. The history of Idona was written on every wall. She could picture the High Queen walking beneath the arched ceilings, running her fingers along the paintings of all those who had lived before her. Statues of fallen heroes sat on every floor, each of them with a different story to tell. The historian in Constance wanted to marvel in it and ask as many questions as her mouth would allow.

Lincoln was a silent statue himself beside her, a shell of the man he once was. Constance tried to avoid looking at him if she could help it. The sight of his face only broke her heart, and his grip on her arm shattered her soul. She doubted whatever bruise he'd left would disappear easily. Perhaps it would brand her forever.

The corridor he led her through, or dragged her through, was dark and lit only by sconces along the wall. Night had fallen outside, the entire city silent after Ash…

Ash. Constance was still blinking back tears at the thought of the woman she'd once known. She hadn't been able to breathe as she'd watched King Loren Mason place that crown of diamonds upon her head. *Ash is High Queen.* She shook her head, unable to believe it.

The villager Constance had rivaled had looked so different. Far more beautiful than when she'd last seen her, bleeding from the nose and begging to go on the hunt to find the Werewolf. She'd never returned after that, and now it was clear where she'd gone. To Dracus. To fight this war and *win*.

Constance pulled in a painful breath as Lincoln came to a halt, raising a fist to knock on the large oak door in front of them.

"Enter!" a nasty growl of a voice responded.

Lincoln opened the door and thrust Constance inside, where the Dark King rose from his desk, his dark eyes scanning her from head to toe.

Another man stood in the room, his eyes on the floor. His dark hair fell limp around him, the same shade and length as her own. Constance eyed him for a moment, her heart thundering against the walls of her chest.

"A spitting image of your mother," the King seethed. "Don't you think so, Malachai?"

Constance trembled as Lincoln dragged her toward the man, forcing her to stand at his side, his grip never leaving her arm.

The man beside her finally took his gaze off the floor, his eyes meeting her own. Constance held her breath, her blood turning to ice as she stared into his red eyes. She didn't miss the pain that lurked within them before he broke their stare, looking toward his father.

"I suppose," he replied in an emotionless tone.

"I certainly see the resemblance," Xavier insisted, crossing his arms. "Tell me, other than those beautiful features of yours, what else did you inherit?"

Constance bit her tongue so hard, she drew blood. Lincoln's grip on her arm tightened once again, and she cried out in response, tears springing to her eyes.

"Address your King," he ordered.

Shaking her head, Constance prepared for whatever blow was to come. Who would kill her? The man she loved beside her, the Prince, or the King? Which one would hurt her the most?

"I can smell it, you know," Malachai told her softly. He seemed so depleted. Defeated, even. "The Magic."

Constance scowled at him, fighting the urge to spit at his feet or perhaps in that familiar face of his. "What of it? I won't be using it on your behalf," she finally spoke. "Not after what you did to her."

The Prince frowned, the pain returning to his gaze.

"She was pregnant, you know," Constance continued between clenched teeth. "My father wept over that nursery for *months* before he finally took the crib down."

Malachai refused to meet her gaze again, and only looked toward his father, who was smirking as he lowered himself into his oversized leather chair.

"I do not care who my mother was to either of you," Constance declared.

"You can't change the blood in your veins," Xavier told her. "I suggest you make yourself at home. Perhaps show your dear cousins some forgiveness. Get to know them. Though I'm afraid Malachai won't be around for you to bond with."

Constance hissed, "As if I care."

But Xavier didn't respond to her. He merely looked toward his son, who stared back, so still it was almost as if he'd been carved from ice. But he was melting beneath the fiery stare of his father. The Prince may try to hide it, but

Constance could see. He was weak in the presence of the Dark King. No more than a trembling, beaten dog.

"You will leave this kingdom," Xavier's voice was so low that it was terrifying, "and you will not return. Not unless you have that bloody Messenger's *head* in your hands, and her *Sectra* around *my* neck. Do you understand me?"

Malachai nodded, perhaps too quickly.

"If you fail again," the King hissed, "it will be your head. You've served your purpose. Don't forget that. Lincoln can easily do whatever it is that you do in the next Realm, you useless fucking runt."

The Prince said nothing. He only stared back at his father. Constance wasn't even sure if he was breathing.

"Leave," Xavier snapped. "Now. All of you."

Lincoln pulled on Constance's arm, her eyes wide with horror. "You'd speak to your own *son* that way?" she roared, rage roiling deep in her gut.

Malachai ceased his walking, having gone rigid, his hand still wrapped around the doorknob.

"Lock her up," was all Xavier said before they all filed out of the room.

Constance was writhing beneath Lincoln's grip as they entered the hall. "Let me go," she ordered. "I'd rather escort myself to the dungeons than spend another second with you." She hadn't realized that the Prince was still there, staring at her.

"I didn't know she was pregnant," he told her. "I do not harm children."

"Well, you did," Constance retorted, fighting to hold her chin high. "And while you might not have killed the McBride family, you still killed Pat. Left his children orphans. This man right here, dragging me through the

Realm and through this castle, grew up without a father because of you."

Malachai's face twisted, the only form of true emotion he would reveal. Annoyance. Perhaps hatred.

"And there's no doubt in my mind that he's in this *state* because of you," Constance hissed. "Now you're off to go and kill Ash. Another child, left an orphan, because of *you.*"

The Prince turned his back on her, preparing to storm down the hall, but Constance didn't care that she might have hurt his feelings and called after him.

"When are you going to stop ruining lives?" she thundered.

"When someone does me a favor and ends mine!" he shot right back before fading into the darkness.

Sighing, Constance waited for Lincoln to continue with marching her to whatever horrific dungeons lay beneath the castle. She looked up at him, only to find him staring back at her, his expression blank. "What?" she asked.

"I've just never seen anyone daft enough to talk to a king, or a prince, that way." He shrugged. "It's nearly amusing."

Constance snorted, rolling her eyes. "Family is a complicated thing," she said. "You'd know that if they hadn't replaced your brain with whatever is rolling around in your skull now. A pea, perhaps?"

And with that, they were off. Constance walked and was partially dragged, to a bedroom. Not a dungeon, to her surprise. Lincoln threw her inside, allowing her to tumble onto the stone floors, and locked the door. He did not return. Later, when a servant came to deliver her supper, she said he'd left again to finish his task.

The thought gave her chills. She'd seen the faces of the other Mortals he'd captured. Alrich had said they had abilities, courtesy of the king. Constance hadn't witnessed anything strange about them but didn't doubt it. Her stomach churned at the thought of what might become of them, or how many more Lincoln would drag to this kingdom. Some of them had been little more than children. She'd seen one of them, taken straight from school.

Now lying in darkness, Constance curled up onto the rough sheets atop the bed, bringing her knees to her chest. She allowed herself to cry. Not only for herself, but all the others Xavier would force into war. She had never known her aunt. Her mother had told her next to nothing about the woman who was married to Xavier, who had birthed his children. She knew only that she was a powerful Witch, and an even more powerful mother. She'd given her life for her children. The most honorable way to die for *any* woman.

Constance wondered how Soroya Trevayne would feel if she knew what her husband had done after her death. If she knew that he'd forced his children into war. That one of her sons had even gone missing, likely dead. Constance could only assume so after hearing how Xavier spoke to Malachai.

Though as she drifted off into sleep, she hoped that wasn't the case. Perhaps there was another relative of hers out there, somewhere. One who wasn't tainted by whatever darkness lurked in the veins of those here, in the Idonian Kingdom.

55

enjamin had given Ash likely more than she'd ever need. Her pack was now filled with gadgets she'd never understand, and most of them she hadn't the slightest clue how to use. As usual, she supposed she would figure it out. She didn't have much of a choice now, as she watched the gates to the Unity Bridge creak open in the dead of night.

The guards said nothing as they obeyed Benjamin's command. They simply turned their backs, more concerned with trying to shield themselves from the raging storm.

"Use your air ability to push the snow out of the way so you can have a better view as you cross the bridge," Benjamin directed, shivering, even beneath his thick wool jacket. "And Alistair, use your fire ability to melt the snow and dry the bridge."

"For someone who doesn't possess an elemental ability, you sure do have a lot of tips," Alistair teased, elbowing the Head of Communications in the ribs.

"That does not mean my abilities are less than helpful," Benjamin glared. "Without me, our Realm would be at a serious technological disadvantage."

"And we appreciate you," Ash assured him. "Endlessly."

"Just be careful," Benjamin ordered. "Make the punishment I'm about to receive tomorrow for this worth it."

"I'm forever in your debt," she insisted, pulling down her mask so she could reach up and plant a kiss on the Council Member's cheek. He blushed, his lips curling upward into a smile. "For what it's worth, I'd think you'd make one hell of an advisor," she said, refastening her mask and turning to face the bridge before her.

The storm raged, and Ash's visibility was wretched, even with Elven vision. She held on to Alistair's hand while holding the other to the air, summoning a breeze strong enough to blow the snow away as best as she could, while he used Dragon's Breath to melt the snow away and dry the bridge.

"Do you *ever* use your fire abilities?" Ash asked, gripping his hand harder. She fought not to focus on the icy waterfalls around her, or their mist freezing her to her very core.

"Sometimes." Alistair shrugged, continuously waving his sword back and forth. "But to be honest with you, I had a hell of a lot of fire beforehand."

Despite Lucinda's wishes, the Allies were celebrating, as best as they could without drawing too much attention to themselves and disturbing the Elves, most of whom were celebrating too. The streets throughout the City of Gold were lined with Elves and

Mortals alike, lifting glasses into the air and thanking the Moons for the woman who'd save them all. Ash VanCamp.

Marcus, however, was far too focused on planning their next task. Whenever Ash arrived to join them, he wanted to have a sound plan waiting for her. One that would work without a hitch.

The Elven Library offered a plethora of information, and despite Vincent's desire to celebrate himself, he was the best person for Marcus to ask for help. While Lucinda would hold the most knowledge about Veda the Red Witch, the last thing the Mentor wanted to do was stress her out more. Therefore, he left the Sorceress to her own devices and hit the books.

Census Records. That's where they'd started.

"When my great-grandfather outlawed the Witches," Vincent began as he poured over the records, "he made them each sign a census, so he knew exactly how many lived in his Realm. It was either that or die."

"Gruesome." Marcus cringed. "Though I can't say I blame him."

"Perhaps if they'd kept their heads down, none of that would have ever happened," Vincent suggested, running a hand through his dark auburn hair. "It says here that at the time of registry, sixty years ago, Veda registered as *Veda Terranova*. She was five hundred and eighteen at the time."

"Damn, she's *ancient*." Marcus let loose a long whistle. "And from what I've heard, Witches only get more powerful with age."

"Indeed," Vincent paled as he closed the census book, pushing it aside as if he never wanted to look upon it again for as long as he lived. "I remember Cedric mentioning her once, during our lessons together. He said she led a Coven. *The Crimson Coven*. They live in the Regal Mountains, in the mountain city of Aren. Thousands of them."

"And if Veda has struck a deal with Xavier…" Marcus didn't want to even consider what that would mean for the Dark King, though he was a king no more.

Vincent gulped, reaching for another book. "The Grimm's had called for her aid once. Alexi had tried to strike a deal with her. She said that she'd send who she could to assist him. No one ever showed, and the entire Grimm family perished, leaving only Blair, who later married a VanCamp."

"Perhaps if she'd shown up, the Grimm's might still rule."

"Well, it's history." Vincent shivered. "We're making our own history now. The VanCamps are back in business."

Marcus chuckled and said, "Indeed they are."

"Are you familiar with how to kill a Witch?" Vincent asked, reclining in his chair.

Blinking, Marcus hadn't considered it. "Can't we kill them the same way that we kill other Immortals?"

Shaking his head, Vincent released a frustrated sigh. "It depends on the Witch. Younger Witches are easier to kill, like us, unfortunately. Older Witches, such as Veda and perhaps Irina Phantom, who supposedly runs the city of Aren, would need to be beheaded and then burned. Just to make sure."

"The amulet possesses fire." Marcus's eyes narrowed. "Perhaps Ash can just set her aflame with it, reduce Veda to dust, and then we can rob her."

"I'm sure Lucinda would love that," Vincent snickered.

"Something tells me that *she* wants to give the killing blow," Marcus told him, a shiver running down his spine after all he'd learned the other morning in the healing springs. "And we should let her."

"If it's an option. We have no true idea what Veda is

capable of. She exists in the shadows. She hasn't gotten in the way of any high standing noble. She keeps to herself," Vincent reminded him, his gaze cold. "We've never seen her fight."

Marcus nodded slowly, knowing this to be true. Even as a Black Knight, and as much of a threat Veda was, she was never a target of his. Never a person to keep an eye on. Perhaps they should have.

THE BLIZZARD WAS TOO MUCH FOR LILLY TO BEAR. HER teeth were chattering so hard she feared they might chip, her father's book frozen as she pressed it against her chest. Sam kept a tight grip on her as they passed through the borders, entering the village of Olaigon with hope that they'd have enough coin to purchase a room for a night.

Sam did the talking while Lilly remained silent at his side, her eyes on the snowy ground. After a few moments, they were directed toward an inn, and trekked the remaining distance across the village.

The wind was harsh enough to nearly blow the front door to the inn straight off its hinges as Sam thrust it open it, ushering Lilly inside. Another villager helped him shut it, locking the door so the fierce weather wouldn't open it on its own again.

A woman behind an old, weathering desk rose to her feet. She eyed Lilly, her nose wrinkling.

"Seeking refuge from the storm?" she asked.

"We are," Sam answered for her. "What would it cost for us to stay here until the storm subsides?"

The woman snorted, falling back down into her seat. She was older, her long dark braid speckled with streaks of silver. Her coffee-colored complexion was adorned with wrinkles in the shape of crow's-feet beside her eyes. Yet, despite her age, she seemed to radiate with youth and warmth. Something about the woman, despite her wrinkling nose, made Lilly feel safe.

"Well, don't expect for that storm to subside any time soon, children," the woman replied, reaching to fondle a golden necklace around her neck. Lilly eyed it warily, a dull ache arriving in her head. The same headache she'd received since the storm had begun mere hours after she and Sam had left Crane. "This is no normal storm."

The lights in the inn flickered as the wind continued to push against the establishment. The entire building creaked, the cold air seeping through every available crack. The fire in the nearby hearth began to dwindle.

"What's that supposed to mean?" Sam growled.

"Magic." Lilly's eyes bulged at the realization. "Someone is causing the storm."

"Indeed," the woman drawled. "One heck of a Sorcerer, if you ask me."

"Great," Sam grumbled, reaching to rub the back of his neck. "It doesn't change anything. We can't stay here more than a night."

The woman snorted, glancing toward the trembling windows. "You might not have a choice," she warned.

Lilly pulled in a breath, her father's book warming beneath her cloak. She hadn't read the entire thing, but she'd learned enough about spells to know that they could *always* be broken. "If it's a spell that's causing the storm, it could be broken." Her voice wavered as she spoke.

The woman's brow raised. "Do we have a Magic wielder in our midst?"

Shaking her head, Lilly swallowed hard against the lump forming her throat. "But if *you* have noticed that it's a spell, others have too. Perhaps our Realm Sorceress will notice and break it," she suggested.

"We can only hope, child," the woman replied soothingly. "But for now, you two looked starved. Perhaps we should get some food in you."

A sigh of relief escaped Sam, and Lilly looked up at him, offering him a faint smile. "That would be wonderful."

"Right this way." The woman waved for them to follow, and they did without question. Lilly examined the inn around her as they walked. The halls were long and dark, lit by melting candlesticks, the flames flickering, casting eerie shadows on the worn wood floor they walked upon.

Sam kept his grip on Lilly's arm, and she could see he was nervous. She bit her lip to keep herself from laughing at him. How many times had this man beside her fought the Pandora? Hadn't he so easily taken off into the mountains to search for a Werewolf? Yet here he was now, fearing an old woman.

As they were led into a tavern of sorts attached to the inn, Lilly stifled a gasp, having never been in such a place. She doubted it was a place that any young woman should set foot in. Men sat around tables playing cards and drinking ale. None of them bothered to look up to view who entered or seemed alarmed by the storm causing the lights to falter every few moments.

"Briggs, fetch us three bowls of your rabbit stew," the woman called to the barkeep as she guided them to an empty table. Lilly hesitantly lowered into a seat, allowing her father's book to fall into her lap.

"So, what are your names?"

Lilly's eyes widened with surprise. Had she forgotten to introduce herself? Her cheeks flamed red with embarrassment. She'd never needed to give her name before, as she'd never met anyone new. "Lilly McBride," she replied, and the chattering throughout the inn came to a deadly halt. She allowed her gaze to drift throughout the room, only to find that each man stared back at her, something like fear flashing through their eyes. "Is something wrong?" she whispered to the woman.

"McBride, you say," the woman said breathlessly. "You share the same surname as Xavier's Dark Recruiter."

The woman's words struck Lilly as if she'd sent a blow straight to her gut. She steeled herself, fighting to keep her lip from quivering beneath all their eyes. She wanted to scream. To tell every soul in this inn and its adjoined tavern that Lincoln was *not* who they thought he was.

"I'm Sam Waters." Sam grinned, trying to change the subject.

"I know who you are." The woman's eyes narrowed in his direction. "We received a message, here in Olaigon, from the Justice Keeper in Witherow. He says that you're aiming to take Walsh's place and want to ready the Rebels. Raise an army."

"No." Sam blinked, shaking his head. "I'll be replacing our *true* leader, not Walsh. I'm sure that the people of Olaigon were smart enough not to follow that rancid bastard when he decided to take control after the Grimm Estate's Fall and Cedric returned to the Kingdom of Elves."

The woman nodded slowly, as did the men scattered throughout the tavern around her. "We never saw you at any of our gatherings at the Grimm Estate," she mentioned as Briggs trudged over, placing three bowls of steaming stew before them.

"We weren't permitted to leave our village," Sam revealed easily as he dug into the soup without a second thought. Lilly watched him, her eyes narrowing. They were dangerously close to revealing Crane's secret. If he wasn't careful, the entire Realm would know of the village's existence, and their life of secrecy would come to an abrupt end. "You probably saw my father, though, Drake Waters."

The woman gave him a curt nod. "A pleasant man."

"I agree." Sam snorted.

"And Witherow has chosen for *you* to lead us?" Her brows furrowed.

"Someone has to do it," Lilly said. "I didn't hear of anyone else offering."

One of the men at a nearby table growled in response. "Would you be so willing to step up, after what happened to Walsh *and* Cedric?"

"We've been lying low long enough," Sam insisted, wiping his mouth with the back of his hand. Lilly frowned at him. Just because they were surrounded by brutes, didn't mean that he needed to act like one. "And now the war is getting worse. Whatever Xavier is doing to Mortals across this Realm has brought his minions right to our doorsteps. They're snatching people from their beds, putting them in chains, and whipping them all the way to the Idonian Kingdom."

"Do you *know* why the war is getting worse?" the old woman inquired. "Did you see the announcement from Dracus earlier today?"

Lilly felt the blood rush from her face, her breath growing uneven. "What happened?"

"Briggs," the woman called once again. "Can you replay that broadcast?"

"The storm might interfere," the barkeep warned her as he reached for some sort of control and turned on the screens. Lilly froze in her chair as she stared up at the screen hanging on the north-facing wall of the tavern.

"The Draconian King," she breathed, her eyes wide with wonder.

The connection was glitchy at best, but Lilly didn't have any trouble hearing the king and all he said. She began eating her stew, filling her empty stomach as she watched Princess Penelope walk down an aisle with a sparkling crown atop a velvet pillow. Lilly was in awe of everything she saw on the screen. The Draconians, the magnificent throne room, and the Princess herself. But it wasn't until Lilly saw who approached behind the Princess that her spoon fell, clattering into her bowl of stew.

"Ash." Sam blanched beside her. "Lilly, that's Ash!"

Nodding, Lilly's mouth opened to speak, but no words came out as she watched Ash kneel before the Draconian King. An amulet hung from her neck, swaying above the floor of the dais. *The Idonian Sectra.* Lilly gaped.

"You know her?" The woman's eyes were wide now as well.

"Yes!" Sam beamed.

Lilly listened as Ash took her oath, tears spilling from her eyes. She raised a trembling hand to her mouth, holding back a joyous scream. She was not only alive but was given the Sectra as well. Yet, when Ash turned to address the Realm that sparkling crown of diamonds now resting upon her brow, what she said next was far more shocking than anything that had led up to that moment.

"Ash is the Messenger," Lilly whispered, reaching for Sam's hand. "She's the bloody Messenger!" She shot out of her seat.

"This is what we were waiting for, you see." The woman smirked. "This is why we were banded together. For this moment, and to keep the faith throughout our Realm. Our founder saw a rift developing in our Realm. The Mortal and Immortal populations grew distant. He wanted to prevent that. He wanted to keep the peace, and to rise up against the Dark King. He wanted to deliver the VanCamps to the High Throne, where they should have always been. Now that the Messenger has arrived, and this war will soon come to an end, it's time for us to rise as well."

Lilly's heart was in her throat as she stared at the woman, only to find kindness staring back at her.

"And, Sam Waters," the woman continued, her smile widening, "if you would like to lead us, then we will gladly accept you."

Sam was still, his grip tightening around Lilly's hand. "Well then," he grunted. "I might need to ask for your assistance, Miss—" his brow furrowed. "You never told us your name."

The woman rose then, her hand rising to the golden necklace hanging around her throat. Lilly examined her for a moment, her stomach fluttering. Power practically radiated off of her, though not the sort one would find in a Sorcerer or any of the Idonian Immortals across the Realm.

"I am Lady Evanora, of the house Ivanenko, Zerinian Empire," she announced, flicking her brows upward. "I came here nineteen years ago to aid Gideon VanCamp. Idona and Zerin have always aided one another, and when my brother couldn't come himself, he sent me instead to offer guidance. Gideon sent me to the Regal Mountains to gather intel about the Pandora and track their movements. I settled here in Olaigon while I continued with my investigation. By the time I discovered Xavier's plans to move toward the Idonian Kingdom, it was too late. The gates were shut. I was trapped here. And so, I've made it my home. I wept over the Idonian Kingdoms fall. But, when an Elf arrived here in our village to recruit, asking if anyone might want to join his cause, I finally found a way to make up for how I'd failed to help before. So here I am, at your service."

"You're King Sampson's sister," Lilly gawked.

"He's my pesky little brother, yes." Evanora laughed.

"Well, Lady Evanora," Sam rose to his feet, giving her a respectful nod, "I must ask you a favor. My younger sister was taken by the Dark Recruiter. Lilly and I intend to head to Dracus to ask for their aid."

Lilly nodded. "My older brothers are there," she added.

"I plan to ask the Draconian King if we can align our forces," Sam admitted. "So that we might work together to stop Xavier from continuing to take these Mortals. But now that we know the Messenger has arrived, I suppose we'll be joining our forces for much more."

"Indeed," Evanora agreed. "So, what would you like me to do, General?"

"General?" Sam's brow furrowed.

"If we are forming an army, we'll need a General," Briggs said from behind the bar. "Might as well be our proclaimed leader."

Sam's jaw clenched. "Fine then." His voice wavered slightly. "Evanora, I'd like you to summon the Rebels. Every last one that you can find. And more so, find people who would like to join us. If you can do that while I'm forging our alliance with the Draconians, we'll be ready in time for the siege of the Idonian Kingdom."

"I can do that," Evanora agreed with a bright smile. "But how do you expect to get to Dracus in this storm?"

Lilly shivered at the thought, her eyes drifting toward one of the windows. The blizzard continued, as angry as ever.

"We'll manage," Sam replied.

"I'll send a warning to the Idonian League of Sorcerers," Evanora revealed. "If anyone can undo whatever this
spell is, it would be one of them."

"Perhaps our Realm Sorceress herself," another man
added excitedly.

Lilly breathed a sigh of relief. Hopefully, the storm
would cease before they were lost in it tomorrow. She tried
not to think of it as Evanora led them to their room later
that evening, and though she missed her bed back home,
she collapsed onto the one she'd been given, falling into a
deep sleep within a matter of seconds.

56

Ash was sure that she could find a way to regret every decision she'd ever made. Especially now, as she and Alistair pushed through a Magic-fueled blizzard. They'd crept along the side of the Strip, using the mountain range to block out the harsh winds rushing from the south. Witherow had come and gone, and she wished she had stopped at the village for temporary cover from the storm.

All efforts to reach Lucinda had failed. The storm had likely affected the three towers Benjamin had told her were positioned throughout the Realm. The towers were what allowed his communication devices to work across the Realm. Without them, live broadcasts, video calls, and other forms of contact with the other kingdoms wouldn't be possible. Now, they were clearly out of order, which meant both Ash and Alistair's chips weren't functioning. Any messages they typed out wouldn't send, and any calls they tried to make failed to go through.

The only hope the pair had was that the Sorceress would notice the storm soon enough. The fact that she hadn't already surprised Ash. But perhaps the blizzard hadn't made it to the Kingdom of Elves yet. It didn't matter, either way. She'd need to push forward whether there was a vicious storm or not.

The force field Benjamin had gifted them projected from a small black square at the end of Ash's sleeve. It was enough to keep the snow from falling directly upon them but did nothing for their visibility. Every so often, the field would flicker, and her breath would hitch. They were the first people to test the new feature, and the thought made Ash's chest grow tight. Now was not the time for trial and error, and if the force field failed, their journey to the Kingdom of Elves would turn from dangerous to downright impossible.

"I'm going to hunt whoever caused this storm down," Alistair growled furiously at her side. "And when I do, I'm going to cut them into tiny pieces and feed them in parts to Willa."

"Would she even eat another person?" Ash inquired nervously.

"Probably not," he huffed in response.

Relieved, Ash kept pushing forward. She ignored the dull ache in her side and scanned their surroundings, or what she could see of them. "It's getting worse by the hour," she admitted, her teeth chattering, either from fear or the deep chill sinking into her bones.

"We should find cover," Alistair suggested. "It would have been smart to stop in Witherow. Or, I don't know, turn around and head back to Dracus."

Scowling, Ash chose not to reply. Instead, she peered through the snow, searching desperately for any sort of shelter. She'd take anything. An abandoned, decrepit barn. A hole in the ground. As the thought swam through her mind, she found herself gasping.

"The tunnels!" Ash grinned. "If we can find a way into

the tunnels, we could follow them all the way to the Kingdom of Elves."

"That would be great, and all," Alistair told her, "but we don't know where any entrances are around here. And there's the fact that the Dark Army has found a use for them. How do you think they're sneaking up on the villages so easily?"

"By people, you mean Lincoln," Ash accused with a glare in the Rider's direction. "I overheard it in the infirmary, you know. The healers were talking about him. How one of the Archers was working with Xavier, acting as some sort of recruiter for whatever fucked-up army he's creating."

Alistair was silent beside her. He kept his focus on the path in front of them, refusing to meet her gaze.

"You knew," she accused sadly.

"There's nothing we can do about it right now, Ash. We need to let the others handle it."

"Others?" She ceased her walking, holding the force field back with her. Alistair walked straight into it, the entire field flickering from his touch. He hissed, reaching to rub a sore spot on his head.

"No one is going after Lincoln," he assured her, holding up his hands. "They're sending Humphrey into the Idonian Kingdom to investigate a portal Xavier has created. It's laced with Black Magic and sending waves of dark energy out into the Realm. It's what's causing the Mortals Lincoln is taking to have abilities they shouldn't have."

Ash gaped at him, her heart thundering in her chest. "And you didn't tell me this, *why?*"

"Because I didn't want you any more stressed than you already are. Your focus needs to be on finishing these tasks, so you can get to Xavier before he uses that portal for *other* reasons. There's enough Fae Magic running through it to rival the Galactic Gates themselves. He could use it to flee into the other Realms."

Stunned silent, all Ash could do was stand there in the cold, allowing everything Alistair had just said to sink in.

"And they think Humphrey can shut the portal down from the inside," Alistair added for good measure. "He knows the Idonian Kingdom better than anyone else."

"They're sending him in alone?" She could hardly believe it.

"He'll draw less attention if he's on his own," Alistair told her. "And you need to get that Scepter, bless it with that Moonshade, and end this before Xavier inflicts any other pain on the other Realms. You're High Queen now. You're supposed to protect them all."

Gulping, Ash's stomach twisted into knots.

"Humphrey, as much as we care for him, is one man," Alistair continued, nudging Ash forward. She began to walk, again, albeit slowly. "There are billions of other people's lives at steak. All of their fates depend on you ending this war, and Humphrey disabling that portal. Whichever happens first."

Pulling in a deep breath, Ash gave her fellow Ally a nod and pushed forward. If they were to find shelter, it would be a saving grace. But, if they couldn't, then they would continue. Nothing would keep her from completing the remaining two tasks. Not now. Not while Humphrey was laying his life on the line for something she could end herself had she fulfilled the prophecy already.

They continued in silence. The only sound to be heard was their uneven breathing as the cold began to set in. Even the temperature control fabric of their uniforms did little for them now. The snow was turning to ice, and Ash fought not to slip and fall. Tearing her stitches was not an option. Not only for reasons pertaining to her health. If she was forced to head back to Dracus, they wouldn't let her leave, especially since they hadn't let her leave the first time.

A black flash flew through the blizzard, causing Ash to slide to a stop. "Did you see that?" she asked in a whisper.

"See what?" Alistair matched her soft tone.

She peered out into the sea of white, a shiver skittering down her spine.

A second flash of black, and then another immediately after had Ash drawing Lionheart. The weight of the sword was excruciating, and she doubted she'd be able to fight with it well enough if need be. But the flashes continued, red now visible amongst the black.

"Pandora," she seethed.

"Can they get through the field?"

Ash shrugged, the sound of their heartbeats pounding in her ears. The storm wasn't enough to fool her. They were surrounded. She could feel it. She began to count one heartbeat after another.

Fifteen. A chill skittered down her spine. Normally, the number wouldn't faze her, but the weather and her current condition put them at a serious disadvantage. Her muscles grew tense, and her chest grew tight as her grip tightened around Lionheart's hilt.

"If we leave the field up, they'll claw their way through it anyway." Ash eyed the force field warily, watching as it flickered once again. "The best we can do is shut it off and burn them."

"Are you sure?" Alistair gave her a long look.

"Have another idea?" she croaked.

"I wish," he replied with a hiss.

Glowing red eyes began to pierce through the wall of white before them, revealing the forms of fifteen large wolves. Ash rolled her shoulders, her brows pulling together. She looked toward Alistair one last time, watching as he gave her a nod, Dragon's Breath already glowing in his grip.

Ash's gloved fingers hovered over the small black square on the end of her sleeve. The moment she pressed down on it, the force field would vanish, and the Pandora would strike. She tried not to imagine that Malachai might be among them, and that he'd returned to finish his task.

"Now," Alistair ordered, his blue eyes taking on an orange hue as the light of his sword surrounded him.

Without another thought, Ash pressed down on the field and released it. The moment she felt the snow upon her face she aimed her palm, releasing a ball of fire that flew toward the beasts. She caught one of them, and the beast's scream echoed throughout the night, ringing in her ears and rattling her bones.

Alistair lunged at them with his sword, barely flinching as they leaped toward his face, dragging their claws down his uniform jacket. The fabric didn't splinter, courtesy of Benjamin once again. But that wasn't to say that it wouldn't over time.

Fire was the easiest way to kill the Pandora, yet the snow interfered. Each time Ash attempted to use the ability, it was weakened by their damp surroundings, just barely singeing the beasts' fur.

"It's not working!" she shouted in a panic, lifting Lionheart into the air while she reached for the dagger strapped to her thigh. She had no other option but to use the Mason family sword and pushed any thoughts of her stitches from her mind. If they tore, then so be it. She'd rather bleed to death than be shredded by Pandora teeth and claws.

Ash drove her sword into the throat of a wolf and sent her dagger flying toward another. She didn't need to look to know that she'd hit her target. The sound of the beast's skull crunching, and the black mist swirling in the air a moment later was enough of a confirmation.

Every time Alistair swung his sword, Ash drove hers into another skull. She ignored the pain overwhelming her and the scent of her own blood lingering in the air. Clenching her teeth, Ash lifted Lionheart one last time and sent the sword crashing down against a wolf's neck. She watched its head roll beside her feet and fell into the snow herself, sucking in quick breaths.

"That was alarming," Alistair admitted, pulling down his mask for a moment to take a proper breath.

Nodding, Ash took a few moments to catch her breath. Tears stung her eyes as she endured the constant wave of pain radiating from the wound she knew was bleeding once again. She didn't dare reach her hand up her uniform to see if she'd torn the stitches. She already knew that she had.

"Are you alright?" Alistair asked.

"I am," she lied, pushing herself to her feet. She fought to master her agony as she looked toward the Rider, forcing a smile to her face. "We make a good team. Now, let's try and find some shelter for the night."

Ash enabled the force field, and the pair continued through the atrocious weather in silence, scanning their surroundings for any form of shelter. The sensation of something warm, wet, and delicious running down her side and onto her uniform pants led Ash's breath to grow uneven. Her stomach burned, yearning for one of the thermoses of blood in her pack. She bit her lip, fighting to remain focused on searching for some sort of haven they could lay in for the night. Then, and only then, would she indulge in an entire thermos full of blood. She'd sort out her wound afterward. Somehow.

"If I remember, there should be a cave up this way." Alistair gestured to the mountain path spreading upward onto the Strip on their left.

"*If* you remember?" Ash glowered.

"I'm fairly certain."

"*Fairly* certain?"

"Unless you'd rather continue toward the Kingdom of Elves, where we won't come across another village until we find Blackbay in the Lakelands four days from here, I'd say it's our only option," Alistair countered, glaring right back at her.

The incline, as subtle as it was to start, led Ash's stomach to churn. She fought to calm her shaking limbs as she pushed herself upward, every muscle in her tired body screaming as she forced them into use. Her body begged her not to continue, so much so that she trembled, falling into the snow.

"Whoa." Alistair reached for her, wrenching her back to her feet with ease. "Are you sure you're alright?"

She clenched her jaw, her teeth chattering behind her mask. She didn't need to respond for him to realize what she'd done. He could smell it. She could tell by the way his eyes widened, his grip around her arm tightening and pulling her toward him. The sensation of his fingers on her sore flesh as he reached beneath her jacket to inspect the wound caused her to cry out in pain, tears springing from her eyes.

"Fuck." Alistair retracted his hand, staring at his blood-covered fingers, his complexion turning ashen.

Darkness began to creep around the edges of Ash's vision, her mouth growing dry as her legs wobbled beneath her. The Rider kept a firm grip on her jacket, holding her up as the faint sound of wings and wind began to echo around them.

THE SCENT OF MUSK AND DAMP EARTH DREW ASH AWAKE. Her eyes fluttered open to the cold walls of a cave and the warmth of a campfire burning a few feet away. The scent of her blood flooded her nostrils as she forced herself to sit, her eyes falling on Alistair, who was now hovering over her with his gleaming, burning sword in his grip.

Ash looked down at herself, the cold air nipping at her exposed stomach. Her jacket was in a bloodied heap to her right, beside her pack. Her mouth watered at the sight of it, as she knew the amount of blood waiting for her inside.

"I'm going to cauterize it," Alistair told her, gesturing to the bloodied mess of a wound on her right side, just below her ribs. "It's going to hurt like a bitch."

"I'm assuming you don't have a first aid kit in your pack that involves sutures?" Ash gulped.

The Rider only shook his head.

Frowning, Ash looked him over. She could see that he was serious by the way he held his sword. "That's an enchanted weapon," she mentioned softly.

"I'm aware," he replied dryly. "But I won't be stabbing you with it, so I think you'll live."

"Can't you just use your fire abilities?"

"And give you a burn in the shape of my hand?" he scoffed. "Listen, we don't have the time to argue. If we don't do this, you'll just lose more blood and I'll have to have Willa take us back to Dracus."

Ash shook her head, knowing if they went back the odds of her leaving any time soon were slim. "Fine," she said through clenched teeth.

"Fine," he replied, preparing himself above her. The heat of the sword was enough to wipe away any chill lingering from their hours traveling in the storm raging outside. Ash began to tremble beneath it, her breath catching in her throat as it grew closer. "Brace yourself," he warned, barely giving her a chance to do as he said before he pressed the sword to her wound.

Ash bit back a scream, tears rushing from her eyes as she endured the burning. She writhed beneath the sword before he lifted it, returning it to its sheath and setting it beside the cot.

"Blood please," she said, gesturing to her pack.

"It won't do you any good," Alistair revealed. "Not what's in there."

Unable to stop herself, Ash gaped at the Rider, her mouth falling open. "And I'm supposed to drink *your* blood?" she asked, shaking her head. She recalled all Craven had once said in the library, her mind racing as she imagined what drinking his blood would do to her. To *them*.

"It wouldn't be the first time," he admitted.

Ash's brows raised, and the realization hit her hard enough to steal her breaths straight from her lungs. The blood lingering on her tongue when she'd awoken in the Infirmary had been *his*. She swallowed as hard as she could, her mouth beginning to water as she recalled the substance and how it had tasted.

"And you're willing to do that?" she inquired, her voice wavering with nerves.

"If it can heal you," he began. "And get us to the others so we can finish this war, then yes."

ALISTAIR'S HEART WAS RACING SO TERRIBLY FAST THAT HE thought he might faint. He hoped she was too weak to realize how he truly felt about the matter. The feelings he'd endured in the infirmary had never faded, though he'd fought against them with all his strength. The moment she'd sunk her fangs into his wrist had changed everything. Even the way he'd felt about her. He could hear the blood rushing through her veins. He yearned for it, as if it was a key to whatever unfinished business his mind convinced him he had with her.

"Then fine," Ash agreed, her breathing ragged.

"You're aware of what that'll do to you?" Alistair lifted a brow.

"Completely." She gulped as the words left her mouth.

Alistair's heart began to race. "How would you like to proceed then?"

"However it was done the first time," she replied quietly.

Pushing up his sleeves, Alistair sat down on the cot beside her and offered her his wrist. His prior wound had faded quickly, though he could feel it beneath his healed flesh. Waiting. Begging for more of whatever he'd felt that day that he'd fought so angrily to bury in the presence of those around him.

"Are you sure you're alright with this?" Ash mentioned, taking his wrist in her warm hands. A shiver ran down his spine at the sense of her touch, one he couldn't have hidden if he tried.

Nodding, Alistair sighed. "I am, as long as you are."

"And if this heads in an odd direction?"

He looked toward her, though he wished he hadn't once he did. The blush on her cheeks was brighter than he'd ever seen. Her eyes as bright as green meadows in the spring. "It doesn't have to," he told her, and meant every word. He'd contained himself before, and he could again.

She never replied.

Instead, she drove her fangs into the flesh of his wrist without another word. Alistair's heart dropped into his stomach, the same way it always had when Willa dove off a cliff. His heart pounded angrily against the walls of his chest, as if it were a wild Idonian horse grinding its hooves into the earth as it raced, indulging in its freedom. He forced himself to let her continue, when all he wanted to do was turn to face her and take her blood for himself. He hated himself for hoping, but as his desire for her intensified, he doubted he could stop himself, even if he tried.

It was just the two of them. There were no others watching, threatening to hit him over the head if he so much as extracted his own fangs. And he wanted to. More than he wanted to do anything else in all his miserable life.

Time passed so slowly that it was pure agony. Alistair trembled, his uniform constricting him. He was boiling, suffocating beneath the fabric by the time she abandoned him, retracting her fangs and collapsing back onto the cot with a breathless sigh.

Without thought, he turned to her and caught sight of the flesh around her neck. She watched him, her gaze glassy, her lips quivering, coated in his blood.

She's a VanCamp, he told himself. *And the High Queen, even if it's only temporary.*

But the way she looked at him made the Rider forget all of that. Her surname slipped past his mind as he shed himself of his uniform jacket and tossed it to the ground before climbing on top of her. He stared down at her, each breath he inhaled like fiery wisps sailing into his lungs.

There was no clue as to what was running through Ash's mind as she wrapped her fingers around his thin thermal shirt and pulled his lips down to hers. The sensation of her lips against his was enough to send the entire Realm spinning around him. As he kissed her, he forgot about the storm raging outside the cave, or the Dragon standing guard outside the cave. He forgot about what uniform he wore each day, or the silver badge upon it. He forgot he was an Ally, and only remembered that he was a man, and the woman who writhed beneath him was stunning in every way.

When he broke their kiss, she didn't complain. She didn't stop him as he trailed kisses down her neck, his fangs grazing her soft flesh. And when he bit her, the sound she made was one he never wished to forget. The taste of her blood was unlike anything he'd ever had before. A far cry from the blood they filled the thermoses with. It sent him into an entirely different *Realm* as he filled himself with it.

Whatever happened next, Alistair didn't care. He'd do whatever necessary to keep this moment from becoming a distant memory. Even when he released her, and his lips found hers again, his lust for her blood fading, he refused to stop. She tore at his clothes, and he hers. He reveled in the way she touched him, and the noises she made as his fingers ran down every inch of her flesh.

For three years, Alistair had been alone. He'd found himself with only the company of Dragons. But even their fire couldn't compare to the flames igniting with him now. He wasn't sure he'd ever felt so close to someone as he was to Ash right now. He wasn't sure whether to laugh or cry when they finally pulled apart, panting and with no sense as to how much time had passed since they'd begun.

Too weak to even reach for his clothes, Alistair stared into nothing as he fought to calm his racing heart. A sea of emotions raged within him as he shook his head in silence. Without words, Ash handed him his pants before slipping into her own. And when she laid back down beside him, he reached for her once again. But not to kiss her, though he wanted to. To hold her until they fell asleep. And she let him.

There was nothing but silence in the Kingdom of Elves in the dead of night. There wasn't a soul to be seen walking along the cobblestone streets as Lucinda wrapped her black cloak around herself, concealing the uniform beneath it. She pulled her hood over her head, hiding her unusual shade of hair as she kept to the shadows, approaching the snow-covered fields on every edge of the city, stretching for miles before the golden walls.

Moonlight coated the field, causing the snow to sparkle like fallen stars as Lucinda reached into her pocket, wrapping her fingers around the chrome sphere within. She wouldn't use it to get to the Regal Mountains. If Veda sensed the Magic, she'd know she was coming. The only other option was to travel to Dairth.

Sucking in a deep breath, Lucinda looked over her shoulder, her eyes falling on the castle that loomed over the kingdom off in the distance. Her Allies would be furious with her. But this wasn't their fight. And if there was one thing the Sorceress could to do aid the Messenger, it would be to spare her from Veda the Red Witch.

Tossing the sphere onto the ground, Lucinda watched

as a shimmering portal to Dairth appeared. She passed through without another thought, only to find herself walking straight into a blizzard unlike any she'd ever seen.

Magic pulsed in every flake of snow, causing Lucinda's brow to furrow. She *knew* that Magic. "Every Magic wielder has a thumbprint," she muttered as her stomach twisted with dread. "And I know that thumbprint."

Though she wanted nothing more than to track the spell and discern where it had come from, time was of the essence. Growling, she allowed her wand to fall into her hand and whispered a spell she knew would disable the storm. She often used it when training Sorcerers in her league, as her instructors had once done to her. When spells got out of hand, or went wrong in any way, the disabling spell acted as a manual override.

With a hiss, Lucinda whispered the words and held her wand into the air. The wind fueling the blizzard halted, leaving only gracefully falling flakes of snow. With a sigh, she slipped her wand back into her sleeve and turned toward the mountain range stretching for miles. She could see the peaks of the tallest mountains, capped with snow, and smiled.

Home. A shiver swam down her spine as she began her journey, forming her plan along the way. She'd make it to Veda's cottage by tomorrow evening, and then she'd kill the Red Witch. She'd behead her with her scythe, or she'd burn her alive. She supposed it would depend on what mood she was in when the time came.

ANASTASIA'S HEAD WAS SCREAMING AT HER THE MOMENT she opened her eyes to begin the day. Perhaps she'd had too much to drink last night. She hadn't particularly kept track of how many glasses she'd filled with both wine or blood as she was too busy sharing battle stories with Beck and Craven. She'd rather enjoyed her time in Beck's pub, though she was surprised his uptight parents had allowed him to have one.

The story of how the General acquired his pub would forever make Anastasia laugh, and she certainly chuckled as she climbed out of bed, her eyes falling on the empty bed across the room. At first glance, she supposed the Sorceress had gotten up early, as she often did to head to the healing springs each morning they'd been in the Kingdom of Elves. But as the Draconian walked closer to the bed, she noticed something amiss.

The bed hadn't been slept in. A bag of chocolates and the small bundle of baby's breath the maids put on the pillows whenever they came to make the beds each day still sat where they'd left it. Untouched.

Ana's stomach churned as she glanced around the room, her smoldering eyes darting in every direction. There was no sign of the Sorceress. Everything from the book she read in the evening and the brush she left on their bathroom counter was gone, along with her pack.

There wasn't even a strand of blood-red hair to be seen.

"Fuck!" Ana thundered as she raced to brush her teeth and pull her uniform on. She didn't bother to braid her long white hair, or tie it back at all, as she darted out of the suite and raced down the hall.

When the Fire Clan Leader barreled into her targeted suite, she watched as both Quinn and Marcus sprung from their beds, reaching for their weapons.

"Relax," Ana directed with her hands on her hips. "If I wanted to kill either one of you, I'd have done it by now."

Marcus scowled at her as he reached for his shirt,

pulling it over his head. "Is there a reason you're barging into our suite in uniform so early in the morning?"

"Lucinda is gone," Ana told him.

"What do you mean *gone?*" Quinn's cerulean gaze narrowed in her direction, his sandy hair messy from his tossing and turning throughout the night.

"I was afraid of this." Marcus shook his head, his eyes wide with fear as he raced for his own uniform. "Summon the others. We're going after her. Now."

"Where exactly did she go?" Quinn asked.

"To Veda," the Mentor told him, his face drained of color.

"You've got to be shitting me!" the Archer insisted, now fetching his uniform as well.

Marcus slipped into his jacket, the Ally badge shining bright against the white-lined black stripe running across his torso. "I wish I was," he replied, running a hand through his own messy hair.

"We don't know when she left," Anastasia mentioned as she watched the two division leaders rush to ready themselves. "What if she's already *there?*"

"If she is," Marcus told her softly, "let's just hope she won the fight."

WHEN DAWN ARRIVED, ASH SLIPPED OUT OF THE COT she'd shared with Alistair and blushed furiously as memories of the night flashed through her mind. However, she didn't particularly regret it. She doubted she'd ever enjoyed something quite so much, and the absence of pain on her side was relieving. Whatever they'd done had worked, and as she approached the mouth of the cave where the massive black Dragon was slumbering, she nearly cried out with joy to see that the blizzard had disappeared.

"Alistair!" Ash shouted, rushing back to their cot.

The Rider's eyes flew open and Ash felt a tinge of shock swim through her, as if she'd been startled. Confused, she shook the feeling away and said, "The storm is gone."

"Oh?" Alistair grinned, dressing himself quickly.

Relief washed over Ash, and her stomach fluttered. She stared at the Rider as he armed himself, fastening his mask around the lower half of his face and pulling his hood over his golden hair.

"About last night," she mentioned, her heart dropping into her stomach as Alistair froze at the sound of her words. "What are your feelings on the matter?"

"Well," Alistair began, swallowing hard enough for her to hear. Ash could *feel* how nervous he was. She could feel his pulse racing and sense the sweat emitting from his palms. "I think you and I are both aware that what occurred was the result of potentially life or death circumstances."

Nodding, Ash's lips pursed. "And it's best we probably put it behind us."

"And never speak of it again," Alistair added sheepishly.

Before she could reply, she felt yet another emotion that wasn't her own. Sadness. Her eyes bulged, her hand raising to her mouth to keep herself from gasping.

Alistair's brow furrowed as he turned to her, crossing his arms. "Is something wrong?" he asked, his voice wavering.

"Alistair," she said slowly, her hand falling to her side. "I think we might have made a mistake."

"Well, if you *really* think it was a mistake." He sighed.

"No, that's not what I mean." Her cheeks heated with an embarrassed blush.

As if he could feel how embarrassed she'd become, Alistair tilted his head to the side and peered at her with a furrowed brow. For a few moments, they stood there in silence as the sun rose higher into the sky, casting more light into the cave. Willa stirred outside, having awoken for the day.

"Then what do you mean?" he finally asked.

Ash released an annoyed huff. She wasn't sure if she'd lost her mind or not. Last night had been hectic, for more than one reason. She considered the fact that she might be tired and slightly overstressed. After all, being the Messenger *and* the Interim High Queen was a lot for just one person to handle. But she couldn't rid herself of the idea gnawing at the back of her mind.

A light bulb seemed to flicker on within her mind, and Ash realized there was only *one* way to confirm her suspicions. She closed her eyes for a few moments, imagining the most painful moment throughout her life. The moment she'd returned from the Harvest Festival two dreadful years ago to find that her mother had passed while she was away. Her heart broke all over again as she thought of walking onto that porch, only to have Quinn block her way into the house.

"Ash..." It was clear that Alistair had caught on to what she was doing. She opened her eyes to find him staring at her with misty eyes. "What is this?" he asked, holding a hand to his chest.

"We have a Lover's Bond," she told him quietly, turning away from him and pinching the bridge of her nose, squinting her eyes shut. *How* could she have let this happen? She groaned, her stomach now in knots.

Alistair's footsteps sounded from behind her, and to

Ash's surprise he placed a hand on her shoulder and squeezed it gently. "If we do, then we do," he told her. "If anything, it'll just make us stronger on the battlefield, as we'll know exactly how the other feels at any given moment."

"I suppose," she replied, turning to retrieve her belongings from the cave. She took a few moments to arm herself, strapping Lionheart's scabbard to her back and placing a dagger everywhere her uniform would allow her.

"If it makes you feel better," Alistair told her as he rolled up the cot and attached it to the bottom of his pack, "we could always get married."

"Very funny." Ash grunted with a heavy sigh.

The pair vacated the cave, and Ash took one look at the Dragon waiting for them and froze. She'd seen the beast before and knew that without her she wouldn't have made it back to Dracus in time. But she couldn't wipe how the magnificent beast had appeared in the skies above Crane, raining blue fire down upon them in a storm of bone-melting heat.

Willa's nostrils flared as she inched toward Ash, stretching her long, black scaled neck. Ash barely allowed herself to breathe as she reached forward and placed a shaking palm to the Dragon's snout. The beast's eyes shut, and a strange humming sound vibrated against Ash's hand.

"She's purring like a cat," Alistair announced with a wide smile. "After saving your ass twice, she's probably grown to like you."

"Perhaps she'll like me more than you, and I'll become her Rider," Ash teased, wiggling her brows.

"As *if*," the Rider scoffed as the Dragon outstretched her wing for him to climb. He settled himself on her back, taking a moment to stretch before giving her a good pat. "Her eggs will hatch soon," he revealed, his sky-blue eyes shining with pride. "Right now, one of the other Dragons is keeping them warm so she can take us to the Kingdom of Elves."

Ash couldn't bear the idea of letting another soul take care of her newborn, if she were ever to have one. She frowned at the idea, unable to foresee a moment in the future where a family might be possible for her. Though, she hoped one day that it would be.

"I'll owe her a great deal for sacrificing her precious time with them." She sighed, taking note of Alistair's outstretched hand. She hesitantly backed away from the Dragon's snout and walked over to Willa's wing. She stepped carefully, worried she might injure the Dragon as she inched upward, far enough to take the Rider's hand and allow him to hoist her up.

"She doesn't mind," Alistair replied as Ash fought to get comfortable in front of him. "It's time we all do our part. I bet once the war is over, the other Dragons will come down from the den and choose Riders for themselves. At least, I hope they do. And I think they *want* to."

Ash's stomach fluttered at the idea. "Do they truly only choose Riders with Dragon's blood running through their veins?"

"Normally, yes," he told her sadly. "But it's said that you're great, great-grandfather, Graham VanCamp, had Dragon's blood, as his mother was from Mayfire. The city of Dragons. Maybe you do too."

"Your city," Ash mentioned softly. "Will you ever return to it? You are its Lord."

Alistair was silent for a moment, shifting uncomfortably behind her. "I'm not sure I will," he admitted, and Ash could feel the sadness evolving in his soul as he thought of the city. "If I truly can't, I'll appoint someone else to take my father's place one day. But right now, we have to concern ourselves with other things. Like flying to the Kingdom of Elves and *finally* reuniting with the others."

Smiling at the thought, Ash prepared herself for flight. "Let's go then."

ASH WOULD NEVER BE ABLE TO PREPARE HERSELF ENOUGH for a flight on a Dragon's back. She learned, as Willa dove into the skies, that she had a fear of heights. They'd flown so high in the sky that she'd been able to touch clouds, and with her Elven eyes, she felt as if she could see every inch of Idona. Wild horses running in the pastures below looked more like ants, and the Edge of the Underworld hiding behind the Regal Mountains revealed itself, surrounded by an eerie orange glow that sent Ash's heart thumping against her chest. She silently hoped she'd never see the wretched place up close.

The Kingdom of Elves fell into view and Willa lowered to land, just outside of the golden walls surrounding the massive city. Ash held her breath as she examined the rooftops and the white marble castle looming off in the distance.

Ash could have sworn the massive walls surrounding the kingdom swayed when Willa landed, the entire Realm trembling around them. The Elves took notice of them quickly enough and were opening the gates by the time Ash dismounted, rushing out to view the beast they'd thought was extinct.

"Magnificent!" an Elf with long red hair gasped as he approached, remaining a safe distance away. Willa paid the Immortal no mind and instead stretched out upon the snowy earth, as if she were ready for a nap after flying halfway across the largest Realm in Si Realtra.

"Don't feed her ego, Red," Alistair directed, tilting his head toward the Elf by the way of greeting. "It's been far too long, old friend. Tell me, you wouldn't have happened to see any extinct Arebus Archers walking around anywhere, would you?"

Red nodded, but as he took notice of Ash as she moved to stand beside her fellow Ally, he dropped into a low bow, as did the other guards behind him. She cleared her throat, hoping she wasn't blushing as she waved the Elves to stand.

"It's a pleasure, Your Highness," Red told her.

"Ash is fine."

The guard's eyes widened with surprise. "As you wish."

"So, have you seen our fellow Allies then?" Ash asked, hoping her impatience wasn't showing. All she wanted to do was hug each one of them, even if Anastasia would push her away. High Queen or not.

"I regret to inform you that they left early this morning." Red frowned, his gaze falling to his feet. "They left in a hurry."

Ash's chest grew tight as she looked toward Alistair, clenching her jaw. "Any idea where they went?" The question was pointless. She already knew. Lucinda had gone after the Red Witch.

"You'll want to speak with Princess Mika," Red told her. "She was there when they left. She would know why."

"If you wouldn't mind summoning her," Ash began, and a guard standing toward the back immediately rushed back through the gates. Ash began to pace, unable to help herself. Her mind was already racing with possibilities. Lucinda could have used Magic to travel quickly, which meant by the time any of the others got to her, she could already be dead.

There was a reason it was decided that the divisions would reunite *before* the second task. It was best to approach the Red Witch as one, and hope that the sight of all ten Allies would scare her into handing over the Moonshade willingly. Now, if only Lucinda approached Veda, it could easily turn into a death match.

It might have been minutes, but it surely felt like hours before the guard returned with an Elf cloaked in crimson velvet lined with white fur. Ash eyed her curiously as she dropped her hood, revealing a head of long golden hair to match her piercing gaze. Two braids ran from her temples before joining at the base of her skull in traditional Elven fashion, and a silver tiara sat above her brow, shining in the bright midday sun.

The Princess bowed, though it seemed half-hearted. Ash's brow furrowed. She'd never liked when people bowed before her, but if they were going to do it, they might as well do it right, not half-assed. "Your Majesty," Mika drawled. "We've been expecting you. King Loren informed us that you might be approaching."

Ash bit her inner cheek, now wondering exactly how furious Loren was. "I am told you know where my Allies ran off to?"

"This morning, they became aware that our Realm Sorceress, Lucinda Cross, had disappeared during the night. Marcus believed she'd left to face Veda the Red Witch on her own, so we allowed them to use our portal rooms. They used one to get to Mayfire and planned to use Immortal speed on their way to the Regal Mountains."

Mika eyed the Dragon behind Ash and Alistair, her golden gaze filling with both fear and curiosity. "Would you like to use our portal rooms as well?" she added, her tone far too sweet for Ash's liking. "I can escort you myself. Though I'm afraid they left nearly six hours ago."

"Which would be faster?" Ash asked Alistair. "The portals or Willa?"

"Willa?" Mika's high-pitched tone rose another notch. "Is that what you've named this beautiful beast, Alistair?"

The Rider gave the Princess a nod but quickly turned away, staring off into the distance. He was deep in thought. Ash could feel it, though the sensation was still incredibly unnerving.

"We'll fly," he revealed.

"I can provide you with the fastest route," Mika told them, taking another step toward the pair. She held out her hand and said, "I'll add it to your communications chip. I've learned a great deal about the machines over recent months."

Hesitantly, Ash reached into her pocket and retrieved the device, gently handing it over to the Princess. She watched as Mika fidgeted with it for a moment.

"I've marked two routes for you," she chirped, moving closer to Ash so she could see. "The red route will be the fastest. It'll take you over the Lakelands and over Greystone Ruins, but our weather trackers have noted that a storm is evolving over Death Valley. If it becomes too much to withstand, or if you'd rather not risk it, you could always take this blue route. That will take you east until you fly over the Strip and toward Dairth. It'll be slower, but the weather is clear."

"We'll take our chances with the first route," Alistair insisted as he climbed onto his Dragon, already outstretching his hand toward Ash. "I think we can handle a little storm."

58

It wasn't the storm that had turned out to be the problem but the forest below that caught Ash's attention. She gazed down at it, her blood chilling in her veins. Green, misty clouds radiated above black, decrepit trees. The stench of it alone led Ash to pull her mask back over her face, bile creeping up her throat.

"It's like it's rotting!" Alistair called, the wind roaring around them drowning out his voice.

Nodding, Ash couldn't disagree. The forest looked like it truly *was* rotting. If they weren't already hours behind the other Allies, she might have suggested stopping to investigate it.

"What could cause something like that?" she asked, the forest now miles behind them as Willa pushed forward through the chunks of ice and snow falling from the clouds above them. The Dragon was flying as fast as the speed of light itself, or so it seemed. If Ash didn't squint her eyes, she was sure her eyelids would flip.

"Black Magic!" Alistair sounded sure of himself, his grip around her tightening as Willa dipped further beneath the clouds, attempting to distance herself from the harsh conditions.

The Regal Mountains highest, snow-capped peaks were visible in the distance, and Ash released a sigh of relief at the sight. They'd made it. She just hoped that they'd made it in time.

A holographic map began to project from Alistair's sleeve, revealing a glowing red target. The cottage where Veda supposedly lived, ten miles outside the mountain city of Aren. Ash's eyes narrowed at the sight of it, her blood beginning to boil in her veins.

"If that wench lays a hand on one of my Allies, I swear I'll give her a Sectra show!" Ash declared, the heat of the amulet around her neck making itself known. She could feel the box, deep within her gut, unlocking to release the Berserker rage she would use to tear the Witch apart with her bare hands if she had to. Her eyes burned, and Willa grew uneasy beneath her.

"Ash!" Alistair tugged on her jacket, forcing her to look back at him. The way his eyes bulged made her heart falter in her chest.

"Your eyes!" he roared. "You're connected to the Sectra!"

Shaking her head, Ash felt an overwhelming sensation of power flowing through her veins. She hissed through her clenched teeth, fighting to control it before the Dragon panicked. *Disconnect,* she silently begged, flexing her fingers. *Wait for Veda.*

As if the Sectra could hear her thoughts, the heat coursing through her vanished. She shivered because of the weapon's sudden absence, her chest tightening as the Dragon pushed toward the mountains, closing in on the range with impeccable speed.

The sun was dipping beneath the mountains as they

landed. Ash rolled off the Dragon, waving her goodbye before darting off in the direction of Veda's cottage. She couldn't wait to see it *burn*, or to see the Witch burn with it.

Marcus fought to catch his breath, his entire body aching from his nonstop run across the Realm. He looked toward Morghan, who walked beside him, panting in his Mortal form. He imagined he would transition at any time now. They were nearly there. And though Marcus had hoped to hear a fight echoing throughout the mountains, the night was silent.

"Get into the trees."

The Archers and Vincent obeyed his command as soon as the words left his mouth, but Craven, Anastasia and Morghan remained at the Mentor's side. The wolf transitioned at the sound of Anastasia's chains unraveling, and the Electric Immortal unsheathed Shadowstrike in one swift movement.

"Remember the plan?" he asked the others, watching as Craven nodded slowly. "We distract her with flames so she doesn't notice the Archers in the trees. One of those arrows to her heart, and she's done."

"She's strong, Marcus," Ana reminded him from behind, her chains dragging in the snow beside her. "We're going to have to behead the bitch and incinerate her to be sure she's through."

"Are you sure we don't want to keep her head and put it on display?" Craven asked with a devilish smirk. "I have an empty place on my mantle."

Marcus held back a snort as he focused on the path before him. The Witch had chosen her location wisely. Her cottage was built in a small ravine, the pathway leading toward it lined with trees—thankfully pine trees. Without their needles, the Archers would stick out like a sore thumb.

If their glowing eyes hadn't given them away already.

"We're within three miles," Ana mentioned. "They can shoot whenever they feel like."

Marcus's breath escaped him the moment he heard the whine of bowstrings being pulled taut. Veda might be strong, but she would surely be weak against the original Immortals. There was a reason the Sovereign designed them the way that they were today. If they could protect *the Messenger* and kill *her* enemies, they could face Veda and walk away unscathed. Marcus was sure of it.

The mountains shook around them, and Marcus nearly lost his balance. He kneeled on the ground for a moment to brace himself, his heart in his throat.

"What the hell was that?" Craven asked in a whisper, looking over his shoulder.

Morghan yelped softly beside them, now looking back toward the path they'd come down as well. Marcus followed his gaze, noting the atmosphere changing around him. The air thickened, pulsing as if it had a heartbeat. The trees trembled, snow and pine needles falling from their branches.

The path began to glow both blue and orange off in the distance, and Marcus shot to his feet, his eyes widening as he drew Whitefire. The glowing intensified, burning brighter. Whatever was racing toward them was moving *fast*. Too fast.

"If that's who I think it is…" Craven shook his head, his lips stretching into a smile. "We should probably get out of the way."

WHATEVER HAD CAUSED THE MOUNTAINS TO QUAKE SO terribly had nearly knocked Quinn from the tree he was perched in. And while he was curious about what it was, whether it be enemy of foe, he couldn't stray from the task at hand. He flew through the trees, unsure of whether the other Allies were still following or not.

Cooper traveled in a tree across the pathway, his gaze occasionally meeting his brother's. They'd both drawn their bows, arrows already loaded within them as the cottage came into view. It was quaint and built with sturdy gray stone. Lights were strung along the edges of the red-shingled roof, twinkling in the fading sunlight. Candles were lit, flickering in every window.

If Quinn hadn't known any better, he'd say the cottage was warm and inviting. It looked like the sort of place a humble newlywed couple would settle down in and grow old together.

On the ground, in the tree line on the south side of the cottage, lay a heap of black cloth. Quinn's stomach dropped at the sight of it. "No." He shook his head, releasing his arrow without a word to warn the others. He watched as it shattered one of the windows, sailing into the cottage as the candlestick tipped over, lighting red-laced curtains aflame.

A cry of sheer agony was the Archer's signal to drop from the trees and race over to the black cloth. He slid into the snow, catching sight of the long red hair splayed on the snow beside him. "No, no, *no!*" he hissed as he rolled the Sorcerer over. She was freezing and pale, her breathing weak but stable. He released a relieved sigh as Cooper dropped onto the snow beside him.

"Did you kill her?" his brother asked, eyeing the cottage with fearful eyes.

"I definitely hit her," Quinn replied as he worked to

shake Lucinda awake. "Come one," he growled. "Wake *up*."

Rustling from within the cottage drew their attention, and Quinn stifled a panicked gasp as he turned just in time to watch the front door fly open.

"You guys need to get out of here, now!" Vincent ordered from above as the Witch sauntered out onto her front porch, red velvet robes billowing around her.

Cooper loaded his bow, his breathing ragged as the Witch's fiery gaze fell upon them. Her lips twitched into a smirk as she surveyed the Archers. Black mist began to seep from her fingers in tendrils, creating a wall of pure darkness that stretched from the ground to the trees above.

Fear began to grip Quinn, his entire form trembling as he looked toward his brother. The wall was beginning to thicken, strengthening. He didn't doubt that once Veda released it, it would be upon them in less than a second.

"Cooper," he rasped. "You're going to need to take Lucinda and teleport the fuck out of here, *now*."

The Archer didn't waste any time kneeling beside the Sorceress, pressing a trembling hand to her shoulder. "Get her sphere!" Vincent called.

Growling, Quinn eyed the wall as he did what was asked of him. He dove his hand into the pocket of her cloak and wrapped his hand around the sphere, pulling it free just as the wall twitched.

"Vincent, run!" Quinn ordered as Cooper disappeared beside him.

The Archer braced himself as the field surrounding the cottage began to glow blue, and he found that he was frozen with shock as he watched Ash barrel into the wall of Darkness, surrounded by burning sapphire fire just as a hard body crashed into him, sending him flying into the nearby brush.

"We need to get out of here. The others are waiting on the path," Alistair insisted, now crouching.

"Where the hell did you come from?" Quinn gawked. "I thought you two were in Dracus."

"It's a long story," the Rider replied.

ASH'S HEART WAS BURNING IN HER CHEST, ALONG WITH every inch of her flesh. Before, she'd been teetering along the line of sanity, and realized wholeheartedly that she'd finally crossed it. She must have lost her mind, to allow herself to barrel into a wall made of pure Black Magic.

She rolled onto the ground beside the Witch and forced herself not to think of the powerful being her opponent truly was as she reached for her, wrapping her fingers around her neck as her Magic withered, carried away by the winter breeze.

Veda didn't burn because Ash didn't want her to. Not yet.

"One wrong move and I'll turn you into dust." She hissed the warning through clenched teeth.

The Witches yellow eyes flashed orange, and Ash's grip tightened around her throat. She could crush her windpipe in an instant, as her Berserker rage was viciously flowing through her. She was furious. Furious to have seen Cooper disappear in a flash with an injured Realm Sorceress.

"What did you do to her?" Ash snapped, loosening her grip enough for the bitch to speak.

"You wouldn't understand, baby Queen," Veda insisted.

Ash's brow raised at the title. "Do I look like a baby to you?" The question sailed past her lips in a drawl as she reached for one of her daggers. She dragged the enchanted blade along the Witch's cheek with her free hand, watching as her lip began to quiver in fear.

"I put her under an eternal sleeping spell," Veda barked. "I wouldn't give her the courtesy of killing her. Now, she'll be trapped in her subconscious until someone has the guts to drive a knife through her heart."

"All spells can be broken," Ash reminded the Witch.

"You might be right." The Witch dared to laugh. "But few people know how to break this spell. Two people to be exact. I do, and the only other person is the victim herself."

Ash debated slicing her with the dagger, now yearning to see a line of scarlet blood running down her cheek. But her task wasn't complete, and she needed the Witch alive. Though the wound she could smell on Veda's chest told her that she'd already managed to escape death once. Though the fact that she'd survived an Arebus arrow was concerning.

"Where's the Moonshade?" Ash snarled.

"I'll tell you, at a cost," Veda chuckled.

Running low on patience, Ash flipped the dagger in her hand and sent the butt of the hilt crashing down onto the Witch's skull. She watched her eye's roll as she released her grip on her throat and rose to her feet. She waved her hand around in a circle and watched as a ring of blue fire surrounded them, her amulet glowing on her chest.

Veda remained on the ground in a daze as Ash passed through the fire, reaching out with her palm to summon the air around her. The cottages front door flew off its hinges, slamming against the trees bordering the clearing. Without another thought, she crossed through the threshold and into the Witch's home, hell-bent on tearing it apart until she found what she wanted.

CRAVEN WASN'T SURE HE'D BOTHERED TO BREATHE WHILE he watched Ash tackle Veda to the ground in a whirl of blue fire and Darkness. There had been no hesitation, only rage fueling her as she wrapped her hand around the Witch's throat and dragged a dagger down her cheek.

It wasn't until he watched Veda's front door fly into the trees that he finally inhaled a sharp breath, looking toward Marcus with wide violet eyes.

"I've never seen anything like that," he admitted, his voice wavering.

"I'd pay any amount of coin to see it again." Morghan laughed.

"Let's just hope she finds the Moonshade," Marcus grumbled. "With our luck, Veda will have moved it far away from here."

If the Witch had been smart, she would have, but something told Craven that Veda's pride might have gotten the best of her. Why wouldn't the strongest Witch in Idona think that she could face the Messenger and win? He chuckled as he examined her, lying lifelessly in the snow, surrounded by a ring of fire. The perfect prison for an Immortal like the Red Witch.

The Allies continued waiting in silence, and eventually Quinn began to pace in front of them all. "Should we help her look? She's been in there a while," he asked nervously.

Craven could see the worry wrinkling in the Archer's brow and was beginning to consider heading into the cottage himself when he heard a laugh echo from within it. His gaze snapped in the direction of the gaping threshold just in time to watch Ash emerge victoriously, holding a large glass vial in the air for them all to see before quickly placing it safely in her pack.

A long sigh of relief escaped the Draconian as everyone else cheered. They'd completed the second task, but not unscathed. His mind drifted to Lucinda and how they hadn't made it in time to help her face her nemesis. He recalled what she'd told them about Veda, and all the Red Witch had done to her. His stomach churned as he took everything in. She'd had the chance to end the Red Witch for good. And she'd failed.

"If I were you, I'd get back," Ash warned, pulling Craven from his thoughts. He did as she requested, stepping back and watching her warily as she turned to face the cottage, a ball of blue fire evolving in her hands. It grew, larger and larger until she needed two hands to thrust it toward the cottage. In a matter of seconds, it was imploding, burning as bright as a star.

Craven hit the ground, covering his head with his arms as bits of stone and rock flew through the atmosphere. His heart raced as he recalled what had occurred at the base, but as he looked up, he found himself smiling at the sight before him. The cottage was gone. Nothing remained but the broken foundation it had been built upon.

"Good work." He patted Ash on the shoulder.

She scowled at him. "That's all I get?" she growled. "A pat on the shoulder? Do you not realize that I just raced across the bloody Realm on a Dragon to get to you guys?"

Without another word, he pulled her into the best hug he could summon, squeezing her as much as he could without breaking a bone. He listened to her laugh and then sigh. For a moment, the Realm seemed normal around them.

"Now I'm *really* going to confiscate those daggers, just so you're aware," he said upon releasing her.

"I'd like to see you try," she scoffed before turning to her other Allies and hugging them one by one. Anastasia was, of course, as stiff as a board as she endured the embrace. And when Ash nearly tackled Quinn to the ground the same way she did Veda, the sight made Craven snort loud enough to earn a glare from the Archer.

While it was wonderful to see such a reunion, Craven couldn't forget that they weren't whole. "We should get going," he mentioned. "This isn't over yet."

Vincent's suggestion to obtain Lucinda's chrome sphere had certainly proven to be useful. Quinn had tossed it to the ground and opened a portal to Olaigon, where they'd found a quaint inn to stay in. After they filled themselves with food and perhaps some well-deserved ale, they planned to only stay for a night before moving on to the third and final task.

While Ash appeared to be relieved to raise a glass of cold ale to her lips, Quinn could see the shadows in her eyes. They sat in silence around an old table in the back corner of a small tavern attached to the inn.

The barkeep, a man named Briggs, eyed them nervously as he prepared eight bowls of beef stew for the new High Queen and her Allies. Quinn's mouth watered as the scent of it wafted over to their table. It hadn't been so long since he'd had a hot meal, as they'd been well-fed in the Kingdom of Elves. But it *had* been too long since he'd had a wonderful beef stew.

His stomach growled as he thought of Lilly's cooking. She would always make stew on the coldest of winter days.

"When do you suppose Cooper will be back?" Vincent

asked softly as he ran a finger around the rim of his mug, likely expecting it for dust.

"He said he wanted to stay with Lucinda a while longer," Ash muttered softly as she scrolled through the messages on her chip. She winced every few moments. Ever since the towers across the Realm had been repaired by Benjamin's communications officers, her chip had buzzed endlessly. From what Quinn had gathered, Loren was incredibly disappointed with her, and he could recall, painfully, how it felt to have anyone *disappointed* in him. He'd rather they be angry, instead. Somehow that felt easier to cope with.

Nodding, Quinn chugged the remainder of his ale and gave a nod to the barkeep for another. Briggs gave him a nod in return and moved to fill another glass while a woman sauntered over, a tray with their stew in their hands.

The woman set a bowl in front of each of them before setting a basket of fresh bread in the center of the table. "Enjoy." She smiled before turning to assist the other tables.

"So, there's really only two people in the Realm that know how to break the spell? Veda and Lucinda?" Alistair asked softly. "That doesn't sound right."

"It's true," Vincent confirmed. "The eternal sleeping spell is rare. A five-caliber spell to be exact. Everly Cavanaugh herself forbade the Magic wielders from using it and teaching it to their fledglings after a Witch placed one of her fellow Sectra Holders under the spell during the destruction of Amoria."

A chill ran down Quinn's spine at the mention of the forgotten sixth Realm. "Yet Veda knew how to use it, and so did Lucinda. Perhaps more people throughout the

Realm know too. And if they know how to cast it, they know how to break it."

"Veda knows everything about *everyone*," Morghan revealed from his seat beside Ash and Alistair. "She would know if someone knew."

"Who knew such a hateful bitch would bother to tell the truth." Craven frowned.

"We'll find a way." Ash sounded so sure of herself as she dipped a piece of bread into her stew. "If anyone can figure that out, it's Hartford, Ebony, and Vincent."

"Me?" Her twin gaped at her.

Ash nodded slowly and said, "You're the smartest person I know."

"Now that's just offensive," Craven complained with narrowed eyes. "I'm rather intelligent too, you know."

"Then you should help him," Ash countered before turning toward the Wolf. "And you know a great deal about Magic yourself, it seems. You should help too."

Morghan shrugged as he shoveled stew into his mouth with a crooked spoon. "I suppose I know a thing or too."

At last, Ash turned toward Marcus, who sat directly across the table as still as a statue. "And you should go with them."

"Have you lost your mind?" Quinn winced as Marcus asked the question. "I'm not letting you walk into the Forest of Fools without me. Not after what happened the last time we were all apart. There's no way. Not in all the eight layers of the Underworld."

Ash's scowl was enough to rid Quinn of the rest of his appetite, and he was glad when Briggs finally delivered his requested ale.

"Now that she's finished two tasks," Anastasia began, leaning back in her chair and rubbing her full stomach. "Xavier and his minions are going to be doing *everything* they can to take us down. We'll need the protection in Dracus. Who's to say they won't strike our home base?"

Marcus's glare faltered at her words. "I suppose you're right," he replied. "But she'll need just as much protection as she moves to get the Scepter."

"I'll have both Archers." Ash crossed her arms, offering Quinn a devilish grin. "And I think Anastasia and Alistair will prove to be enough protection on their own. Not to mention, I've already called in for some extra assistance."

A commotion out in the village pulled the Allies from their conversation, and Quinn reached for his bow and traveled outside without a second thought. The other Allies were following at his heels, weapons drawn and ready for whatever they were about to meet.

When Quinn caught sight of what was waiting for them, he held out a hand to keep Ash from taking another step, and silently prayed she wouldn't connect to her Amulet. Pandora in their Mortal forms stood around a single man, who was calling out names in the center of the village.

"He's come," Briggs mentioned from behind the large group.

"Who?" Ash snapped.

"The Dark Recruiter."

Ash was in shock.

Nothing could have prepared her for what was happening in the center of Olaigon, and as much as the sight enraged her, it made her sick to her stomach as well. Tears were already brimming her eyes as she stood on the tips of her toes, fighting to peer over Quinn's shoulder.

"We can't just let him take them," Anastasia hissed from Ash's side, her chains ready to unravel in her hands.

"He's guarded by ten Pandora in their Mortal forms, which means they could be something else, as well. Sorcerers, even," Marcus warned.

"We took down three bases *full* of them," Vincent argued. "Why wouldn't we be able to handle the ten of them and Lincoln?"

He'd said his name, and the pain that shot through Ash's heart was too much for her to bear. She shook her head, willing the sensation away. "I would be the worst High Queen in the history of Si Realtra if I didn't stand up for these people right now," she told them all. "Let me through."

Quinn gave her a pleading look as she pushed past him.

"Follow me, and draw your bow," she instructed. "Ana, get on the roof of that bakery over there. Vincent, get on the roof of the Justice building across the street. Marcus, Alistair, and Craven, draw your enchanted swords. We'll surround them."

"What about me?" Morghan asked.

"You stay here," she revealed. "Transition at the first sign of trouble, and if you see me connect to my Sectra, tear them all to shreds."

"What about Lincoln?" Craven inquired.

"Try to knock him out." Ash shrugged. "If not, do anything in your power to keep him from drawing that bow on his back."

Vincent and Anastasia scattered, rushing toward Ash's chosen locations for them. Lincoln was in the process of dragging a girl no older than twelve from her parents grasps. She watched lightning flicker in the sky as the tears flowed from the girl's eyes and felt Craven stiffen beside her as they began their approach.

The girl's ability was the closest to his own that he'd ever seen, and Ash reached toward him, taking his hand in her own and giving it a gently squeeze. They'd stop him. She knew they would.

It took no more than a few seconds for Lincoln's guards to notice them, and they drew their weapons quickly, baring their teeth as they took in the three enchanted swords pointed in their direction. If that wasn't bad enough, the loaded Arebus bow beside Ash could certainly disturb them, as well as the Sectra hanging around her neck.

"Let the girl go." Ash's voice broke as she said the words.

Lincoln's gaze met hers, and the girl's wrist fell from his grasp. She stumbled back to her parents, who rushed her from the village square as fast as they were able.

"Ah, if it isn't the High Queen," he sneered, and her heart thundered against the walls of her chest. He was looking right at her, yet no recognition flashed in his haunted red eyes. She thought of the last time she'd seen him, turning his back on her and fleeing into the forest. She thought of the hateful things they'd both said, and how none of it mattered now, for he couldn't remember any of it, anyway.

"You're surrounded," Ash told him. She did not expect to fight him, nor did she want to. "I suggest you leave, so you might live long enough to see us take back our kingdom."

Lincoln laughed, a musical sound that vibrated in Ash's ears. "Oh, I plan to be there. I'll greet you at the gates!" he announced. "With an Arebus arrow aimed directly at your heart. Though, I doubt you'll live that long yourself. Not with Malachai out here looking for you. I'll have to tell him you're here and perhaps stay to watch him finish his kill."

Ash found herself smiling, her hand resting atop Lionheart's shining hilt. "Go right ahead," she drawled. "I've missed that prince of yours dearly."

"At least he gave you one wicked scar to remember him by." Lincoln's brows waggled. "Or so I've heard."

"Would you like to see it?" Ash lifted a brow. "Just come a little closer and I'll show you."

"No, you won't," Quinn muttered beside her.

"Lincoln, let's just go," the man beside him suggested, his brow wrinkling with worry. Ash examined him, her eyes narrowing. He was tall, his dark hair cut incredibly short, his eyes the same haunting shade as the others beside him. Scars peppered the visible parts of his flesh, pale against his bronze complexion.

Lincoln looked toward the man, his nose wrinkling. "I have orders."

"You won't be completing them here," Ash declared. "I'll give you until the count of five to leave Olaigon's borders."

"You're not going to try and capture him?" Marcus gave her a disbelieving look.

"Not until we know how to fix him," she replied in a whisper.

"And how do you expect to find out how to do that?" His brow furrowed.

Ignoring the Mentor, Ash turned her gaze back toward Lincoln and the Pandora in front of her. "One," she said and heard Quinn pull back his bow string.

Lincoln continued to stare at her, smirking.

"Two," she said, taking a step forward as Dragon's Breath began to glow in Alistair's grip.

The Archer's smirk faltered ever so slightly.

"Three," she continued, electricity surrounding Shadow Strike's obsidian blade.

"Lincoln let's *go*," the Pandora nearly begged.

"Four." Ash chuckled, Whitefire lighting aflame.

The Pandora backed away, their fearful gazes looking toward their leader. Lincoln remained still, his smirk vanishing.

"Five." Ash felt the power of her amulet course through her and summoned the air to knock the Archer onto his back. She watched as he fell to the ground and rushed to his feet, the Pandora reaching to grasp his uniform. They pulled him away, though it was clear he wanted to stay and fight. He looked over his shoulder at her, staring her down with eyes that weren't his own.

Ash held his stare as his minions guided him from the village. She held her breath until he was out of sight, and then expelled it the moment the villagers began to clap, applauding the Allies as Anastasia and Vincent dropped from their places on the rooftops. Morghan sauntered up to them, a tall glass of ale in his grip.

"Alright, now that *that's* over," he said in between sips. "What assistance did you call for *exactly*?"

60

ries was far from thrilled when he appeared in Olaigon the next morning. Ash watched as he ruffled his wings, eyeing the wavering inn around them. "What exactly do you need me for?" His face twisted with disgust as he leaned against the wall of her suite, smoothing his black uniform, which was similar to her own.

"I need you to teleport us directly to that wretched beast in your forest. The one guarding the Sovereign's Scepter," Ash told him, her tone flat. She didn't bother to look for his reaction and instead moved to arm herself.

The Fae was silent as she strapped Lionheart to her hip and slipped an enchanted dagger into her boot. The other Allies were all crowded in the room next door, their ears likely pressed against the walls. None of them thought Aries would agree to do such a thing. What they failed to realize was that while the Fae might all bow down to Cleo, Ash was currently Cleo's superior, and she would pull the rank card if she had to.

"Is that all?" Aries inquired.

Ash's brow raised as she glanced toward him, only to

find the Fae staring back at her with a faint smile. "Would you prefer to do *more?*" She gave him a disbelieving look as she threw her pack over her shoulder.

The Fae kicked at the frayed carpet beneath his feet, deep in thought about her question. "It's been fifty years since I've fought in a war," he told her softly. "We were backed into a corner, and though we don't indulge in violence, we needed to fight to protect our Realm. I would like to do it again, by being an Ally to the Allies. So, anything you ask, I'll do."

"All I need you to do is teleport me and some of the Allies to the cavern that beast is guarding," Ash told him softly. "And if I don't make it out, to teleport inside the cavern and use my blood to break the spell around the Scepter."

The Fae paled at the sound of her words.

"It's the only way," Ash told him, not at all minding if the Allies were listening in the other room. "If that beast bests me, kill it and use my blood to break the spell. That's what I was designed for. To break the spell. I do not need to be the person that wields the Scepter. Don't forget to take the Sectra, as well."

"Who would you prefer for me to give the weapons to?" Aries asked in a whisper.

Ash was silent for a moment. She hadn't really thought that far ahead, likely because she was hoping that wouldn't be the case. "Give the amulet to Vincent, and give the Scepter to Marcus," she said. "So he can avenge my mother's death and bring her children home."

Cooper arrived in Olaigon; his expression dark as he approached Ash. She'd been waiting for him in the fields behind the village with the other Allies. She observed him, clad in his Ally uniform, equipped with the armor Benjamin had designed for their final task and the raging battle that would occur afterword. They were all wearing it. The black breastplates, pauldrons, and gauntlets. They would have full suits of it when they approached the Idonian Kingdom, but for now, protecting the vital organs was all that was needed.

It was decided that Ash would approach the beast on her own as the prophecy directed. The idea made her nervous as she'd heard of what it had done to Alistair. The Rider was silent as they all prepared for the final task, while those who wouldn't be joining them bid their goodbyes.

Ash's jaw clenched as she watched Marcus approach her, a deep frown upon his face. She surveyed the scar on his eyebrow and recalled how he'd said he'd once gotten it. The day he'd died. She was happy knowing that today he wouldn't risk his life. For once.

"What's your plan?" he asked, his voice low.

"To teleport to the cavern, enter it, slay the beast, and get the Scepter. After that, I'll head to the center of the Realm in Crane and fill it with moonlight." Ash recited her plan with ease, her heart swelling at the thought of returning home, at least for a little while. If she made it that far. "What's your plan?"

"Scour every book in the Realm until we can find a way to break the sleeping spell cast on Lucinda. We've summoned her league to Dracus. We're hoping one of them will know what to do," Marcus told her. "But don't worry about her. Worry about what you're about to do."

Nodding, Ash pulled in a shaky breath. "Once that Scepter is freed," she told him, "we end this war."

THE FOREST OF FOOLS WAS TERRIFYING.

Ash fought to not look around as Aries and Cooper finished transporting the other Allies to the cavern. So far, there was no sign of the beast that had nearly torn Alistair to ribbons. There was only the cavern. Dark, damp, and filled with nightmares.

The forest around her was alive, in a deadly way. Butterflies appeared to be normal and friendly until they landed on the ground by Ash's feet and revealed their true forms—poisonous scorpions ready to pounce. The moss on the trees reeked of acid. It ate away the bark on the trees, slowly growing over time until it swallowed everything whole.

The birds that flew through the trees were abnormal. Some had two heads, and some were stripped of feathers, nothing more than bags of sagging pink flesh.

The ground wavered, bubbling to reveal yet another trap. Ash poked at it with the toe of her boot, only to be submerged by camouflage tar. She'd wrenched her foot free, nearly dislocating her ankle in the process.

"Stop touching things," Aries barked at her as he delivered Anastasia, the last of the Allies attending the mission.

The Fire Clan Leader was less than thrilled to be in a place like this. Her nostrils flared as she tucked her arms around herself, a fiery rim emerging around her charcoal irises.

"Any sign of that... thing?" Alistair asked, his complexion pale.

"He's in the cavern." Aries' nose wrinkled with disgust. "I can smell him."

"He's probably waiting for Ash." Quinn's eternal frown

deepened. "Are you sure you need to go in there alone? I'm sure between all of us, we could take him."

"He wouldn't be susceptible to Arebus arrows," Aries revealed with a scowl. "It seems Xavier and his Dark Army know a way around that. In case you haven't noticed, the people you've shot with them that weren't your run-of-the-mill Pandora haven't perished immediately as they should have. I doubt this beast will be any different."

Quinn glared in the Fae's direction. "I'm still shocked my arrow didn't take that Red Witch down immediately."

"At least I was able to kill a Warlock with one of mine," Cooper bragged.

"You're wrong," Aries insisted. "Savron Phantom was spotted in the Regal Mountains a few days ago, walking on two feet."

"That's impossible!" Cooper growled. "We watched him die!"

"Well, we have eyes all over the Realm. We're Fae. Even the animals report to us." Aries crossed his arms, lifting his chin with pride. "Our scouts have seen Savron in the village of Aren."

Ash's blood ran cold at the thought. "Well, he'll be looking for vengeance," she whispered, her eyes drifting toward the cavern. "But we don't have the time to worry about him right now. I have a task to complete. I'm going to need you all to listen carefully," she began, her voice trembling. "If I'm not out of this cavern in one hour, assume me dead. Cooper will teleport you back to Dracus, while Aries teleports inside the cavern to retrieve my Sectra and the Scepter."

Quinn gawked at her then, the color draining from his cheeks. "Why does he get to do that?" he asked. "We're your... family!"

If any words could have broken Ash's heart any more

than it already was, they were the ones Quinn had just spoken. She looked toward him with misty eyes, her stomach in knots. "I know," she told him. "But it will be less scarring for Aries to do this. We barely know each other. He could hate me for all I know. I *did* beat his ass once," she told him with a forced smile. "If the worst happens, help Dracus win this war, and then return home to Crane and live your Immortal life in the best possible way. Marry Constance, if you still wish to. Have your babies. And please, find a way to save Lincoln and bring him home as well."

"Ash." Alistair said her name as soft as a feather. "That's a very depressing thing to say."

"I'm not done yet," she declared. "I want you to return to Mayfire. Face your pain and become the Lord they need you to be."

The Rider's eyes bulged at the sound of her words, and as he began to shake his head, she held up a hand to cease him from speaking any further. She looked toward Anastasia next, and the Draconian shifted uncomfortably beneath her gaze.

"Tell the council I'm sorry," Ash told her. "And try not to burn down the Idonian Kingdom in the process of taking it back."

The Clan Leader's lips curved into a smile. "I can try my best."

"Cooper." Ash eyed the youngest McBride brother. "I might have shared a womb with Vincent, but I shared a cradle with you. You're a part of me. I hope you remain optimistic for the rest of your days, and that you never change. Not for anyone, or for any reason."

Aries sighed, clearly bothered by all the sadness now lurking around him.

"And you." Ash scowled at the Fae, and he mimicked

her expression within an instant. "Thank you. You may not have been chosen as an Ally, but I proclaim that you *are* one. An extended Ally of sorts."

His burgundy eyes brightened at the idea.

"Now," Ash breathed. "I am going to go into this cavern and tear that beast to shreds. If I can. The rest of you, don't touch that tar over there. Or those butterflies. Or anything, for that matter," she ordered before turning toward the cavern and sucking in a shaky breath. As she took a step toward its dark entrance, she steeled herself, preparing to complete her third and final task as Idona's Prophesied Messenger.

61

The cavern was dark, and deep. Ash noticed upon entering that stalactites dripped from the ceiling, and that the ground sloped downward. She braced herself, placing one hand on the earthy wall as she descended the slope, her eyes darting in every direction. She used her free hand to light a flame to guide her through the Darkness. Her breathing was ragged by the time she made it to the bottom, nearly slipping and sliding the entire way there. *Perhaps that would have been easier,* she thought as she eyed the small, underground lake in front of her.

There was no exit on the other side of the body of water. For a moment, Ash considered that Aries might have brought her to the wrong cavern. But as she peered through the water, focusing her gaze on the button, she saw that the path continued beneath the dark depths.

Frowning, Ash wished she would have asked Craven how long a Draconian could hold their breath. But she wasn't *just* Draconian, though she would admit she was more unified with *that* part of herself. She was a Berserker. And if she drowned down there, well, she'd eventually wake back up and try again.

The beast could be anywhere, even hiding somewhere in the water. A chill swam down Ash's spine as she slipped into the lake, her heart pounding. She pulled in the deepest breath her lungs would allow before completely submerging herself, her gaze fixed on the exit as she swam.

A small tunnel sat at the bottom of the lake, large enough for her small form to fit through. Was the Sovereign and her Sorceress Siobhan small as well? She thought of them, and how they'd delivered the Scepter here so long ago. She imagined how painful it must have been for the creator of their civilization to say goodbye to her cherished weapon. Ash would have felt the same if she were to say goodbye to her daggers, though they were small in comparison to the weapon she was about to retrieve.

The water around her felt leaden as Ash pushed forward, as if it were designed to keep people out. But it wouldn't deter her. She'd continue, even if it grew to be as thick as tar and swallowed her whole.

As Ash pushed toward the tunnel, she wondered if anyone else had come this far before. Had people traveled to the Enchanted Forest before Cleo had turned it into a trap to keep her enemies away? Had they swam through this lake? Were there bones lurking at the bottom from people who had tried, yet perished? She shivered at the idea as she thrust herself forward, reaching toward the tunnel and grasping the earth around it with her ragged nails.

The water continued, filling the tunnel completely. Ash felt the desire to breathe, though she wasn't in danger of needing to. Her lungs simply missed the sensation of being filled with air as she continued swimming through the dense water. Light began to glow on the other side, and her pulse quickened, pounding in her ears. This was it. Was the beast waiting for her? Or had it vanished?

Wouldn't that be something? She smiled. *But it would be too easy.*

The tunnel widened as Ash approached an incline that would lead her back above the water. The moment she was able to rise to her full height she gasped for air, shuddering with relief that she'd managed to swim for as long as she had. She wasn't sure how much time had passed since she'd begun but didn't have the time to ponder it as she peered toward the very end of the cavern.

Nothing but silence surrounded Ash as she began her final steps toward her destination. She held her breath, catching sight of the Scepter driven into the earth at the very back of the cavern, gleaming in the light of two torches burning with eternal flame on each of its sides.

The beast wasn't in her line of vision, but Ash didn't have a full view of the cavern from where she stood in the tunnel. She drew her largest dagger from her boot, and the weight of it in her grip offered a strange form of comfort. She stared down at it as if it were her oldest friend and supposed that no matter what magnificent weapons she obtained; she would always cherish the ones she had started with. After all, the set of enchanted daggers that the old crazed bookkeeper had given her had saved her life for years, and they would protect her now.

Ash pulled in a shaky breath and took her final step into the cavern where the beast was indeed waiting for her.

But he wasn't a beast at all. He was a man, tall enough to rival a giant, with flesh so pale that it was nearly translucent and waist-length snow-white hair to match. His eyes were nothing more than black orbs, scanning her up and down from where he stood against the wall.

"So, you've finally come," a deep, raspy voice greeted her.

Ash fought to hide her fear as she held his stare. "Indeed, I have," she replied slowly, the hairs beginning to raise on the back of her neck. "Are you the welcoming committee?"

The man's lips twitched toward a smile. "No."

She shifted her weight, her grip tightening around her dagger. The torch light bounced off its shining blade as she turned it over in her hand. "Do you have a name?"

The man's muscles were rigid, and it was clear that he was fighting to restrain himself. Agony flashed through his dark eyes, his throat bobbing as he crossed his arms, digging his nails into his flesh as if to keep himself from launching at her.

"My name was taken from me when everything else I cared about was as well," the man told her truthfully. "I've been here for twenty years. Waiting for you."

Ash's chest grew tight as she considered who this man might have been before he'd arrived here. The pain in his gaze told her more than she wished to know about a man she was preparing to kill.

"You were brought here by force." It wasn't a question.

The man shifted uncomfortably, trembling as he was fighting not to transition into the beast he truly was.

"If you were only put here to keep *me* out, why attack Alistair Ward?" Ash's blood was now boiling as it raced through her veins. "Or anyone else for that matter? You've killed hundreds of people who have come to this place, hoping they were the one destined to save the Realm. And you slaughtered them all."

The man's gaze fell from her then and drifted toward the Scepter. "I am spelled," he told her. "I am not allowed to disobey. I cannot leave this place, and I'm to kill anyone that tries to get close to it. I cannot control myself."

Ash's brow raised. "Yet you're controlling yourself now," she mused. "You haven't tried to kill me yet."

"The second you take another step forward; I won't be able to stop myself. Unless you're hiding a wand somewhere upon yourself and can spell me," he admitted, his tone cold.

"Has someone done that before?" Ash asked, her eyes widening.

The man nodded, his face twisting into a scowl. "I wish he would have killed me," his voice wavered slightly, "so that I might have been able to escape this punishment."

While Ash wanted to ask the man a plethora of questions about who that man might have been, and why he was receiving such a punishment, the others were waiting for her. And if an hour passed, Aries would appear in this cavern and likely get himself slain by the beast. She couldn't allow that to happen.

Daringly, Ash took another step toward the Scepter and watched as the man cringed. She eyed him, her dagger ready in her hand as he scowled, sweat beginning to form on his brow as he trembled. He was trying to resist. She could see how hard he was fighting the spell upon him. For a moment, she felt bad about taking yet *another* step.

The man transitioned then, revealing the form of the beast who'd slaughtered so many. A Hybrid of sorts. He was a wolf, with the mane and tail of a lion, and so large that when he rose on his hind legs he appeared to be as tall as a bear.

The beast snarled, its lips pulling upward to reveal rows of razor-sharp teeth. Ash watched as it dropped onto all four legs, crouching, its claws digging into the earth as it readied itself. She prepared herself as well, unlocking the box within her and allowing her inner-Berserker. She felt her eyes burn, her heart racing so quickly she feared it might explode.

She didn't wait for the beast to strike. Instead, she launched at it with a battle cry that reverberated throughout the cavern. He met her head on, and they tumbled to the ground. Clouds of dirt rose into the air around them as his claws dug into her shoulders, pinning her down as his teeth inched closer to her throat.

Ash released an agony-filled scream as his claws grazed her bones, dragging against them. She summoned her fire, allowing it to surround her hands as she reached up, pressing her burning palms against its ribs.

The beast leaped off her with a yelp, and Ash reached for the dagger lying on the ground beside her and lunged toward him. The beast growled as it jumped over her before she had a chance to bury the weapon into its flesh.

A frustrated grunt escaped Ash as she whirled in time to view the beast as it barreled toward her in a blur of white. She braced herself for impact, tears streaming from her eyes as he sank his claws into her gut. The blow was enough to drop Ash to her knees, blood pooling around her as the beast paced back and forth, trembling with rage.

Ash hissed as she felt her flesh fighting to knit itself back together. If she could sit there for a few moments and allow herself to heal further, it would surely be beneficial. But the beast wouldn't allow that. Instead, he went in for his final blow.

Ash held her breath as she watched him jump, drawing Lionheart the second he dove into the air. By the time the beast realized what she'd done, it was too late for him to change his course. He fell onto the blade, roaring as she drove it deeper into his chest.

Pain radiated through Ash's form as she pushed herself

to her feet, fearing her innards might seep through the gashes in her stomach. She stared down at the beast and watched as it transitioned back into a man, panting as she wrapped her hand around Lionheart's hilt, preparing to rip it from his chest.

"Wait," he rasped.

Ash paused, her knees wobbling as she looked into his dark eyes.

"Thank you," he said as he began to weep, reaching with his hands to feel the blade. "My name is Archibald," he revealed. "I'm an Amorian who swore loyalty to Aiden Cavanaugh before my home Realm's destruction."

Gaping at him, Ash found herself falling to her knees.

"I left Amoria in hopes to give my species a better life," he explained. "We lived happily in Death Valley before our fellow Amorians came back to destroy us all. They punished me for my abandonment by putting me here and turning me into this Hybrid." His voice grew weaker as he spoke. "They compelled me to kill anyone who came near this cavern, to keep the Messenger from getting the Scepter. All my life, I had refused to take a life outside of battle. I had only ever killed to protect myself, and they made me kill innocent people."

"You were a Werewolf." She could hardly believe it. She thought of Morghan and found herself swallowing hard against the lump forming in her throat. "I'm so sorry." Her lip quivered as he surveyed the sword protruding from his chest.

Archibald managed to smile, and Ash could hear his pulse weakening. "The spell was only able to be broken by death," he told her. "Now I'm going to be free."

The life left his eyes, and Ash bit back a sob as she rose to her feet and freed the sword from his chest. She'd hated Xavier before, but now, she was trembling with rage. The

Werewolves, all punished for only wanting to lead a peaceful life. She shook her head, tears clouding her vision. She'd just been forced to *kill* one of the few wolves left.

A scream fueled by anger escaped Ash as she threw Lionheart to the ground. She'd end him. And now, she would have the exact weapon to rid him from Si Realtra forever.

Ash approached the Scepter, holding a hand against her bleeding gut as she dropped to her knees before the ancient weapon. She'd done it. She'd finished all three tasks, but the Prophecy had yet to be fulfilled. She gulped as she examined the Scepter, noting the smears of old, dried blood upon it. Her brow furrowed as she attempted to inhale its scent, a faint smile arriving on her lips. Someone else had made it this far. Someone else had tried to save the Realm.

The Scepter was truly beautiful. It was nearly as tall as she was, and though one end was buried in the earth, the top of it alone was enough to take Ash's breath away. An orb hovered in the center of an impeccable blade adorned with diamonds that sat at its very end in the shape of a crescent. Four large crystal spikes protruded from the blade, with smaller sapphire spikes in between. The staff, covered in blood that wasn't her own, was a shiny silver so pristine Ash doubted that it had come from anywhere in Si Realtra.

Ash recalled all Valentina had told her about the spell the original Sorceress Siobhan had placed on the soil around the Scepter, and her hand trembled as she pressed it against her wound, covering it in her blood. She placed her palm against the earth and released a sigh of relief as it trembled.

The moment she curled her hand around the Scepter's staff, Ash felt the Realm stop around her. She lifted it and found herself weeping as she felt its weight in her hand. Her eyes drifted shut as she whispered a silent thank you to the Moons and to all those who had helped her make it this far.

Finally, Ash sighed as she rolled onto her back, laying the Scepter across her chest. Exhaustion gripped her, and though she wanted to swim back through the lake and rejoice with her fellow Allies, she knew she wouldn't make it that far. Instead, she would lie there in silence and wait for Aries to teleport into the cavern. *Then* she would celebrate and return to Dracus. *Then* she'd end the war.

62

The sensation of snow falling onto her face drew Ash into a conscious state. She shivered, her stomach burning with an angry hunger for blood as she opened her eyes. A forest canopy hovered above her. Pine needles drifted down to the ground as they broke loose from their branches. Ash watched them fall, swirling in the air before finally landing atop her.

Every part of her body was either sore or screaming in pain as Ash forced herself to sit. She looked around, expecting to see her fellow Allies standing nearby. Instead, she found no one.

The scent of pine and snow overwhelmed Ash as she struggled to her feet, slowly turning in a circle to examine her surroundings. Her brow furrowed, her heart beginning to race in her chest as she took in how familiar the forest was. He breath caught in her throat as she reached for the Scepter lying at her feet and forced herself to walk.

Impossible. Ash breathed as she exited a tree line and found herself standing on Crane's East Cliff. She was home. Exactly where she needed to be to fill the Scepter with Moonlight. The center of Idona, and the Strip's intricate swirl. Her journey had brought her full circle, and she wasn't sure whether to weep with joy to have finally found her way back to the place she loved, or to cry out in frustration. She was separated from her Allies and it was likely that they believed her to be dead. And though Ash had certainly traveled throughout most of Idona during the last few weeks, she doubted she'd be able to make it back to Dracus on her own very easily.

The sun would set soon, and Ash supposed she should sit and wait. She would fill the Scepter and then she'd head to the village and try to find a map of the Realm. Perhaps Drake knew of a way to contact the Kingdoms, and she might be able to find a way to reach either Cooper or Aries so they could teleport and retrieve her.

Sighing, Ash's stomach grumbled again. She growled, wishing she wouldn't have left her pack with the other Allies. She supposed she'd have to hunt the old-fashioned away and find an unsuspecting deer.

The sound of someone approaching drew Ash's attention, and she found herself smiling as she thought of who it might be. Sam Waters often hunted in this area of the mountains. Perhaps she'd be able to reunite with him and tell him all that had happened since she'd left Crane.

But as she turned around to greet whoever had come, Ash found herself with a desire to leap off of the cliff she was standing on. It wasn't Sam Waters, or anyone from Crane that she loved. It was the last person she expected or *wanted* to see.

"Hello again, Ash." Malachai smirked.

M.L Darlow was whisked away at the sparky age of seventeen and embarked on a magical journey called The Five Realm Chronicles which came to light seven years later in 2019. Since then, she has continued her mission and pursued A Wicked Fairytale along the way.

M. L Darlow plans to take The Five Realm Chronicles as far as she can, with no end in sight.